Strangers

Books by Mary Anna Evans

Artifacts
Relics
Effigies
Findings
Floodgates
Strangers

Strangers

A Faye Longchamp Mystery

Mary Anna Evans

Poisoned Pen Press

First Edition 2010

10 9 8 7 6 5 4 3 2 1

Library of Congress Catalog Card Number: 2010923848

ISBN: 9781590587423 Hardcover
      9781590587447 Trade Paperback

Poisoned Pen Press
6962 E. First Ave., Ste. 103
Scottsdale, AZ 85251
www.poisonedpenpress.com
info@poisonedpenpress.com

Printed in the United States of America

For all the Americans who saw
those first tall ships crest on the horizon…

Acknowledgments

I'd like to thank everyone who reviewed *Strangers* in manuscript form: Michael Garmon, Erin Hinnant, Rachel Garmon, Amanda Evans, and Carl Halbirt.

I'd also like to thank these folks for their expertise on archaeology, rare documents, and the history of the St. Augustine area: Dr. Robert Connolly of Chucalissa Archaeological Museum; Carla Summers of the Matheson Center in Gainesville, Florida; Carl Halbirt, St. Augustine's City Archaeologist (which I think is one of the coolest jobs on Earth); Melissa Dezendorf, Assistant to St. Augustine's City Archaeologist, Forrest County, Mississippi Coroner, Butch Benedict; and Dr. Jerald Milanich of the Florida Museum of Natural History at the University of Florida. I also appreciate the assistance of the staff of St. Augustine Historical Society Research Library and the tour guides at the St. Augustine Ripley's Believe It Or Not! Odditorium, The Fountain of Youth Archaeological Park, Casa Zorayda, Ghost Tours of St. Augustine, and Old Town Trolley Tours.

These people helped immeasurably in making *Strangers* as accurate as possible, but all errors are completely mine.

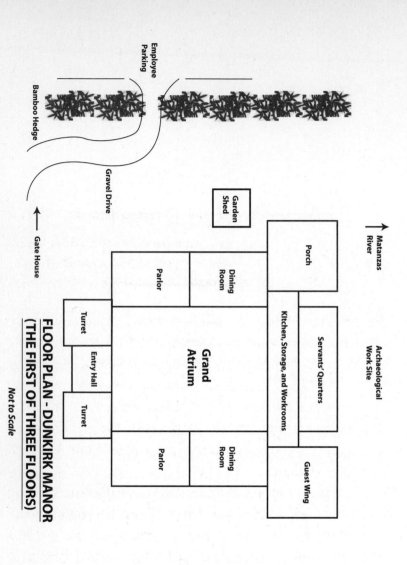

FLOOR PLAN - DUNKIRK MANOR
(THE FIRST OF THREE FLOORS)

Not to Scale

Matanzas River

Archaeological Work Site

Gate House

Gravel Drive

Bamboo Hedge

Employee Parking

Garden Shed

Porch

Dining Room

Parlor

Turret

Entry Hall

Turret

Grand Atrium

Kitchen, Storage, and Workrooms

Servants' Quarters

Parlor

Dining Room

Guest Wing

From the journal of Father Domingo Sanz de la Fuente

Translated from the Spanish by
Faye Longchamp-Mantooth, Ph.D.,
and Magda Stockard-McKenzie, Ph.D.

The favor of the Lord shone down on the fleet of our admiral, Captain-General Pedro Menéndez de Avilés, on that bright July day in 1565 when I was a young man of two-and-twenty. With ample supplies of wood and water laid in, we waved a brave farewell to Mother Spain, setting sail with the noble intent of conquering Dominica from the infidel Caribbee Indians.

Within a week, the Lord's favor faded. Two of our ships were lost, and days spent searching did not reveal them. Only then, standing on a ship that had looked impossibly large when I boarded her, did I realize the boldness of our journey. The blue water stretched out so far that, for all I knew, it was washing the face of God on its other shore.

A third ship soon sprang a leak. Its pilot wished to continue sailing, seeking repair at our destination, but the crew instructed him at swordpoint to return to Spain, lest they all be drowned. We could offer no assistance beyond prayers for their safety.

Our remaining ships sailed on until the most frightful hurricane imaginable raised the sea to the very clouds. I admit that I was soon on my knees, begging the Lord and his Mother for mercy with no less cowardice than the most beardless deckhand. It was then that I fully appreciated the faith and power of my superior, Father Francisco López de Mendoza Grajales.

Father Francisco stood bestride the deck as the waves washed fully across the ship, exhorting the men to repentance and spending all that long night in taking their confessions. I confess that he took mine, and my greatest confession was that of utter cowardice.

To keep our ship above the sea, we cast great barrels of drinking water overboard, and seven millstones, and all the reserve rigging. Our ship's captain was resolved to throw the men's chests into the ocean. The news brought a great wail from the mouths of those who owned no possessions beyond the contents of those chests.

Father Francisco urged the captain to trust in the Lord's mercy and to spare the men their meager belongings. I make another confession here: I would not have had Father's compassion. I was in such depths of fear that I would have cast overboard any inanimate object that fell into my hands. I might have been craven enough to throw an animal or even a human being into the waves, if it had improved my chance of enduring that great storm. Since then, I have felt great sympathy for the faithless disciples who awakened Our Lord and begged him to calm the raging sea.

Day came and still the storm raged, though light made the terror easier to bear. Then night fell again, and day broke, and darkness descended once more. When the Lord at last stilled the tempest, I asked myself why our prayers were not answered for so long, until suddenly they were. There are many things I do not understand.

The morning light showed us only water. We were alone in the infinite waves. Days passed before we encountered our missing companion ships.

Fatigue and confusion and long darkness left our pilots with no notion of our location, but the Holy Ghost led us on to Dominica, where we kissed the ground in gratitude. My faith tells me that the Holy Ghost—and, truly, the other two members of the Blessed Trinity—accompanied us on the next leg of our journey. For They are with us always, even unto the ends of the earth.

I cannot fathom what Those Three must have thought of the horrors we saw there at the western end of the earth, nor the horrors we ourselves inflicted.

I, Father Domingo Sanz de la Fuente, attest that the foregoing is a statement of actual events.

Chapter One

Faye Longchamp-Mantooth was capable of lust. Her handsome husband Joe could turn her head without even trying, just by stooping down to tie his moccasins.

Since Faye was an archaeologist, sometimes the things that inflamed her passion weren't even alive. She had a specific fetish for handcrafted homes that bristled with wretched excess.

She lived in just such a home. Joyeuse, the two-hundred-year-old plantation house that had been handed down through her family for generations, was in the midst of an extensive restoration. It would *always* be in the midst of an extensive restoration. Quite frankly, it was a money pit. But she loved its finely restored spiral staircase because she and Joe had restored it themselves, and she adored the frothy perfection of the murals on its bedroom walls.

Her home had been built by slaves who were her ancestors. It had been built for those slaves' masters, who were also her ancestors. Joyeuse and its complicated history were as much a part of her family as her mother and her grandmother had been.

As Faye walked through the grand doorway of Dunkirk Manor, she felt a familiar quickening of her pulse. This, too, was a house worthy of lust.

The heavy door swung wide, and Faye walked in. The high-ceilinged entry hall functioned as a library and art gallery. Its ornate wooden staircase climbed past a fine collection of early-twentieth-century oils so vibrant that Faye made plans to come back and enjoy them more closely.

The staircase rose a balcony that circled the room and provided access to thousands of old books. Burgundy, navy, black, cocoa, crimson—their faded leather bindings were as colorful as the paintings on the walls below. The gilt lettering on their spines was worn, but it still sparkled.

Faye didn't just lust after old houses. She also lusted after books. Joe didn't mind. He knew she lusted after him, too.

He walked beside her through this living museum. His handmade moccasins didn't make a sound on the burnished oak floor. Faye and the rest of her work crew—Magda Stockard-McKenzie, Kirk Graham, and Levon Broome—clattered carefully across the gleaming floorboards in their work boots. Magda clutched her daughter Rachel's hand as if she were afraid the child would leave behind a trail of little-girl-shaped smudges.

There wasn't a speck of dust on those shiny oak floors. There wasn't a mote of dust in the cool quiet air. The wood-paneled walls gleamed behind gilt-framed paintings, and the leaded glass windows on either side of the enormous front door were surrounded by flawless velvet hangings in an unexpected but perfect shade of burnt orange. It was as if the Gilded Age had never ended, and an army of chambermaids prowled the house constantly, armed with feather dusters and lemon oil.

It was as if the phrase "minimum wage" had never been coined.

Glynis Smithson ushered them through all this perfection. She was the perfect person to do it. Glynis was tall. She was slim and willowy. Her sleek waist-length hair gleamed silver-blonde. Pale feathery eyebrows said that her hair color was natural. If she had piled that hair atop her head and pulled on a high-necked and bustled gown, Glynis could easily have stepped back to the time this house was new. Faye had the feeling that her clients had chosen their assistant for her retro glamour.

"Daniel and Suzanne will be right down," she said, leading them from the high-ceilinged entrance hall into the stupendously high-ceilinged atrium at the center of the house.

On cue, Daniel and Suzanne Wrather appeared on the third-floor landing and began making their way down one of the two mirror-image staircases that encircled the atrium. This room, too, was completely paneled and floored in oak. The banisters and stair rails were oak, too, ornately carved in a gothic style. An entire forest had died to build this house.

Looking at the enormous antique rug spread across the atrium floor, Faye saw that it was made of hand-knotted silk. Faye figured an entire army of Persian women had gone blind for the cushiness under her feet.

No windows lit the atrium, only a ceiling filled with stained glass skylights. In the absence of windows, more lush velvet hangings were draped around the doorways, their bittersweet orange bringing sunshine into a room that might otherwise have felt dark.

Daniel and Suzanne were navigating the stairs very, very slowly. Having just turned forty, Faye knew that her clients weren't much older than she was, but they seemed so. Suzanne was very thin, almost bird-like, and she had a habit of hugging her arms close to her body, elbows bent, like folded wings. Daniel's sandy hair was thin and it was the same graying shade of mid-brown as Suzanne's. Though Suzanne was tall, he was taller. Daniel's head bowed a bit, as if he were tired, but he retained a spring in his step as he descended the stairs. Perhaps his pace was hampered by Suzanne's slower movements.

Daniel's devotion to his wife of many years was palpable, and Suzanne never looked at him without smiling. As a newlywed herself, Faye just liked to watch the two of them together.

"You must be exhausted," Suzanne said, extending a maternal hand toward Faye.

Faye had found that her advanced pregnancy affected older women in this way. They urged her incessantly to sit down and put her feet up. As the months passed, this advice became more and more welcome.

"Let me show you all to your rooms. I see that *you* need some rest," Suzanne continued, looking at Faye with concern. Then she turned that same concerned focus on a monumental floral arrangement sitting on a plant stand between the two grand staircases. A full-blown pink rose was beginning to fade, and Suzanne apparently couldn't have that. She plucked the drooping bloom out of the arrangement and tucked it in her pocket, studying each of the other flowers for flaws before she turned away.

Then Suzanne led them out the right side of the atrium, through a vast dining room that was as shiny and oaky as the rest of the house. They walked toward the rear of the house, past a doorway to a modernized kitchen that extended across the full width of the atrium, shiny with immaculate stainless steel. Then they passed through a door that was finished in gleaming oak on the front and painted a nondescript brown on the other. It passed into a hallway painted dun-beige, with a ceiling so low that six-and-a-half-foot-tall Joe had to stoop.

An imaginary line seemed to run across the threshold of that door, and all the dust that was missing from one side of that line appeared to have been shunted to its other side. Cobwebs clung to the ceiling and dust was matted into their silk.

Suzanne was saying, "I apologize for our housekeepers. We just can't get them to come back here. If they only knew. *This* is the part of the house that *isn't* haunted." She took the teeth out of this statement with a quick laugh.

Faye didn't know how to respond. Should she say, "I can see that!"? Or should she lie and say, "Why, it's perfectly lovely back here!"? Instead she just smiled and opted to sidestep the issue. "Thanks so much for hosting us. We're a new business and it helps a great deal for us to have our travel expenses covered."

A row of white doors extended down each side of the dun-colored hallway. There were a whole lot of them. No wonder Suzanne had offered private rooms for each member of Faye's field team. Faye's internal compass told her that the hallway paralleled the back of the kitchen, which meant that the doors on the left opened to windowless rooms the size of monks' cells, judging by the short distance between doors. The rooms on the right were small, too, but there was at least a chance that they had windows…presuming that Gilded Age employers had thought their household staff merited the luxury of a few panes of glass.

Suzanne and Daniel operated a bed-and-breakfast in Dunkirk Manor, so Faye had innocently expected fluffy pillows and fine linens and lots of chintz in her room. *Au contraire.* Now she knew what it was like to be the hired help.

Suzanne pointed to one of the identical doors—thankfully, on the side of the hallway where she might hope for a window—and said, "This one is for you and Joe," so Faye stepped in.

The paint around the doorknob was worn away to the bare wood. The drab wallpaper around the light switch was worn through to the bare plaster. A single light bulb hung from the ceiling. The only things of light and color in the entire room were the curtains surrounding the hoped-for window, which had once been a bright and sunny yellow-and-blue calico, and a tiny watercolor painting of a woman strolling on the beach at sunset. Judging by the style of the woman's dress, the painting had been done during the Depression, and Faye figured that was about the last time somebody had tried to make this room pretty.

Two narrow, iron-framed beds clung to the walls on her left and right. Pregnancy was wreaking havoc on her back and hips. Just looking at the thin, sagging mattresses on those beds made Faye hurt from her rib cage down.

As soon as the door closed behind them, Joe dragged one bed across the room and snugged it up against the other one. Joe wasn't real big on sleeping in separate beds. He wasn't even real big on staying on his own side of the bed.

Faye had been so excited to land this job. She still was. With her newly minted Ph.D., she and Joe had started their archaeological consulting business just in time for the economy to tank, taking with it the property development industry that fueled so much archaeological work. Excavating the rear garden of Dunkirk Manor to the strict standards of St. Augustine's archaeological preservation ordinance wouldn't be a quick job, and Faye's crew billed by the hour. This was a very good thing.

Her preliminary library research on the property said that the existing mansion had been built on undeveloped property in 1889—brand-spanking new, for St. Augustine—but that it had figured significantly in the city's history until the Depression. Henry Flagler, who'd kick-started the juggernaut that was Florida tourism, had been a frequent visitor at the Dunkirks' gala parties. Thomas Edison, Henry Ford, and virtually every other celebrity who had ever hit town—and there had been a lot of them before Palm Beach and Miami sprang up to steal the tourists away—had graced Dunkirk Manor with their presence.

Robert Ripley had been a guest here. He'd enjoyed St. Augustine so much that he'd bought the Castle Warden, quite near Dunkirk Manor, and used it as the home for his first permanent museum of oddities. He'd even featured the Dunkirk house in one of his Believe-It-or-Not columns, saying:

"Each staircase has thirteen steps to the second floor landings in the atrium and thirteen steps to the third floor landings. Thirteen leaded glass skylights shine above them, and each is adorned with thirteen peacock feathers. Thirteen paintings ring the walls. The inlaid mahogany rosettes in each corner of the floor have thirteen petals. Yet everything else in the room is perfectly symmetrical, making these odd-numbered features feel just…wrong. It's the spookiest room in America. Believe It…or Not!"

But, fascinating as Dunkirk Manor itself was, Faye wasn't working inside the house, so these things were just background for her project. Dunkirk Manor's glamorous history gave Faye historical justification to launch a significant field effort for a project that, in truth, wasn't glamorous at all…but it was work.

For a consultant who got paid only when a client appeared with money in hand, work was work. And work was good.

Daniel and Suzanne wanted to build a swimming pool for their bed-and-breakfast guests, and Faye and Joe had been hired to make sure that the construction wouldn't be destroying anything historic. Or prehistoric.

Ordinarily, St. Augustine's City Archaeologist would have done the job herself, funded by the property owner, but Daniel and Suzanne had met Faye and Joe by chance two months before, while they all waited for seats at an overcrowded restaurant in the historic district. At the time, introverted Faye had wished the friendly couple would let her enjoy a rare evening on the town with her husband before the baby made date nights hard to do, but now she saw that business owners need to network all the time.

On the strength of that one casual encounter, Daniel and Suzanne had remembered her when they needed an archaeologist, and they'd gone to some effort to get permission to use her firm instead of using the city's staff. Hiring her through the nonprofit organization that maintained the house made a difference with the powers-that-be, for some reason Faye didn't understand. Mainly, she was just glad the job had come through.

She looked around the dreary little room, planning an immediate assault with a feather duster. Then she slid an arm around the waist of her tall, handsome, and sexy business partner.

"Well. At least it's free."

Chapter Two

Somewhere in St. Augustine, Florida, right this minute, someone is murdering history. It happens all the time.

When this city was founded, Elizabeth I was Queen of England. It was a single year after the death of Michelangelo, and the Renaissance had seized Europe with no intention of letting go. In other words, it was a very long time ago.

Since then, the Spanish built their city atop the site of a Native American village. Then the English came and went, and the Spanish came back. And now the Americans have held the land for nearly two centuries.

In St. Augustine, it is possible to drop your car keys and destroy something irreplaceable. Actually putting a shovel or a bulldozer blade into the soil…well, such activities are highly regulated.

Some people resent being told what to do. And some people are capable of doing bad things…evil things…when they have dollar signs in their eyes.

Somewhere in the countryside outside the old city, a bulldozer is scraping away the topsoil to build an upscale development. A human finger bone, a broken war club, a few musket balls, two pieces of a long stone blade, a corroded crucifix, a scattering of silver rosary beads, and a startling amount of very old trash—the discovery of these things causes the developer a moment of consternation, but only a moment. They are quickly discarded.

The man in charge has just one thing to say.
"What the historic preservation people don't know won't hurt 'em."

Chapter Three

Faye knew that billions of women had been pregnant in the past. Millions of women were pregnant at any single point in time... including, at the moment, her.

This meant that many, many people were precisely as physically miserable as Faye, and at precisely the same time. This didn't mean that she should be happy about the fact that her feet hurt. Nor that her ankles were so swollen that they felt squishy to the touch.

Faye's legs ached. Her back felt exactly as crummy as one would expect, considering that she spent her workdays in the classic pregnant woman's pose: feet slightly apart and pelvis tilted until her lower back was swayed into the shape of the letter *C*. As much as possible, she kept both hands pressed into that swayback, for support.

Soon, her crew would be finished with the test pits that she was watching them dig, and they could get to work doing some serious excavation. Faye knew she had no business standing on the lip of an archaeological unit and barking orders. If this baby gained one more ounce, her swayback routine wasn't going to be enough to counterbalance the extra weight. That ounce would pull her forward, right onto her face, which would be bad enough if she were standing indoors on a plush carpet. If Faye plunged forward, landing deep in a dirty hole, the situation would be damn near catastrophic.

The worst part of this situation was the fact that she had a whole month left to be pregnant. More than a month, actually. She was due to be pregnant another five weeks and six days. But who was counting?

No. Those five weeks and six days were *not* the worst part of the situation. Joe…the love of her life, her husband, the man with whom she hoped to spend the rest of her days…

Joe was driving her stark raving nuts.

He asked, "Can I get you a chair?" about every five minutes, despite the fact that she'd told him that sitting made her hips ache.

"Would you like another glass of milk?" he murmured periodically, despite the fact that she'd drunk so much milk to please him that she was pretty sure she was turning into a cow.

And if he brandished any prenatal vitamins in her direction, ever again, she was going to yell at him until *he* was the one with iron-poor blood.

Faye was sweltering. There were two reasons for this. She was very, very pregnant, it was true. But she could also blame geography. In Florida, May was not springtime, no matter what the calendar said. May was full-out summer by any definition that counted, and it always had been…even in 1565, just before the conquistadors stepped ashore in August of that year and founded St. Augustine.

If it hadn't been for the gracious old homes and spreading trees that dotted this neighborhood, Faye could have looked south and seen the Castillo de San Marcos, the great stone fort that had guarded this old, old city for most of its existence.

And if she'd had a clear view north, she might have seen the very spot where Pedro Menéndez de Avilés once claimed some unspecified but extremely large portion of the New World for His Majesty Philip II of Spain. If a giant were to magically remove all those interfering houses and trees, Joe could have probably shot two arrows and hit both historic sites, without taking a step from where he now stood.

It made Faye smirk to remember that the conquistadors came ashore smack in the middle of hurricane season, when the heat and the mosquitoes and the tempestuous storms must have made the bravest among them wonder whether it would be best to just pack up and head back to Spain.

It was a little early for hurricanes at the moment, but Faye was enjoying the sea breezes.

Actually, the water lurking behind the wall enclosing this garden wasn't the sea. It was the storied Matanzas River, named for the massacre of men more than four centuries dead. Faye sometimes got the shivers when she remembered the things that had happened in this very old town.

The site her crew was investigating wasn't nearly as old as St. Augustine itself. Dunkirk Manor was a massive fake-stone Gilded Age mansion, but it was flimsy and new compared to the Castillo de San Marcos. She could hardly expect to find anything at this dig older than a century or so, but stranger things had happened in these parts. She knew an archaeologist who had gotten major publications from a site under the bathroom of an old roadside motel, not far from the spot where she stood.

Faye had the feeling that she could find anything today. And she loved that feeling.

"Sit down, Faye," Magda barked.

It must be ten o'clock. Faye had made Magda and Joe swear that they would only nag her once an hour, on the hour. And she'd made them promise to take turns. Clearly it was Magda's turn to tell her what to do.

She was opening her mouth to bark back at her oppressors when Joe said, "Would you look at that?"

This phrase was music to any field archaeologist worth her salt.

He was digging a test pit, and he was hardly a foot beneath the ground surface. The primary reason for a test pit wasn't necessarily to look for artifacts, though those were always nice to find. Digging a set of narrow-but-deep holes spaced in an orderly grid would give Faye and her crew a good idea of the site's soils.

Were they sandy?

Here? Practically on the edge of the Atlantic Ocean? Yeah, probably.

What did the stratigraphy look like? Was there an orderly, well-defined sequence of soil layers, or had the soil been disturbed?

Well, they were just about to find out.

Did the people who had used the land over the years leave any of themselves behind?

Faye sure hoped so. She rushed over to see what Joe had found.

As he cleared a razor-thin layer of soil, a sharp dividing line appeared. On one side of the line, the soil was undisturbed. On the other side, it had been churned, a long time before.

Faye, Magda, and their field techs Levon and Kirk dropped everything and watched Joe work. The sea breezes took a break and silence descended.

Joe was stooped so low that his long black ponytail dragged the soil. The sun had risen in the sky while they worked, and it chose this moment to shift the shadow of the tree limb that had shaded Joe all morning. He had to be feeling the heat, but he was too intent on his work to even wipe his face. Sweat from his chin dappled the dusty ground.

Before long, Joe had cleared a few more layers of dirt. Everyone could see that the sharp, straight line between the two soil types continued to slice downward below-ground, and it continued indefinitely in either direction. A few broken bits of tile embedded in that dividing line told a story.

"I think there was a pond or a fountain or maybe even a swimming pool here," he said, standing up to give his back a rest. He looked at Faye. "Don't you?"

Faye nodded. Magda took a tile fragment from Joe and studied it a moment. Then she handed it to Faye and cocked one eyebrow, wordlessly testing her powers of observation. Faye was trying hard to behave like her image of a Ph.D.—confident and decisive—and Magda didn't help matters when she refused to stop acting like Faye's professor.

The tile was coated with a glaze that was still bright white beneath the clinging dirt. Along one unbroken edge ran a black border in a clean, geometric design that fairly screamed

Art Deco. Faye ran a finger over the smooth finish and said, "It looks expensive."

Squinting at the house and at the brick wall surrounding the garden where they stood, Faye said, "If it's Art Deco, then it's not old enough to be original to this house. And tiles this nice would have been used for something special. A pond or pool or fountain, like Joe said."

Scanning the garden again, she said, "We're right in the middle of the back yard. A fountain or fish pond would have looked nice here, but there's room enough for a swimming pool. Wouldn't that be a funny thing?"

Considering that they'd gotten this job because the B&B's guests had been complaining to Daniel and Suzanne about its lack of a swimming pool, Faye found it rather poetic that Joe might have uncovered one.

Faye thought the planned pool construction could probably still move forward. Surely an old, filled-in pool wouldn't have enough historical significance to put a halt to the project, even in this history-obsessed town. Her clients would build an elegant new pool, right next to the spiffy tennis court that was Daniel's pride and joy, and it would have all the most sought-after extras: a hot tub and a waterfall and a bunch of picturesque boulders and a dark paint job that made it look like a natural pond….well, sort of natural.

Then, a few years down the road, this new pool would develop cracks. Its pump and plumbing would grow creaky, and its design would stop being stylish. Someone would say, "I'm sick of cleaning this thing. Let's just fill it in." Soon there would be more broken tiles stirred into the soil, and this spot of ground would become an even more interesting place for future archaeologists to dig.

It occurred to Faye that her clients would want to see what they'd found. Even if this wrecked pool was as historically insignificant as she thought, it was still pretty cool. The people who were paying for the work should get a chance to see it.

It only took Faye a moment to fetch Daniel and Suzanne. Suzanne was trailed, as always, by Glynis, who moved so gracefully that her bosses looked lead-footed by comparison.

Faye found the fact that her clients consulted each other publicly over the smallest business decisions especially endearing. While waiting for Daniel and Suzanne to show her crew around the garden that morning, she'd heard the following exchange, and she'd had the feeling that such conversations happened daily:

"I've been thinking we should add smoked salmon to the breakfast menu," Daniel had asked, touching Suzanne's arm. "Should we keep serving bacon, too?"

Suzanne had said that bacon was hardly optional, because people expected it, but she couched the statement with a respectful, "Don't you think, dear?"

She'd then launched into an impressive display of mental arithmetic, calculating how much the salmon would cost and adding in the price of bagels, onions, and capers, because people would expect those, too. And Daniel had watched her silently, still amazed after thirty years by how smart she was. When they finished their decision-making, Suzanne had looked to Daniel for approval, then she'd met eyes with Glynis and nodded, knowing that Glynis would make it so.

Faye and Joe were in business together now, just like Daniel and Suzanne. She'd decided that she could learn a thing or two from this couple. Faye tended to make a decision and tell Joe about it at some undetermined time in the future. Like, maybe, when the bill landed in their mailbox.

As Faye led Daniel, Suzanne, and Glynis into the back garden, she got a sudden, gut-level sense that something had changed. It was as if the sun had moved behind a cloud, but it hadn't. Its bright rays still shone hard on Joe's sweaty face. Black shadows clung close to her crew's legs, under a sun now hanging almost straight overhead. What was wrong?

She rushed to Joe's expanded test pit and saw Levon leaning over his own test pit, several feet away from Joe's discovery. He too had found tiles, but they were larger and hewn of rough stone, suitable for wet feet. They'd been set flat on the ground, and Levon had expanded his pit outward, uncovering several tiles before prying one of them up and setting it aside.

No one was looking at the tile he'd removed. They were all looking at the exposed soil where it had been.

Faye's hips protested as she squatted beside him. "What'd you find?"

The young man gestured at the soil and Faye understood what had disturbed her crew so badly. An infant's silver rattle protruded from the dirt. A multicolored collection of diaper pins with decorative china heads were carefully arranged in a rectangle beside it.

Why was this so upsetting? Faye felt the dark undercurrent in the air, but it was in her nature to want to explain it. Maybe this cluster of artifacts raised all their hackles because the rattle rising from the dirt looked more than a little like a headstone, and the rectangle of pins looked like they could enclose a tiny grave.

Also, the question of *why* somebody had buried these things hung in the air like incense. They had obviously been put in the ground intentionally.

Faye remembered her grandmother saying that her boy cousins had enjoyed torturing her by burying her dolls and holding mock funerals. But there was no sadistic fun to be had in burying the toy of a child too young to be angry.

She lightly fingered the corroded wire of a diaper pin. Why? What was a good reason to bury a baby's things?

She could imagine a child playing in the dirt with his baby sister's stuff. It would have taken a very orderly child to lay out these pins so neatly, but such things were possible.

Faye's dear friend Dauphine was a voodoo mambo, so Faye had more knowledge of sympathetic magic than the average non-mambo. Maybe this arrangement of baby things was intended to help someone get pregnant. Maybe the voodoo practitioner herself wanted a baby.

Faye knew from experience that when Dauphine thought somebody needed a baby, Dauphine got busy. And she didn't always ask whether the person being charmed *wanted* to have a baby right then.

A well-timed kick in the guts from the inside reminded Faye that she wanted this child more than anything else in the world, except for Joe. She was glad Dauphine hadn't asked permission before she worked her magic.

The last possible explanation for the subterranean arrangement of baby things hit Faye like a different kind of kick in the guts. The buried rattle and diaper pins had the feel of a shrine, a memorial to a lost loved one.

Faye knew that if she were to lose this baby, she would never want to look at the nursery full of baby gear waiting for her back home at Joyeuse, not ever again. She could absolutely see herself digging a big hole and throwing in a stroller and a car seat and a playpen. Nowadays, such a purge would take a bulldozer, but babies had required less merchandise in days gone by.

The curved shape of the rattle spoke of Art Deco. Its tarnished silver spoke of money. If the person who buried it had done so out of grief, then that grief might be eighty years dead and gone. Still, it reached across the years to Faye.

She rose to her feet and gathered herself together, determined to show a businesslike face to her clients. Guiding them away from the silver rattle, she showed them Joe's two-colored dirt, studded with broken tiles.

Daniel and Suzanne made the appropriate noises about the interesting information an archaeologist could glean from dirt that looked like…well, dirt…to the ordinary observer.

Glynis clearly didn't want to just stand around and talk. Ever since Faye and her crew had arrived that morning, she'd made it clear that she found their work fascinating. Once she got wind of Joe's and Levon's discoveries, she'd dragged the hem of her spotless ivory pants in the dirt and squatted right down, so that Faye could explain what they'd found. Then she'd gotten her hands grubby and risked the destruction of her manicure, just so that she could fully experience the difference in color and texture between the undisturbed dirt and the scrambled soil that had been used as fill dirt.

There were few character traits that Faye appreciated more than curiosity, so she instinctively liked Glynis a whole lot. Levon's face was alight as he crouched beside the young woman to explain what she was seeing.

"See the change in color? Here? And here? That's a dead giveaway. It would have been obvious to Joe, even without the tile fragments to mark the dividing line. "Now, over here—"

Levon shifted Glynis' attention to the rattle and diaper pins and kept talking without missing a beat.

Levon loved his work, so he always answered questions with a smidge more detail than needed. Glynis seemed to actually be interested in his archaeological minutiae, so ecstasy spread over Levon's pudgy baby-face. Glynis was also very pretty in an ethereal way that contrasted sharply with the flushed and sweaty archaeologists. From the look in his eyes, Faye would guess that Levon fell hard for the ethereal type.

The shadowed glances Suzanne was casting toward the baby toys showed that she was too creeped out to feel much curiosity. Levon's monologue was flying right over her head. Faye could see that Daniel sensed her unease, and she wasn't surprised when they retreated quickly into the big house to tend their paying guests, with Glynis in tow.

Faye was left to wonder what else might be buried with that silver rattle. She'd dug up potentially spooky things like skulls and bones and religious totems and voodoo offerings at various times in her career. She tended to look at them through a scientist's eyes. They were interesting fragments of the past and no more.

Being pregnant put a different spin on the discovery of a baby's toy. It made her want to set down her trowel and walk away. It made her wish she were working anywhere but here.

Nothing else turned up before quitting time, but she spent the afternoon hugging her bulging belly just a little tighter than usual.

Chapter Four

Alan Smithson was well prepared for his meeting with the county's growth management people. He was always well prepared for everything he did.

Anything worth doing is worth doing right. That's what his late father had always told him. So he'd prepared a top-flight presentation for this evening's meeting, even though he already knew the outcome. His development application would be approved. A new strip mall would take the place of a scrubby and unkempt strip of natural Florida that was currently earning nothing for the local government in terms of sales taxes and impact fees. The government would benefit substantially from Alan Smithson's strip mall, and Alan Smithson would benefit substantially more. This was as it should be.

His applications were always approved, no matter what he wanted to build and no matter what county he wanted to build it in. This was because he hired top-flight people to fill out his development applications, people who knew how to say whatever it was that the permitting people wanted to hear.

Alan Smithson did *not* hire people who were more concerned about bald eagles and Indian mounds than they were about their employer's pocketbook.

His daughter Glynis did not understand this concept. She understood that Daddy paid her credit card balance in full every month, but she didn't seem to grasp the connection between those pretty dollars and the ugly housing developments and shopping malls that Daddy's development company built.

Glynis had been spending way too much time with her tree-hugging friends lately. They reminded Alan of his late wife's do-gooder cronies, but the prattling women of an earlier time had limited their charity work to people so down-trodden that his wife and her friends would have never have even hired them to scrub their toilets. Those unwashed charity cases had never crossed paths with Alan, and they certainly had never hampered his business interests. Glynis' volunteer work, by contrast, had the potential to be very costly.

Her friends were out-and-out dangerous. They truly thought Alan should shut a project down every time an arrowhead surfaced. Did they know what it cost to have a backhoe and its operator sitting idle while some archaeologist dithered over whether his multimillion dollar project could proceed?

Fortunately, Alan knew which county officials could be bought, and he knew how much they cost. The outcome of today's meeting was a slam-dunk.

Nevertheless, Glynis' new obsession was getting tiring, so Alan had found her a boyfriend who could be bought, just as surely as most politicians had a price. And if Lex couldn't keep Glynis from running off to her historic preservation society meetings and her Audubon Society gatherings and her archaeology club parties…well, there were other men on the auction block. How hard could it be for a red-blooded American man to date Alan's gorgeous daughter?

Of course, if things got serious, that red-blooded American man was going to have to swallow a bitter pill in the form of a finely detailed pre-nup, but still…Glynis was sweet and she was beautiful and she was loaded. What red-blooded American was going to turn down *that* combination?

Chapter Five

Joe and Magda had spent the morning tracing the edge of the swimming pool. Or goldfish pond. Or whatever the heck it was.

Faye guessed that the Art Deco tiles were made in the 1920s, and swimming pools had been popular at that time. Of course, anything expensive had been popular in the status-seeking Roaring Twenties, including reflecting ponds and elaborate fountains, so the jury was still out.

Faye was having a Great Gatsby moment, picturing handsome Jazz Age ladies and gentleman playing tennis in spotless whites and lounging beside a swimming pool while they smoked cigarettes in long holders. At the moment, reality was less enchanting. Daniel and Suzanne were playing tennis in t-shirts and ratty shorts, and the archaeologists were sweating unglamorously as they worked.

Kirk and Levon were clearing dirt off the stone tiles, one by one, that had paved this portion of the garden. Their curving pattern seemed to match the line in the soil that Joe and Magda were following. A web search had turned up lots of photos of pools from the Roaring Twenties. The ones that best matched this site were a long, narrow oval shape that Faye found particularly elegant. Maybe Daniel and Suzanne could propose a new pool with a retro design. The historical review committee should just love that.

Faye hated watching her crew work, while she just stood around and sweated for no good reason. She wished she could be more help, instead of just managing a staff of people who didn't need her to tell them what to do.

After lunch, she'd succumbed to Joe's nagging and collapsed into a stylish lawn chair he'd dragged over from the back porch. Magda's daughter Rachel was playing at her feet, singing to the baby doll in her arms. It was astonishing to Faye as a not-yet-parent to see how much a child could grow and learn in three years. Faye remembered when this little goddaughter of hers had been a fairly useless lump of adorable flesh.

The sun played on the child's russet hair, and Faye simply sat there and loved her. If she felt this way about someone else's child, what would it feel like to look at her own?

Magda had stopped teaching summer classes when Rachel was born, and she'd cut her office hours back as far as the university would tolerate. Since she'd waited until she was way older than Faye—forty-five—to give birth, her intended goal had been to enjoy this child as much as possible. Her husband, Sheriff Mike McKenzie, had been on the far side of sixty when this last child was born, so his stated goal had been to spoil Rachel just as badly as he spoiled his grandchildren.

Magda obviously enjoyed the heck out of being Rachel's mother, but she enjoyed her work, too. She'd seized on Faye's first big contract as an opportunity to mix business and family and friendship and pleasure.

"Hire me," she'd said. "I'll work cheap. It'll be the perfect summer project for me."

That offer had silenced Faye's first objection. She couldn't afford a Ph.D. other than herself, but if Magda was willing to give her expertise away, who was Faye to say no? Still, there was the question of Rachel. Faye just couldn't imagine Magda staying in St. Augustine, hours away from her daughter in Micco County, possibly for weeks.

Magda was ahead of her, but what else was new? "If I hire somebody local to watch Rachel while I work, will the boss-lady let me bring my kid?"

Faye silently added up the cost of a full-time babysitter. "I thought you said you'd work cheap."

"I will. I don't expect to come out too far ahead, money-wise. But—" She held up a hand and began ticking off the job's benefits on her fingers. "One, I'll have some time with my daughter. Two, if I hire a babysitter, I'll have some time *away* from my daughter. Three, I'll get to work with you and Joe, which is always fun. Four, you can give me a fancy-schmancy title, so I'll have a nice-looking consultant job to add to my curriculum vitae. Five, I'll surely make at least a little extra pocket money to spend on my charming husband."

Magda had run out of fingers, so she started counting them again. "Six, if my boss-lady puts me up someplace nice, that same charming husband can drive over and spend some romantic time with me, now and then."

Thinking of their not-luxurious quarters, Faye realized that she'd failed to hold up this part of their bargain.

"Seven," Magda had continued in her customary relentless manner, "Rachel's godmother, my boss-lady, will have plenty of chances to take her goddaughter off my hands and practice her childrearing skills. *And...*" She held eye contact with Faye as she stuck up an eighth finger and landed hard on the word "and." "...you and I can surely get a publication out of this job."

Motherhood or not, Magda never stopped being an ambitious academic.

"Magda, it's a routine consulting contract. We're just digging up somebody's back yard. What could we possibly find worth publishing?"

"You never know what you're gonna find. That's why I love this line of work. And we're talking about St. Augustine. There are four hundred and fifty years of European history to uncover, and only God knows how long the First Americans were piling up oyster shells beside Matanzas Bay. Besides, you and I have been known to get papers out of just about anything. We wrote up that stuff you uncovered in *your* back yard, you know."

This was true.

"We published your work on that eagle effigy mound in Mississippi. Well, *you* think it looks like an eagle."

"It does, and you know it."

"Pregnancy makes you tart-tongued, does it? I've got no excuse for my own tart tongue."

Both these things were also true.

"We'll find something worth writing about, trust me. And I'm going to keep bullying you into publishing your work until you see reason. I'll turn you into an academic, Faye, if it's the last thing I do. Digging up back yards that probably don't need digging up is a waste of a fine mind, if you ask me."

Faye hadn't asked her, and she was gratified to hear her old friend admit to being a bully. But she didn't like to argue with Magda, so she just said, "If we find something interesting, I'll help you with the article. But I doubt it'll come to that."

So Magda was here working for peanuts, and Rachel would be toddling around underfoot for a few minutes each morning and afternoon while her hardworking babysitter Lynne took a break. Faye was glad to have them. Maybe she was hormonal, but this just felt like a time when she wanted to be surrounded by her loved ones.

Magda stood up and chortled, "Hey, look!" in the shrill tone she'd cultivated to convince students she was half-witch and fully intimidating.

Faye hauled herself to her feet and shuffled over. "What've you found?"

"A pipe. Since it runs that direction," she said, pointing toward the rear garden wall, "instead of toward the house, I'm thinking they pulled the water right out of the river. The Matanzas is tidal, so this would have been almost like a saltwater pool. Certainly brackish, at least."

"Unless there's a well out there somewhere." Faye followed the line of the pipe with her eyes. "Seems unlikely. Pulling water out of the river would've made a lot more sense."

The two women stood with their backs to the house, wondering whether the old pipes still lay underground and trying to imagine what path they might take if they did. Faye felt like she jumped a foot when the slim cool hand landed on her shoulder.

The other hand had touched Magda's shoulder, and Magda had done the same.

Glynis was the culprit. Faye felt completely stupid for being spooked by someone so nonspooky. By contrast, Magda made it a professional point to be as scary as possible.

Suzanne's elegant assistant gave the impression that she'd rather be on Faye's crew than working indoors. She'd already strolled out to the excavation several times that day—before work, at lunchtime, during coffee breaks—just to chat with the archaeologists and watch them work. It made Faye laugh to see Levon wipe his hands and smooth back his hair when Glynis appeared on the back porch.

Faye had let the young people be, chatting with Magda while Levon and Kirk talked to Glynis about their work. The twenty-somethings were friendly enough to the two older women, but their chatter over which nightclub had colder beer and which cell phone company gave the best deal on unlimited Internet access made Faye feel elderly. She'd felt so elderly, in fact, that she spent one of her own breaks learning to text, just to prove that she wasn't old yet. As if being pregnant didn't serve the same purpose…

When Glynis saw how badly she'd startled Faye by simply touching her on the arm, she'd lost her breath from laughter.

"Daniel would like to see you," she said to Faye.

Glynis offered no reason for this summons. Faye was new to business, but she wasn't stupid. When her client called, she needed to appear promptly and with a smile. She turned and walked alone to the house while Glynis interrupted Levon's work yet again.

Joe brushed his hands on the rag hanging out of his back pocket as if he planned to escort her. She shook her head as she passed him, saying, "Don't worry, Joe. I really am capable of walking across the yard."

It was quite a deep yard, since the old house occupied a city block, but Faye wasn't concerned about the distance. Walking would probably relieve the pressure of the baby's weight on various portions of her anatomy. It was the staircase that loomed large in Faye's mind.

Daniel's office was on the third floor, and Faye had gotten a good eyeful of the atrium staircase when she first arrived. It was a typical Gilded Age monster—two stories of hand-carved oak balusters and railings and banisters and wainscoting. The stair treads were narrow and the risers were steep by modern standards, a bit of a problem for a woman who could no longer see her feet, and the swooping curves required triangular treads that were downright treacherous.

She counted those stair treads as she climbed. Ripley's Believe-It-or-Not had been right. There were thirteen of them.

Faye could have been happy, lying on the polished oak ground floor and staring up at the stained glass ceiling overlooking Dunkirk Manor's grand atrium. Hauling herself up the stairway overlooking that atrium was quite another thing. Nevertheless, her client had summoned her. With sufficient effort, she could get herself to Daniel's office, and she would by God paste a smile on her face when she got there.

She was halfway up the second staircase, still counting steps. *Seven, eight, nine...* Looking upstairs she could see that, again, there were thirteen of them. Her voodoo priestess friend Dauphine would have cautioned her to skip that last step, because a person's future was determined by where her feet fell. It was too late. She'd already stepped on the thirteenth step of the first flight of stairs, because it was too much of a stretch for her aching body to skip one for no good reason.

She trod hard on that thirteenth step, and prepared herself mentally to meet and impress her client. She reminded herself to smile.

Her hips might be screaming bloody murder but she was smiling.

Faye had paused and caught her breath before knocking on Daniel's office door, and the man hadn't seemed to notice her discomfort, so the pasted-on smile must have worked. Unfortunately, their errand required Faye to navigate yet another flight of stairs.

Again, there was a clearly demarcated line where Dunkirk Manor's housekeeping staff's responsibility ended. The soles of her shoes had more traction on this last flight of stairs, because no surface could be slick underneath a thick and downy coating of dust. Those dusty stairs had been narrow, twisting, and rickety as Faye and Daniel ascended to the attic. As it turned out, climbing them had been worth every painful step.

Behind a paneled door coated with flaking and powdery white paint, a treasure trove was waiting.

The walls were lined with shelves, and the stuff loading those shelves had overflowed and spilled onto the floor. Somebody had cleaned out a path through the narrow room, so Faye and Daniel were picking their way down the full impressive width of Dunkirk Manor's kitchen. This cluttered and dusty room looked like most people's attics, except that it had been the attic of people who could buy anything they fancied for more than a hundred years.

Faye saw trunks spilling over with yellowed silk dresses. She saw moth-eaten buffalo heads and the tusks of elephants. Tucked among the junk were boxes of file folders, probably the complete tax records of a wealthy family, dating to the time when the 16th Amendment first turned the Bureau of Internal Revenue loose on an unsuspecting public. Most of this stuff would probably be worth a few dollars at one of the antique stores on San Marco Avenue, but no more.

Still, Faye would have sold her mother for a chance to plunder through it. And her history-loving mother would probably have understood, if she were still around to be sold. Maybe if Faye exercised a little salesmanship, she could get paid for this work that she was dying to do anyway.

"We could curate this material for you, Daniel. Some of the papers might be worth archiving, and there could be artwork that you'd want to display for your guests." She pointed at a pile of ornate frames sitting in a dormer.

Daniel was silent longer than he needed to be.

"Maybe." Daniel seemed to waver. "I'm not sure Suzanne and I can afford such a large project yet—not until you finish the one you're working on now, anyway—but I do have one thing to ask you. I mean…" He swallowed hard. "I have something to show you."

He waved vaguely in the direction they'd been moving. Then he started walking briskly down the length of a huge room in an attic so big that there was yet another door in the far wall. Faye looked lovingly at the door—what could be behind it?—but forward progress stopped when Joe opened the door behind them.

"You were gone for awhile, Faye, and I got worried. Glynis told me where you were." He looked at Daniel. "It's a powerful long hike downstairs from here for a pregnant lady. Maybe you've got a freight elevator we can use to get her back down?"

Great. Her handsome and sexy husband was talking about her in the third person, and he was saying that she needed to be hauled around in a freight elevator. Was the romance truly that dead?

"Oh, I can do the stairs," Faye said, though her hips were arguing with her.

"Didn't you use the elevator to get to my office, Faye?" Daniel asked. "There's no way to get up this far without that last flight of stairs, but we added an elevator that serves the guest areas on the three main floors."

Faye's back was yelling at her, saying, *Idiot. You should have known a place this luxurious would have an elevator.*

A tiny bit of irritation seeped into Daniel's habitually calm voice. "This house was built with a freight elevator. A dumbwaiter, too. But the freight elevator wasn't good enough for the government, so we installed a passenger elevator in the turret on the right side of the entrance hall. We did it right, too. We hired a historic restoration firm to design one that wouldn't destroy the aesthetics of the house. That atrium is featured in architecture textbooks, you know."

The restoration architect must be really good, because Faye had never even noticed the elevator. Clearly, it was damn near invisible.

Joe looked behind him, through the open door, obviously looking for the easiest way to get his elephantine wife safely downstairs. Faye could see that she had no choice but to clamber back down the attic stairs. After that, though, it couldn't be far to the elevator.

An odd quiet hung in the air. Faye took it on herself to break the awkward silence.

"You said you had something to show me?"

Or had Daniel said he had something to *ask* her? Which was it?

Logic said that Daniel had wanted to show her something, because he could have asked her a question downstairs or outside in the rear garden. He could have asked her a question on the telephone or by email. He could have even texted her a question, now that Faye knew how to answer it. No. Daniel had asked to see her face-to-face.

Daniel eyed Joe for a second. Why did Faye have the feeling that this man didn't want to speak in front of Joe? Joe was her business partner. If Daniel wanted to talk to Faye about curating this glorious roomful of junk, he could certainly say so in front of him.

Or maybe he had truly just wanted to show Faye something interesting, and he was finally getting around to it. Instead of speaking, Daniel took a tentative step into the midst of the junk to his right and grabbed a book off a dusty shelf, deep in the alcove formed by a dormer window.

And not just any book. It was beautifully bound in worn blindstamped calfskin that was still mostly black. Faye reached out both hands to grasp it safely, cursing the skin oils on those hands and on Daniel's. Daniel handed it over casually, like a man with no idea what he had.

Faye hesitated to touch the pages, but they looked like very old vellum. They had been bound together in a day when books were precious and their craftsmanship reflected that value. Wishing for cotton gloves, she gently opened the volume. The ink had faded from black to brown, but the words were still clear on the old paper. The text was handwritten in Spanish.

Faye thanked God that the university had forced her to study a foreign language and that she'd chosen Spanish. And she thanked Magda, especially, for refusing to let her stop her Spanish studies after she'd met the two-year foreign language requirement imposed by the graduate school. Despite the antique script and archaic language, Faye knew that she could read the words written in this very, very old book.

The narrative began by stating that, "*The favor of the Lord shone down on the fleet of our admiral, Captain-General Pedro Menéndez de Avilés,*" and Faye lost her breath. The baby had a habit of kicking her in the diaphragm, which sometimes made breathing difficult, but this was a different kind of gasp. This was the kicked-in-the-stomach breathlessness of a history geek who recognizes a name from her textbooks.

Pedro Menéndez de Avilés was the founder of St. Augustine.

The next words were even better. If her translation was accurate—and why shouldn't she be able to translate words so simple that a small Spanish child might use them?—then the next phrase read, "... *on that bright July day in 1565.*"

Menéndez de Avilés had sailed for the New World in July 1565. Was it remotely possible that this book had come with him and his crew?

"Would you like me to take a look at this for you?" Faye asked, though she hardly supposed Daniel could understand her, since her lips and tongue were so dry. "Is this why you brought me up here?"

Daniel drew the book back and laid it atop a cardboard box. "Not this book, especially, though I do love the look of that old leather. I was thinking it might look nice in the guest library downstairs."

Faye groped for the right words. It was a completely awful idea to expose this priceless journal to the dirty and careless hands of bored tourists. But it was Daniel's book.

Daniel grasped Faye's elbow with a gentle but firm hand, guiding her toward the door where Joe stood. "I really just brought you up here to see this room. In the future, Suzanne and I might want to hire your firm to sort through this junk and tell us if there's anything worth preserving. Right now, though, we need to focus our money on getting permission to build that swimming pool."

They took a step away from the book. Faye was in agony.

She couldn't possibly leave the priceless manuscript in these awful surroundings. The book had probably languished here for decades, it was true, but now she knew it was here. She couldn't leave it for the bugs and the humidity and the dust to destroy. The sunlight streaming through the dormer window onto the leather binding made her physically ill. And that cardboard box beneath it…the acids in the cardboard would give her nightmares tonight. If anything, by moving the book onto that box, Daniel had put it in even more danger now than before.

"Daniel?"

Faye thought quickly as she spoke. If this man told her to mind her own business and get back to the work she was being paid to do, there wasn't a thing Faye could do about it. She'd need to choose her next few words carefully, because she might not get another chance. "I'd like some time with that book tonight, after I've finished monitoring my field crew for the day. I think it might be significant enough to get some publicity for your business—"

Daniel perked up substantially. Faye had chosen just the right approach.

"—and I won't charge you for my time."

Daniel, the consummate businessman, absolutely glowed.

Faye had decided that maybe she was pretty good at fostering good client relations. All she had to do was promise to give her clients something for free. Of course, this would mean that those clients would expect her to keep right on doing that, but she'd cross that bridge when she came to it. Right now, she was just happy to *have* clients.

Surely this was a most diplomatic way to get her hands on the book. And it was a lot more ethical than sneaking back up here tonight and…um…liberating it.

Faye could see that Daniel was thinking. And while he was thinking, the sunshine was doing its damage to the front cover of a book that might be irreplaceable. And the cardboard was taking its own toll on the back cover. Faye prayed for the right answer…

…and she got it.

"Okay. Take it with you." He grabbed the book and handed it to Faye as casually as if it were a sack of potatoes. "Just stop by my office later in the week and let me know what you find out about it." He glanced behind him and fetched another book out of the stack. "This one looks interesting, too. Let me know if it's worth anything."

It was a blue cloth-bound copy of an early Nancy Drew mystery. Even given all the various editions and printings and changes in artwork, it would be far easier to establish the age and value of this book than the old leatherbound journal.

Faye accepted the second book and gave her client an ingratiating smile, as she promised to do a little more work for free. "I'll do that."

Picking her way through the junk on the floor, Faye let Joe lead her by the hand. With his arm around her waist, he gave her just enough support to make the trek downstairs easier.

He knew her well enough not to even try to carry the books for her.

◇◇◇

Faye would have said that it was impossible for Glynis' voice to be anything but sweet. She would have been wrong. The young woman's sharp tone was evident and audible, even from the next room. Faye lingered in the atrium, wishing that she'd just stayed in her room with Joe, instead of venturing out to scavenge an after-dinner snack.

She was hesitant to walk into the dining room and let Glynis see that someone had overheard her argument, so she just lurked and wished she were somewhere else.

"I told you I was busy tonight! I have a board meeting."

Glynis was angry and upset, and she was doing a good job of communicating that. If she was trying to sound forceful, though, she was missing the mark. Faye remembered that she'd been well over thirty before she'd gained the strong tone of voice that caught the attention of people who were busy dismissing her.

"And I told you that I wanted you at home."

The voice was calm, as if to suggest that Glynis was the unreasonable one. "I just want us to have some quiet time together. A drink. A nice meal—"

"Of course, you want a nice meal, Lex…as long as I'm the one that cooked it. Make your own damn dinner. And mix your own damn martini." Sweet little Glynis might not sound convincingly bitchy yet, but she was getting closer. "I'll be home early. I'm always home early. What's your problem?"

The male voice shifted into an ingratiating tone so quickly that Faye knew he was faking it. The man wasn't just angry over Glynis' rebellion. He was outraged.

"Sweetheart…the preservationists can get along without you just this one night. I just want to look at your pretty face over the dinner table, and I want to watch old movies while we hold hands. Like we used to do."

Why wasn't Faye picturing a happy couple, hand in hand? Why was she picturing a big angry man holding both Glynis' dainty hands in one of his huge ones? What did this guy look like, anyway?

Faye edged closer to the open archway separating the atrium from the dining room. The arguing man and woman were standing on either end of a serving table. They were looking at each other, not at her, but the painting above the serving table *was* looking at her. The dark-eyed woman in the image looked just as unsettled as fair-haired Glynis sounded. Actually, she looked terrified. Faye remembered why she wasn't such a big fan of expressionist art.

Interesting…the man wasn't as big as he sounded. He was several inches taller than Glynis, who was not a short woman, but he had the kind of slender build that looked good in a suit. He was fair-haired, and his tanned features were cleanly sculpted. She caught only this glimpse before Glynis delivered her final word.

She said, "I'll be home by nine. If you'd enjoy a quiet dinner together, then have it cooked when I get home." Then she showed him the door.

Faye backed into the shadow of the staircase, so as not to detract from Glynis' sweeping dismissal of her idiot boyfriend, but she wanted to give her a standing ovation.

Joe watched Faye trudge into their shabby room. She was five feet tall in her sock feet and, until eight months ago, she'd tipped the scales at a hundred pounds. Joe, on the other hand, was never allowed to forget that he was six-and-a-half feet tall, since he spent his days stooping down to hear the conversation of normal people and tiny folk like Faye.

There was a very real possibility that Joe's baby would be just too big for Faye to carry.

They didn't talk about it. They *couldn't* talk about it, because that would require Faye to admit there might be something in this world that she simply couldn't do.

It would also require her to admit that she was forty years old. Joe was only thirty-one, but he could already feel time making a difference in his strength and endurance. They were both still prodigious, but there was a difference.

When Faye was twenty-five, maybe she could have carried and delivered this baby easily. Now, he could see the toll her pregnancy was taking. She groaned when she rolled over in her sleep, because her hips pained her. She rubbed her aching back all the damn time. She wasn't eating as well as she should. And he was frankly scared to keep shoving prenatal vitamins her way, because one day she was going to bite off the hand holding them.

He'd wanted this baby so badly, and so had she. She'd gotten pregnant as soon as they said, "I do," because they wanted more than one kid and they thought there might just be enough time for that.

Now he was wondering. Maybe this should be it. He'd been an only child, and so had Faye. They'd both turned out okay. Yeah, he liked the idea of listening to two kids laughing and playing all over the wild island where he and Faye lived, but he wasn't sure he wanted to take another big risk with the health of the woman he loved. If Faye came out of this pregnancy with a ruined back or wrecked hips, she'd live with the consequences for the rest of her life. And there were worse things that could happen.

He knew this, because he'd bought every pregnancy manual on the bookstore's shelves. For a man who'd spent his first quarter-century running from books as if they were bears, Joe had found that knowledge had a pacifying effect. When he was worried about Faye, he could find a book to tell him that most women came through childbirth just fine, even women who'd waited till they were forty to find the right man and start making babies.

Unfortunately, those books also told him about women who needed Cesarean sections to birth babies who were too big. And other women who got dangerous infections afterward. And still other women whose blood pressure spiked so high that they got strokes and kidney failure and—though he told himself to stop brooding about it—sometimes they died.

He blamed himself, every time she bent over and her face twitched in pain. If something happened to Faye, Joe would always blame himself.

From the journal of Father Domingo Sanz de la Fuente

Translated from the Spanish by
Faye Longchamp Mantooth, Ph.D.,
and Magda Stockard-McKenzie, Ph.D.

The Captain-General, Don Pedro himself, visited our vessel as we prepared to sail from Dominica to La Florida. Having secured weapons from our stores, as well as taken two soldiers from among our number to care for the ordnance he took from us, he gave a most stirring speech.

Upon hearing of his plans to force our way past a seaport armed with two thousand Frenchmen, Father Francisco had the bravery to speak his opposition, begging the Captain-General to remember that he must give a good account to God for his care of a thousand Christian souls. It speaks well of the Captain-General's respect for the Father that he listened to his appeal, though he did not heed it.

Our passage to La Florida was yet another succession of omens, good and foul. Near the entrance to the Bahama Channel, God hung a comet in the heavens, where it shone long enough for a penitent soul to repeat two Credos. The sailors spoke of this as a good omen, yet the next day found us utterly becalmed. Father Francisco prayed ceaselessly, and shortly after the sun passed its highest point, Our Lord sent a fresh wind and we were under full sail again.

This miracle continued, for we soon sighted land. Taking anchor, we found ourselves miraculously near the enemies we sought, without any need to thank our pilots. These benighted men had pretended that they knew our location, while claiming that we were yet one hundred leagues from La Florida. I confess that I fully believed them, up till the moment that La Florida's coastline crested on the horizon like the monstrous whales we encountered while far at sea.

And then the evil omens resumed. For four days we remained at anchor, thwarted by contrary winds. When they abated, we had no winds at all.

As we waited, the Captain-General sent scouts ashore to seek the location of the French port, and I asked to accompany them. I confess to a burning curiosity to see this wild country and the wild people who lived there.

We first built a large fire on the shore in hopes of attracting Indians who could lead us to our destination. When no one appeared, the lead spy cried out—

"There is proof of their ignorance. They are too dimwitted to wonder who has landed on their shore!"

I wondered whether their absence might be more due to caution than ignorance, but I do not have Father Francisco's boldness, and so I held my tongue.

The decision was made to penetrate the interior, and we arrived at the village of a tribe of Indians

known as the Timucua. They received us kindly,
serving us abundant food and embracing us as
friends. Through sign language, they asked us for
gifts in return, as I have learned is their custom, and
our soldiers complied with trinkets such as beads
and mirrors. In return, the natives handed our leader
two pieces of gold. They were small nuggets and not
of the highest quality, yet I now believe that this
gift marks the natives' true moment of ignorance.

How could they have known how much blood
had been spilled—and would soon be spilled again—
for this substance that is, truth be told, not very
useful. You cannot eat gold. You cannot build a
house of it. You cannot clothe yourself in it. You
cannot burn it for warmth. Why do we kill for it?

I am now at the end of a long life, and still I
cannot answer that question.

I do admit that gold feels warm and wordlessly
lovely in the hand. When we returned to the ship, the
Captain-General's eyes glittered over the glowing
lumps of metal. How he gloated over the unequal
exchange: our trinkets for their gold! And this is
the tragedy underlying everything I have seen in
this strange new world. I do not think the Timucua
saw the exchange as unequal. They returned trinkets in exchange for the trinkets they were given.

How could they have known that we would
destroy them in the name of this luminous and
glistering plaything... gold?

I, Father Domingo Sanz de la Fuente, attest
that the foregoing is a statement of actual events.

Chapter Six

"You look terrible this morning, Faye."

As usual, Magda minced no words. She leaned in the doorway to the room where Faye and Joe were staying, with the relaxed demeanor of the mother who has just handed her cherished offspring over to a trusted babysitter and who is, therefore, drunk with freedom. Clearly enjoying her responsibility-free moment, Magda lounged, waiting for Faye to respond.

"I look terrible? Why, thank you. Now let me check *you* out for physical flaws, okay? Where shall I begin—"

Joe nudged her with his foot, and she knew this was a warning not to hit Magda in her soft spot. The older archaeologist was strong, smart, and tough, it was true, but she was a woman. She would have liked to have been pretty, too. And she *was* pretty, if you liked short, stocky, freckle-faced women whose beauty regimen consisted of washing their faces and wrapping a rubber band around their long bushy locks. Sheriff Mike thought Magda was ravishing.

Nevertheless, it would be best to leave physical flaws out of this conversation, even if Magda did have personality flaws that included a distinct lack of tact.

For once, Joe did the talking for the two of them, and Faye didn't like what he had to say.

"She doesn't look terrible. But she does look like she was up most of the night."

"That's why I'm here. When Faye sends you to my door asking for white cotton gloves, and it's way after quitting time, I know something's up. I would have come back with you last night, but Rachel was already asleep and I couldn't leave her."

Faye was actually glad Magda was here to pry into her business. She had something big to share.

"Check this out."

She put on the borrowed gloves and carefully folded back the acid-free paper she'd wrapped around the journal.

Magda let her breath out in a slow hiss, but she turned her head, so as not to breathe on the old book. Faye gently opened it to the title page. When Magda saw the date "1565," the rest of her breath left her with a whoosh.

"Do you think it's really that old? It sure is in good shape."

"The condition of the paper is one clue that it really might be that old. Paper from the last couple hundred years ages a whole lot faster than the really old stuff. The wood pulp makes modern paper too acid. Back in the day," Faye patted the book with her gloved hand, "and I mean way, way back in the day, they made paper with cotton rags, and that stuff lasts. But you know that."

"I know that intellectually," Magda said, pulling on another pair of cotton gloves that she'd brought with her, just in case, "but just look at that paper. It's so white, and it still bends. Just *look* at it…" She stopped to look at Faye. "Can you still read it? You're smiling. And you were up all night. That means it's still readable. I'll be damned. What does it say?"

"Well, it's in Spanish…"

"Tell me you're grateful that I didn't let you quit taking Spanish after you met the grad school's minimum requirements."

"I'm grateful. Now, do you want to hear what it says or not."

Magda raised her bushy eyebrows, which was her way of saying yes.

"It's the memoirs of a priest who landed here with Don Pedro Menéndez de Avilés in 1565. It's got everything—the ocean voyage, the founding of St. Augustine, first contact with the

Native Americans, the Matanzas massacre. Everything. But it's going to take me a while to translate it. Can I do that?"

"Not if it means you won't be sleeping." Joe's voice had an edge to it that contrasted sharply with his usual good-natured warmth.

The women ignored him.

Magda was talking fast, but her eyes never left the manuscript. "Well, you're good at Spanish, but that doesn't make you a specialist in Renaissance Spain. So if you're planning to publish that translation, be prepared for serious criticism."

"The manuscript, Magda. Should I get the manuscript to an archivist before it self-destructs in my hands? What's the ethical thing to do here?"

"Where was it stored?"

"In a hot, humid, dusty attic. Just inside a sunny window. On top of a cardboard box."

"Well, that was a crime against humanity. You're already on the side of the angels, just because you got it out of that attic. Let me think."

Magda stooped over the desk and studied the book's leather binding through the strongest part of her trifocals. "Who owns it?"

"Daniel and Suzanne, I guess."

"Maybe. If the author is a priest, the Catholic Church may want to argue with them about that. There's a precedent for ceding ownership of such things to the Church. Or sharing it. But if it gets that far, Daniel and Suzanne might just sell it before the lawyers even get started jousting over the legal fine points, and all the information between these covers could disappear into a collector's library. With all that in mind, I think you need to do three things."

"I'm listening."

"First, keep it here in this cool, dark, humidity-controlled room for the time being. It ain't the National Archives—which may actually be where this belongs—but it'll do for now. Do not under any circumstances let those people put it back in that damned attic. Second, convince them to donate it or sell it to someone who will make sure that it's properly preserved, maybe even to the Catholic Church. And third…you're going to like this one, Faye."

"Am I going to like it?" Joe asked.

"Well, I don't know, Joe. I think Faye should learn as much about this thing as she can, right now, in case it disappears into the collector's market."

Joe snorted. "You're just giving her permission to work all night, and you know she needs her sleep."

"Tell you what, Joe. I'll help her with her day job so she can devote some time to this project. You take over responsibility for my rebellious friend at night. Your job is simple: make the woman go to bed at a reasonable hour."

Poor Joe. Faye had already seen enough of Father Domingo Sanz de la Fuente's story to know that he would be keeping her up nights for quite some time, despite the efforts of her husband and her best friend to get her to act like a feeble pregnant woman.

As Joe watched Magda and Faye fuss over the old journal, he could see that they were going to be very late for work. It was a good thing one of the two was the boss, or else they'd both be out of a job.

When the workday had officially begun at eight a.m., Magda and Faye had looked up from Father Domingo's memoirs just long enough to ask Joe if he'd go outside and manage the field techs. He didn't mind. Since he didn't read Spanish, this suggestion had made perfect sense. Somebody needed to manage the project that would be paying his and Faye's grocery bills for the summer, and it might as well be him. He knew that nothing short of a shrieking police siren could have ripped the two women from their new intellectual toy.

Two hours later, that siren sounded. Many sirens, in fact, and they all converged directly in front of Dunkirk Manor. The sound was incongruous on this windswept, shady, and affluent street.

Joe saw the cook look out the back door. Seconds later, Magda darted out onto the back porch, looking to make sure the field crew was safe. Several heartbeats passed before Faye appeared. It was a shock to realize how very slowly she moved these days.

Joe barked at Levon and Kirk to hustle themselves to the house. He felt responsible for them, and he knew that Faye wasn't going to retreat into the safety of Dunkirk Manor until she knew her crew was safe, too.

The sirens hadn't stopped and, even in the large empty yard, he was worried. The tall brick wall surrounding it was sturdy enough, but he knew that Daniel and Suzanne left the iron gate onto the street open around the clock. Rain had washed soil around the base of the gate and clumps of grass grew out of that soil. It had been years since the gate had been closed, probably more years than Daniel and Suzanne had owned Dunkirk Manor. In this neighborhood and in this fortress of a house, crime seemed a distant worry. Yet the sirens continued to sound.

Who knew why the police had descended upon this street?

Faye let Joe help her find a seat in the crowded living room of Suzanne and Daniel's private quarters, which took up the entire streetside half of Dunkirk Manor's second story. The Wrathers had asked their employees to wait there while they dealt with questions from worried guests, who were gathered in the home's two dining rooms.

Suzanne had obviously redecorated the owner's suite to her own taste. The upholstered furniture was leather-covered and Scandinavian in design, and the wooden end tables were sleek and light. The crisp window hangings were striped in white and cornflower blue. Though simple, everything in the room was elegant and obviously expensive.

Only the artwork looked like it belonged in Dunkirk Manor. Judging by the gilt frames, which matched those in the atrium and the entry hall, Faye would say that they were part of the early twentieth-century collection that dominated the house with its color and energy. They were all full-body portraits, and the faces were expressive and finely wrought, but the poses were vaguely unnatural and disturbing. Combined with the flashing blue lights on the street below, the paintings made Faye feel even more creeped out. However, on the dubious strength of four graduate classes in art history, Faye would say that many of the works were of museum quality.

The elegantly appointed room overlooked the front yard, which meant that everyone sitting inside could look down on the cluster of police cars out front. Faye was sitting on a settee overcrowded with nervous people, so her right side was jammed against the front wall. She could look down and watch the police as they looked everywhere for…something.

The wall was cold against her cheek, reminding her that Dunkirk Manor was made by a building technique firmly associated with St. Augustine: poured concrete. The wall was utterly solid beneath its generous coating of plaster and blue paint. She shifted her head, leaning it on the wall behind her. It, too, had the solid feel of poured concrete. This house would stand until Doomsday.

The five archaeologists plus little Rachel and the babysitter, added to two chambermaids, a cook, and a hostess, filled the living room to capacity. Gossip couldn't have failed to flow in a room that full. Ordinarily, Faye hated gossip, but she made exceptions at times like this.

The cook whispered that Glynis had failed to show up for work. Faye heard one of the chambermaids add that the gardener was being questioned, because he'd found Glynis' car in the lot reserved for staff parking. The car was where it was supposed to be, but Glynis wasn't.

Joe was thinking like a predator.

People were saying that Glynis had gone missing from the staff parking lot. Being a hunter, he compulsively focused on how this could have happened. The lot was on Dunkirk Manor's grounds, inside the brick wall that enclosed the rear garden where the archaeological crew was working. It was accessible from a gravel driveway that entered from the street through the open gate, but a thick hedge of bamboo camouflaged it from the eyes of passersby. People who entered the parking lot generally found it only because they already knew it was there. This told Joe something about how Glynis could have been taken with no one knowing, if she'd even been abducted at all.

The bamboo hedge even camouflaged the parking lot from people who did know it was there, blocking it from view within Dunkirk Manor's extensive grounds. Without the hedge, Glynis' abandoned car would even now be clearly visible from the site of the former swimming pool where the archaeological crew had been working. Joe stirred. With this realization, he knew that danger had crept too close to Faye for his comfort.

"I don't know what the gardener saw, exactly," the hostess offered to anyone willing to listen, "but I did hear that there was blood on the front seat. Glennie has dove-gray leather seats, so you know the blood showed up. He couldn't have been wrong about that."

Joe's throat hurt. Glynis must have arrived at work early, before he started work at eight, or he'd have seen her drive in the gate and disappear behind the hedge. By then, Glynis' car was already sitting there, empty and with bloodied upholstery. What had happened to that poor woman? And now that violence had come so close, what was to prevent someone from hurting Faye?

Violence against women affected Joe viscerally. If someone had hurt fragile, gentle Glynis, then he needed to go hunting for the son-of-a-bitch. The very idea made it hard for him to sit still. A crowded room full of scared, gossiping people was the last place he wanted to be right now...except for the fact of Faye.

If she'd been annoyed by the way he'd dogged her every step lately, then her life was about to get worse. Yes, there was a tall and stout brick wall around their worksite, and maybe Daniel would start keeping the damn garden gate closed, but that wasn't enough. From now on, Faye would be protected by a tall, stout brick wall and a tall, brawny husband. She could argue all she liked but, even at her currently inflated size, he was still way bigger than she was.

◇◇◇

Faye felt a cold breeze on her face. She rose to her feet and Joe followed without any need for her to ask him. She needed to tell the police about what she'd heard last night, when dainty Glynis told her large boyfriend where to get off.

If the gossip was true, if Glynis was missing, then the police would eventually want to talk with everyone who'd been at Dunkirk Manor that morning. Eventually. But Faye had information that couldn't wait.

When she stood, every eye in a room full of tense, nervous people swung her way. Feeling as conspicuous as a whale swimming with a school of sardines, she maneuvered her swollen body through the crowd. Joe was three inches behind her, where she suspected he would remain until Glynis was found or the baby came, whichever came last. This made her trek even more conspicuous, if such a thing were possible.

"Excuse me," she murmured, as her belly brushed against the cook's arm. "Pardon me," she said as she stepped over Kirk's outstretched legs. "I just need some air."

Faye could hear her mother's voice in her head saying, "Can't you just, for once, do as you're told? The police will get to you eventually, if you'll just wait your turn."

But she could also hear her grandmother's voice saying, "Do what you think is best, baby. God gave you a brain. He expects you to use it."

Faye knew that when a person was missing, every second counts. Every second could be taking Glynis further away. Every second, more of her blood could be flowing. Every second could be her last.

Faye and Joe stepped out of the owners' suite and onto the balcony that encircled the atrium. Two policemen, one in uniform and one in a golf shirt and slacks, stood talking on the ground floor, so Faye clattered heavily down the staircase instead of taking the elevator. From below, she probably looked like a zeppelin, descending out of the sky.

How much longer would she be pregnant? Oh yeah…five whole weeks. And five days.

The plainclothes officer looked up at her and said, "Ma'am, if you'll just wait with the others, we'd like to talk with you eventually. But right now—"

"I think you need to talk to me now." She reached the bottom step and suddenly, he was no longer looking up at her. She saw now that he was almost as tall as Joe, although considerably wider.

"Now why exactly do you think that?" Spoken by a different man, in a different tone of voice, his words could have been confrontational or dismissive. Not, however, when spoken by this man. He just wanted to know the answer to his question.

"Is the gossip true? Is Glynis Smithson missing? And do you have reason to think she's been hurt?"

The big cop cocked his balding head down at her and said, "I see that there are no secrets in this house. You know something and you think it's important. Tell me what it is."

"The last time I saw Glynis, she was standing in that room there," Faye pointed at the dining room to the right of the staircase, "and she was arguing with her jerk of a boyfriend."

There it was. Faye had dragged herself down that staircase, burning to tell this to someone in a position to help.

The detective gave her a long evaluating look before speaking. "When?"

"Last night."

"Lex Tifton?"

"She called him Lex, yes."

"Did he hurt her? Or threaten her?"

"No, but he was overbearing and controlling. That's why they were arguing. She had plans for the evening, and he wanted her to come home. I'm pretty sure he lost the argument. I am *dead* certain that Glynis did not go home and cook him the romantic meal he wanted. She said something about a board meeting, and he said something about preservationists. So I guess maybe it wouldn't be too hard to find out where she went last night after she left here."

The uniformed officer looked very interested in what she had to say, but the big man in the golf shirt was the one doing all the talking. He must be in charge.

"She looked okay physically when you saw her?"

"Yes."

"And Tifton didn't hurt her while you were watching?"

"No. They were standing on opposite ends of that table." She pointed through the open passageway into the dining room. "He didn't even raise his voice, but he was angry."

"I've only talked to a few people so far, but, if Lex Tifton has a fan club, I'm not sure it has but one member. And even that presumes that his girlfriend likes him."

"After last night, I'm not so sure he still has a girlfriend."

Faye stopped short, horrified by what she'd just said. She hadn't meant that Lex might not have a girlfriend because something terrible had happened to Glynis. She'd simply meant that Glynis had sounded like she was about ready to cut Lex loose.

She tried again. "That came out wrong. I meant that Glynis sounded like she'd enjoyed just about as much of Lex's company as she could stand."

The officer chuckled. "I knew what you meant." He extended a hand. "You know, I think we've settled in to work here and I haven't properly introduced myself. I'm Donald Overstreet, and I appreciate a witness who tells me the truth without pulling any punches."

Faye shook the hand. "I'm Faye Longchamp-Mantooth. I think my husband sometimes wishes I'd pull a few punches."

She didn't have to look behind her to know that Joe was nodding.

Overstreet laughed out loud. "Well, I'm not your husband.

Joe stuck out a hand. "Joe Wolf Mantooth. *I'm* her husband."

Overstreet chuckled and said, "Lucky man."

Faye wasn't sure how to take that comment.

"Tell me what you overheard of Glynis' and Lex's conversation. No holds barred."

Before doing that, Faye interrupted the interview to blurt out an idiotic question. "Why would someone want to hurt a twenty-something-year-old girl?"

Overstreet just looked at her and shook his head, and she felt completely stupid. She knew the answer to her question, and so did he. Any woman alive who'd ever wished she wasn't alone in a dark place could answer it.

◇◇◇

Overstreet noticed that Faye Longchamp-Mantooth's husband was standing right behind her, with his hand resting lightly between her shoulderblades. He remembered how he'd felt when his wife was this pregnant. If a violent kidnapper had suddenly turned up in the neighborhood when she was in that condition, he'd have probably turned paranoid and homicidal. Only in a good way.

Joe Wolf Mantooth looked constructively paranoid and homicidal. Overstreet had no doubt that this man would be protecting this woman. He wished he had enough officers to protect all the other women within striking distance of Dunkirk Manor.

Surely, Mother Nature had had her reasons for making women smaller and weaker than men. And surely she'd had her reasons for making some men aggressive enough to use that imbalance in ways that weren't very nice or even very human, but Donald Overstreet couldn't imagine what those reasons were.

Why would someone want to hurt a twenty-something-year-old girl?

Alas, the answers to that question were age-old.

Chapter Seven

By noon, the gossip machine had spread the word that Glynis' boyfriend Lex was not a nice man. Faye had seen Lex exactly once and she knew that already.

A single glimpse had told her that Lex Tifton was tanned and as handsome as she'd expected. Women like Glynis attracted high-status men.

Glynis was pretty enough to satisfy the male urge to crow, "Look what I've got!" but her attraction for powerful men would have gone beyond mere looks. She was smart enough to make pleasant dinner party conversation. And she was soft-spoken enough to avoid challenging her boyfriend in any meaningful way at all. Or she'd seemed that way until she'd gotten her dander up last night.

Faye was not surprised to learn that Lex was a lawyer, because Glynis would be the perfect lawyer's wife…if they found her… when they found her.

The scuttlebutt said that Lex was the kind of boyfriend who complained when his girlfriend was just a few minutes late getting home from work. He was the kind of man who didn't like the idea of a girls' night out. Again, Faye had seen Lex just once, and she knew that already.

Those who knew her well said that Glynis didn't talk about these things, but people notice when a woman is constantly on her cell phone, saying things like, "Suzanne wanted me to work a few minutes late, but I'll be right there," or "I'd love to have dinner with you and the girls, but Lex and I enjoy our evenings together." People notice, and they talk about it.

Glynis said and did these things with a gracious smile. And there was nothing wrong with showing your partner the courtesy of telling him you'd be late for work, or with preferring to spend most of your time with him. Still, a certain kind of man has been controlling a certain kind of woman for all of human history. People who care about a woman notice the signs when she's been backed into that kind of corner.

Glynis' friends didn't like Lex. Faye knew this meant that the police were giving him an uncomfortable amount of scrutiny.

Or they would be, if they could find him.

Daniel and Suzanne had been sitting on the porch glider for two hours, motionless. Faye had been watching. She wasn't sure they'd spoken to each other in all that time. They'd just sat side-by-side in the wrought iron glider, hands folded in each of their laps. Only the sides of their thighs and their upper arms were touching.

Faye hadn't been married as long as they had, but she knew the comfort that came with the wordless touch of that one chosen someone. Every atom in both their bodies seemed to cry out, "Where is Glynis? How could something like this happen here?"

She didn't want to disturb their pain, but she'd waited as long as she could. Pregnant women can only go so long between visits to the bathroom, and Daniel and Suzanne were sitting directly between Faye and the facilities.

She trudged across the lawn and up the porch steps. She wasn't sure whether it would be better manners to exchange some quick pleasantries, or to just pass them quietly

Daniel solved that problem by asking her a question as she passed. "Faye, do you know anybody on the city commission?"

"The county," Suzanne said. "I think it was the county."

He nodded. "Maybe so."

"Besides, this guy said he lost the election. So he's not on any commission, anywhere. And I'm glad." Suzanne crossed her arms across her chest and nodded hard.

Faye wasn't quite sure whether they were actually still talking to her, or whether she should resume her bathroom dash.

"You probably come across these guys all the time, Faye," Suzanne said, angrily pushing against the porch floor with her feet and setting the glider in motion.

"I hope the police are grilling him right now," Daniel said. "Poor Glynis."

"*Grilling who?*" Faye said a little more forcefully than she should have. "And what did he do to Glynis?"

"Last Friday, Daniel had to go out to the parking lot—right where they found Glynis' car—and ask a man to quit badgering her," Suzanne said, still pushing the glider back and forth, hard. "His name was Dick Wheeler, and he was a real horse's ass."

Daniel looked gape-jawed at his suddenly foul-mouthed wife.

"Well, he was!" Suzanne insisted. "Tell her."

"Dick Wheeler sat on the Board of County Commissioners for fifteen years," Daniel said. "I figured he'd be there till he died. The developers loved him so much that I think they'd have kept him on the board even after that."

Suzanne giggled. "You think they would've just propped his corpse up and let him keep rubber-stamping their projects?"

Daniel nodded.

Suzanne giggled again.

"Why was he bothering Glynis?" Faye asked.

"Because her historic preservation group campaigned against him, and he lost." Suzanne couldn't keep from smiling as she delivered this news.

"I don't think his secretary's sexual harassment lawsuit helped his campaign any," Daniel pointed out.

Faye still wasn't completely sure she was part of this conversation, but it was interesting.

Suzanne waved her hand in a dismissing gesture. "Oh, that. He flirts with anything in a skirt, but he's all talk. The voters have always known what he was like, but they kept electing him. You stay away from him, Faye. He'd even hit on a woman in your condition. Nope. The lawsuit didn't sink his political career. Glynis did."

Daniel nodded. "You're right. She did. You should have seen her preservation group's commercial, Faye. It just destroyed Wheeler's façade of being a moderate when it came to growth management. Actually, the PR firm that Glynis' group hired gave me a copy of it, since we were the corporate sponsor. It was just hilarious."

Suzanne nodded emphatically.

"Glynis and her friends are very clever with computers," Daniel continued, "so they put together some video that made it look like the developers had just trashed St. Augustine. The PR guys loved it, so they took the original idea and spruced it up into something TV-ready. Golden arches over the Castillo de San Marcos. Strip joints on either side of the Bridge of Lions. A casino in the Old Slave Market. Then they filmed footage of lovely Glynis walking through the real St. Augustine, talking about how the city's preservation ordinances had saved it for all of us. She begged county residents to elect commissioners who would do the same for them.

"And they did," Suzanne said. "Much to Dick Wheeler's disappointment."

So Glynis had been the face of a controversial political movement, and that face had cost some influential people dearly. Faye knew what that might mean, and so did Daniel and Suzanne. Their pride in Glynis and her accomplishment faded from their faces, and they returned to sliding slowly to and fro on the glider.

"You've told Detective Overstreet all this?"

The dejected couple nodded silently.

Faye, like many people, had strayed from organized religion, despite all the efforts of her mother and grandmother to keep her on the straight and narrow path. That didn't mean she never prayed. Thinking of Glynis lost and alone and maybe hurting, Faye prayed more fervently than she had in a long time.

◇◇◇

When Detective Overstreet returned in mid-afternoon, Faye worried that he'd come back to harass Levon or Kirk or even Joe. Her interview with the detective had gone well, up until the point where she was forced to answer some very pointed questions about her crew:

Where had each of her employees been during the hour before the police arrived, especially the men?

They'd been working since at least eight, according to Joe. But from the police's standpoint, even Joe was suspect. If forced to tell them only what she'd seen with her own eyes, she could only say that Joe was with her when she woke up about six. After that, he'd gone to the dining room, loaded up two breakfast plates, then come back to the room to eat with her. He'd left her and Magda just before eight, and Faye'd seen nobody else from that time until the moment the house staff had come to tell her that they heard sirens outside.

She suggested to Overstreet that he check with Suzanne and Daniel to confirm Levon's and Kirk's alibis. Both of her technicians had the typical appetite of the very young man. She felt sure that they'd taken advantage of Dunkirk Manor's generous breakfast spread before coming to work. The people feeding them couldn't help noticing diners who ate so very well.

Had any of her employees shown an unusual interest in Glynis?

She'd felt compelled to mention that Levon had obviously found her attractive, but she felt silly and disloyal doing it. Of course he did. Glynis was an unusually pretty woman and any man would show a noticeable interest in her.

Kirk had certainly perked up whenever he saw Glynis coming, as well, so she told Detective Overstreet that she thought he'd been interested in her, too. Faye had bristled a bit when Joe's name came up, but she'd assured Overstreet that her husband had barely ever spoken to the missing woman.

Had any of them ever shown signs of having a temper?

This was a question Faye felt comfortable answering. She couldn't imagine three mellower men than Joe, Levon, and Kirk. The only ill-tempered person on her crew—other than, on occasion, Faye herself—was Magda. And Magda, who knew that Faye and Joe got up with the chickens, had been standing on Faye's doorstep shortly after sunrise, demanding to know why Joe had borrowed her cotton gloves. Therefore, Magda had two people to give her an alibi, Faye and Joe.

Then came the question that Faye couldn't possibly have anticipated.

How close were you, personally, to the missing woman?

There was only one answer. "Not at all."

Faye thought back over the past week. "I only knew her for a day. Well, we spoke on the phone a few times while I was bidding this job, and afterward, while I was planning the field effort. I don't think Glynis and I ever had a personal conversation, though. She delivered messages to me from her bosses, and she said hello when she came outside to visit with Levon and Kirk. That's about it."

"Well, you may have been the last person she communicated with before she disappeared."

The officer paused a minute, looking at her with a neutral expression. With his salt-and-pepper hair, plain features, bland expression, and receding hairline, Detective Overstreet could have been a television policeman, acting out the role of competent supporting cop to the dashing and glamorous star. Only there was no dashing and glamorous star at his side. Glynis' safety depended on this calm, deliberate man who couldn't have been less dynamic.

Faye couldn't make sense of his confident statement that she was among the last people to talk to Glynis. "But I told you this morning that I hadn't seen her since yesterday evening."

She realized the omission in her statement and hurried to fill it. "Even then, I didn't talk to her, and I haven't talked with her since. Or emailed or texted or twittered. I wish I *had* talked to her, so that I could help you find her, but there's been no contact of any kind since yesterday. She must have seen and spoken to people since then. Her boyfriend, for sure. Didn't they live together? And the rumor mill says that she spoke to a convenience store clerk right before she disappeared. I can't possibly have been the last."

Now she was talking too much. It sure was easy to look guilty.

"Oh, I believe that you haven't communicated with Ms. Smithson." He gave her a "Trust me," smile. "It's just that I know something you don't. *She* communicated with *you.*"

"Come again?"

He used the touch-screen on his phone to pull up a document and read aloud. "Dear Dr. Longchamp-Mantooth—"

"Are you saying she wrote me a letter?"

He nodded and kept reading. "Dear Dr. Longchamp-Mantooth," he began again. "I've been up all night, wondering what's the right thing to do. I really don't know, so I'm asking you. Can you look at these things and tell me whether they're as important as I think they are? I don't want to get anybody in trouble, but it's wrong to destroy history, just because somebody wants to build something. I've looked all over the Internet, trying to figure out what's legal, but I just don't understand the laws well enough. Can you help me? I want to do the right thing."

Detective Cole looked up at Faye and said, "It's signed Glynis Smithson." Then he laid a damaged crucifix, and a handful of beads on the table. Beside them, he placed a bone, three musket balls, the bottom half of a broken stone blade that had once been very large, and a piece of a broken battle club. Then he handed her a photo. The photo showed another piece of a damaged battle club, probably the same one. From the looks of it, the two pieces, when fitted together, would be a complete reconstruction of the original club. It hadn't been shattered in a million pieces. Sometime in the past few hundred years, it had simply been broken in two.

Overstreet said nothing, letting the artifacts speak for themselves.

Faye picked up the crucifix and the musket balls, one by one. They were all Spanish, she'd guess, and really old. She'd also guess that the filigreed beads had once dangled from this crucifix as a rosary.

The bone bothered her. She picked it up and rubbed her fingertips over it. It was a phalange, one of the small bones in the hands and feet of humans and other mammals. It was old and worn and one end was broken off. It might have been part of a pig or a deer, but she was more concerned about the possibility that it was part of a human being. Humans were more like pigs and deer than most people would like to admit. Sometimes and with some bones, only lab work could distinguish the species.

Faye wasn't a walking analytical lab, but she had handled a lot of bones. She'd want lab data or detailed taxonomy before she'd sit on the witness stand and say for certain that this bone was human. But her experience and the tactile memory in her hands said that it was. "Have you reported this?"

"The medical examiner's office said we should."

If anybody should have developed the ability to recognize a human bone on sight, it would have been a medical examiner. "Then I'm sure you followed that advice. If this is a human bone, the legal ramifications of Glynis' letter skyrocket, from an archaeological standpoint. At the very least, the construction project she mentions would need to be shut down right away."

She could tell that she wasn't telling Overstreet anything he didn't know already.

She switched her attention to the battle club, more accurately called a "celt." She'd guess that it was Timucuan, but she found it difficult to date without access to reference materials. Still, she could tell that the old weapon was large and heavy and beautifully made.

She glanced at the photo of the celt's other half. It would have taken a major blow to break a piece of stone this size into two pieces like this—this chunk alone was as long as Faye's palm—but even big, heavy pieces of rock can break. The Timucua had designed these things for bashing in skulls on the battlefield. If this celt had been used in battle, it had taken many blows and the last one had ruined it.

"Why didn't you show me these this morning?"

"Oh, don't worry. I wasn't keeping anything from you. It's just that the lab hadn't released the materials. Besides, we didn't know what we had."

"Come again?" Faye said, one more time. How could the police not know about the artifacts Glynis had apparently wanted her to see?

"Ms. Smithson had written her note, then folded it up and put it in an envelope with the smaller stuff—the crucifix, the musket balls, the beads, the bone. The broken blade and the pieces of the—um, did you call it a celt?—were a little too big for the envelope, so maybe she was carrying them in her hand when she was…kidnapped…or attacked…or whatever it was that happened to her. We found the broken blade and this piece of the celt on the passenger seat of the car, resting on a pile of wadded-up wrapping paper. The chunk of celt in the photo was on the ground outside. I was wondering if you could tell whether the celt was broken recently, maybe during a struggle this morning, or whether it was already broken."

"Let me see." Faye reached for the photo and the hunk of stone.

Overstreet pulled a few more photos out of his file, showing the two weapons from all possible angles.

Faye pulled a magnifier out of her purse and studied the celt's fracture plane, both on the physical piece of rock and in the photo. "I'd say it's been a real long time since this club was in one piece. A lab could tell you for sure."

"I had a feeling that interviewing you would be useful."

"I can't imagine that knowing the age of the celt, or whether it had been broken for long, would give you much that would help you find Glynis."

"The celt is rather…important."

Faye turned her attention to a photo that focused tightly on the celt's blunt edge. A smear of blood resolved itself in front of her eyes, and she set the magnifier down with a clatter.

Steeling herself, she picked it back up. "I think this celt looks like it has been…used for its design purpose."

"*That* is, peculiarly scientific way of saying that you think someone was bashed with this stone club."

"I'm a scientist. So sue me. And I don't deal on a day-to-day basis with weapons that have been recently used."

"Believe me when I say that I wish I didn't."

She turned her attention back to the blade. "If I really wanted to hurt somebody, though, I don't think I'd club them with the celt. I'd use this. Even though the pointy business end of it is gone, the part that's left is still a fearsome thing."

"There's not a trace of blood on it. Believe me, we looked. Because we think somebody got hurt this morning with something a lot sharper than a broken Indian war club."

"Oh, Glynis." The words escaped Faye's lips like a sigh.

"No, not Glynis." Detective Overstreet paused, then he back-pedaled. "Well, maybe not. Two people got hurt this morning. We know that because the blood we found wasn't all the same type, and most of it wasn't hers. I'm hoping the lab can tell me whether the blood got on this celt because it was just…everywhere…or because somebody used it as a weapon. It's certainly solid enough to do some serious damage if someone decided to bash someone else in the head. I guess I never really answered your question about why I didn't tell you about the note when I was here this morning. That's why."

He rubbed a finger on the photo, as if trying to wipe the blood off the celt's blunt edge.

Faye wasn't following him. "*What's* why?"

"We didn't know that Miss Smithson had written you a note this morning, because we hadn't opened the envelope yet. We couldn't open it right then because…well…"

Faye waited.

"Aw, ma'am, I don't like to say such things to a pregnant lady. But there's no help for it. You may be able to help us get that young woman back home to her family. The more I think about it, the more I think I need to get the department to issue you a consultant's contract. You know stuff about the potential murder weapons that I just can't know. And you understand the ramifications of Glynis' artifacts, in terms of money and politics, in ways that I don't."

He shuffled the rosary beads around the table, and Faye wished he weren't spreading his skin oils all over things that were potentially so old.

"It's like this," he said. "We didn't know about the note this morning, because we didn't want to open the envelope until the forensics lab could process it and open it under a controlled environment." The detective lowered his calm voice a single decibel. "Because it was saturated in blood."

◇◇◇

Dr. Faye Longchamp-Mantooth put a hand on the table in front of her, using the leverage to hoist herself out of her chair. Detective Overstreet thought she looked like the events of the day had sapped her last erg of energy.

He rose, too, walking with her toward the door. She tottered a bit and he reached for her arm.

She smiled and her teeth gleamed white in her golden-brown skin. "It's okay, Detective. My husband's out back with our crew. I can walk that far. Really."

He was sure she could. Nevertheless, he was going to dog her steps until he placed her in the care of that big, strong husband. Then he was going to remind Daniel Wrather to get a contractor out here to install a lock and a key-coded opener on the iron gate leading to the parking lot and back garden, so that he could control access to his property. Never mind that the gate hadn't been locked, or even closed, in fifty years. Something terrible was afoot.

Detective Overstreet walked at Dr. Longchamp-Mantooth's side until he had shaken hands with her husband and handed the pretty doctor over to him. He had seen the things that one human being could do to another, and just because this woman thought she could take care of herself didn't mean that it was true.

Chapter Eight

Faye had learned early in her career that moving dirt around was a peaceful thing. Glynis' disappearance had fouled her mind considerably, so she'd set aside her plan to spend the rest of the afternoon translating Father Domingo's memoirs. Instead, she was on her knees, clearing away the dirt atop more of the stone tiles so that Levon could pry them up to see what was underneath.

Joe had spent the first half-hour after her return telling her to go sit down. He'd shot her disgusted looks for another hour and a half, then he'd given up. She hoped he forgave her by quitting time, because she was going to need help standing up, and he was the only person close-by who was big enough to give it to her.

Her work crew had a spectator this afternoon, an elderly busy-body named Victor. After Victor took up residence in Dunkirk Manor's back garden, Faye had sent Kirk to ask Daniel to *please* shut the garden gate, but she hadn't had the heart to send the feeble man packing.

Daniel had come out to tell Faye himself that he was having a keypad entry system put on the gate. He'd brought one of the police officers who were still searching the grounds for signs of Glynis to check out the interloper, but it hadn't taken any of them long to figure out that a ninety-year-old man had not attacked and wounded young, strong Glynis. And if Victor had seen anything that morning that would help find the young woman, it was lost in the clouds of senility where he floated so happily.

Faye had asked Victor where he lived, and she'd gotten a vague reference to a boarding house downtown where he'd eaten for a while after World War II. She sure hoped he wasn't sleeping under a bridge somewhere, and that he owned more possessions than the scraggly junk in his Piggly-Wiggly shopping cart.

Victor, however, wasn't worried about where he slept nor whether he owned anything he couldn't push around in his shopping cart. After the police officer left to resume the gargantuan effort of searching Dunkirk Manor, Victor had shoved his cart into the shadow of a tree, then trotted across the garden lawn at an astonishing clip to take a gander at the archaeologists' work.

Faye would never forget his happy, burbling tone as he cried out, "What are you folks doin' back here? This looks *interesting*."

Not wanting to encourage him, Faye had given a polite but brief answer to the question of "What are you folks doin' back here?" She'd learned that it didn't take much to encourage Victor.

For a no-nonsense scientist, Faye was a little soft-hearted so, though it had taken her an hour to train him to stay out of her crew's hair, she couldn't bring herself to chase Victor away.

"Never was sure whether the Mr. Raymond Dunkirk I knew in the Twenties was the man who built this place, or whether it was his father—"

Faye knew that it was his father, because she'd seen the deed and she knew both Dunkirks' birthdates and death dates. She wondered just how old Victor was, if he remembered the 1920s so well. If he was over ninety, it was indeed possible that he remembered the Jazz Age.

"—but I do know that the railroads must have paid the people that ran them a powerful lot of money back in those days. You could tell, just by the way they flung cash around. That's where Mister Raymond's father got all his money. Mister Raymond... he doctored people. That's where he got his money.'"

Faye had inventoried the Piggly-Wiggly shopping buggy. There was nothing in it but a pink wool sweater, a stack of Captain America comic books, and an electric skillet. She wondered what "a powerful lot of money" was to Victor.

"Miz Dunkirk—she used to let me call her Miss Allyce—went around in fancy dresses, a-drippin' with jewels. Then, at night, she changed into even fancier dresses and put on different jew'lry that she saved just to wear at night. And she did that every night, even when nobody wasn't coming to eat at that big long table but her and Mr. Dunkirk. Used a different dining room at night, too. There was times after my folks died when I ate there with 'em. Me and my raggedy knee pants."

Victor shook his head at the thought, then he just kept shaking it for awhile, as if it felt good to work the kinks out of his aged neck.

Faye eyeballed the back of the hulking Dunkirk mansion. She imagined that the people who had lived there could have afforded to behave exactly as Victor described.

Still shaking his head a little, he asked, "Tell me one more time why you folks are digging back here?"

"Mr. and Mrs. Wrather hired us. They want to build a swimming pool back here for their guests, and—"

Victor couldn't be bothered to wait for the answer to his question. "What in the heck they need another swimming pool for? Mr. Dunkirk—the one I knew—he tore up the one he had. Tore it up and filled it in with dirt."

There, from the mouth of a man who was possibly both homeless and senile, was the answer to the question of the hour…the month, actually. Well, except for the bigger question of Glynis' whereabouts.

Faye didn't know why it hadn't occurred to her to ask Victor what he remembered about her worksite. Probably because she'd had no way to know that he was so familiar with Dunkirk Manor and its inhabitants.

For the next hour, Victor was the center of attention, as he led Faye, Joe, Magda, Levon, and Kirk on a tour of the great house's rear garden, saying things like, "Wouldja look at how big Miss Allyce's camellias have got? I helped her plant that one there. It blooms red, all winter long. And just look at her crepe myrtles getting ready to bloom."

After a few minutes of listening to Victor, Faye called Suzanne and Daniel. She knew they'd enjoy Victor's stories.

"The swimming pool…it was a big one. And deep. Mr. Dunkirk could dive like a seagull going after its dinner. I saw him do it lots of times when I was a little kid living down the street, 'cause Miss Allyce used to let me come swimming. She'd swim, too, like a fish, wearing one o' them old-timey bathing suits that looked like long dresses with pants under 'em. Salty, that water was."

Magda grinned at this confirmation of her theory that the pool had been filled with water piped from the brackish river.

"Allyce Dunkirk was my great-great-aunt," Suzanne said. "I don't remember her, but my father inherited this house from her and her husband. It's so nice to talk to someone who knew my family. Did you know my father?"

"That may be. I knew a young scamp who used to climb that tree there and drop right into the pool." He pointed to a massive live oak.

"Does this look familiar to you?" Faye asked, holding out a fragment of one of the black-and-white Art Deco tiles.

The wrinkled face softened. "Yes. Oh yes, it was such a pretty thing, that pool. Them black-and-white tiles ran around the rim, and all the others was snow-white. The walls and the bottom and the wide steps where the pretty ladies walked so careful into the water—they was all slick and white. And the railings for them to hold onto were all shiny and silvery. The men…they jumped and dived and jack-knifed right into the deep end, else they would have looked all sissy-like, creeping down the steps a-clutching the hand-holds like a girl."

He took the broken tile in his hand. "Betsy would like this. She's a pretty girl and she does like pretty things. She should really be more careful what she does to get 'em, though." His gaze turned to Faye's face. "Listen. Folks should listen more better when I talk to 'em. You should all be more careful what you do for pretty things."

Faye wasn't sure how to answer him, but it didn't matter. Victor just kept talking.

"You people, for example," he said, gesticulating first at Faye, then Joe, then the rest of the archaeologists. "What call do you folks have to come here and disturb the dead?"

Magda leapt into the conversational breach. "Now, Victor, it's not like we're digging in a graveyard here. We're not disturbing the dead. We're just digging up their stuff."

Daniel and Suzanne nodded vigorously, as if to say, "Besides… it's *our* stuff now!"

Victor's mood had darkened. He had no more stories to tell about little boys leaping into a gleaming saltwater pool. Now he was shaking his grizzled head and muttering about dead people and foolish girls and greed and death.

He shuffled over to his Piggly Wiggly cart, saying, "Time to go. Time to go."

Go where? Faye wondered. *Where did this very old and sometimes very confused man sleep?*

She didn't like to pry, but no one should be homeless, especially not someone so feeble and fragile. "Victor," she began in a light tone of voice, "do you live near here?"

He glared at her as if she'd asked the most personal question imaginable. "Sure do. Always have." This didn't answer Faye's real question, which was whether the place near here where he lived had an actual roof.

Victor was still muttering under his breath but, after a moment, the words grew loud enough to understand. "Gotta go. Gotta go. But I gotta do something for the children first."

He reached deep into the pocket of his baggy black pants and came up with a handful of coins.

"…something for the children…" he crooned the words softly.

Walking from person to person, he carefully set a coin on the palms of Levon and Kirk and Faye and Joe. She found it interesting that a ninety-year-old man drew the line between children and adults at the onset of middle age. Forty-year-old and pregnant Faye was one of the "children," but forty-eight-year-old Magda and fiftyish Daniel and Suzanne missed the cut.

Faye watched Victor wander out the gate, and she resolved to ask Detective Overstreet if he knew where the old man lived. She glanced down at the coin on her palm. It was a dime, but the gleam of the sun on its worn surface was all wrong.

Looking more closely, she saw why the light reflected strangely from the dime. It was silver.

Minted in 1941, Faye's gift coin was a Mercury dime, adorned with the head of Liberty, wearing a winged cap. Looking over Joe's shoulder, she saw that he'd gotten a modern Roosevelt dime, while Levon held an older Roosevelt dime, also with the unmistakable sheen of silver.

"He does that…gives away dimes, I mean," Suzanne said. "The cook grew up here, and she says he's done that for as long as she remembers."

Faye didn't know much about American coins, but even this worn silver dime in her hand might be worth ten or twenty bucks. Who knew what else Victor was carrying around? If he was destitute, the answer to his problems might be found in the pocket of his worn black pants.

Faye's day was ending in the best way possible, considering the way it had started. She'd given their room a good dusting, which had gone a long way toward making it comfortable. Now, it was quiet and peaceful, except for the sound of the television.

She was curled up in bed in front of the TV, her head on Joe's shoulder and a chunk of blueberry coffeecake on a plate in her lap. More accurately, the plate was sort of balanced on her belly, because she couldn't actually see her lap any more. Even *more* accurately, the blueberry coffeecake on that plate was crowned with a dollop of ice cream, thanks to Suzanne's amply stocked kitchen.

The coffeecake was so good that she wanted to grab it with both hands and shove the whole thing into her mouth at once.

She might be sleeping in a dump, but the leftovers at an upscale bed and breakfast were divine.

Her mind was calming itself after a tough day…a tough week…a tough year. Okay, a tough life. She'd traded the worries of a grad student for the worries of a business owner, and now she was trading her life-long grief over parents who had died too young for the typical towering pile of parental fears.

Would the baby be okay? Would she know how to take care of it? Oh, God, would she drop it or do something else stupid that would maim it for the rest of its life?

Should she have let the doctor tell her its sex, so she could stop calling her baby "it"?

Joe seemed to be exercising his own particular brand of Creek zen, because he looked completely calm. She had always liked to look at him, but now she could play the completely distracting game of "What-will-our-baby-look-like?"

It was a pretty safe bet that the baby would have dark hair, since Faye's hair was black and Joe's hair was as close to black as brown could get. There wasn't a curl, wave, or bend to be seen on either of their heads, so she guessed the baby's hair would be straight. The skin tone would likely be some kind of mid-brown, though it was anybody's guess whether it would lean toward the bronze of mostly Native-American Joe or the milky-tea brown of Faye's personal African-European blend.

As for the baby's facial features, Faye hadn't a clue. She and Joe both had strong jawlines and prominent cheekbones, so she was guessing this would be no round-faced cherub with dimples. Beyond that, the biggest question was whether the baby would be a big, strong physical specimen like Joe, or whether it would be a scrawny thing like Faye.

Even if it turned out to be a girl, Faye hoped the poor thing was at least a little bigger than she was. It was difficult to be a strong-minded woman without the physical power that would be such a help when she needed to bend the world to her will.

The TV newscaster's voice wormed its way into her brain. "There have been reports that blood found at the scene spurred the early involvement of law enforcement in this case. Police have released no information on the disappearance of Glynis Smithson, daughter of local land developer Alan Smithson."

Faye was repulsed by the image of Glynis struggling with an assailant, struggling hard enough for one or the other one to shed enough blood to stain those gray leather seats. Or both of them. Detective Overstreet had said that two people lost blood in Glynis' car that morning.

Maybe she should hope for a boy, a large boy. His size would make him just that much safer in this dangerous world. But not really. Being large had its limits. Size meant nearly nothing when one's assailant held a gun. It hadn't been so long since someone turned a gun on Joe, and Faye had come a breath away from losing him.

Faye snuggled closer to her husband. Her mind was all snarled up again, and even the ice cream on top of her blueberry coffee cake wasn't going to be enough to soothe it. She was going to need a distraction.

"I'm not going to be able to sleep for a while, Joe. I think I'll do some work on Father Domingo's memoirs."

Joe was not pleased. He had already suggested that she should go to bed. Twice.

She knew she wasn't going to be able to rest until she told him about Detective Overstreet's proposition. There was no point in putting it off any longer.

"We have a new client, Joe."

"See," he said, pulling her closer. "I told you not to worry so much about getting business. We do good work, and people will want to hire us."

Faye was charmed by Joe's Pollyanna-ish view of the corporate world.

Joe was, however, businessman enough to want to know whose hand held the cash. "So who's the new client?"

"The St. Augustine Police Department."

Wrinkles appeared on Joe's smooth forehead. Faye reached up to smooth them away.

"What do they want?" Joe's voice usually sounded so calm, so…so different than it did right now. "If it's a dangerous job, I want you to turn it down. We'll be fine."

"Joe. We've worked for the police before. Remember? Sheriff Mike asked me to look at some broken china one time, hoping I could tell him whether somebody had been digging illegally. That's not dangerous work, but it does pay well."

She omitted the work they'd done for the police in New Orleans, which had been inarguably dangerous and had nearly gotten them both killed.

Joe wasn't going to be mollified so easily. "The main thing I want to know is this: Will this work put you cross-wise with some dangerous criminal?"

"I don't think so." Faye decided to try humor as a negotiating strategy. "Maybe it'll put *you* cross-wise with some dangerous criminal."

"Well, that would be okay."

Faye didn't think so, but she saw no point in picking a fight. "Nobody's getting cross-wise with any criminals. The police just want me to look at some artifacts they found in Glynis' car. According to a note they found, she'd brought them to work with her that day, because she wanted to show them to me. She wanted me to tell her whether any laws had been broken when they were dug up. My job…*our* job as a company…would have been to answer that question. Now that Glynis has gone missing, the artifacts are secondary. The police want my input on whether those artifacts might somehow be related to her disappearance."

She left out the fact that the musket balls and the crucifix and the rosary beads had been soaked in blood. And she also left out the fact that all the blood had not belonged to Glynis.

Would the lab eventually be able to tease out the identities of the two people who had lost blood in Dunkirk Manor's parking lot that morning? Detective Overstreet had said that the DNA tests would take some time, but the test for blood typing couldn't be any quicker.

The preliminary results were back and they had been clear-cut: the smears of blood found on Glynis' driver seat were A-positive, just like Glynis' blood. There are a lot of people walking around the world with A-positive blood but, given the circumstances, Detective Overstreet expected DNA testing to confirm that these smears did come from Glynis herself.

The blood that saturated the package of artifacts, though—this blood was B-positive. So were the traces of blood on the celt. And the blood that had soaked into the soil outside Glynis' driver door…well, there had been a lot of it and the samples had all come back B-positive. This didn't mean that there wasn't some amount of A-positive blood there, but it didn't show up in the two samples collected. Lots and lots of B-positive blood did.

Detective Overstreet had said simply, "It looks like somebody bled out here."

The person who might have bled to death on that spot had carried B-positive blood in his or her veins.

Faye didn't tell Joe these things. He was her business partner and they'd work through this case together, by the light of day. Tonight, he was her husband, and he didn't need to go to bed thinking about sordid details that had nothing to do with their marriage. Joe had a tender soul and there had been times when she forgot that she needed to pick and choose what she told him. From here on out, she planned to do better.

He'd pulled her close for a moment and said, "It's good that we're getting some business. I guess. I'll be outside."

Chapter Nine

Joe never argued with Faye, not when it could possibly be avoided. And arguing usually can be avoided between two people willing to talk things through. Still, he had his ways of expressing himself. When Joe was mad, he could generally find a way to let Faye know about it.

Sometimes, when he said, "I'll be outside," he just meant that he'd be out enjoying the night air. Other times, he meant he needed some time to meditate beside a roaring campfire. Built with the proper wood and made more fragrant with the addition of just the right herbs, a campfire could make the world feel like a more hospitable place.

Joe got a lot of comfort out of the old Creek ways, but he was pretty sure there were ordinances against campfires within the St. Augustine city limits. And he wasn't free to chop down a small tree here on the grounds of Dunkirk Manor whenever he ran short of firewood, either.

Ceremonial herbs? He didn't see any of those growing in the mansion's formal and well-manicured flower beds, and he doubted Suzanne would appreciate it if he pilfered stalks from the rare salvias in the butterfly garden she tended so fervently. The woman spent so much time in Dunkirk Manor's gardens that he was pretty sure she'd notice if individual leaves were missing. Joe knew better than to come between a woman and her obsession.

There was only one traditional herb readily available here in the city, and it made Faye speechless with frustration when he bought it. Tobacco smoking was an age-old spiritual practice in the Americas, and Joe indulged on occasion, but only for ceremonial purposes.

His "ceremonial purposes" excuse for smoking never failed to make Faye laugh herself silly. He'd smoked a couple of times a month since he was twelve and wasn't hooked yet. Joe figured addiction just wasn't in his nature.

Faye said he was being stupid. Yes, tobacco was an age-old tradition, but so was dying young, until the advent of modern medicine. Why did he want to risk addiction and blacken his lungs and maybe die young, for no good reason?

Now that the baby was coming, she could bludgeon him with the dire effects of second-hand smoke, like low birth weight and asthma and crib death. These arguments were moot, since he only smoked alone at night under the open stars.

In the past, he'd used Faye's age to excuse the risk in his mind. She was nine years older, and he didn't care to outlive her, so what would it hurt if his occasional cigarettes shaved a few years off his life expectancy? If something happened to Faye, his plan had been to start smoking around the clock and see how fast he could choke himself to death.

Now there was the baby to consider. He wanted to be around to see his child grow up. Beyond that, he wanted to see his grand-children and his great-grandchildren. Once he figured children and family into the picture, he had all the reasons in the world to try to live as long as possible. Long life and cigarettes—those two things didn't really belong in the same sentence, much less the same life.

There was no good reason for Joe to be lighting the cancer stick in his hand, but he was doing it. Why?

Because he was pissed off at Faye, and this was the best way to let her know it.

If she wanted to abuse her over-stressed pregnant body by sitting in a straight chair all night, hunched over a dusty old book, then she could just go ahead. In the meantime, he'd show her what he thought of that by standing out here and puffing on a cigarette he didn't even want.

Within an hour, Joe saw the light go off in their room, and he knew that Faye had done the sensible thing and quit working. She'd made her point by refusing to listen to reason when he wanted her to go to bed. He'd made his point by smoking a cigarette, which had been stupid but it was done and he couldn't take it back.

It was time to get rid of these clothes and brush his teeth, so that the lingering tobacco odor didn't disturb Faye's sleep. It was time to go to bed. It was time for peace.

Joe had the eyes of a great horned owl. He could see perfectly well by the light of a quarter moon. He leaned against the trunk of a massive magnolia tree and listened to an armadillo move through the bushes in the far corner of the garden. The bushes' glossy leaves reflected the moonlight and Joe could track the armadillo's location by their movement.

By contrast to the quiet rustling of the armadillo, Suzanne's headlong rush across the back porch was as loud as a fighter jet. The kitchen door slammed shut, and her dainty sandals clattered on the flagstone walk.

Joe could see Suzanne clearly in the reflected moonlight, struggling with the door of a garden shed standing between the gravel drive and the manor's kitchen. She first grasped the handle with both hands and pulled hard, proof that she was familiar with the door and knew how heavy it was before she even tried it. Nothing happened. Suzanne just kept pulling.

Again and again, she yanked on the door with enough force to make its old wrought-iron hinges creak, but nothing happened. Joe could see her hunched-over shoulders shake, and he knew she was weeping. He took a step out of the magnolia's shadow toward her. There was no way he could open a door that was obviously locked, but he could certainly escort a distraught lady into the house, where her husband would give her the comfort she needed.

Fortunately, the radar of the long-married was working, and Daniel stepped out of the same kitchen door that had just slammed behind his wife. He rushed to her side, saying, "Baby, it's locked, and it's gonna stay locked."

Between sobs, Suzanne said, "But…I need my *place*."

"It's not a good place for you. If you need to cry, you can do it in the house. You've been spending too much time out here." He pulled her to him and started walking, forcing her away from the locked door.

"But I *don't* just come out here to cry. I'm not so lonely out here, Daniel. It just melts away. Sometimes…" and the sobs began to shake her again. "…sometimes I don't feel alone at all. I think she's here, too. Sometimes…"

"Baby, Annie's gone. You've got to stay in the real world. Stay with me."

Daniel walked his wife in the house. Or maybe he just walked her body in the house. Joe had the feeling that Suzanne herself stayed behind, wishing she could just go in the garden shed and close the door behind her.

People said cigarettes helped them think, but Joe thought that was a load of crap. Joe thought cigarettes were an excuse to let the mind go blank…which made it way easier to ignore the looming specter of lung cancer.

So Joe's mind had been comfortably blank since he finished his cigarette. The nicotine couldn't wipe away his worry over Faye, but it had allowed him to think of something else. Then, a couple of puffs later, it allowed him to stop thinking altogether.

He was picking up the root beer can he used as an ash tray, preparing to go inside and face a woman who was mad at him for smoking, when his mind woke up and asked him why Daniel had picked tonight to lock the garden shed. Suzanne seemed to have been going there for a long time, maybe years. The only thing different about today was that two people were missing.

He reached for his phone and dialed the phone in their room, because he knew that Dunkirk Manor's great concrete bulk rendered Faye's cell worthless. Quietly, he said, "Faye. Get your detective friend on the phone."

Joe sat on the damp grass and watched the stars wheel overhead. Faye had seriously suggested that she should join him in this vigil.

He didn't often use a deep, forbidding, manly tone of voice with her—mostly because it didn't work—but he hadn't been able to help himself tonight. No, she wasn't going to torture her overworked body by sitting on the cold ground. No, she wasn't going to risk herself and his unborn child by sitting outside in the open, waiting for the police to come check this shed for an imprisoned woman, or worse. Just no.

Faye wasn't completely unreasonable, so she had agreed to his terms. She would call Detective Overstreet. She would then call Joe back and tell him what Overstreet had said. He knew that nothing he could say would keep her from peering out their tiny window, but he knew that it pointed the wrong direction. She'd be looking across the back garden in the direction of the river. The garden shed was on the other side of the house, near the gravel drive to the employee parking lot.

The tiniest edge of panic had entered her voice, and that was so unlike Faye. "Glynis could be in that shed, Joe. We can't just leave her in there. She could be hurt."

"You know Overstreet said not to do anything until he gets here, and it's gonna take him awhile to get a search warrant. I'll just sit here and watch. If somebody opens the shed door and Glynis is in there, I won't let them take her away or…hurt her. You know that. But if they don't, we need to sit tight."

"Overstreet said he searched the shed this morning and it was empty. Nothing but a dirt floor and yard trash. If she's in there now, where was she this morning?"

Daniel and Suzanne certainly hadn't acted like they had anything to hide while the police were searching the house. They'd welcomed them, begging for help finding their friend Glynis.

Joe shifted his weight, so that his legs wouldn't stiffen. A lifetime of woodcraft had taught him to keep his body useful at all times. "Suzanne and Daniel are going to feel a lot different when the police come to their door at three in the morning. Overstreet needs his warrant. While he gets it, I'll be out here, making sure nobody goes in that shed and nobody comes out of it." Then he said something loving but futile. "Baby, if you can't get some sleep, will you at least lie down and rest? I'll call you if anything changes."

She snorted. He had heard her snort before. He thought the sound was adorable. "I'd rather eat dirt than lay here and think of what Glynis might be suffering. Father Domingo's journal will keep me company."

Joe didn't even argue with her.

"And Joe…" Faye sounded oddly like a little girl, not like herself at all. "Would it be safe for you to go over to the shed and talk to her? Maybe she can hear you through the door, even if she can't talk back. Can you go tell her that we're getting her some help and that you're there, waiting with her?"

Yes, he certainly could do that, and he was ashamed that he hadn't already thought of it. So, though he'd seen no sign of anyone watching, Joe had used all his woods skills to creep silently from shadow to shadow until he sat here, with the shed shielding him from even the moon's faint light.

He'd tapped lightly on the shed's wooden siding and murmured Glynis' name quietly, getting no response. He did that periodically, adding comforting words like, "The police are coming to help me get you out," or sometimes just, "It's going to be okay, Glynis."

He leaned his head on the siding and kept it there, knowing that he could sense faint vibrations through his skull that he'd never hear with his ears. He heard nothing. He felt nothing.

If she was in there, she wasn't talking. Or she couldn't.

The baby was so active inside her that Faye knew she wouldn't have slept this night, even if she'd known Glynis was safe. Joe was outside, hoping to help bring the missing woman home, but that meant that his side of the bed was empty. This fact, too, would have robbed Faye of a good night's sleep.

How fortunate it was that Father Domingo had written his thoughts down, all those centuries ago, and left a piece of himself to keep Faye company through this dark night. And how appropriate it was that Father Domingo had written stories that left Faye in no doubt that he had spent many lonely, dark nights himself.

From the journal of Father Domingo Sanz de la Fuente

Translated from the Spanish by
Faye Longchamp Mantooth, Ph.D.,
and Magda Stockard-McKenzie, Ph.D.

The natives who foolishly tempted my countrymen with gold were anxious to feast us. They urged us to pass the night with them, but our leader declined, as he was anxious to deliver the good news of treasure found.

When our Captain-General and Admiral, Don Pedro, saw the two tiny golden prizes, he rose from his seat and made a plan to go ashore immediately. He himself led a party of men to the village, taking with him a goodly quantity of linen and knives and other little things of that sort. These gifts bought him the location of the French settlement, a piece of knowledge that would cost many Frenchmen their lives.

While we were in transit, the natives had fetched one of their number who had traded with the French and thus spoke some of their language. I was able to communicate with him, to a degree, and thus added a sin to my soul so large that it challenges my faith in our Savior's ability to forgive it. I learned that a party of the French remained five leagues behind us, at the precise spot where God conducted us on the day we first sighted land. Hundreds of men died because I passed that information to Don Pedro.

God help me, but I never once considered the consequences of those words as they crossed my lips. Or, if I did, I excused myself with the knowledge that we Spaniards serve the Lord with so much more purity of spirit than the French ever could. How ironic it was that the French flagship was named the Trinité!

On our first encounter with the Trinité, we expected her immediate surrender, as they were accompanied only by a single galley, and we were five ships. Yet in the midst of parleying, they abruptly shipped their cables, spread their sails, and passed through our midst.

The Captain-General called after them to drop their sails by order of King Philip II, and he received an impertinent answer. Perhaps this behavior was prompted by the Captain General's assertion that we had come to protect the rightful territory of the King of Spain, and also to hang all Calvinists.

We fired our cannons upon the retreating French and I saw a single shot carry away five or six men. Though we gave chase all night, they maneuvered so well that we could take neither the flagship nor its galley. Even Father Francisco was heard to say that the miserable devils were very good sailors.

I, Father Domingo Sanz de la Fuente, attest that the foregoing is a statement of actual events.

A few quiet words emanating from her cell phone in Joe's voice…Faye had no other evidence of the arrival of the police. They weren't visible out her window. The stout walls of Dunkirk Manor blocked their voices and the sound of their tires on the gravel.

A few minutes after Joe phoned to say, "They're here," she had seen a reflected glow where their flashlights played on the vine-covered garden wall. Other than that, the police could have come and gone, and she would never have known.

Time dragged and stopped. Were they finding Glynis right now? Or Lex? Were either of them still alive?

Her phone, over-loud, broke the silence. "There's nobody in the shed, and nothing in there but yard trash and tools and the gardener's stuff."

Joe sounded tired, devastated. In her mind, and just as surely in his mind, Glynis had been in there, safe and waiting for them. Faye didn't know whether she'd thought Lex might be in there. Half the time, she thought that Lex was the kidnapper—or worse—and she was convinced that he was either with Glynis or on the run from a murder charge.

The rest of the time, her sensitive, feminine side—and she did have one—reminded her that large volumes of blood that wasn't Glynis' had been found. The man could have bled to death just a day before. Faye reminded herself to give him the benefit of the doubt.

She crawled into bed, not because she thought she might sleep, but because it would make Joe happy if he saw here there.

Chapter Ten

Overstreet had called Faye at seven sharp. She knew he thought he was being considerate by giving her time to sleep, but she'd been waiting for hours to hear from him.

"You didn't find *anything*?" she asked, even as she hated the edge to her voice.

"Not much. The shed is original to the house, so that dirt floor is packed so hard it might as well be stone. There's a sink and a drain in the floor and a hose, because Suzanne and the gardener pot some pretty good-sized plants in there. The shelves are overflowing with stuff, but the floor's pretty clear, except for some landscaping rocks and a big pile of cedar branches and boxwood trimmings smack in the middle. Suzanne says she makes decorations for the bed-and-breakfast out of the stuff the gardener prunes out of the yard. Seems kinda cheap for somebody that owns a place like this, so I'm not actually sure I believe that…"

"No, Suzanne makes beautiful floral arrangements. She's telling the truth. But can't you move the stuff and look for evidence under it?"

"Now, you know we did that. It was such a big pile there could have been…anything…under it."

It was odd to hear a police officer be delicate about saying there could be a dead body in a pile of trash. She'd noticed that, as she got more pregnant, people got prissier.

"Did you find anything under it? Hair? Blood? Footprints? Fibers?"

Maybe if she got him to focus on something specific, he'd drop the prissy act.

"Hair? No. And Glynis' hair, in particular, would be hard to miss. White-blonde, and more than two feet long, if her pictures are any indication."

"Yep. If you saw a full-grown hair from Glynis' head, you'd know it."

"We got no fibers, either. As for blood, well…that pile of yard trash is a problem."

"Well, shove it out of the way and spray that luminol blood-detecting stuff on the floor. Or won't it work on dirt?"

"Shall I just hand you my badge and quit the case? Of course, we moved the yard trash and used luminol. We didn't get much, but it did fluoresce faintly in a couple of spots. Unfortunately, there's quite a long list of things that can cause false positives with luminol. Cedar and privet—also known as boxwood—are both on the list. So's poison ivy, but here's hoping we didn't get into any of that. We've got troubles enough."

Joe came in with two plates piled high with rich and expensive breakfast food. Faye snagged a cup of coffee as he walked past. He stopped and swapped cups with her. Apparently, she'd nearly swiped his caffeine.

"So you can't say for sure whether there's any blood in the shed or not?"

"I really don't think there's any blood out there. Even if there is, it ain't much, and we didn't find anything else. All we did was alienate Glynis' formerly cooperative employers."

It occurred to Faye that Daniel and Suzanne also employed a gardener, the man who had reported Glynis missing. That didn't necessarily mean that he was innocent of her abduction.

"Do you think the gardener knows more than he's saying?"

"Well, if we'd actually found anything in the gardening shed, I'd have his butt across the table from me right this minute, and he'd be telling me *everything* he knew. But I actually think the

gardener's okay. He has a decent alibi. A hardworking guy…
lives fifty miles out in the country. Drives into town every day,
which can't be fun."

"Gas prices must be brutal on a gardener's salary," Faye
pointed out.

"No kidding. Anyway, we have video of him from the morning Glynis went missing. At the most likely time for her disappearance, he was gassing up his truck forty-five miles from here.
We have video of Glynis getting gas that morning, too. When
you put the time and location of the video of the gardener up
against the time and location of our video of Glynis, there's just
no way to put him in town at the right time."

Faye said good-bye and scanned the morning paper, and
she saw that Overstreet had revealed some details about Glynis'
disappearance to the reporter, in hopes that an eyewitness would
come forward, but he'd also kept some things to himself. Faye
read every word, hoping that the answer to the puzzle would
jump off the page at her. No luck.

The news story confirmed reports of the existence of the
convenience store video Overstreet had mentioned. The clerk
was a high school classmate who knew her well, and the store's
surveillance cameras corroborated the clerk's story. Those same
cameras showed that Glynis had been alone in the car when she
arrived at the convenience store and when she left. The car's
gas tank had still been full when it was found in the employee
parking area at Dunkirk Manor.

The article mentioned that the driver's seat was smeared
with blood. Apparently, Detective Overstreet had decided that
the presence of the artifacts was nobody's business but his and
Faye's, because the reporter didn't mention those. No mention
was made that a goodly volume of blood that wasn't Glynis' had
been found at the scene.

A brief allusion to evidence collected outside the car didn't
give away much, either, saying only that "there is a possibility
that Ms. Smithson left the vehicle on her own power, but it is

impossible to confirm this or to determine whether she was alone at that time."

Faye trudged to the worksite, where her crew was in the process of expanding the test pits in the area of the possible pool. She was lost in thought, still in the process of planning her day. Overstreet had given the consultant's contract to Joe during his early morning visit, so her timesheet for the day would be divided between two clients. This was a heady feeling for the owner of a fledgling start-up. But what was the best way for her to help Overstreet with his investigation?

Faye's interpretation of Glynis' note was that someone had dug up the dagger and celt and other artifacts, and that Glynis thought that person was hiding the location of a possibly important archaeological site. Perhaps Faye's most useful action would be to try to find out where that site was. It wouldn't be the first time a person had covered up an archaeological site that might prevent a valuable piece of property from being developed.

Joe's voice broke into her thoughts. For the second time in three days, he was saying, "Hey! Would you look at that?" The excitement in his voice told her that his passion for archaeology was his own. He hadn't just fallen into this profession because it was what his wife did.

He carefully pulled a small object from the soil and held it up for everyone to see. Faye hurried over and he held out his hand to show her something resting on his palm.

In its current condition, the artifact looked like a black crusty disk. A nonprofessional might not even recognize that it was a coin.

"Let me take it inside," Faye said. "I can start cleaning it up. While it's soaking, I won't be wasting my time. I can work some more on translating Father Domingo's story."

Joe shot her an unreadable look. Knowing him as she did, she figured he was thinking that she'd be better off in a straight chair, hunched over a book, than she was right now, kneeling in a dirty excavation. He nodded once, and she retreated, coin in hand.

◇◇◇

After some time spent soaking, the coin looked a lot less like a black, crusty disk and more like a silver, crusty disk. It was Spanish.

Of course, it was Spanish. Florida joined the United States in 1821, and St. Augustine *still* hadn't lived under the American flag as long as it had under the Spanish colors.

The coin was crudely shaped, like the "cobs" that were hand-stamped in Mexico on disks sliced from round bars, and those could date back to the 1500s. She couldn't make out a date, but then she could hardly even see the Spanish shield that covered the back of the coin. Four or five centuries could be hard on a thin slice of silver.

She was pretty sure it was a four-*real* coin. The romantic in her wished it had been an eight-*real* coin, because it would have been just so cool to find a piece of eight. The very words carried with it a whisper of pirates and tall ships.

Nevertheless, it was an exciting find, and an unexpected one. As far as she knew, this property had been undeveloped until the late 1800s, long after Spanish money had dropped out of circulation in Florida, but maybe its last owner had been strolling through the woods and this thing simply dropped out of his pocket.

Rushing out to show Joe how pretty the coin was, without its top layer of grime, she was astonished to hear him say, again, "Would you look at that?" He had found a shapely and unbroken tool made of chipped red stone, hardly two feet away from the spot where he'd found the Spanish coin.

Most days, archaeology is a colorless, dirt-brown science. The most spectacular find of the day might be a dried-up corncob that someone gnawed in colonial times. More often, a day might pass with nothing that reached even that level of excitement. This site—with its shiny black-and-white tiles and its silver coin and a silver rattle and a handful of colorful china safety pins and, now, an unusually pretty carmine-red stone scraper—had a Kodachrome quality that you might expect in the movies, but not in real life.

Wondering what on earth might have happened here to leave behind such exciting finds, Faye dropped to her knees beside Joe.

"Where exactly did you find this stuff?"

"Here," he said, stretching out a big, well-shaped hand adorned with ground-in dirt. "And here."

Faye's heart sank, just a little.

The scraper had been in the undisturbed earth that had lain underneath a stone tile for decades. The Spanish coin, though, had been hiding in the area of churned earth where the swimming pool had been. So it had only been on this piece of property for maybe seventy or eighty years. Maybe less. This was disappointing, but sadder still was the possibility that the fill dirt brought here eighty years before had come from someplace where the Spaniards and their pieces of eight had collided with Native Americans and their finely chipped stone tools.

Any artifacts found in that fill dirt had lost most of their history when they were dumped in this hole. But that didn't mean that Faye didn't want to find out as much about them as she could.

Now Faye knew what she was going to do with her day. She was going to talk to some people with workboots-on-the-ground experience in St. Augustine. Local archaeologists were accustomed to sites layered with hundreds of years of debris from four or five separate cultures, and she needed their help. She might only have two names on her client list, but she had some fascinating artifacts in-hand—the rattle and the diaper pins, and especially the rosary, the celt, the scraper, the musket balls, the stone blade, the silver coin, and that fascinating journal. Not to mention a possibly human bone. And it was still only Wednesday.

It was starting to look like Faye would need to read up on all of American history to do a decent job for her clients. This was definitely going to cut into her profit margin.

It wasn't every day that a woman got paid to visit The Fountain of Youth.

Faye had been there before. Every schoolchild in Florida took a pilgrimage to St. Augustine, and those field trips almost always included a visit to The Fountain of Youth. The venerable tourist attraction featured moth-eaten models of nearly naked Native Americans, which never failed to ignite giggles from preteens. Standing beside them were life-sized models of armor-clad Spaniards. Well…more or less life-sized.

Faye used the term "more or less" because the plastic chief of the Timucua and the plastic leader of the conquistadors stood eye-to-eye. Modern science believed that the Timucua ate so much better than the sixteenth-century Spaniards that the natives must have looked like giants towering over the men from Spain.

The other exhibits, a big creaky globe showing the path of European conquest of the Americas and an even creakier planetarium, looked exactly the same as they had when Faye was twelve, so she felt no need to tour them. Her superstitious side sent her into the Spring House to take a sip from the sulfurous spring that a century of tradition and hucksterism had proclaimed to be the Fountain of Youth. Granted, Faye had drunk from that spring during her last visit, in 1982, and she was still aging. But it never hurt to hedge her bets.

After swigging the sulfur water, Faye headed through the beautiful gardens, past the bleating peacocks who lived there, and toward the river, where the *real* history was.

She felt absolutely wonderful. Maybe it was the water. More likely, she was, praise God, entering that last phase of pregnancy—the one where the nesting hormones flowed freely and women suddenly decided to scrub their whole house from top to bottom, even behind the refrigerator.

She was also feeling a guilty thrill of independence. Glynis' disappearance had rendered Joe barely capable of letting her out of his sight, but he'd been willing to drive her here if she promised to be good and stay within eyeshot of a crowd of tourists at all times.

Or maybe it was the fresh air blowing off the river that made her feel so alive. It stirred the red hibiscus flowers studding the garden of the Fountain of Youth. The animated conquistadors in the Spring House might be cheesy, but Faye couldn't fault the place for its gardens. Palm trees swayed overhead. Aged anchors and cannons sat tucked amidst tropical foliage. And in the distance flowed the broad Matanzas River.

An entrepreneur had decided in 1901 that the spring on this property—which she coincidentally owned—was the actual Fountain of Youth visited by Ponce de Leon. This was an interesting hypothesis, since modern historians believe he never set foot within a couple hundred miles of this spot. It was God's cosmic joke that the woman's property *was* the site of another, inarguably historic, event.

In 1565, Pedro Menéndez de Avilés had stepped ashore right in this very spot, said hello to the Indians who were already here, and founded the first permanent European settlement in the territory that became the United States.

Dr. Elizabeth Schneider, St. Augustine's city archaeologist, had inherited the job of overseeing the archaeologists ferreting out the secrets of this place that she called "Ground Zero for the European Invasion." And yes, she knew that there were other spots whose proponents thought had a better claim to the title, and she was happy to debate them at a moment's notice.

She was known far and wide for her early career in academia, centered on bringing archaeology to the public, which had made her the perfect person to head up archaeology here in a city that had enthralled archaeologists and tourists for more than a century.

Faye spotted Dr. Schneider's famous gray curls from far away and hurried to greet the woman under those curls.

"It's good to finally meet you in person, Dr. Schneider—," Faye began, only to be quickly interrupted.

"Is that sulfur I smell on your breath, young lady?"

Faye knew that she couldn't possibly look much like an esteemed fellow Ph.D. when she gaped. Should she feel guilty for paying her respects to such a silly legend?

The older woman laughed and said, "Call me Betsy. I always accuse newcomers of having sulfur breath, and I'm always right.

Nobody really believes the water from that spring will give them eternal youth, but I have never met anybody that was willing to walk past it without taking a drink. Just in case."

Faye gave her a sheepish smile.

Betsy ran a hand through her curls. "I drink a cup of it every time I come out here. Wipe my face in it, when I get sweaty. Just in case. I've found that sulfur water can't keep your hair from turning gray, but it must give you buckets of vitality. I sure don't feel sixty-five. And I like what it does for my skin."

Betsy's face was remarkably unlined for a woman older than the Atomic Age. Faye thought maybe she'd take a bucket of that spring water home to Joyeuse. Just in case.

"I'd love to see what you've got going on here," Faye said, "but I'm here on business. Do you mind taking a look at a few things for me?"

She opened her tote bag and pulled out a collection of carefully wrapped artifacts. "We found these things behind Dunkirk Manor."

Betsy fingered the rattle and diaper pins delicately. "Not much to say about those, except that they probably belonged to a rich kid back in the Jazz Age."

"This is how we found them." Faye produced a photo showing the grave-like arrangement of the baby things.

"Oh." Betsy drew back from the photo. "I nearly lost a child once. My youngest came early, and that was back before doctors could work miracles with premature babies. Standing beside the incubator of a critically ill child feels...like that."

The look in Betsy's eyes prompted Faye to turn the photo over on its face. She said, "Burying a baby's toys feels to me like something a person does to exorcise pain. Maybe the child died."

Betsy had a storyteller's light in her eyes. "Or maybe he was taken from his parents by people who judged them unfit."

Faye imagined that Betsy could come up with seven unlikely scenarios for every artifact she uncovered. And one of them would probably be right.

"Or maybe," Betsy continued, breathless, "the baby grew up to be a person who shamed his parents, and they buried his toys so that they could put away the memory of him."

All Faye knew was that she could think of no happy reason to put a silver rattle in the cold ground. All the fears of late pregnancy surfaced and a chill ran down her spine.

"Where'd you find 'em?"

Betsy's no-nonsense manner brought Faye back to the concrete matters of science and history. Talking to Betsy was like talking to Magda's older, dreamier sister.

"I think somebody pried up a tile that was part of a patio surrounding a swimming pool. They arranged the diaper pins and rattle just so, then covered them up with dirt and laid the tile on top."

"Is that where you found all this stuff?" Now Betsy was fingering the carmine-red scraper. "This sure is a pretty thing. Amazing that it's in one piece." She flipped the scraper over, examining the other face. "It looks more like something you'd find much further west, not within the Timucua's usual trade routes at all. I think it's old, too, way before European contact. Even if the Timucua did make it, I'm not sure where they'd have gotten this stone."

"Yeah, we found it near the rattle and diaper pins, though it seems like a stretch to think that they're related. And we found this in the fill dirt somebody used to fill the swimming pool, sometime in the mid-twentieth century." She handed Betsy the Spanish coin.

"Too bad. It lost its archaeological context way back then, but you knew that already. That doesn't mean it's not pretty."

Betsy continued to play with the scraper, running her finger down an edge that was still sharp. Then she held the four-*real* coin up at an angle to the sunlight, letting the shadows enhance the coin's surface markings. "The coin's old, for sure. When you get it cleaned, we'll be able to see whether it has a date. The oldest ones didn't. I'd say there's a good chance it *is* really old, maybe late fifteenth-century. I don't even want to think about what those people destroyed when they dug up the dirt to fill that pool. Reckon where they got it?"

"Probably from the *real* Fountain of Youth."

Betsy let out a giggle that sounded younger than she looked. She reached for the envelope of artifacts and photo in Faye's hand. "And what are these things?"

She let out a low whistle when she saw the crucifix. "I'd bet anything I own that this was made in Spain, a very long time ago, and it wasn't made as a trinket for trading with the First Americans, either. Look at the filigree-work on those beads. I bet this came over with an officer or a priest or, later, with a prominent family coming to claim their piece of the New World."

Faye had been thinking pretty much the same thing.

Betsy's eyes got a faraway look. "One of my friends has done a lot of work around the cathedral in New Orleans. She found a crucifix, not so different from this one. She found postholes nearby that were carbon-dated to the time of the first European settlement. And the earliest expedition's priest was known to have camped in a pavilion in that area, possibly in that very spot. Can you imagine?"

Faye could.

"Can you imagine how my friend felt when she knew that she could put a name on the person who, three hundred years before, had probably owned that crucifix? How many archaeologists go for their whole career without having a moment like that?"

"Pretty much everybody."

Betsy caressed the crucifix a bit as she carefully wrapped it and put it back in its padded envelope. "Anything else?"

Faye laid Glynis' broken celt and the photograph of its mate in front of Betsy, alongside the broken stone blade.

Betsy picked up the photo of the celt. "I've seen lots of these before, some of them right here. They were made right around the time of European contact. Some of them are so very big that I have to wonder whether they were really used as weapons. It would be tough to handle something that heavy. What would they have needed with something that size? You could take down a deer or even a boar with something smaller than this."

"Manatees?"

Betsy grinned and continued scrutinizing Faye's artifacts.

"Maybe the celt was ceremonial," Faye offered.

"Presuming something is 'ceremonial' is the last refuge of the lazy archeologist."

"So Magda says."

"You know Magda Stockard-McKenzie? She does top-quality work. "

"She will soon be the godmother of my first-born," Faye said, patting her belly. "She's working with me at Dunkirk Manor. Come meet her."

"Well, now, you can count on that." Betsy squinted at the photo of Glynis' celt piece. "I think I've even seen another one broken in half like that, right across the middle, when I was in graduate school," she said. "Just like this one. It's deep in the bowels of the university museum now, I expect. Maybe the construction technique left them vulnerable in just that spot."

"Makes sense," Faye said.

Betsy pulled a magnifier out of her pocket. She turned it onto the photo, then turned questioning eyes in Faye's direction. "Is that blood?"

"Yes, it's blood. Besides the Wrathers, I'm also working for the police department. They think this blade was used to hurt somebody yesterday…maybe to kill somebody…maybe a friend of mine, Glynis Smithson. The celt and the crucifix and the beads and these," she held up the musket balls, "were all found in or near Glynis' car. She left this behind."

Faye handed a copy of Glynis' note across the table.

"The missing girl…" Betsy laid a palm flat on the paper, as if to feel the voice of the writer. Then she fished some reading glasses out of her pocket and read the note.

The reading glasses went back in Betsy's pocket and she stared over Faye's shoulder at the river. "The girl—her name was… is…you said it was Glynis, right? She thought somebody was disturbing an important historical site, probably while doing construction, but she wasn't sure. She wanted you to tell her what to do."

Faye nodded a couple of times before saying, "Yeah. But what *should* I do? How can I find out where she got the crucifix and all those other artifacts? You know archaeology in this area better than anybody. Can you help me?"

"There are ways, but you're looking for a needle in a haystack. No, a whole barn full of hay. There's history everywhere around here, so the City of St. Augustine has a very restrictive ordinance to protect archaeological sites, but you know that. It's the reason you were hired to do the Dunkirk Manor project."

This was true.

"Darn Daniel and Suzanne Wrather, anyway. *I* wanted to do that work, but they were dead-set on bringing your company in to do it."

Faye loved hearing people say "your company." When other people acknowledged her business' existence, it made her new venture seem real. And a little less scary.

Betsy grinned. "That's okay. There's enough interesting stuff in this town to go around, and if I'd been doing the work, then I'd have been the one in the middle of a kidnapping investigation. Instead, you're doing it. Lucky you."

Betsy was running a thoughtful finger over the photo of the celt's bloodied surface. "We've got some potent historical preservation rules here in the city. Out in the country? Not so much. The cultural resources protections aren't nearly so strict, though I give them credit for recent reform. So my guess is that this stuff came from somewhere out-of-town. There's not a lot of oversight out there, and folks are afraid they'll lose the use of their land if they tell anybody they own an archaeological site."

Faye had encountered plenty of people like that in her career. "So those people, by definition, ain't talkin'."

"Yeah. Obviously. But there are ways to find these things out. You can check the official list of known sites in the county and other counties thereabouts. You can find the locations of active construction sites where these things might have been uncovered. And I can put you in touch with people who know about sites on private land that will *never* make any government lists. The best place to start is with the county's environmental services office. The archaeologist there is quite good, and he knows these things as well as I do."

A sing-song voice sounded behind them, proclaiming, "Beautiful day! Oh, it's such a beautiful day!"

The familiar squeaky wheels alerted Faye that Victor was present before she even turned around. The noise settled somewhere in the middle of her spinal cord and sent miserable shivers down her arms and legs. Faye knew she had an oil can in her tool kit, back at the excavation. Next time Victor showed up at Dunkirk Manor, she was going to desqueak that Piggly Wiggly cart, if it was the last thing she did.

"Ah, Betsy, you are such a lovely thing! You have the bluest eyes in town," Victor warbled. "Can you imagine a lovelier place to be than this? Sparkling water! Grass a-growing! Purty red flowers on the bushes!" His watery eyes focused on Faye. "And here's the other lovely young lady who likes to dig around in other people's business."

"Victor, you should be nicer to Faye. Those people at Dunkirk Manor *asked* her to dig around in their business. And the people around here—" she gestured at the excavated units behind her, "—well, they've been dead for centuries. Maybe they enjoy our company. Sometimes, late in the evenings, I see strange things here…a palm tree standing stock-still in a heavy wind…shadows that just look like they're in the wrong place."

Faye lived with Joe on an island far from people with only the trees and wind for company. Somehow she found Betsy's images of Nature thrown out-of-whack to be more disturbing than the conventional picture of a white-sheeted ghost.

"My work keeps me walking a tightrope between the living and the dead," Betsy was saying. "If the tourists only knew what they were walking over, right there in the historic section. The area around the fort and gate is wall-to-wall with the unmarked graves of British soldiers and Spanish soldiers and American soldiers and poor people who died of yellow fever without the money to buy a cemetery plot. Lord knows how many prisoners the Spanish garroted, in front of cheering crowds. The spirits of the dead are just everywhere in this city, four centuries of them, plus millennia of Timucuan ghosts. But you know, I think the dead like having me around. I never feel afraid, not even alone out here beside the river, and I never get the sense anybody... or anything...wants me to go away. They know I'm just trying to dig up their stories. Nobody wants to be forgotten."

Victor didn't respond. His eyes were pointed in Betsy's direction, but they were unfocused. She peered at him for a second before putting a gentle hand on his shoulder and saying, "Here, sweetie, have a grape soda."

As Victor sucked the cold drink down greedily, Faye said, "I thought he liked Coke. I watched him drink four of them yesterday."

"If it's cold and sweet, Victor likes it." Betsy handed the police department's photos back to Faye. "I shoulda known Victor would've found you by now. He's a walking history book, and he's always looking to add new chapters to his historical knowledge."

"Have you been careful since I was here last, Betsy girl?"

Faye did a double-take. So *this* was the Betsy who Victor had been mumbling about just the day before. When he'd groaned over Betsy, the "pretty girl who should be more careful," she really hadn't pictured a grey-haired woman with a little pot belly and the beginnings of a dowager's hump.

"I'm always careful, Victor. And I'll make sure Faye is, too."

Betsy drew closer, so that she and Faye could continue talking business while Victor slaked his thirst.

"I understand your husband is quite the expert on lithics. Haven't you asked him about the two stone tools you showed me?"

"He said pretty much the same thing you did. I just wanted a second opinion. And I wanted you to see the other artifacts, including this one."

She'd been saving Father Domingo's journal for last, because it wasn't strictly a part of her ongoing project, nor the murder investigation, and because it was such a stunningly cool piece of history. Donning gloves, unwrapping it, and opening it gently to the first page, she held it out for the older archaeologist to see.

Betsy's jaw dropped open so far that Faye could see every last filling in her molars. "Where on earth did you get this? And where has it been all these years?"

"It's my client's. It was stacked in a pile of junk he and his wife inherited, right next to an old Nancy Drew mystery. I had to promise them my firstborn to get them to let me take it off their property."

"No shit. And it looks like that firstborn might come any minute."

"Five more weeks." Faye patted her belly. The baby was quiet at the moment, just giving the occasional companionable squirm to let her know he was okay. Or she. Whatever.

"Magda and I are doing a first-cut translation, while I try to get the client to donate it to a museum that can preserve it properly."

"Don't tell me. You found it in a hot, muggy, buggy attic."

"I didn't see any bugs, but otherwise, yeah."

Betsy leaned in and put her face close to the leather binding. Whether she intended to study the book or smell it, Faye had no idea.

"I want to see that translation, young lady. As much as I'd like to keep talking to you about it, and as much as I'd like to pore over this book myself, I'm going to do the noble thing and send you to some people who are actually qualified to advise you."

She finished sniffing the book and pushed it back in Faye's direction. "Go to the St. Augustine Historical Society's library and ask for the director, Rosa Mazza. When she and her assistant Harriet get an eyeful of that book, they're going to have twin myocardial infarctions, but they'll survive. And when you've finished talking about the book and you're sure you don't have any more billable work to do, ask Rosa's assistant Harriet to tell you what she knows about Dunkirk Manor. Harriet's stories will make you want to crawl back into that attic and go looking for flapper dresses and feather boas. Now, young lady, get this priceless book out of the sunshine before I have a myocardial infarction of my own."

Chapter Eleven

St. Augustine's historical society had a library worthy of a town that labeled itself "The Ancient City." Rosa Mazza was its queen, and she guarded her library as staunchly as the lion statues on the city's gateway, The Bridge of Lions, guarded the entrance to their home.

"Leave it here."

The tone of Rosa's voice said that she now viewed Father Domingo's journal as integral to St. Augustine's history and, thus, part of her domain.

"I can't. It's not mine. It belongs to my clients."

"Your clients owe it to the world to make sure it's preserved and that it doesn't end up in the hands of a...*collector*." She pursed her mouth as if the word tasted bad. "They don't know that and you do. This is your responsibility."

The book lay on the table between them. Faye reached out her gloved hand and took it back. "I know my responsibility. I am looking into the most suitable home for the book, and I will advise my clients accordingly."

This was going swimmingly. Rosa had been cordial, if a little stiff, as she piled Faye's study table high with books on Timucuan stone tools and Spanish coins and Art Deco tiles and early twentieth-century children's toys. Faye had only stopped poring over them because it was lunchtime and because Joe would have a spasm if she didn't eat.

She'd been saving the journal to show Rosa after they'd discussed all the other artifacts. She was very glad she did, because now she just wanted to get the heck out of Dodge, away from the librarian's disapproving gaze.

She laid a business card on the table and said firmly, "I want to do a good job for my client and for St. Augustine. My report will be filed with the city archaeologist and I'll be happy to donate a copy of it to the library, if you'd like. If you think of anything that will make that report better, please don't hesitate to call me."

Then she collected the journal and her notes and tried to exit gracefully. The part of her that despised conflict just wanted to bolt for the door and put herself far away from Rosa's disapproval.

Advanced pregnancy did not make for a quick or easy retreat, however. The library was housed on the second floor of a Spanish Colonial home, and it was accessed by an exterior staircase that was tough for Faye to navigate in her oversized condition. If there was an elevator for handicapped access, Faye didn't want to take the time to look for it.

The open courtyard at the foot of the stairs was a calm and lovely place to catch her breath. She leaned against an arch made of local coquina rock and decided to just enjoy the flowers for a minute…until the clattering of hard soles on that old wooden staircase made her want to flee. Was Rosa really going to chase her, demanding custody of a book that (probably) belonged to Daniel and Suzanne Wrather?

Faye could flee, but she wouldn't get very far and she wouldn't get there fast. Because Joe had refused to let her wander the town alone with a kidnapper on the loose, she had no car and was thus trapped in the library's courtyard. A rebellious part of her was pretty sure that Joe was using the notion of a free-range kidnapper wandering the streets to accomplish what his overprotective self had wanted to do all along: put his pregnant wife in a padded box and keep her there till the baby arrived safely.

St. Augustine was a small town, so it had taken Joe ten minutes, tops, to pick her up at the Fountain of Youth and drive her into the historic sector so that she could make this library visit. That was pretty darn quick, but it still meant that, even if she called him right now and he left instantly, she was still trapped here for longer than she wanted to be.

Oh, she could leave on foot and call Joe as she walked, telling him just to pick her up somewhere on Aviles Street north of the library, but she could only waddle so fast and so far. If Rosa came after her, the stern librarian would surely catch up with Faye, the evildoer who wasn't treating Father Domingo's manuscript properly—which was to say that she wasn't treating it the way Rosa wanted it treated.

As the footsteps neared the bottom of the staircase, Faye detected the distinctive tapping of a pair of stiletto pumps. What a relief. Rosa had definitely been wearing a staid pair of lace-up flat shoes.

"Dr. Longchamp-Man...uh..."

"Longchamp-Mantooth, but call me Faye. My married name is a real mouthful."

"Okay, Faye." Seeing Faye heft her tote bag onto her shoulder and hold it close to her body, Rosa's assistant Harriet laughed. "Relax. I didn't come to swipe your book. Rosa can be a bit... intense...when it comes to local history. So can I, actually, but I like to think I have more perspective on the matter."

Harriet's sundress and shoes were brand-new and expensive, but the dress' dropped waist and the pointy-toed pumps gave her style just a whisper of an earlier era. Her long frosted hair, however, bore no resemblance to a flapper's bob. Faye hoped she had as much fashion sense as Harriet when she hit her sixties. Heck. She wished she had it now.

Harriet was overloaded with an armful of books.

"Listen, I heard you say you'd been in the attic at Dunkirk Manor. Did you see anything interesting? Anything related to the murder?"

"Murder?" Faye's throat constricted. "Did they find Glynis?"

Why did Faye's hand clutch reflexively at her swollen belly so often these days? She forced herself to let it hang by her side.

"No. Oh God, no. I'm sorry to startle you. You look like you've seen a ghost. Here, sit down."

Harriet helped Faye take an uncomfortable seat on a lower stair.

"I was talking about the murder of Lilibeth Campbell, back in the Twenties. You haven't heard about it?"

Faye shook her head. She knew she didn't have to speak, because she could see that Harriet had plenty to say.

"Oh, this story has it all. Glamour, money, sex, blood, death. Did you know that St. Augustine was a major player in the early days of the movies, before Hollywood?"

"I've seen some cool still shots of the *Creature from the Black Lagoon* being filmed at Marineland."

"That was later. I'm talking way before that, back in the silent era—Theda Bara, Ethel Barrymore, Rudolph Valentino. They all made movies here. And so did Lilibeth Campbell. She would have been that kind of a star if somebody hadn't knifed her to death and left her body on the bridge that crosses the moat of the Castillo de San Marcos."

"Nobody knows who killed her?"

Harriet sat beside her, books on her lap, and opened the top one. "Nope. Maybe it was the director, a well-known lecher. Maybe it was her co-star, a cut-rate Rudolph Valentino clone. Maybe it was one of the men bankrolling the movie. From these pictures," Harriet held the book so that Faye could see, "it looks like the financial dudes thought their money gave them the right to rub their paws all over Lilibeth every chance they got."

"Ick," Faye said, looking at a photo of three portly old men clustered so closely around a pretty young woman that they'd all managed to get a proprietary hand on her. Her sleeveless, knee-length dress was modest by modern standards, but to men who grew up in a world where corseted women were covered from their necks to the wrists and ankles, she must have looked half-naked. Touching her bare arm, to them, would have been like public sex.

"Why did you ask if I'd found anything related to her murder at Dunkirk Manor?"

"Because Raymond Dunkirk was one of the prominent men who worked so hard to bring the movies to town. He turned that fabulous atrium into a ballroom and threw over-the-top parties to lure all those disgusting old men here."

She waved her hand at the photo of the three Hollywood moguls lusting after a young girl. "I've seen photos of some of those parties…oh, you wouldn't believe the ballgowns and the jewelry and the jazz bands perched up on the stairway landing. Dunkirk Manor was well-known for having the best bands south of Charleston. Look, here's a picture. And there Lilibeth is, standing next to Raymond Dunkirk."

Faye felt the weird sense of recognition that comes with seeing a very old photo of a familiar place. The people in this photo were adults in the 1920s, so they were likely all dead. But Dunkirk Manor's burnished magnificence was unchanged, even when depicted in faded black-and-white.

Lilibeth Campbell was standing in the shadow of the grand staircase, partially obscured by a crowd of admirers, yet her pale oval face was the first thing Faye's eyes lighted on. This quality of being impossible to ignore was called star power.

The man standing a respectful distance from her right elbow had it, too. His chiseled face was as pale as Lilibeth's, and his black eyes were set in that face like twin chips of onyx. Faye suspected that Lilibeth didn't need to fend off the attentions of elderly drunks when Raymond Dunkirk was around.

Harriet kept talking. "There's the director, here in the foreground. His name was Timothy Selby. And there's the star—Randolph Terracina. Don't you know they gave him that screen name so people would associate him with Rudolph Valentino? Hollywood thinks people are so stupid."

"The movie industry has made many fortunes by underestimating their viewers' intelligence."

"True," Harriet said, lightly brushing the photographed faces of Lilibeth and Raymond. "But Randolph Terracina was not the man with the most sex appeal in this room on that night."

And she was right. Randolph Terracina had the big eyes and the over-pretty features and slick hairstyle that were the epitome of male beauty in that day, but Raymond Dunkirk would have been head-turningly handsome in any age.

Harriet's finger traced the two faces lovingly again. "I think it was a crime of passion. Everyone did at the time, actually. Newspapers were willing to publish lurid speculation in those days—and lately they've started to do it again—but their prose was really purple when they described the violent death of this sexy starlet."

Lilibeth Campbell was still looking at them out of the old photo, and she always would be.

"They said that someone had washed her wounds clean," Harriet said with an unseemly degree of relish, "and wrapped her in a silk sheet before dumping the body. So, yeah, there could be information on her murder in Dunkirk Manor, since this isn't the only photo taken of her there. I heard you say that the owners inherited a pile of junk. I'm sure they did—there's a lot of room for junk in that big old house. I imagine Lilibeth spent a lot of time there, and not just at parties." She cocked one eyebrow.

Faye cooperated and asked "Why?" even though she knew where the conversation was going.

"Because the whole town knew she was having an affair with him. With Raymond Dunkirk."

"He was married."

It wasn't a question. Victor had mentioned "Miss Allyce," but who knew when Victor knew her? There was no reason to believe that Raymond Dunkirk was already married when this photo was taken, but Faye thought he was. She knew that men who owned mansions like Dunkirk Manor almost always owned a high-society wife as an ornament to the home. If he was lucky, that wife was more than a social asset. She had the judgment and smarts to run a small business, which is what a household of a dozen servants was.

Faye had already spotted the slender figure on the staircase above Raymond and Lilibeth. She was graceful and smiling, but her eyes were locked with the band leader's in a way that said she needed a word with him. This was not a woman who could be pushed around by the hired help.

"Yes, he was married," Harriet said, pointing to the figure on the staircase. "That's Allyce Dunkirk, there. The whole town was apparently talking about it. When Lilibeth was killed, several people came forward with their suspicions of Raymond."

Faye could tell there was more scuttlebutt, but Harriet wanted to continue playing the gossip game, and gossips dearly love to be asked for their fascinating information. So she said, "There has to be more to the story."

"Exactly!" Harriet said, exultant. "I looked up Lilibeth's death certificate. It's signed by Dr. Raymond Dunkirk."

Faye cocked an eyebrow. "Would a doctor stab somebody to death?" she mused. "He wouldn't be squeamish about the blood, but would he randomly hack somebody up like that? Or would he do something cleaner, like maybe using poison?"

"When it comes to crimes of passion, I don't think a person's brain is really operating, do you?"

Faye was too startled to respond. She was staring at Harriet's book.

Harriet had turned the page to a full-page photo taken at a party in the back garden of Dunkirk Manor. Again, though Lilibeth Campbell was doing nothing more attention-getting than lolling on a chaise lounge, her beautiful face drew the eye. And, again, Raymond Dunkirk hovered at her side.

The chaise lounge sat on a pavement of hewn stone tiles surrounding an elegantly oval swimming pool that was rimmed with familiar Art Deco tiling.

"I'm going to need a copy of this photo for my project report."

Chapter Twelve

Faye was hardly back from her trip to town when Daniel and Suzanne brought the leftovers from breakfast out to Faye's work site and treated the archaeological team to lunch.

"We can't serve this stuff again tomorrow. People will notice, and they expect fresh food at these prices. It's still good, and it tastes wonderful, if I do say so myself. You people might as well eat it."

Suzanne handed Faye a loaded plate and added, "Especially you, Faye. Here's some protein and iron and vitamin C and calcium and a whole lot of other good stuff."

She placed a sprig of parsley on the plate then, thoughtfully, she picked it up and moved it a half-inch closer to the plate's rim. Faye didn't think the placement of a bit of green stuff rated the intense concentration on Suzanne's face, but she had to admit that the plate looked noticeably better after Suzanne moved the garnish.

Next to the parsley was a big chunk of egg casserole and a dollop of fruit salad with sour cream dressing. The baby would thank her, but her arteries might not.

The aroma of bacon and cheese rising from the eggs made Faye hungry for the first time in days. Hang the cholesterol. Today, she'd act like a pregnant woman, instead of a 40-year-old hoping to avoid a stroke. This food smelled *good*.

She took the fork Suzanne offered. "Thank you so much. I could sure use some protein and iron and all that jazz."

"And some calories. You could sure use some calories, too."
Suzanne cast an evaluating eye on Faye's body, head to toe.
"That baby's not much smaller than you are. Eat up. I promise
it'll taste better than those pregnancy vitamins. I remember that
awful iron after-taste…"

Suzanne drifted away, dispensing already-loaded plates from
a rolling cart. Faye stood, plate in hand, watching her. Daniel
and Suzanne had no children. If Suzanne was intimately familiar
with the flavor of prenatal vitamins, then that meant…

"We lost a child," Daniel said, answering her unspoken question. Faye blushed, realizing that she'd been staring at Suzanne.
"Annie had leukemia. She was ten. That's when we sold everything
up north and moved down here. I just couldn't stand practicing
law for another second. I was never the tough, driven trial attorney
in the family, anyway. Suzanne was the brilliant litigator, not me.
I'd rather play tennis. Suzanne left our practice to take care of
Annie, and she was too fragile after we lost our little girl to even
consider going back in the courtroom. There was an awful time
when I thought I'd lose her, too. She'd inherited this place when
her father died a few years back, and we both wanted to leave
everything behind. Sometimes, you need to start over."

A tall man flung open the back door of Dunkirk Manor,
making just enough noise for everyone in the garden to notice
and lingering just long enough in the open doorway for everyone
to see him. Then he strode across the big yard, heading straight
for Daniel and Suzanne. They rushed to meet him.

"Alan," Suzanne said, "we've been so worried about you. Did
you get my call? Has there been any word on Glynis?"

Alan Smithson shook his dark-haired head wordlessly in
her direction, the action of a man who knew the rules of polite
behavior but who had been pushed to the brink.

He spoke instead to her husband. "I waited for a ransom note
for twenty-four hours. *Twenty-four hours*. It didn't come. So now
I know they weren't after my money." He shook his head again,
as if he could hardly believe it. "They weren't after my money.
They were after my daughter."

His mouth worked, but it refused to form any more words. Suzanne ran for the cart, poured a glass of ice water, and thrust it into his hand. Alan gulped the whole thing down.

"I think it's your fault, both of you."

Daniel took a step back in the face of Alan's anger and put a hand on the small of Suzanne's back.

Alan moved like a man trained in hand-to-hand combat. He stepped into the space vacated by his adversary, Daniel, and kept talking. "You put her in that ad. You let her be the face of something controversial."

"Why should preserving the past be controversial?" There was a slight quaver to Suzanne's voice, but it somehow made Faye want to congratulate her for speaking up in the face of Alan Smithson and his practiced intimidation techniques.

Alan looked at Suzanne as if she were a five-year-old. "Because preserving the past costs money. The preservationists who hid behind my daughter's pretty face know how much money is at stake in the development business. They knew it then, and they know it now. The new preservation-friendly board that rode to election on my daughter's elegant coattails will cost me something on the order of six figures, maybe seven, but I'll survive. With the economy like it is, some of my competitors won't be able to do that. They'll be bankrupt in a year. You don't think one of them might want to scare the new board into voting the right way…their way?"

Faye was struck by Alan's certainty that Glynis' disappearance was linked to money. In his world, either someone kidnapped her because they wanted some of his money, or else they did it because they blamed her for the loss of their own money. He could think of no other possible motive.

What about Glynis herself? A woman that beautiful would always be sexually vulnerable. Had her father not thought of that? Or maybe he just couldn't bring himself to think of that.

The first suspect in any crime against a woman is generally the man in her life. In this case, the man in Glynis' life was missing, too. Detective Overstreet hadn't said he was focusing his investigation on Lex, but he'd be a fool if he didn't.

Faye couldn't help herself. "Why are you blaming Daniel and Suzanne when your daughter's boyfriend is missing, too? Don't you think Lex might have taken her?"

"Impossible," Alan stated with the blustering certainty of a rich man. "I know the man. He…" The bluster faded. "Well, frankly, I'm concerned that he's been harmed by the people going after my daughter. I can't believe…"

He cleared his throat and tried again. "Lex has been part of my daughter's life…my life…for two years now. His parents are my friends. I just can't believe he would have hurt Glennie. If he did…"

Suzanne stepped forward, as if to touch his arm, but she didn't follow through. Her hand hung in mid-air, touching nothing.

Alan found his voice. "I've spoken with Lex's family and they're outraged that the media is treating his disappearance like a footnote to my daughter's. So am I."

Faye wasn't at all convinced that Alan's concern extended beyond his daughter's safety to Lex's.

And what about the possibility of random violence? Was Alan really ignoring the possibility that Glynis and Lex had been caught up in a purse snatching gone bad? Or the possibility that they had crossed paths with a serial killer who murdered for no reason at all?

Faye suspected that Alan Smithson couldn't comprehend the notion of killing for no reason at all, because it didn't fit with his world view. And that world view was simple: Alan Smithson and his money sat squarely at the center of the universe.

Detective Overstreet reached for a cigarette, but pulled his hand away from the pack without touching it. He was a nicotine addict, for sure, but he wasn't so much of a junkie that he'd let a pregnant woman sit cooped up in his car beside him, breathing his second-hand smoke. He was having second thoughts about the wisdom of hiring a pregnant woman to help him in the first place.

The woman was interesting, he'd give her that. "The crucifix is probably very old," she was saying, "maybe as old as St. Augustine itself. There's a decent chance that all the artifacts you found are that old—musket balls, crucifix, beads, celt, blade, bone. The age of the crucifix alone ramps up the significance of Glynis' note. If someone was tampering with an unreported archaeological site of that age…"

Detective Overstreet had grown up in St. Augustine, and that upbringing generally put you in one of two camps. You either had a certain reverence, even awe, for the cool old stuff you saw every day. Or you were thoroughly bored with the constant carping over how old the bricks were in the pothole-strewn street in front of your house, which did nothing but make you wish for some nice smooth asphalt. And you wholeheartedly wished the flippin' tourists would go home and stay there.

Overstreet liked the old stuff, himself, and if there were people out there abusing it, then he wanted Dr. Longchamp-Mantooth to help him find them.

"Betsy says that this visit to the county growth management people will tell us where construction is going on in the county." She patted one slender, short-nailed hand on her armrest. Its skin was the color of dark honey. "Nothing we see today will tell us much of anything, though. Nobody's going to put a piece of paper in their file that says, 'Dug up a real old crucifix today. Tossed it in the landfill to keep the damn preservationists off my back.' Today, we'll find out where the currently active construction projects are, and that's all. We're going to have to go out and look at the construction sites themselves. Even that won't tell us much, unless somebody's raping history at the very moment we arrive."

"Then why did you suggest that we do this?"

The honey-colored hand rubbed a cheek made puffy and blotchy by hormones. Overstreet remembered when his wife had been this pregnant. Three times, she'd looked this tired and this uncomfortable.

"We're going out there because people have consciences," she said. "Somebody dug up those artifacts. What did they do with them? Throw them away someplace where Glynis found them? Give them to Glynis because they knew she cared? Somebody knows where those artifacts—museum-quality artifacts, from the looks of some of them—came from. That somebody probably knows that Glynis had them. Now that her disappearance has hit the media, that person's conscience is going to be screaming, right about now. Anyone in that position who isn't feeling some blame for her predicament is a sociopath."

"So you think that if we go out to the site and just…hang around…someone might come to us privately and spill the beans?"

"It would probably be smarter if I went without you. People get very quiet when the police come around. Maybe you've noticed that?" She crossed her arms and grinned like a woman who knew what he was about to say.

And she did. Overstreet wasn't about to be distracted by her smart-ass tendencies.

"That's what Miss Smithson was trying to do, and look what happened to her."

Damn. He was right back where he'd started. Despite the fact that they had no plans for this day beyond paperwork, there was still a danger that he might be putting his civilian consultant in harm's way, and he didn't want to do that.

There was no way in hell he would ever show her the photos stored in his phone's memory. The wide shot of Glynis' sleek expensive car sitting empty with the driver door hanging open. The close-ups of blood smeared across the pristine leather seat. The mid-range shots depicting the positions of the broken celt and the broken blade and the blood-sodden envelope. And the very graphic shot showing just how much blood had soaked into the ground in Dunkirk Manor's employee parking lot.

"Has the lab come up with anything, based on the samples they took from the parking lot?"

Overstreet could see that she was going to keep poking into the most gruesome parts of this crime until he told her to shut up, or until he broke down and told her the whole bloody truth.

"Footprint analysis from the parking lot hasn't been all that useful. The forensic technicians were dealing with pea gravel and patches of weedy grass and soil packed hard as iron. They did find three partial footprints—"

"Wait. Let me guess. Glynis, the gardener, and...Lex?"

"Close. Glynis and the gardener were gimmes, although the conditions were so bad that the technicians could even have missed those. But no Lex. Just Sara the housekeeper."

"She walks through that lot twice a day, at least."

"Exactly." If he closed his eyes and forgot Faye was an archaeologist toting a Ph.D. and a nearly done bun in the oven, Overstreet could believe he was talking shop with another detective, a partner. "Sara was seen arriving at work at six-thirty, about the time Glynis was on film at the convenience store. So her footprints were *supposed* to be there. There was also plenty of scuffing that proved what we already knew—the entire staff of Dunkirk Manor comes through there every day. Beyond the expected amount of scuffing from foot traffic, I'd say there was enough evidence to suggest a struggle near Glynis' car, but we've basically got nothing useable, footprint-wise."

"Tire prints?"

"The only interesting tire print data that we have is negative. The whole parking lot is covered in a web of tire tracks, and not many of them are readable. Those that are readable seem to belong to cars that had every right to be there, the cars of Dunkirk Manor employees. Lex Tilton, however, drives a vintage Corvette with extremely expensive specialty tires. We see no sign that his car has ever been in that lot."

Faye hadn't even thought about Lex's car. "Do they know where that Corvette is?"

"In the driveway of the very nice historic home where he lived with Glynis, not three blocks from Dunkirk Manor. Apparently, she hardly ever drove to work."

"Does it mean anything that she drove yesterday?"

"Maybe she had a fight with her boyfriend and left in the car just so she could get him out of her sight. That would explain why she was out and about so early. Or maybe her car was running on empty and she just needed to get some gas. Or maybe she's addicted to convenience store coffee. We just don't know."

"So we know that she got gas on her way to work, although we can't be sure where she was coming to work *from*. Probably from her house, but we don't have proof of that. Her car got as far as Dunkirk Manor, and its seats are smeared with blood that's Glynis' type. We don't really know where Lex slept or where he's been since..."

"You are the witness who saw him last," Overstreet pointed out.

"Then we don't know where he's been since night before last. But we know he's missing and that he's not in his own car or in his girlfriend's. Do we know his blood type?"

"B-positive. Which isn't good news for Lex Tifton."

The pretty doctor nodded her agreement. "So we know that it's completely possible that he lost a heckuva lot of blood yesterday morning. So I guess you used the same magic blood-detecting fluorescent chemicals in the parking lot that you did in the gardening shed. Those two people that were bleeding have gone somewhere. Did they leave a trail?"

Overstreet liked to talk shop with a cigarette in his hand, and he was really missing it about now. "That fluorescent stuff only works well in the dark, so we had to wait hours to use it in the parking lot, and who knows what data we lost in the meantime? The bed-and-breakfast's damn sprinkler system ran at 7:30 a.m., according to a maid who got wet trying to take out some trash. God only knows what the sprinklers washed away before we even knew Glynis was missing."

"I remember Kirk grumbling about an inch of water standing in the test pits that morning. I asked Daniel to change the sprinkler schedule, but it never occurred to me that this water had made Glynis harder to find."

Overstreet nodded and continued walking his consultant through the evidence, as he knew it. "The B-positive bleeder left a clear trail for the first few feet away from the car, but everything's been washed away once the trail leaves the lot. The A-positive person, probably Glynis, also left a few drops until she got to the sprinklers. That's all we got."

"So we know that two bleeding people walked—"

"—or were carried—" Overstreet interjected.

"—across the parking lot. Big hairy deal. Of course, they left the parking lot. They certainly weren't there any more by the time anybody realized there was a problem."

The woman didn't miss much, and she didn't mince words.

"That's about all the physical evidence we've got right now. The lab's working on some hair and fiber evidence from the car, but every indication is that the hairs belong to Glynis and Lex, two people who had every reason to be sitting in that car and leaving hairs behind. I—"

Faye looked out the window, then interrupted him without a visible qualm. It occurred to him that she might need to learn to kiss up to her clients if she hoped to be successful as a consultant. Blithely ignorant of her client-relations *faux pas* she said, "You know, we're almost at the growth management office. We really should talk about what we're going to say to these people."

The egg-headed archaeologist was doing a better job of concentrating on the reason for this interview than he was.

The closely trimmed fingernails were still drumming on her armrest as she talked in that singsong tone people use when they're really just thinking out loud. "We want to talk to somebody who knows how the artifacts were found. Was the cross just lying on the ground? Or did someone dig it up?"

He nodded and just let her keep thinking aloud.

"Was that someone working on a large development that required permit approval? Or was it just someone with a shovel in his back yard? The laws distinguish between those things."

Despite their very short acquaintance, Overstreet felt completely confident that Dr. Longchamp-Mantooth would thoroughly investigate the fine points of those laws.

This brief conversation had more than discharged her duty and earned her paycheck, but God love her, now she'd moved on to ruminating over the list of suspects, and she was doing a damn fine job of it, too.

"If you could've heard the argument between Glynis and Lex…" she mused. "I'd be tempted to just presume he took her and be done with it, but that would be intellectually dishonest. There are the antipreservationists to consider, with Dick Wheeler the ex-commissioner first among them. And I really don't like her father, but maybe I'm just prejudiced against self-involved rich people."

Overstreet allowed as how she was not alone.

"I don't know what to think about Daniel and Suzanne. They were close to Glynis, and I can't think of any reason for them to hurt her…"

"But you include them on the suspect list out of…let me guess…intellectual honesty?"

She smiled at his teasing. "Yes. So we have to include Levon and Kirk to maintain that honesty." The smile dimmed. "The poor guys are beside themselves with worry. They really liked her for herself, aside from that pretty face."

"And your husband Joe?"

She was woman enough to bristle at the suggestion. "Yeah, but then we'd have to include Magda and me. We are each other's alibi, and we could be in cahoots, you know."

His cell phone chose that moment to ring, and in that moment Overstreet and Faye lost their leisurely afternoon surrounded by boring files.

The voice of Overstreet's boss boomed out of his cell phone. The boss never had much to say when he was pissed off. Like now. He just got straight to the point. "We've got a body, and that's all I know. Some old fart called in, damn near hysterical because he found a rotting corpse in his usual fishing spot."

Overstreet wondered if Faye could hear the grisly information moving out of the phone and into his ear.

"You know the boat ramp at Lighthouse Park? The medical examiner's office has somebody there already, talking to the guy that pulled the body out of the river. Get over there now."

No wonder the boss was so thoroughly pissed off. The poor guy that found the body was probably just a nice retired man out for a day of fishing. He'd done what he considered to be the right thing by hauling the body out of the water and getting it to shore…and it couldn't have been an easy or fun job.

The guy was probably a pretty fine boatman, come to think of it, if he managed this without capsizing his craft. But his good deed meant that every abrasion on the body would come with a question. Did it happen when the body was salvaged from the water? Did it happen during the past day-and-a-half, while the body was presumably floating free in the river? Or did it happen as part of an assault or murder?

Overstreet was almost as pissed off by his own awkward situation. What precisely was he supposed to do with the highly paid and well-qualified consultant sitting to his right? It wasn't fair to shut Dr. Longchamp-Mantooth out of the investigation, not when she was truthfully a real asset to the team, and he had no time to drop her off on his way to the boat dock, anyway.

He looked her over. She looked about as emotionally stable as a person can look, which was quite some accomplishment in her condition. And the woman's air of quiet security said she was convinced that she could take care of herself, no matter what. But she was wrong.

Faye Longchamp-Mantooth sat in the car next to him, barely big enough to carry the child in her belly. Even when she wasn't pregnant, an average-sized man with no scruples could flatten her without half-trying. There was a reason that some policemen kept their own women on a short string, constricting their social circle and limiting their freedom to move around the world until there was really nothing in their lives but their husbands. It was sick and it was wrong, but Detective Overstreet could understand it.

In a law enforcement career, a person saw up-close what havoc an evil person could wreak on a woman. Or on a man.

Still, there was no help for it. He was going to have to take a pregnant lady to see something awful.

Chapter Thirteen

The condition of the body was…well, no corpse that had been in the Matanzas River for that long was going to look good. Faye would have thought she'd be nauseated by such a sight but adrenaline seemed to be keeping her lunch in her stomach.

The body, still dressed, was wrapped loosely in a blue tarpaulin. The skin was white and flabby. The throat wound seemed to have monopolized the attention of the fish and crabs attracted by this big tasty morsel of dead human being, which might have been a good thing and it might not. The medical examiner and the CSI people and Detective Overstreet had all commented on the corpse's exceptionally good condition.

"That brackish water in the Matanzas keeps a floater looking good for an extra day or so," the medical examiner, Butch Benedict, had said.

Sometimes, when Faye got all dolled up for an evening on the town, Joe whistled and said, "Mmmm, looking good…" She devoutly hoped that his definition of "looking good," was night-and-day different from Butch Benedict's.

Not wanting to seem like a prissy girl, Faye leaned over the side of the boat one more time and took a good long look at something mind-bendingly terrible. Squinting at the body's destroyed throat, three words came out of Faye's mouth without conscious thought.

"Call my husband."

Overstreet lurched in her direction. "Are you sick? Do you need to sit down?"

Bewildered, Faye blurted, "What? Oh, that. You know, you should really just try to forget that I'm pregnant."

He looked at her as if she were speaking Sanskrit. He also looked like he expected her to faint and hit the ground at any moment.

"Okay, so maybe you can't help but notice that I'm as big as a barn. But try." She waved a hand in front of his mild blue eyes, with their incongruously long gray lashes. "And try to focus on what I'm saying. Let's call Joe. It may be that this throat wound was made with that stone blade that Glynis found. The other half of it, anyway. I don't see anything about that wound that says it wasn't."

Faye thought that maybe talking about mortal wounds and how they were made might start him to thinking more about their job and less about her condition, which would be a nice change. Most detectives spent a fair amount of time obsessing over the murder weapons that generated their caseload.

Faye plowed ahead. "Joe knows more about primitive tools and weapons than most anybody. He makes them. He uses them. He digs up old ones. High-falutin' archaeologists pay him outrageous sums for his opinions on flintknapped tools. Let him look at that wound and tell us what he thinks about how it was made."

Overstreet seemed like an innately reasonable man, and that trait won out over his innate need to protect her. His gentle eyes just looked at her, while he nodded his head. Faye snatched her phone out of her pocket and speed-dialed her husband.

She looked the body over one more time, then she went back to the car to wait for Joe—not because she couldn't handle the corpse's horrific condition, but because there was no sense getting in the way when she couldn't think of anything else helpful to do. And because she was dead-certain that Overstreet would get progressively happier with every step she took away from the rotting human being who had, until an hour before, been floating free in the Matanzas River.

◇◇◇

Joe and Benedict and Overstreet were crouched in the boat, talking and scrutinizing and squinting at the corpse like some kind of biology project. Faye had never liked biology class, because she always felt bad about the frog or earthworm or cat or whatever it was that she was dissecting.

Her feelings about the body they were examining were more complicated. She was deep-down glad that it didn't belong to Glynis.

Should she feel guilty about that?

She should definitely feel guilty if she believed that it was extra-sad for Glynis to be chewed on by fishes, just because she was young and pretty

She'd known Glynis for a day, but that was enough for her to know that the woman was more than pretty. She was smart and competent and interesting, and Faye had liked the way she supported her employers, particularly gentle and vulnerable Suzanne. Faye had seen that Glynis was also well able to stand up for herself in the face of her obnoxious boyfriend.

This last fact made Faye's feelings at the moment particularly confusing. Because the corpse rotting on the bottom of the boat *was* Glynis' obnoxious boyfriend.

Faye watched Joe and Overstreet rise to their feet and strip off their rubber gloves. Benedict tossed the other two a bottle of hand sterilizer and a towel. He probably figured that, though the gloves had protected their hands, they were both feeling fairly icky right now. And a medical examiner ought to know.

Joe was gesturing with his hands as he wiped them, making long, powerful stabbing motions. Benedict and Overstreet leaned in close to watch the demonstration.

Faye hauled herself to her feet. If Joe was pantomiming a murder, then she wanted to see how he thought it was done.

Now he was pointing to Overstreet's throat, tapping at its soft hollow. "Yeah, I think the killer used the pointed end of that broken blade, or something shaped a whole lot like it, and I think it hit Lex hard right there."

Joe was still pointing his index finger at the detective's throat. "That scar on his neckbone was deep, but a blade that size could certainly have gouged it out. If I had to guess, I'd say Lex was already down when that blow was struck. You'd have to be damn lucky to strike someone dead center in the throat and drive the blade straight in, if the person was standing and fighting back. That wound looks like it was made by someone straddling somebody who was already pretty helpless."

Overstreet wiped his hands down and handed the towel back to Benedict. Then he stared at the river for a moment. The slow-moving blue Matanzas seemed to help him think. "So you think the person who stabbed Lex wasn't necessarily someone who had a lot of experience with a knife?"

This scenario would have made the murder easier for someone less physical than, say, Joe. Someone like Glynis.

Joe nodded slowly, still picturing how the killing might have been choreographed. "Yeah. See that big bruise on his forehead," he said. "If he got hit hard there, it might've immobilized him long enough for someone to finish him off. Would've taken something bigger and blunter to make that lump, though. Something like that celt Glynis found. You did find blood on one piece of it."

All three men and Faye peered over the side of the boat.

Faye's imagination was a little too good. She concentrated her energies on not picturing what this experience would be like for Lex or for his killer.

"You sure know a lot about deadly weapons," Overstreet observed.

"Many's the time I fed myself with 'em. Deer. Squirrels. Rabbits. Duck," Joe said. "But in case you're wondering," Joe said. "I didn't use any weapons on Lex Tifton. I would've just used the sharp edge of that blade to cut the carotid, myself. It's a lot more certain than striking hard and maybe missing."

Faye decided to focus her mind on *not* picturing a man bleeding to death from an arterial neck wound.

◇◇◇

Faye leaned in through the open driver's window to say good-bye to Detective Overstreet. She'd hardly known him a day, but when that day was punctuated with the discovery of a murdered man's corpse, the bonds of friendship formed pretty quickly.

His thin gray hair was stuck tight to his sweaty forehead and his fingernails looked freshly gnawed. She opened her mouth to tell him to go home and get some rest, but he beat her to it.

"Tell that husband of yours to take you home and let you put your feet up. Make him get your supper for you. He should also talk to you about something more pleasant than prehistoric murder weapons and how to murder people with them."

"You mean that we shouldn't discuss the best way to slice someone's carotid artery while we're sipping our after-dinner coffee?"

"Now, you know that man's not going to let you have any coffee." He nodded in the general direction of Joe, who was using hand gestures to help an ambulance driver thread his way through the parking lot serving the ramp where the boat and its cargo waited.

"Okay. I promise that we won't talk about blood and guts while we sip our tea."

"Caffeine. Joe's not going to let you have any caffeine till you have that baby. Longer, if you're nursing. My wife's in the La Leche League. I think she nursed ours until they got on the school bus."

"That's a heckuva long time to go without caffeine."

Overstreet laughed. "I didn't think she was going to survive the withdrawal…which lasted maybe three years." He reached for his cigarettes and stopped short for about the thirtieth time that day. "I hope you survive till you can have your coffee—"

"Coke. I'm dying for a real Coke."

"—your Coke. I hope you survive till you can have some real Coke again. Tell Joe I said good-bye and that it was a pleasure working with him."

"I'll do that—"

Benedict interrupted Faye by politely tapping her on the shoulder, and she stepped away from the car window. "Detective, could you come with me for a second? We were getting ready to move the body, but something just fell out of his pocket."

"What was it?"

Overstreet was out of the car and had taken three steps in the direction of the boat before Benedict could answer his question.

"I think it could be important. I mean, I can think of two or three ways this thing could get somebody mad enough to do murder."

Overstreet had pushed his weary body to a jog, but he still had enough wind to say, "Come on, Butch, don't make me guess. Money's plenty good enough to trigger a murder, but you're not going to come grab me out of my car because the man had some Benjamins in his pocket."

"Well, I might if he had a thousand of 'em."

The two of them reached the boat, with Faye close behind, pushing her own legs as fast as they'd go. A crime scene photographer was pointing her camera at something protruding from a pocket on the chest of Lex Tifton's sodden golf shirt. A slender blue-tipped piece of white plastic showed stark against the black fabric. The familiar thing struck at a place in Faye's heart that, until now, had only been associated with happiness.

Even from this distance, she could see three letters clearly through the window in that little piece of plastic. They said, "YES."

Why had Lex Tifton been carrying a positive pregnancy test in his shirt pocket when he was killed?

Chapter Fourteen

The vampire was unexpected.

In her lifetime, Faye, like all Americans, had seen many people parading around outdoors in sweeping capes and an unhealthy pallor. But always in October, never May. Well, maybe occasionally outside movie theaters when certain movies were playing.

The woman on the front doorstep of Dunkirk Manor looked out-of-place, standing in front of a froth of Suzanne's white daisies and pink sweetheart roses while dressed in jet black satin. There were a dozen people standing around her, dressed normally (for tourists) in shorts, sandals, and t-shirts with risqué sayings across the chest. They seemed to see nothing odd in the woman's clothing, not even when she called their attention to it by spreading the cape wide with both arms, then crossing them across her chest to furl it around her body.

Faye usually parked in the employee lot but, since she'd left that morning, Daniel had finally gotten the garden gate closed and a keypad installed. With no access code, she and Joe had no choice but to park on the street.

After conferring for a moment in the parked car, they'd decided they'd rather pay for takeout than eat yet another meal from the bounteous leftovers of Dunkirk Manor's breakfast. So Joe had driven away to scout out nearby restaurants, and she was on her own, with no way to enter Dunkirk Manor other than to wade through the crowd on the porch. So she did so.

The cape-wearing woman was delivering a speech that she'd obviously given a hundred times, but her delivery was fresh and convincing.

"Thank you for joining me for this evening's ghost tour. The costume's just for fun…and it *is* fun, isn't it?" she said, twirling in place to spin out the hem of her trumpet-shaped skirt. "But I'm serious about ghosts, and this city is full of them. We begin our tour tonight with Dunkirk Manor, one of the most haunted homes in town. Our tours begin at dusk and I'm here to tell you that I start here because I want to move on before the sun goes all the way down. I'm afraid of this place after dark."

She paused to let her customers titter and whisper among themselves. Faye took this opportunity to politely wend her way through the crowd toward the front door.

The vampire assailed her as she approached the door. "Faye!"

Faye was pretty sure that she didn't know anybody with fangs.

"It's me, Harriet!"

And indeed it was. Faye recognized the librarian's long frosted hair and trim figure, but her daytime look had lacked the gothic glamour and exposed cleavage of these vampire threads.

Harriet gave her a quick hug and whispered in her ear. "I'd love to talk to you sometime about the inside of this house. I'm only allowed to take my guests into the entry hall for the tour." Then she turned her attention back to the paying customers.

"Dunkirk Manor is one of the poured-concrete buildings characteristic of St. Augustine. When Henry Flagler brought his railroad down the east coast of Florida in the late 1800s, opening up the Sunshine State to tourists…like you wonderful people—" Harriet gave her audience a welcoming smile. "—he chose our city as the grand destination. And in those days, the word 'tourist' wasn't in common use. Here in St. Augustine, we were still using the older word, 'stranger,' which I find interesting as a real-life librarian. If you start researching the history and etymology of the word 'stranger,' you find yourself taking a side trip through synonyms to 'guest' then through 'host' and even to 'ghost.' So bear in mind as we enter the house that we may not be the only 'strangers' in the room."

The tourists laughed.

"Our next stop," Harriet continued, "is St. Augustine's city gate, one of the most haunted places in town. I see it as a symbol, because this place is one of the first gateways from the Old World to the New. This is where the European invaders stepped ashore and stayed. And when you think about ghosts and guests and strangers…well, from the First Americans' point-of-view, weren't the Europeans the ultimate strangers?"

She flung open the front door, motioning to Faye to enter ahead of them. Faye hadn't used the front door since she first arrived, and the sumptuous entry hall seemed cold and empty and filled with echoes, compared to the warm conviviality on the flower-draped front porch.

"As I was saying, the poured-concrete construction of Dunkirk Manor is characteristic of Gilded Age St. Augustine. Henry Flagler's Hotel Ponce de León was the nation's first major poured-in-place concrete building and it was among the first major buildings to have electricity. I'm told that Flagler employed electricians whose only job was to go from room to room, turning the lights on and off for the hotel's guests…tourists…strangers…ghosts. Whatever."

Motioning her tour group into the house, Harriet flicked the wall switch and the electric wall sconces flickered spookily. "Don't tell the owners I did that, Faye."

"I'll take your secret to the grave." Faye was tickled to see that her weak ghost joke got some giggles from the tourists.

"Dunkirk Manor is the home of several ghosts. The first Dunkirk couple who lived here are said to have shared their wedding night with a bunch of angry spirits who whispered in their ears for hours in foreign languages that neither of them recognized. They moved to another room, then another, but the constant chatter continued until dawn. Mrs. Dunkirk announced the next morning that she was returning to Pennsylvania on the first train and invited her husband to join her. This put Mr.

Dunkirk in a major bind. As one of Henry Flagler's top officers in the East Coast Florida Railway, he made plenty of money, but you can see how even a rich man could sink his entire fortune in this house."

Harriet extended her long arms toward the walls, covered from polished floor to high ceiling with hand-crafted woodwork. "And he had no hope of selling it, because nobody in town had enough money but Henry Flagler, and Flagler had his own mansion. Mr. Dunkirk persuaded his bride to go to her parents' home in Pennsylvania for a few months while he consulted a priest for an exorcism. The priest said the place was full of really pissed-off Timucuans who had been killed off by the Spanish. He did the best he could, but he advised Mr. Dunkirk to just give the house over to the ghosts at night. The priest told him that if he built a bedroom wing to the rear, he was pretty sure that the ghosts and demons would leave the young couple alone there. You can see in this photo that the rear wing isn't made of poured concrete. It would have cost too much to bring the masons back out to the property, and Mr. Dunkirk had already blown all the cash he could afford."

She held up a large book with a color photo of Dunkirk Manor's rear garden. Faye had spent two days in that garden without paying any attention to the rear wing, but Harriet was right. It was a wood frame structure protruding from the opposite side of the main building from the garden gate and parking lot. Its design was rather plain for the late Victorian era, and it looked out of place stuck onto the back of a building that was otherwise perfectly symmetrical—twin square turrets on either side of a vast rectangular block of a house, with a central rear wing housing the kitchen and servants' quarters.

Faye knew that the interior was just as symmetrical, with the rectangular atrium surrounded by double parlors and even twin dining rooms. The kitchen wing, though larger, balanced the entry hall nicely, and the two identical turrets towered above it all. How interesting that all the bed-and-breakfast guest rooms were in the new wing. Daniel and Suzanne slept in the main house, and so did the archaeology team, but not the paying guests.

"I think Mrs. Dunkirk never intended to come back to Florida, but apparently the ghosts didn't disturb her entire wedding night. She returned to St. Augustine in time for her only child, Raymond, to be born, right here in this house."

"But probably in the rear wing," said a gray-bearded man.

"Probably," Harriet said with a laugh. "They say that she lived here until young Raymond was seven, then went home to Pennsylvania for good. The boy stayed here, to be reared by his father and their servants."

Faye remembered Raymond's black eyes. They had stared coolly out of both photos she'd seen of him, unreadable. Maybe the nameless emotion in those eyes had been the loneliness of a boy whose mother had abandoned him. She shivered, wishing she could just go to bed and lie under the covers until she got warm.

Dummy, she thought. *You can. You're not part of this tour. Stop listening to Harriet's silly ghost stories and go to bed.*

She stepped politely through the crowd and put her hand on the door that opened into the atrium, nodding good-bye to Harriet. Turning its polished brass knob, she took a step into the atrium and stopped abruptly, startled by the whoosh of cold air rushing through the doorway.

Harriet was close behind her, saying, "This is a rare opportunity. I've been in the atrium a couple of times, during fundraisers given by the non-profit that maintains the house. The place is simply magnificent. Everybody try to take a peek while Faye has the door open."

Faye cooperated by lingering longer than strictly necessary on the threshold, willing to give the crowd a chance to see the house's crowning glory.

"This room is considered an architect's marvel. Its proportions are perfectly calculated to make it seem even more vast than it is. The stained glass of the atrium ceiling, made in a peacock feathers pattern, was based on a design by Louis Comfort Tiffany," Harriet said, pointing upward, over Faye's shoulder.

"Like the rest of the house, the atrium is perfectly symmetrical from left to right, as if a mirror were placed in the center of the room, just between the matching staircases leading to the balconies that surround the second and third floors. And try to get a glimpse of the artwork, if you can. You can get a taste of it in here," she gestured to the bold paintings that ringed the entry hall walls, "but everything in the atrium is on a monumental scale, and that includes the art."

Faye hadn't noticed the size of the paintings on her first visit to the atrium. They were the right size for the room, so their scale didn't call attention to itself, but that room was immense. The painting to her immediate right, a surreal landscape under a bronze sky studded with sun, moon, stars, and comets, was taller than she was. The subject, a young man with a flowing beard and long red hair, was shackled to a spreading oak tree.

"All of the art was chosen by Raymond's wife Allyce, who was a talented painter in a day when women of her class weren't ill-mannered enough to compete for gallery space or public attention. Since Allyce and her husband were the second generation to live in this house, and since Allyce as an artist was drawn to the new and avant-garde, she chose expressionist paintings that seem like anachronisms in this late nineteenth-century room. But I like the unsettled feeling they give, and the rich wood paneling sets off their stark colors. See the painting on that far wall that's mostly red and black?"

Faye saw it, dead center between the staircases, glowing like an ember.

"It was painted by Edvard Munch. You know…the man who painted *The Scream*."

"*The Scream* gives me the creeps," said the gray-bearded tourist.

"It's nothing but some pigments smeared on cardboard," was Harriet's breezy response. "If it gives you the creeps, that's because the artist knew how to tap into your soul. Allyce could recognize that kind of talent. Munch isn't the only painter represented in this room who went on to be recognized for his genius. Allyce had the eye of an artist and she had money. My undergrad degree is in art history. I'd dearly love to give a tour of this house, top to bottom, just for the art. The owners won't let me, because they're afraid I'll disturb their guests."

The over-air-conditioned air in the atrium was chilling Faye to the bone. It was time to leave Harriet and her tourists to their ghost tour. As she stepped through the door, the light changed subtly. She supposed the atrium's stained glass ceiling was lit by a collection of skylights, and perhaps they had brightened because the setting sun came out from behind a cloud. Or maybe the streetlights outdoors had flipped on as dusk settled. In any case, the whole room changed before Faye's eyes.

The shadows shifted under the staircases and Faye was suddenly hyper-aware that she was looking at the very spot where Raymond and his mistress, Lilibeth Campbell, had once stood. And above them, his wronged wife had strode up the staircase to have a word with the bandleader, probably because his musicians' work didn't meet the standards of an artist who was forbidden by society to share her own art with the public.

At that instant, Suzanne appeared on the second floor landing, heading upstairs. She was so preoccupied that she never acknowledged Faye standing below her, or even noticed that she was there at all. Suzanne's face was drawn, and she fingered her collar nervously with a pale, white hand. She couldn't have looked less like the photo of her great-great-aunt Allyce, who had strode confidently up that same staircase to chastise an errant conductor, but Faye still felt like she'd seen a ghost.

The moment passed quickly, and the bored mumbling of the tourists behind her told Faye that they'd seen nothing, felt nothing. She became aware of a hand gripping her arm, and she knew that Harriet *had* felt something. Rationality told her that she and Harriet had seen the photograph of Raymond and Lilibeth and Allyce in this very room, and that they'd both experienced a split-second of *déjà vu*, for the simple reason that they *had* both been here before, in a very real sense.

Nevertheless, Faye did not linger in the atrium, and she didn't tarry as she made her way toward her room. Joe would be back soon with their supper, and she wanted nothing more than his comforting presence and the humdrum taste of run-of-the mill takeout food. Then she wanted to put on her voluminous pregnancy nightgown and a pair of cotton gloves, planning to forget the betrayed Allyce and lose herself in the story of a long-ago renegade priest.

In the quiet of the dusty, dun-colored hall, her bedroom waited. It hadn't occurred to Faye before, but she heard nothing from the other archaeologists at night. No television noises seeped through the walls, not even the beeps and blats of an evening game show. Even little Rachel didn't make enough noise to invade Faye's nighttime privacy, and that was impressive, considering how much noise the child could make in the daylight. This house's interior walls must be of the same concrete as its façade, even here in the servants' quarters.

When she opened the door, she noticed how distinctly the little watercolor painting stood out against the faded wallpaper. She supposed Allyce Dunkirk had even chosen the art in the servants' quarters. Perhaps she'd painted it.

Faye walked toward the painting, intending to check the painter's signature. Halfway there, she realized there was no need. The lissome woman walking in profile down a deserted beach had the same mannerisms as the wronged wife in Harriet's photo—the downturned face, the upturned eyes that looked at the world through a heavy fringe of lashes. She even had the determined stride that seemed so incongruous in such a delicate creature.

Had Allyce intentionally painted herself? Had she walked past a mirror, time and again, just to see how she did it? Or did her brush just naturally paint a woman who moved the way Allyce thought a woman should move? Did it matter?

Just to be sure, Faye checked the signature and saw that it did indeed give the name of the lady of this grand house:

Allyce Dunkirk

From the journal of Father Domingo Sanz de la Fuente

Translated from the Spanish by
Faye Longchamp Mantooth, Ph.D.,
and Magda Stockard-McKenzie, Ph.D.

On the morning after our first encounter with the French, a storm arose so great that we feared to remain on the open sea, and yet we also feared being driven ashore and wrecked. There was yet more to fear, since we could suffer an attack if the French should return with reinforcements. The decision was made to retreat to the Seloy River, below the French colony, where we would build our own fort.

Two companies of infantry were sent ashore to greet the natives living along the Seloy, and they were graciously received. The gift-giving commenced in earnest and, as a result, Father Francisco and I each found ourselves in possession of a piece of property no priest should own. My gift was a woman whose name was a mellifluous thing that sounded something like Ocilla. The Timucua had no notion of the written word, so I am forced to write her name as it sounded to me when she spoke it.

Ocilla looked some years younger than I. As I have said, I myself was but two-and-twenty. Father Francisco's gift-woman was hardly older. I looked to the father to see how he responded to this startling event.

Father Francisco came from a family with far more wealth than mine, and he knew well how servants were to be treated. He handed his woman, Yaraha, his prayer book to hold, then looked at her no more. Anxious to behave well, I did the same.

The Indians also gave our commanders a large house belonging to a chief, which was blessed with a most felicitous location on the river's shore. A smaller house was given to Father Francisco and me, and also to a third priest we did not know named Father Esteban, who had traveled across the ocean on one of the other ships. It was presumed that Ocilla and Yaraha and Father Esteban's serving woman Chulufi would live there with us.

I have heard it said that Timucua women use only enough woven moss in their skirts to keep them honest. Their exposed skin and free-flowing hair would be considered an abomination in Spain, but it suits the native women in a way that I cannot explain. Their nakedness is innocent, and it did not often put me in doubt of my sacred vows. Ocilla and Chulufi and Yaraha settled comfortably into a life as our servants, and I soon considered them an ornament to my own life.

Father Francisco was accustomed to having servants to chop the wood that kept him warm and to fetch the water he drank, and he had learned from the cradle to speak in a voice that servants instinctively obeyed. On that first night, he showed Ocilla and Yaraha and Chulufi where to spread their sleeping mats, in a spot as far from our beds as possible within that small house. They slept there that night, and every night, without questioning him.

Later, Ocilla told me that she and Yaraha had discussed the odd disinterest that Father Francisco and I showed for the pleasures of female flesh. I found it noteworthy that Father Esteban was absent from their conversation. From the bruises on Chulufi's arms and the dead calm in her eyes, I soon came to believe that our brother priest had displayed no lack of interest in the things our women discussed in our absence.

Yaraha, older and more experienced, was of the opinion that Father Francisco was simply too old for such things, but she had no explanation for my celibacy. After watching me sleep for some period of time, she declared to Ocilla that I was assuredly not too old, and she ventured an opinion that perhaps there was someone I longed for, silently, late at night. Perhaps, she suggested, it was thoughts of Father Francisco himself that disturbed my sleep. Or perhaps my unspoken desire was for Father Esteban.

Yaraha could think of no other explanation for my lack of interest in my servant Ocilla.

When Ocilla made this revelation, I laughed until my belly was sore. In all my time with Ocilla, I never convinced her that my feelings were those of a normal man, but of a man who had made a most sacred promise. Anxious to preserve my dignity when in public, she sometimes laid a soft hand on my forearm and looked into my eyes like a lover. While this may have preserved my dignity among her people, it did little for my reputation among mine.

Nevertheless, I could not bring myself to stop her from making those little ministrations. The other men in our expedition would have made their obscene presumptions in any case. I found that I preferred their ribald suggestions to the prospect of hurting gentle Ocilla.

Father and I did not display the amorous energy our serving women expected, and neither did we have the warlike energy of the two infantry captains who were given the larger house. Immediately upon receiving it, they ordered a trench and breastworks to be installed around the house.

From this distance in time, I see their sin in taking a generous gift and making it a thing of war. At the time, I congratulated the commanders on their initiative, which was significant given that their men had no tools with which to work the earth. The Captain-General, Don Pedro, congratulated them upon his return from surveying the countryside, also, and his approval was worth far more than mine.

The Captain-General's return to the village on the banks of the Seloy was lauded with trumpets and artillery. Father Francisco took up a cross to meet him, while Father Esteban and I followed behind, singing Te deum laudamus. The Captain-General, followed by all in his procession, knelt and embraced the cross. A large number of Timucua imitated them, in a way that reminds me to this day of the power of a Christian's example.

The Captain-General took formal possession of all this country on that day, and his captains swore their allegiance to him yet again. Father Francisco celebrated mass, to my knowledge the first such sacrament performed in La Florida. To his everlasting credit, Father Francisco then counseled Don Pedro to allow the troops to rest for the winter and delay his conquest of the French until the promised reinforcements arrived from Spain and Dominica.

But the Captain-General was a man who kept his own counsel, and Our Lord encouraged him in his pride by giving him success after success. Or perhaps He did not. It depends upon how you read the omens and whether you are Spanish or French. Or Timucuan. When it comes to your opinion of omens and events, much depends on whether you were born in this new world, or whether you are a stranger here.

In any case, the Captain-General shortly sent two vessels away, one to Spain and one to Havana. Neither was captured by the enemy, which was seen as a very great omen. And God soon showed his favor in a yet more dramatic way, by sending another great hurricane, one so severe that few French ships survived. Perhaps they were all destroyed. I do not know.

The great faith of our leader told him that the French were without naval defense, so he set out with an expedition of five hundred men, despite the objections of a majority of them and of Father Francisco. And of the humble priest writing this account.

Each man was supplied with a sack of bread and a supply of wine and my feeble prayers. They were guided by two Indian chiefs, who both joined our leader in his implacable hatred of the French.

Father Esteban did not object to this expedition, which seemed so foolhardy to the unbiased eye. In fact, he asked Don Pedro's leave to join him, so that he might pray to the Lord for victory within the very sight of the infidels. The Captain-General gave his permission.

Neither Chulufi nor I were sad to see him go.

This army had hardly walked out of my sight when they were punished with the most horrible tempests I ever saw. The next day, Father Francisco's merciful heart told him to send men with more bread and wine for our soldiers, but I had no faith that they would receive it. Father also sent his prayers for the destruction of the heretics from France.

While we waited for word, a Frenchman approached our camp, bearing a white flag. He was made a prisoner and brought for interrogation. Father Francisco asked if he were Catholic, and he proved his faith by reciting some prayers, so Father consoled him by promising that we would not hang him. He then told us that seven hundred men awaited our troops in Fort Caroline on the river Mai. One-third were Calvinists, including two Calvinist priests.

Eight or ten Spaniards who had been found among the Indians, naked and painted, were also among their number. They had been shipwrecked long before and had despaired of ever seeing their home country again.

When we heard of the number of enemy troops awaiting our men, I retreated in prayer so earnest that time did not seem to pass, until I heard the sound of bells ringing and men shouting in celebration of victory. The French fort, Fort Caroline, was ours.

Concealed by darkness and torrents of rain, our soldiers had surprised the enemy in their very beds. Some of them, quite naked, had arisen and begged for quarter, but more than one hundred and forty were killed, including a great Calvinist cosmographer and magician. Within an hour, the fort, six vessels, much weaponry, and a gratifying amount of food were all ours. But Father assured me that the most gratifying advantage of this victory was the Lord's triumph.

He foresaw this as the means of the Holy Gospel being introduced into this country, a thing necessary to prevent the loss of many souls. He anxiously awaited the return of Father Esteban, so that he could hear more about the vanquishing of the Calvinist heretics.

I confess to you that my thoughts were not on our great victory. They were with the souls of the men killed in their beds that morning. It had been but two months since our departure from Mother Spain and I had already learned that I would be worth nothing as a soldier. Since I knew that many of those poor men were not Catholics and still I grieved their suffering and death, I presume this means that I am also worth very little as a priest.

The night after we took the French fort, I lay awake in the darkness. I looked across our comfortable house with its sturdy mud-daubed walls, and I sought the shadows where Yaraha and Ocilla and Chulufi slept. I could not make myself wish them dead merely because I had not yet succeeded in making believers out of them.

I, Father Domingo Sanz de la Fuente, attest that the foregoing is a statement of actual events.

Chapter Fifteen

Harriet sounded amazingly ordinary on the phone for someone who'd been dressed like a vampire with ample cleavage just the night before. Well, she sounded ordinary but extraordinarily enthusiastic. And Faye felt that it was extremely early in the day for enthusiasm, since she'd been up past midnight reading Father Domingo's memoirs. Joe had been so happy about her late-night work that he'd smoked two cigarettes.

"Did you feel it last night, Faye? I know you did. I saw your face."

"Feel what?"

"The atmosphere in the atrium last night. The unnaturally cold air. The sense of something…other. It was Allyce. You know she was there."

"I know that the air conditioning system was running."

It was running now. No vibration from the central air conditioning unit penetrated Dunkirk Manor's stout construction. Or was that "air conditioning units?" Faye had no idea how many units it took to cool the monstrous house. Nevertheless, the cold air pouring out of the vent over her head was proof enough that the system was on.

"You think that was the A.C.? You are such a scientist, Faye." Harriet didn't sound offended by Faye's disbelief, but she left no room for doubt as to her own opinion. "You didn't look like a scientist last night. Your eyes were big as saucers."

"Thank you. I *am* a scientist. And those eyes didn't see anything that couldn't be explained by regular old science. That

wasn't Allyce on the staircase. It was Suzanne, and there's nothing very spooky about seeing a woman climb the stairs in her
own house. You and I got creeped out because we'd just seen the
photo of Allyce and Raymond and Lilibeth in that very room.
The tourists hadn't seen the old photo of the atrium and they
didn't notice anything odd at all."

"Tourists are so…." Harriet paused to grope for the right
word, which wasn't coming, probably because she was a nice
lady who depended on those tourists for a portion of her liveli-
hood. "Well, they're not real perceptive. Okay, they're pretty
clueless. They expect their vacation experience to be wrapped
up in a neat package and tied with a bow. They expect Disney-
style ghosts that look like regular people, only they're green and
grinning and see-through. Anything less than that, and your
average tourist will just yawn and head for the gift shop. Not
that there's anything wrong with that. If I take my tours into a
gift shop and they buy a lot, the owner will usually give me a
cut. Or some free merchandise."

"Is that how you got your fangs?"

"Absolutely. I may be a fake vampire, but I'm a very real
businesswoman, and one of my businesses is publishing. I want
to give you a copy of one of my books. I think you'll enjoy it
and I think you'll be able to use it in your work."

"Will it help me with *this* job? Because I've got a stack of
books taller than I am that I've got to plow through before I
write my report."

"Sure it will. It's got lots of pictures of Dunkirk Manor and the
Dunkirks themselves, but it's got even more pictures of Lilibeth
Campbell, 'cause it's about her. Every scrap of information, every
rumor, every ugly innuendo…if the gossips of St. Augustine ever
said it about Lilibeth Campbell, it's in this book. I know, because
I wrote it and published it myself. They sell it at the gift shops
around town, and it earns me about enough to pay my light bills.
Which actually ain't bad for a book that has mostly local appeal."

Faye wasn't sure a book written to satisfy the lurid curiosity
of the average tourist was going to be a good reference for her

report. This was surely the reason that snobby Rosa had not brought her Harriet's book to study, though she must have known of its existence. There was no way that Rosa would shelve it in her collection.

She searched for a polite way to decline the offer. "Lilibeth Campbell will just be a footnote to my report, if she belongs in it at all."

"Yeah, but I've got pictures of the house in that book that you can't find anywhere else. I'm local and I know everybody. People dug through their old family albums and lent me amazing stuff that they'd never show an outsider. I doubt photos exist of the servant areas of the house—who would have thought they were worth wasting film on?—but I've got pictures of everything else."

Photos of the house that didn't exist elsewhere? Now Faye wanted Harriet's book. She wanted it badly.

"Shall I come to your house after you get off work at the library?"

"Nah. I eat supper in the old city, then go straight to my early evening ghost tour. But I keep copies in my car. I'll just drop off a book on my lunch hour. Look for it on a table in the entry hall."

Faye was trying to say "Okay," but she was being drowned out by Harriet's infectious laugh. Instead she said, "What? What did I say?"

"Nothing. I was just fixing to say you might want to grab the book sooner rather than later. Otherwise, you might have to walk through that spooky atrium after dark."

"Very funny."

"She was there last night, Faye. You know she was. But somehow, I don't think Allyce would hurt a pregnant lady. I think she'd take care of you, actually. Read my book. You'll see."

And with an ethereal "Bye!!!" like the chime of a bell, Harriet hung up. Faye was left to wonder just how anxious she really was to walk through Dunkirk Manor alone after dark. Even for a firm-minded scientist, the atrium would be a different place after the sun left the skylights and there was no light to be had beyond the dim wall sconces that had been gaslights when Allyce Dunkirk was the woman of the house.

◇◇◇

Overstreet was spending the day interviewing the ne'er-do-wells of St. Augustine, and he had expressly forbidden Faye to participate. "You're my archaeology consultant. These guys may be deadbeats, but they're not dead and buried, so they have nothing to do with archaeology."

When she'd opened her mouth to argue, he'd cut her off. "Doesn't it bother you that whenever something awful happens—a woman disappears or a man is murdered or a child is molested—the police can immediately think of a dozen 'people of interest' that they'd like to talk to? I'm going to talk to twelve people today for no reason except that I think they're capable of harming Glynis or killing Lex or that I think they might know who did. That doesn't bother you? Well, it keeps me awake at night. I do not need your help today, but thank you."

He had, however, agreed with the notion that had struck her around midnight. Their plan for the previous day—to visit active construction sites to see if any witnesses might want to talk about any archaeological sites that were being concealed—had been poorly thought out. Those witnesses weren't going to talk to her in front of a policeman.

He'd conceded that point, but vetoed Faye's first idea, which had been for her to go alone. She'd vetoed his counter-suggestion for her to take Joe, because she just couldn't spare him from the Dunkirk Manor project. The businesswoman in Faye just loved it that her new business was already having to juggle two projects.

They'd managed to agree on a third plan: Faye would take Betsy along. Both agreed that a sixty-five-year-old woman didn't offer a huge degree of protection, but there was safety in numbers.

Safety aside, Betsy knew the archaeology of the area and she'd had dealings with most of the land developers and construction companies that they might run across. And, though sites outside the city weren't within her purview, she had a collegial relationship with the county's historic resource specialist and it wasn't unusual for her to visit a site that might relate to work she was doing within the city limits.

So Faye was sitting in the passenger seat of Betsy's city-owned vehicle, chatting with the woman who had maybe the coolest job in Florida. Maybe in the whole United States of America.

"You know, Faye, I've been thinking about those silver filigree rosary beads. They remind me of a doublet button I found near the Castillo. The work is far finer than any I've found before. Likely, it came from Europe and was worn by a very wealthy man. I think the rosary beads were just as much of a status symbol."

Faye wondered how many places in the New World were littered with artifacts as stereotypically associated with the Renaissance as doublet buttons. It was too bad lace ruffs and farthingale petticoats didn't last as long as metal buttons. If they did, Betsy could have probably dressed Queen Elizabeth I by now.

With Betsy's help, they'd made short work of the property development files, selecting three construction sites to visit personally. With her local knowledge, Betsy had eliminated two other active projects out of hand, because she knew for a fact that they were being built on land that had been created in the mid-twentieth-century by dumping fill dirt into a salt marsh. Modern wetlands regulations would have never allowed that, but what's done is done. Faye figured that this created land was as good a place for upscale condominiums as any.

"I guess Glynis' mystery artifacts *could* have come from one of those sites," she pointed out. "They'd have just been stirred up in the fill dirt that was hauled in from God knows where."

"Yeah, but that would make them fairly useless in terms of figuring out how they fit into local history, which would mean Glynis' efforts to preserve them were pointless."

"The person who took her wouldn't necessarily know that."

"Yeah," Betsy said. "Bummer."

Faye knew Betsy was old enough to remember when "bummer" was the latest slang. The woman was still just hippyish enough to say it without sounding stupid.

Though she hated to turn her back on the sites built on fill dirt, Faye knew they needed to focus on the places most likely to yield results. "I get the impression that Glynis was savvy enough to know what makes a site significant."

"She certainly knew enough to bring you artifacts that had the *potential* for significance, every last one of them."

"You got that right. They're flippin' gorgeous." Just thinking about those filigreed beads made Faye want to go fondle them. "So let's assume she knew what she was doing. Let's stick with locations where those artifacts could have come from an undisturbed site from the sixteenth century. Because finding a site like that *would* disrupt a construction project for a very long and expensive period of time. Glynis grew up with a father in the construction business. If she was concerned enough to come to me with those artifacts secretly, then she felt like she needed to hide them from someone...someone who understood how much they could cost a construction business."

"Times are tough." Betsy's curls flopped, detracting from the gravity of her sage nod. "A person on the brink of bankruptcy could be a dangerous person indeed."

Their first stop had been quick. The project was a gas station being renovated to include a drive-thru fast food joint. The existing store was to be demolished and rebuilt, but Faye and Betsy found that site work hadn't even started yet. The entire property was covered in concrete pavement that had been there for forty years, from the looks of it. If Glynis' artifacts had been dug up in Faye's lifetime, it hadn't happened on that spot.

The second stop had been equally quick. The residential development was to be a riverfront subdivision catering to the richest of the rich. Unfortunately, the file said that the developer had been scheduled to break ground on the development's infrastructure in October 2008, the very month when the stock market took the fortunes of the richest of the rich straight into the toilet, along with the smaller bank accounts of nearly everybody else in America. Faded surveyors' flags and occasional traces of spray paint marked the locations of the roads and sewer lines that would have served this community of mansions.

"They never even broke ground," Betsy had said. "Somebody lost a lot of money here. A lot of somebodies—the developer, the bank, the investors…"

"They're still losing it. Every day this property sits here unused is a day somebody's paying interest on the money spent to buy it."

"Yep," Betsy agreed. "But if their bulldozers never came in here and scraped up any soil—and as far as I can see, not the first spadeful of dirt was turned over here—then Glynis' artifacts came from somewhere else."

"So where do we go next?"

"Right down the road, actually. It was going to be a planned community—houses, retail stores, office buildings, golf course, everything. The houses and golf course will have to wait for the economy to recover, but some of the stores and offices are still worth building. More than that—I'd guess the stores and offices probably *have* to be built."

"Because generating a little income from them may be the only way to be able to pay the interest on the property until people can afford to buy houses again?"

"Bingo. And I think you may know the developer."

"I only know one developer in this town. Alan Smithson."

"Bingo," Betsy said again.

"So where's he building the stores and offices?"

"It's not real far as the crow flies, but we'll have to drive a bit. Smithson's engineers had to get pretty darn creative to keep control of the water on these two properties. They're flat and low and the drainage is iffy. Paving a big chunk of land will leave a lot of rainwater with no place to soak into the ground. My guess is that Smithson's planning a retention pond or three. He'll stick a fountain in the middle of each of them, then jack up the price of the properties on his fake lakes by calling it 'waterfront property.'"

They drove a wide circle around a freshly dug pit, then Betsy parked her car under a shade tree. "Here's where they'll build the office/retail center. We haven't come far. See? You can still see the survey flags for the residential development, on the other side of that big hole in the ground. Doesn't look like much, does it? This particular mudhole—I mean stormwater retention pond—will be hidden behind the commercial buildings, so there've got no need to make it look pretty."

And it didn't, for now. Faye knew that plants covered disturbed land with lightning speed in sunny Florida, so this long, narrow pond—which was a nice word for 'ditch'—would look better soon. If she were an alligator, it might look like home already.

Her heart sank. The fact that so much earth had already been moved here made it a real possibility that she and Betsy had done what they set out to do—find the source of Glynis' artifacts. But the sheer volume of disturbed earth worried her.

Acres of land had been cleared and graded, with high spots scraped down and low areas filled to the same height. Soil from the retention pond had probably already been used to level future roads, and their paths might cut straight across the spot where more rosary beads and the other half of the broken stone blade were waiting. All that history might be gone already, despite the risk that Glynis took to save it.

Betsy didn't look as daunted as Faye felt. She'd grabbed two trowels out of her car trunk and was stepping down the sloped side of retention basin. "Let's see what the soils are like here, anyway. We might learn something useful."

Faye found the next hour totally pleasant in a totally geeky way. She and Betsy prowled the bottom of the basin, scraping at the walls and checking out the soil horizons. At one end, the pond was constructed so excess water overflowed during heavy rainfall into a more-or-less natural creek. In that area, the two archaeologists hit paydirt.

"Oh, oh, oh, oh…oh, look."

Faye rolled her eyes at her own articulateness. What was she going to say next?

Oh, oh, look. See Betsy dig. See Betsy and Faye dig up a wad of priceless artifacts.

Because protruding from the creek's banks were bits of multicolored pottery and at least one lump of metal. The hard glint of sunlight on broken flint and chert spoke of hand-chipped tools. Both women whipped out their cell phones and took pictures, then Faye gently tapped the metal lump with the tip of her trowel. A musket ball rolled out of the creek bank and rested at her feet.

She almost crowed like a rooster. Then she put the thing in her pocket. Comparing the size and weight and metal content of this musket ball to the ones in Glynis' stash would go a long way toward being able to say, "Yes. Those artifacts came from here." And that would go a long way toward helping the police figure out who took Glynis and why.

It took the sound of a car engine to remind them that they didn't strictly have permission to be where they were. Overstreet had okayed their plan to go out to a project site and talk to the people working there. He had not approved any cockeyed scheme to go out and duplicate the action that might have gotten Glynis kidnapped, but there they stood—rather, squatted— poking around in something that might cost Alan Smithson his company and his fortune.

Faye eyed Betsy silently, and they didn't have to say a word. Both women knew that it would be an excellent idea to just hang out for a while in this mudhole and hope nobody up there noticed them.

Chapter Sixteen

Faye thought that cell phones might be the biggest technological advance since the printing press.

Stored in Faye's phone was a photo of the spot where Glynis found the artifacts that might have gotten her kidnapped. Yeah, it was a logical leap, but Faye was willing to take it, until lab analysis of that musket ball proved her wrong.

Since her phone was tapped into the Internet—well, maybe *that* was the biggest technological advance since the printing press—the photo had already been flung at the speed of light in the general direction of Detective Overstreet, with a copy to Joe and another copy to Betsy's assistant.

Because Faye was forty, and thus not born with a cell phone welded to her hand, she had forgotten the tiny *boop* her phone made when she pressed each key. So with her first keystroke, an unnatural *boop* had echoed through the quiet air that caressed this pristine bit of nature.

Betsy had locked eyes with her, both of them sure that they would be discovered by the criminals having a casual conversation just a few yards away from the lip of the retention basin where they hid. But they had been lucky.

They had also been lucky in their choice of a parking spot. The car, clearly labeled City of St. Augustine, must have been hidden by the tree above it and the vegetation around it, at least from the vantage point of the newcomers who seemed to believe they were alone. This was good, because those newcomers would not want anyone who worked for the city to see the artifacts hanging out of the wall of this overgrown ditch. And they would not want anyone at all to hear the conversation they were having right this minute.

How unfortunate for them that Betsy was using the *Record* function on her phone to document that conversation while Faye sent photographic evidence of their wrongdoing all over the World Wide Web.

Having turned off the *boop*ing function on her phone, Faye had finished sending the photos to Joe. Now she was considering using the phone as a sort of periscope, sticking it up over the lip of the ditch where they were trapped and taking a few seconds of video that would have told her and Betsy who was up there. But there was no way to do that without a risk that a flash of sunlight reflected off the phone's glass face might attract the men's attention.

Betsy seemed pretty sure she knew who was there, anyway. At the first sound of the first man's low, cultured voice, she had thumb-typed for a second, then held her phone so that Faye could see the screen.

Alan Smithson.

Faye agreed with Betsy. She'd only heard Glynis' father speak once, but the voice was memorable.

The other man's tone was more agitated and excited, and his words carried better.

"I thought you were paying Lex to keep her quiet. Under control."

"Lex found that Gwennie was her father's daughter. Neither of us knuckles under to pressure. Even if her little political temper tantrum was at my expense, even if it did cost me money I could have spent on another pretty sportscar for my little girl, I didn't care. She was busy showing the world what a Smithson is made of. Keep my Gwennie quiet? Under control? What was I thinking? Lex never had a prayer."

"But she cost me the election. She cost me everything I've worked for."

The word "election" caught Faye's ear. Faye typed *Dick Wheeler?* into her own phone. Betsy read it and nodded.

Alan Smithson wasn't buying into the defeated politician's accusations. "My daughter is beautiful and charming, but she did not go into the voting booth with every last person in the county and help them mark their ballots. She didn't help you any, but you lost your own election, Wheeler."

"I didn't have a chance, not with her telling the world that I thought we should open brothels and crack houses in the Castillo de San Marcos—which is a National Monument and thus not really any concern of county government, by the way. So I resent losing my seat because of it."

"I said it already, Wheeler. My daughter is not the reason the voters threw you out on your ear. Do you understand—"

Wheeler's voice rose in volume and in pitch as he interrupted Smithson. "You said Lex could keep her quiet. You said—"

"Don't interrupt me, imbecile. Listen carefully. My daughter is not the reason for your problems."

A familiar metallic click sounded. It wasn't loud, but it was. There's no louder noise in the world than the sound of a revolver's hammer being pulled back.

"Now. Say that you understand what I'm telling you." Smithson's tone was as cool and even as the constant rustle of wind in the trees overhead.

"I understand. I do."

Faye was pretty sure that she could hear Wheeler sweat.

"Say it again, Wheeler."

The ex-commissioner stammered a bit, then said, "I understand you very well."

Faye was very glad that she'd just used her amazing new phone's GPS capabilities to let Joe know exactly where she was.

Just in case he hadn't already figured it out, she texted him a message that would leave no doubt what she wanted him to do:

come get me

◇◇◇

Faye wasn't sure she could feel her feet any more, but moving them was too risky. Not far from the lip of the retention pond where she and Betsy crouched, Alan Smithson had been haranguing Dick Wheeler for quite some time.

Faye'd had time to think about the best way to get rescued.

It was clear that Alan Smithson was not quite sane, no more so than any man whose daughter was missing. The fact that his daughter's boyfriend had turned up dead had only pushed the man further over the edge.

"They say she might have been pregnant when she disappeared, Wheeler. I guess she's still pregnant. If she's still alive. If she hasn't lost the baby…my grandchild…" Faye heard an ugly choking sound. "What are they doing to her? What do they—"

"Put the gun down, Alan. You don't want to hurt me."

"Are you sure? Where were you early Tuesday morning, Wheeler?"

"What are you saying? Do you think I—"

The voice broke. Now Faye was sure she could hear Wheeler sweat.

"You know where I was, Alan. You know where I always am on Tuesday mornings—the Rotary Breakfast Club. I was the speaker, for God's sake. I couldn't have left in full view of half the businesspeople in the county. Nobody has a tighter alibi than I do, except for the other folks at that meeting. Speaking of Tuesday morning Rotary Club…where were you?"

"I'm just not so sure about that alibi, Wheeler. How long does it take to subdue a young woman? A pregnant, scared young woman? We don't know when Lex was killed, so maybe you had time to…hurt my Glennie…before you bellied up to the podium and gave that same stupid speech you give everywhere you go. What time does Rotary start, Wheeler?"

"You know that. Eight o'clock."

"Dunkirk Manor's five minutes from the restaurant that has served the Rotary Club the same bad breakfast for thirty years. Longer than Glennie has been alive. I think you had time to snatch her. Maybe she was in your trunk while you were eating your powdered scrambled eggs."

Faye heard footfalls. She imagined Smithson taking a step toward Wheeler, and Wheeler taking a step back, but she didn't really know what was happening. She just knew that they were getting closer to the edge of the bank. If they got too close, there was no way they could miss seeing her and Betsy. Setting her feet down gently and slowly, the way Joe had shown her, she began making her way to the spot where the retention basin connected to the creek. Betsy nodded in understanding and followed.

Crouched down with her fingers almost dragging the ground, Faye's motion was more like crawling than walking. Her knees were in agony, but she used those low-hanging hands to clear brittle sticks and dry leaves from their path. If their feet fell only on pine needles, no one could possibly hear them. Well, Joe could, but he wasn't here yet.

Joe. He was on his way, and he would be walking into the worst kind of situation. Two angry men, one of them scared and one of them with a gun. She paused and texted the shortest message that would get her point across.

wait

Then she resumed crawl-walking, an activity that no pregnant body should ever be asked to accomplish.

Angry words spilled down into the retention basin where Betsy and Faye were trapped. The two women stood at the bottle-neck where the basin overflowed into the creek, and the word "overflow" spelled bad news for Faye. The basin was designed to behave like the bathroom sink in the house where Faye grew up.

There had been a little hole in that sink, a couple of inches from the top. If little Faye wanted to float her toy boat in the sink, she could stop the drain and fill it up. But if she filled it too full, the water would flow into the hole. Try as she might—and scientific little Faye had tried hard, resulting in wet floors, high water bills, and spankings—she couldn't fill the sink to the brim and she certainly couldn't make it overflow.

This basin had been designed to hold most of the stormwater that flowed off this large piece of property, which was a lot of water. During an ordinary thunderstorm, the water level would rise, then it would go down later, as the water soaked in and evaporated. But during some major event like a hurricane, it was possible that the basin would fill up, run over, and flood all the pretty houses that hadn't been built yet. So the stormwater engineer had designed this thing so that excess water would flow down the creek.

It was too bad for Faye that this engineer had decided the water needed to be up to her waist before it overflowed. Because this meant that she had to haul herself up to an earthen ledge that struck her at waist-level. She had to do this silently, so as not to attract the attention of the armed man above her. And she had to do it quickly, because the angry voices were getting closer.

She looked at Betsy, nodded, then placed both hands on the squishy ledge and pushed hard. All this accomplished was to lift her feet off the ground, where they flailed, trying and failing to gain a toehold. Digging in with her knees to try to lift herself up to creek-level accomplished just as little.

Fortunately, Betsy had been pregnant—four times, if Faye remembered the conversation correctly. Faye suddenly felt the older woman's shoulders beneath her feet. Betsy had squatted beneath her and was slowly standing, using the strength of her own legs to lift Faye to where she needed to be.

Faye felt her swollen belly clear the top of the bank and shoved herself forward face-first into the creek, holding her left arm high enough to keep the phone clear of the water. Reaching back to help, she only needed to give Betsy's arm a gentle yank before they were both lying in the mud, wondering how hidden they really were. Faye was ever-so-grateful for her preferred work garb, olive-drab Army surplus cargo pants and a matching t-shirt.

Betsy was behind her, but Faye couldn't remember seeing her in a bright color. Maybe she was wearing dirty jeans and a brown t-shirt. That would be fairly unobtrusive.

Without looking back to see, Faye started moving down the creek toward the river. It couldn't be far. Well, she didn't think it could be far, but she'd been tooling around this property in a car. Now she was crawling on elbows and knees through water that was more than a few inches deep, with her cell phone clutched between her teeth to keep it dry…dry-ish. And she had no idea whether their butts were sticking up so high that they could be seen over the creek's shallow bank. She figured it was best to just stay low and get the hell out of there. Betsy seemed to agree. The arguing men had grown louder, if possible, but nothing in their tone had changed to suggest that Betsy and Faye had been seen.

When the gunshot came, it took every ounce of Faye's will to keep from throwing herself face-first into the water, drowning the cell phone that was her lifeline to Joe.

The noise echoed through the empty woods. Faye could almost smell burnt gunpowder.

But then two angry voices burst out again, and one of them said, "Have you lost your mind? You could have shot me. You could have *killed* me."

So she knew that the bullet hadn't found its mark. She also knew that the two men were as completely distracted as they could possibly be, which gave her and Betsy a fighting chance to get away. And she also knew that Joe couldn't be far away by now. Unfortunately, she knew with complete certainty that the sound of that gunshot had deprived Joe of the ability to wait. He would be here any minute, and Alan Smithson might aim better this time.

She took the risk of stopping a moment and she also took the risk that her damp fingers would render her electronic lifeline useless.

still okay…not near gun…wait

This was sort of a lie. She *was* near the gun, but she was safe and if Joe ran toward the sound of that gunshot, he wouldn't be.

She resumed crawling on elbows and knees. Florida is not a rocky place. As a person who spent her days digging in the dirt, Faye knew that better than anybody. Nevertheless, there were rocks in this creekbed, and pine cones and tree roots and prickly sweetgum balls. Her pants protected her legs a little, but her forearms were bruised and she was pretty sure that their skin was being peeled off a piece at a time. Her sodden shirt, riding up beneath her armpits, wasn't doing the best job of protecting her belly, either.

Nevertheless, she kept crawling, because Joe's ability to stand still when he thought she was in danger was limited indeed.

Joe had the eyes of a raptor and the ears of a bat. When the gunshot sounded, he was not fooled by the echo. The sound hit each of his ears a fraction of a millisecond apart, so he knew exactly which direction to look for the shooter. And despite Faye's instructions to wait, he intended to locate that gun.

When he got there, maybe he'd do what she'd told him to do. Maybe he'd wait. Or maybe he'd go for the shooter's throat. But surely Faye knew that he would not leave her alone and in danger.

Never.

He pulled off the road and hid the car in a copse of bushes, then he set off walking through a lightly wooded piece of ground marked for development by surveyor's flags and orange paint. His moccasins didn't make a sound on the pine needles that littered the ground. He could see two men arguing in the distance. One of them was waving a handgun at the other one.

He couldn't see Faye yet, but he intended to get a lot closer.

The creek broadened and picked up speed. Faye was not surprised to see the Matanzas River ahead, the same river that Father Francisco had seen so long ago…the same river where Lex Tifton had floated dead so very recently.

With the river in sight, she sat her butt down in the muck and leaned her back against the creek's low bank. Her jaw muscles were very glad when she reached up and took the cell phone out of her mouth and checked the GPS function for her new coordinates. Zapping them to Joe, she sent the words she knew he was waiting for:

come get me
please
come down the river, not over land
I love you

Chapter Seventeen

Faye was glad that Joe had just picked her up and carried her. She really didn't want to have to tell him that she couldn't stand up and she couldn't walk.

She didn't know exactly how far he carried her, slogging knee-deep in the Matanzas River. Joe had apparently scouted out the area and knew what she'd suspected, that the river wasn't visible to Alan Smithson and Dick Wheeler, because he had just scooped her up and started jogging, without hunching down in fear of being found.

Faye didn't have the energy left to do anything but hang from his arms and drip. She was wet all over. She was muddy all over. But, by God, the cell phone had stayed dry. And it had brought her Joe.

When they reached the car, he had laid her on the back seat, ripping off his shirt and covering her with it. He'd no doubt have ripped off his buckskin pants, too, and used them to cover her, but they were almost as wet as hers.

Then he did something she hadn't seen Joe do in a long time. He looked at Betsy with a face that was completely baffled.

He'd looked like that a lot when they'd first met. Joe had grown up with parents who didn't have much use for education. Even if they had, they wouldn't have bothered Joe with it, because they'd thought he was slow.

How they could have believed something so ridiculous when they saw how quickly Joe absorbed the lessons that nature taught? There was nothing about trees or fish or the motion of the stars or the vagaries of the weather that Joe didn't understand. He'd just been born with a brain that shut down when it was confronted with a letter or a number.

If he'd been born in 1798, Joe would have been a man among men, the best tracker and the finest shooter on the American frontier. If he'd been born in 1998, he'd have been recognized as dyslexic and handed over to a teacher who knew what to do about it. But he'd been born in 1978, and by the time 25-year-old Joe showed up on Faye's island, unemployed, homeless, and barely literate, he'd spent all his life being baffled by the modern world.

Faye felt like she'd done nothing but give Joe a home where he could get his bearings, but her friends had opened up his world. Magda had badgered the university into using him as a glorified lab rat in their special education department, and he'd gotten massive amounts of tutoring. Sheriff Mike had been the encouraging, mentoring father that Joe's own father didn't know how to be.

Faye felt that her primary contribution had been teaching Joe to drive, which had been an adventure in itself. Joe's lightning reflexes had been an advantage on the road, except when they led him to slam on the brakes so that he could focus on a street sign that was just too hard to read at highway speeds.

The two of them had survived. And they would survive this day. But the lost-child expression on his face when he looked at Betsy spoke of a man whose world was threatening to crumble.

"I'm okay, Joe," Faye mumbled from the back seat, aware that she looked completely un-okay and thus she looked pretty much like a liar.

Joe didn't answer.

Betsy reached over, flipped on the car heater, and twisted the dial to "High." Faye was grateful, but it was not a good sign that Joe hadn't already thought to do that.

"Really, Joe. I'm fine." She rubbed her belly and found that it was soft. The baby stirred companionably inside her, just as it had done for weeks. "No contractions. And the baby seems perfectly okay."

She didn't like the way his shoulders were hunched as he put the car in gear and got on the road, traveling way faster than his usual cautious speed.

Betsy reached over the back seat and patted Faye on the knee. She'd been pregnant four times and she'd been married for decades. The reassuring pat seemed to be saying, "Settle down. You're both safe and so's the baby. He'll get over this."

And Betsy was probably right. But the drive home seemed longer than it was, because Joe didn't say a word.

Faye was shivering. Hard.

She'd shivered before, but she'd never before had this sense that she had completely lost control of her muscles. They shook her, head to toe, and any effort she made to fight back only made things worse. She closed her eyes and told herself to relax, but that effort was just as big a failure.

This was bad. If Joe looked back here and saw her shaking like this, he was going to lose what was left of his mind. Then he was going to take her to the emergency room, and she'd rather eat dirt than go there, not when she was so sure that she and the baby were both perfectly okay.

Betsy was prattling to Joe, telling him reassuring stories about three of her pregnancies and conveniently leaving out the story of the premature baby who almost died. All the while, her calming hand gripped Faye's shoulder lightly. This helped. If Faye concentrated on that hand, the waves of trembling eased a bit. And she was really loving the blast of the heater as it blew hot air between the front seats.

Then the car stopped and Betsy got out. The heater was still on, but Faye felt like Betsy had taken a lot of warmth with her, until a car door opened and her friend's smiling face reappeared.

By covering Faye with a dusty tarp that she'd found in the city vehicle's trunk, Betsy accomplished three things: she made Faye feel cared for, she made her feel a little bit warmer, and she completely hid Faye's shivering body from Joe. Betsy gave Faye a comforting wink, then disappeared. A moment later, Faye heard the anemic purr of Betsy's vehicle as the archaeologist drove away.

By the time Joe killed the engine in the Dunkirk Manor parking lot, Faye's shivering had eased and she was just dead tired. When Joe flung open the car door at her feet and shoved the tarp onto the floorboards, she was actually glad he'd decided not to let her get up and walk. Drowsy, she didn't protest when he grasped her with his two strong hands and slid her toward him, gently lifting her out of the car.

She was glad that he took her in the kitchen entrance. She didn't think she could stand the drafty atrium or the cold light streaming through its skylights or the painful energy of the bright expressive paintings on its walls. She didn't want to hear Joe's footsteps stop as he stepped from the polished oak floors onto a rug so deep and dense that it absorbed all sound. She didn't think she could bear the room's chilly beauty.

She wanted to be in the warm, shabby room where she slept wrapped in Joe's arms.

He hauled her across its threshold, closed the door, and gently stood her on her feet. She was surprised to find that her legs were willing to hold her up. He took three steps across the tiny room, threw open the bathroom door, and opened the hot water tap. Steam rose quickly as the old claw-footed tub filled.

Joe took the time to carefully adjust the water temperature, just as he would when they gave their baby its first bath. Then he came back to her, unfastening her sodden shirt and pants and bra and panties, peeling them off her chilled skin before helping her into the rapidly filling tub.

Still silent, he pulled off his own pants, soaked by his hike through the river. Naked, he crawled into the tub behind Faye, cradling her against his chest. The tub was old, and its dulled porcelain finish was worn through in places, but it was big enough for the both of them, and for their baby, too.

"When I heard that gunshot…" His voice broke. He tried again. "When I heard the gun…Faye, I was so scared."

His hand stroked the healed bullet wound near her collarbone. Somewhere near the small of her back, Faye knew that she was touching Joe's own scar, where a bullet had nearly taken his life. She leaned against him.

Joe leaned forward, resting his forehead on the crown of her head and, finally, he cried.

Chapter Eighteen

Faye knew there were worse things than lying propped up in bed on a weekday afternoon, wearing flannel pajamas and listening to Joe snore. Magda had lent her a hot water bottle, scolding all the while, but Faye paid her no attention. If Magda hadn't spent most of her pregnancy on bedrest, ordered by the doctor and enforced by Sheriff Mike, she'd have spent the whole nine months digging and hauling and overexerting herself, just like Faye. Magda didn't tend to find herself in the vicinity of gunfire the way Faye did but, otherwise, their approaches to life and pregnancy were much the same.

Still scolding, Magda had gone outside to supervise the field crew. As usual, she was not behaving like an employee.

"Would you two park your butts in this room and stay here? I'd really prefer that neither of you got pneumonia." Pausing in the doorway, she'd barked, "Get in the bed and get warm, both of you. I can handle this job, or did you forget I have a Ph.D. and a quarter-century of experience? It's not like there's any big trick to uncovering an old swimming pool."

Then she'd departed, and Faye had felt more like a schoolgirl on detention than a small business owner.

Joe might be sleepy, but Faye was wired. She weighed her options—continue reading Father Domingo's diary or check out Harriet's book, which Joe had fetched from the entry hall, right where Harriet had promised to leave it.

She opted for Harriet's book for several reasons. Father Domingo's diary wasn't strictly billable to either of her current projects, so she preferred to work with it in the evenings. Since she worked for herself, she could spend nights, days, and weekends doing billable work, and economics might force her to do that at times. For her mental health, though, it was probably better for her to set some time aside for things that were interesting, but had no impact on her pocketbook. Father Domingo's diary fell squarely in that category.

Uncovering the source of Glynis' cache of artifacts had been a huge chunk of progress on her project for the police department. She'd called Detective Overstreet to talk about it, but Betsy had beaten her to the punch. He'd thanked her for the information and listened for a few minutes to her archaeological ramblings about the damage Glynis' father's project had done to the site's archaeology, but he'd cut her off soon enough.

"Betsy and I will figure out a way to deal with Alan Smithson, without letting him know the two of you were involved in finding the source of Glynis' artifacts. You did a good job locating it, but I'll take it from here. I'd have never put the two of you in that kind of danger on purpose."

She'd tried to keep talking, but he'd cut her off. "You did what I asked you to do. If I need more help, I'll call you. Really, Faye. I will. Would you just let it go? Do some normal, nondangerous archaeology for a change?"

So her police department project was on hold, and she was free to focus on her work at Dunkirk Manor. Harriet's book would be a quick read. She'd have to take the information in it with a professional grain of salt, but you couldn't argue with the historical validity of, say, an unretouched photo documented to have been taken in 1928. The photos alone really might give her some new information on the history of the old mansion.

The sound of Joe's snoring was a comfortable counterpoint to Harriet's grim tale of a murdered girl. Lilibeth Campbell had been barely twenty-one when she was killed.

Harriet had compiled a timeline of the last ten months of Lilibeth's life, based on newspaper accounts, dated publicity photos, and written documentation from eyewitnesses. The written documents were the thing that lifted her book above the typical amateur's attempt to solve a famous historic mystery. For Harriet was not just an enthusiastic believer in ghosts and things that go bump in the night. She was a librarian. And she had uncovered diaries and snapshots and old letters that could not have been available to the police who investigated the murder in 1928.

Harriet's conclusions? Raymond Dunkirk and Lilibeth Campbell had become lovers shortly after her arrival in St. Augustine, and their affair had led to her death at his hands less than a year later.

She dismissed the police's suspicions that the starlet had been murdered by one of the three Hollywood moguls funding the silent film that had brought Lilibeth to town, a silent serial melodrama not unlike *The Perils of Pauline*. Faye thought of the creepy photo of the three portly men with their hands on a woman young enough to be their daughter or granddaughter, and she wondered why Harriet was so sure.

There was no disputing the fact that Lilibeth had been found at dawn, dead of multiple stab wounds, after a party that had rocked a popular downtown restaurant until long after midnight. Even without modern forensic methods of estimating time of death, the police had been working within a pretty narrow time window. Unfortunately, few people have air-tight alibis between the hours of three and seven a.m., when even the most insomniac spouse is probably asleep.

Yet all three of the money men—Leo Lestor, Philip Sansing, and Erving Manson—had produced witnesses saying they couldn't possibly have killed Lilibeth. In fact, they had alibied each other, claiming attendance at a private "party" after the big party, attended only by the three of them and three of the city's most selective prostitutes. Lurid headlines hinted at a drunken and wanton orgy with the kind of suggestive reporting common to the era—the news stories said nothing and implied everything.

The police had been certain all three of them were lying, which begged the question of which man had done the murder... or whether they all had. During the ensuing weeks, the newspaper had printed photo after photo of Lestor, Sansing, and Manson with their wives, silently begging the reader to notice that none of these women had left her husband after his degrading behavior had been revealed to the world. If the men had really been guilty, wouldn't their wives have thrown them out of the house out of sheer self-respect? Wouldn't at least one of them have had the gumption to do that?

The photos of those silent and supportive wives begged a question: Was it possible that there was no private party, no orgy, and thus nothing for the wives to forgive? Except for murder. And perhaps each of the men had convinced his wife that one of the others was guilty.

If so, then any of these men could have murdered Lilibeth Campbell. Or all of them. And, if this had indeed happened, one or all of them had gotten away with murder.

Based on the carefully worded police statements that had survived, local law enforcement was virtually certain that Hollywood had invaded St. Augustine, slaughtered one of their own, then fled, taking their money with them. The police were livid at the old men hiding behind alibis that no one believed.

But Harriet disagreed and, decades after the fact, she had known how to do something about it. She was local. She was related to half the people in town. She was relentless in her search for the truth, when it interested her. And she had the kind of personable manner that said, "Talk to me!" In the early 1980s, she'd combed through the city's nursing homes until she found one of the three prostitutes, and she'd charmed her into talking.

"Oh yes, honey," the feeble old woman had told Harriet. "You bet we told the police the truth about being with those dirty old men that night. Me and Connie and Nettie didn't have no reason to lie. They was too tight to pay us enough money to do that. They didn't hardly pay us enough for what we *did* do. Believe me when I tell you that it ain't fun getting roughed up by an old man that's mad 'cause he can't…well, that's all by the by. Mister Lestor and Mister Sansing and Mister Manson wasn't nice men, none of 'em, but I know for certain sure where they was that night. They couldn't have killed Miss Lilibeth. Poor little thing."

So what *did* Harriet think had happened on that long-ago night?

Harriet thought Raymond Dunkirk had killed his young mistress. This theory was the central thesis of her book. He was known to have been at the party at the restaurant with Lilibeth, and without his wife.

Many reliable witnesses had documented his affair with Lilibeth in writing, and their testimony had survived. Raymond Dunkirk had testified that Allyce had been asleep in her room when he arrived home that night, and he was unable to produce a servant who had seen him come in, yet the police never seemed to take him seriously as a suspect.

Faye wondered why, and came up with predictable reasons. He was wealthy and could buy the right people. He was charming and could talk his way out of a murder charge. Most likely, he was just familiar. It was a small town, so everyone knew him, and it's just so hard to suspect a familiar face of hiding a murderer's soul.

Faye thumbed through Harriet's book, well aware of how such things could be subtly skewed. Harriet seemed to be trying to present her evidence dispassionately, like a true journalist, but she was a human being. She chose the things she put in her book and the things she didn't.

So when Faye's eyes scanned photos of Raymond, all of which showed a blindingly handsome man turning an unreadable glance on the camera, she wondered about the photos that Harriet didn't choose. Maybe there had been photos that showed him smiling and laughing…photos that revealed a certain softness that was invisible in the photos Harriet showed the world.

Neither was there any softness in Harriet's description of Raymond Dunkirk as a person. He was an only child raised by a remote and aristocratic father after his mother fled Dunkirk Manor when he was just seven. He was athletic, winning open-water swimming competitions covering distances that would try a man's soul. He had ruled local society with his hypnotic charm and his good looks and his ruthless willingness to let a less intelligent conversational partner tie himself into knots with his own words.

Harriet's portrayal of Raymond Dunkirk made Faye think of the diamond stick pin he always wore in his cravat: His character was hard and finely honed, distractingly brilliant, and not as transparent as one might think at first glance.

Faye's prejudice against Raymond Dunkirk stemmed from a different source than Harriet's. If he truly murdered Lilibeth Campbell, then she agreed with Harriet's unstated conclusion that he belonged in the deepest pit of hell. But even if he didn't, Faye found that she didn't like him for another reason. She disliked him for Allyce's sake.

Raymond Dunkirk had possessed the wealth and the personal charisma to sway the opinions of the people around him. If he had simply said to his contemporaries, "My wife is a brilliant painter. She doesn't have time to be part of your wives' bridge parties and she most certainly does not have time to organize any cotillions. She needs to paint," then Allyce's ambitions would have been accepted. Begrudgingly, perhaps, but still accepted.

Raymond and Allyce Dunkirk had lived in a time when the role of women in society was being rewritten in bold strokes. In 1925, the United States of America had finally deigned to give Allyce the right to vote. Raymond could have done far more than that. He'd had the money to take Allyce and her art to New York. He could have bought introductions to critics and gallery owners. He could have kicked down the barriers his wife faced, so that she and her work could shine on their own merits.

Instead, he'd kept her in this small town, where she could not possibly have fit in. Faye could see that, simply by looking at the bold, original—and, truthfully, a bit scary—artwork that she had painted and selected for Dunkirk Manor.

Instead of encouraging her in her painting, Raymond had expected a woman with an artist's temperament to throw his parties and manage his house, looking beautiful all the while. No wonder Faye saw an increasing remoteness in Allyce's eyes in photographs taken as she passed into her thirties and then into middle age.

And then there had been Raymond's affair with Lilibeth Campbell. Why? Why would a man turn away from a woman who was still beautiful and who, judging by the tilt of her head and the set of her jaw, was still interesting? Lilibeth's murder, and Lilibeth herself, had damaged the Dunkirks' lives in a way that could never be repaired. Harriet found no record that the Dunkirks ever traveled together after that. Even the parties stopped abruptly, and never started up again.

And Allyce just faded away. There were occasional snapshots of her at home in her beautiful garden, but her lovely face graced no more society pages. Faye couldn't even find any evidence that Allyce continued attending parties. While it was true that women of a certain age were invisible in that society, they were not invisible to the camera's lens. Strangely, Allyce seemed to be.

Raymond, by contrast, grew more visible to cameras and reporters as the years passed. In his forties, his longtime friendship with Robert Ripley blossomed. Raymond was heard to say, more than once, that Ripley was the brother he'd always wished he could have. This statement was the only trace of the lonely little motherless boy that Faye could find in Harriet's entire book. It would have humanized him in her eyes, if it hadn't been from the pain evident in the photographs of Allyce taken during that same period.

Raymond had traveled the world with Ripley, visiting places that Faye knew in her heart that Allyce would have wanted to see…places she would have wanted to paint. They met exotic people with habits that seemed bizarre in the post-Victorian world, and they brought home fascinating things. Actually, they brought home mountains and mountains of fascinating things, the foundation for the museums and "odditoriums" that would give legions of tourists the shivers for decades afterward.

Faye's favorite photo of Allyce in the years after Lilibeth's death was of Ripley, Raymond, and Allyce standing in the atrium, draped in the pelt of a lion so huge that it could be wrapped around the three of them. Victor, in his teens by this time, was standing slightly to the side, petting the dead lion's mane. Allyce looked fresh and alive, so much so that both men's eyes were locked on her bright face. In that moment, at that moment, Faye thought it was possible that Raymond Dunkirk still loved his wife.

Harriet took her suspicions of Raymond's guilt seriously, but she hadn't been able to assemble the evidence to support it. Faye thought that this failure was noteworthy. If the woman who tracked down a ninety-year-old prostitute and pushed her for the truth couldn't find proof of Dunkirk's guilt, then maybe it didn't exist. Oh, sure, maybe Raymond Dunkirk was guilty. But it was entirely possible that the evidence to prove it had not survived, and so Harriet would never know for sure.

Hardly any evidence had been found in Lilibeth's hotel suite, which had been so pristine that, again, Harriet suspected something unprovable but logical. The hotel had provided maid service, but the maid had gone off-duty at seven p.m., long before Lilibeth finished primping for a night on the town. Wouldn't a pampered starlet have left discarded clothing strewn everywhere? Wouldn't her toiletries have been scattered hither and yon across the vanity? Harriet thought that someone had tidied the room, after the fact.

The only scrap of evidence that had remained in the dead woman's room was a piece of blank stationery monogrammed with Lilibeth's initials. An alert policeman had noticed indentations on the paper, made when Lilibeth had written a personal letter on a sheet of paper resting atop this one. It had apparently been a multipage letter, as the indented words began in mid-sentence, and she may never have finished it. The barely discernible words just stopped. There was no *Sincerely, Lilibeth* signed with a flourish at the bottom of the page.

The fragment of her letter had said,

wonder why you stay. The good opinion of society will not make you happy. Look around you and you will see that it is true. Mr. Lestor, Mr. Manson, Mr. Sansing . . . do any of those pathetic men look happy? Do you want to come to the end of your life and find that you've become like them? I don't. And I don't want to keep acting for the cameras, pretending that I have a life when I don't. I want what she has, but I have nothing. I want love. I want you. Surely you can see what must be done. I know you are strong enough.

For decades, people had speculated on who Lilibeth was writing, and Raymond Dunkirk was the only reasonable answer, unless Lilibeth had a secret lover hidden somewhere. Harriet swayed Faye's opinion in Raymond's direction with an interesting bit of detective work.

Raymond had inherited Dunkirk Manor and its property and the status associated with the Dunkirk name. But his family's fortune had never recovered from the expense of building the vast house. When it came to unvarnished wealth, Allyce was the one who had inherited enough money to support their gilded lifestyle. It was entirely possible that Lilibeth didn't know this, and that she was urging Raymond to leave his wife and install her as mistress of Dunkirk Manor. It was also entirely possible that Lilibeth did understand that life with Raymond wouldn't be the glittering spectacle for her that it had been for Allyce, who had bankrolled it all. She might have believed that Raymond stayed with Allyce for her money. And it was entirely possible that Lilibeth was right. The fragment of her letter just wasn't clear.

Much speculation had been wasted over whether Lilibeth's letter-writing had been interrupted by her murderer, or whether she'd simply gotten up from her desk and gone to the last party of her life, intending to finish writing later. The letter itself was never found. Even the scrap of paper with the impressions of a single page of the letter had disappeared from the police files.

According to Harriet, it was rumored that Robert Ripley had acquired it by bribing a clerk. If so, it had disappeared into the vast collection of bizarre rarities collected by the globe-trotting founder of the Believe-It-or-Not empire. Harriet reported that it was speculated that Ripley's friendship with Raymond Dunkirk and his obsession with the Lilibeth Campbell case had sparked the interest in St. Augustine that had prompted him to found his first permanent museum of oddities there.

One interesting angle to Harriet's research was her analysis of the surviving photos of the doomed Lilibeth. They had disproven her most dearly held theory—that Lilibeth had been pregnant at the time of her murder. Faye flipped through the photos at the center of the book. While it was true that the loose, flapper-style clothing of the day could have camouflaged an early pregnancy, and the apple-cheeked ideal of beauty of that day echoed a pregnant woman's lovely glow, the photos told a different story.

Lilibeth had been photographed several times during the weeks before her death, sometimes wearing scanty harem girl costumes from her movie and sometimes draped in revealing evening gowns made by an exclusive couturier. Her small breasts, flat abdomen, and narrow waist could not have belonged to a pregnant woman… at least, not to a woman who was pregnant enough to be aware of it, back in the days before near-instantaneous testing.

The thought of Glynis caught Faye's breath in her chest. Her figure had been as slim and girlish as Lilibeth's, but modern technology had told her she was pregnant, maybe on the very morning she disappeared.

Where are you, Glynis? Faye wondered. *Are you and your baby safe?*

Harriet had been intellectually honest enough to look at the photos and reject her pet theory. She also rejected a variation of it, that Raymond Dunkirk had used his physician's training to abort their child sometime prior to a tumultuous argument that ended in her death. It simply wasn't possible for Lilibeth to have been pregnant enough for either of them to know about it, not in 1928.

Joe rolled over and the old bed squeaked. There was no other sound. The contrast between the creaky spring and the still silence reminded Faye that she was living in a house poured of solid concrete. She might as well have been in a recording studio, completely insulated from the noise of the rest of the world.

The silence gave her the focus she needed to do her best work. She felt at her best as an archaeologist when she could leave the twenty-first century behind and imagine herself in a past she'd never seen.

Joe raised up on one elbow. "Have you memorized that book yet?"

"Nah. I'm just looking at the pictures, mostly. Take a look."

Faye flipped through the photos, looking for scenes of life at Dunkirk Manor to show him. There was no better way to take the traces of the past Joe was digging out of the back garden and make them real.

Besides the photos she'd already seen—of the movie moguls pawing Lilibeth, of Lilibeth lolling by the pool, and of Lilibeth and Raymond under the staircase—Faye found several others to show Joe, some of which were taken by the pool and in the atrium. In one of those, the door to the entry hall was open, giving them a glimpse into a room that hardly appeared to have changed at all.

"That bookcase is gone now," Joe said, rubbing a finger over the page. "Remember? That's where the new elevator is. The elevator shaft runs up the turret on the right side of the entry hall. Other than that, everything looks the same."

The photos showed that the decades hadn't even brought that small degree of change to the atrium. Even the paintings on the wall and the curtains around the doorways were familiar. A photo series of a dinner party that spilled through the atrium and into both dining rooms showed that neither of those chambers had changed, either.

"Daniel and Suzanne don't believe in redecorating, not any more than you do," Joe said. "You folks take historical authenticity to a whole new level."

Faye, who didn't even like mopping her historic home's wood floors with modern cleaner, rolled her eyes at him and said, "Except for the government-mandated elevator and the demolished swimming pool, this mansion might as well have been sealed in amber. The swimming pool bothers me, though."

"Why? It was just a hole in the ground that's not even there any more."

"It bothers me because I didn't even know it existed. Before we got here, I looked at everything I could find online and in the library. Books. Aerial photographs. Property surveys. Old fire insurance atlases. But I missed the pool."

"Nobody's perfect, Faye. I know you'd like to be, but facts are facts."

Faye ignored his teasing, except for a well-aimed kick at his leg under the sheets. "I need to check the dates on the documents I saw, but there's no flippin' way that pool existed more than a few years."

"Well…as long as you weren't *wrong*…"

Joe headed for the bathroom and she swatted at his tight butt as he passed. She missed.

Perhaps the answer to the question of the disappearing pool was as simple as the boredom of the very rich. Perhaps Allyce had begged for a pool because it was such a conspicuous luxury to own a home pool in those days. Then, as her friends began to copy her ostentation, maybe she'd turned to Raymond and said, "Swimming pools are becoming so…common. I simply can't bear it any longer. Besides, we need the space for an oriental grotto. They're all the rage now."

Raymond Dunkirk wouldn't have been the first rich man to spend a fortune trying to keep a difficult wife happy. And in this case, it was his wife's fortune she wanted to spend. Faye's guess was that the pool had been a few years old when the photos of Lilibeth Campbell were made in 1928, and that it hadn't existed much longer after that.

Faye was flipping through the photos yet again when the door burst open. The clatter it made by slamming back against the wall filled the room. Magda thrust her torso through the opening, and the distress on her face caught Faye completely off-guard. She had no doubt that Magda had run full-tilt down the hallway to tell her something terrible, possibly calling her name as she ran, but the massive walls of Dunkirk Manor had soaked up the sound of her voice and made this moment a total surprise.

"We need you both outside. Victor's very upset. So's Kirk. And Levon. I'm having trouble keeping them off each other, and I don't want to have to call the police to settle this. Maybe the techs will settle down if their bosses show up."

Joe appeared outside the bathroom door and she turned to him. "We need you two. Especially you, Joe."

Faye knew what Magda was trying to say. Sometimes, the presence of someone very large could quiet down contentious males. But what on earth could stir up mild-mannered Levon and Kirk to the point where Magda was thinking of calling 911?

And Victor? How could police possibly be required to settle him down? Faye was pretty sure she could subdue Victor, even in her current bloated state.

Joe rushed out the service entrance, with the women close behind. Faye found that she could keep up with Magda if she wrapped her arms tight around her belly and ran hard. Rounding the corner of the kitchen wing, the fracas at the garden gate was abruptly audible.

"Open it! Open it!" Victor was rattling the newly locked gate on its hinges. "It can't be locked, ever again. Mister Raymond said so!"

Everything about Victor was startling. The power of his voice, the depth of his anger, the strength of his withered arms as they rattled the heavy iron gate. People Victor's age lost their physical power as a matter of course, but Faye wasn't sure why they seemed to lose their emotional power, too. Not Victor. Ninety years of emotions seemed to be erupting out of his trembling body.

A musician friend of Faye's had once tried to describe his experience as a performer at a nursing home. "The old folks were there in front of me, sitting in the audience. They must have wanted to see the show, or they wouldn't have come. But they just watched me, with absolutely no expression on their faces. It was like playing racquetball against a rubber wall. I sent everything I had out there to them, but nothing came back. Did they hate every note I sang? Did they love it, but they weren't able any more to show me how they felt? Were they listening at all? To this day, I have no idea."

Victor, on the other hand, had not lost his ability to communicate emotion. Not in the slightest.

Joe's long legs had already propelled him across the lawn. He grasped Victor and tried to pull the old man away from the gate without hurting him.

As Faye and Magda crossed the gravel driveway, the time-worn rocks bruised Faye's bare feet and she prayed that she wouldn't find any sharp objects the hard way. She was suddenly aware that she was wearing her pajamas. They were comfy, but she'd have preferred that her employees didn't see her wrapped in pink polka-dot flannel.

"Why hasn't anybody called the police?" Kirk shouted, shaking a shaggy mop of brown hair. "Why are we protecting this bum? Because he's old? Glynis is missing…maybe dead…and everybody's tiptoeing around this guy. If a homeless guy my age had been hanging around the scene of a kidnapping for no good reason, somebody would've already stuck him *under* the jail."

Victor tried to take a swing at Kirk, but Joe blocked his arm in mid-punch. "Stop it, Victor. I ain't going to let you hurt anybody and I don't want to hurt you."

"Mister Raymond told me to look after Miss Allyce. Always. Told me I could be her little boy. And I was. She loved me. I loved her. I love her."

Victor was crying and his nose was running. Joe had his arms pinned, so Victor tucked his head down and wiped his nose on his shoulder, like a child from another time who had lost his handkerchief. "You can't lock that gate. You can't! She hates it."

"Kirk's right. We've been talking about this since Glynis… disappeared," Levon said. His close-cropped black hair and neatly trimmed beard framed a tormented face. "This old man's angry and he's physical about it. He's not in his right mind. He hangs around here for no good reason."

He walked over close to Victor and got in his face, which was very brave of him, considering that the man was ninety and he was being restrained by someone the size of Joe. "*Why* is no one calling the police?"

"I *am* calling the police," Faye said, pointing to the cell phone in her hand as she dialed Detective Overstreet. Whether she agreed with the young men's suspicions that Victor had taken Glynis was anybody's guess. She wasn't sure what she thought about that, herself. Overstreet could quickly get to the bottom of the question of whether it was remotely possible that a frail old man could have stolen young and vital Glynis.

Faye was curious about other things. What had Victor seen in the years that he was Allyce Dunkirk's "little boy"? Did that rambling and feeble mind hold the answers to her professional questions about the history of Dunkirk Manor?

"Why?" Victor mourned, his tears audible in his voice. "Why did Miss Allyce stay here, all cooped up? Why would anybody take something so lovely away from the rest of the world?"

Overstreet had laughed off Faye's offer to sit in on his interview with Victor. "I hired you to consult on archaeology and you did that. Exactly how do you think questioning this old man has anything to do with your area of expertise? Well, except that he's a fossil."

As an experienced husband, he had fended off her attempt to argue further with a simple, "No," followed by a refusal to listen anything she had to say on the matter.

Frustrated, she'd been forced to listen as he continued to explain why he was rejecting her help. "I am quite able to talk to a crazy old dude. You need to take those pajamas you're wearing back to bed and get some rest. I've spent my share of time watching my wife have babies, and I'm here to tell you this: You do not need to start that process already exhausted."

Faye's sore back was speaking to her, which meant that Overstreet's last sentence made more sense than she liked to admit. So she'd limped back to bed in her bare feet, grateful that Joe didn't scoop her up and carry her. He'd spent most of the day keeping her feet from touching the ground, so she was glad he was showing some restraint now.

Back in bed, after a hearty meal of takeout and with a hot cup of herbal tea prepared by her wonderful husband, Faye resumed paging through Harriet's book. Several of the photos interested her because they featured scenes of Dunkirk Manor's gardens. Allyce Dunkirk was in all of them, spade in hand. When a woman with Allyce's money chooses to get dirty, instead of letting the hired help do it, then she clearly loves gardening.

In one unposed photo, she was wiping sweat off her face and laughing at a little boy in worn overalls, holding a watering can in his chubby hands. He was looking at Allyce as if she were a goddess walking the earth. Faye instantly knew that he was Victor.

Unlike the photo of Victor as a teenager, the resemblance wasn't obvious. It wasn't even there. Little children's faces are unformed, cherubic. It takes time for genetics and experience and sun and wind to give people their faces. Still, Faye had no doubt. This little boy loved Allyce, and she loved him. He might have been born to another mother. He might have lived down the street with his blood parents. Nevertheless, he was *her* little boy, and he always would be, even when he was ninety years old.

Harriet's book included a chapter with short biographies of each of the key characters in Lilibeth's murder case. Allyce's story was especially brief, considering that she lived for more than sixty years. She had been born in New Orleans, where she'd entered society at a traditional debutante's cotillion.

Harriet had dutifully included a photograph of Allyce's debut. The young woman's light eyes gazed serenely at the camera, though Faye couldn't tell whether they were blue or green or grey in the old black-and-white photo. Her slender form was rigidly corseted beneath a beautifully draped white satin gown, and her luxuriant brunette hair was piled high above her finely made features.

Two years after her debut, she'd posed for another picture in white—a wedding gown, this time. She was just as tightly corseted and her posture was just as erect, but there was a softness to her eyes and a gentle smile on her lips. She looked at her husband as if the camera weren't even there. Faye was surprised to see that Raymond Dunkirk looked just as smitten with her. She supposed that cheaters were capable of love; they just weren't capable of maintaining it after the initial infatuation wore off.

As Faye had already seen, Harriet's collection of photos of the Dunkirks was impressive, probably because society people were photographed often, even in those days before paparazzi roamed. Raymond Dunkirk, blessed with the kind of male beauty that grows more rugged with age, but no less handsome, hardly changed over the nearly twenty years between their wedding and Lilibeth's death.

Allyce's looks were more affected by time, but not necessarily in a negative sense. In her late thirties at the time of the murder, she had matured into a Jazz Age beauty, with her hair cropped short and her slender body freed from the corset's whalebones.

Faye would guess that the photo of her in the atrium with Raymond, Ripley, and a teenaged Victor was taken some years after that, but the faint crow's-feet that were beginning to emerge only served to focus attention on those intelligent eyes. A whiff of sadness showed through the smile she gave the camera, and it occurred to Faye that she didn't know whether Allyce and Raymond ever had children.

She checked the book, and she found that the mention of Allyce's most personal tragedy was as brief and circumspect as the rest of her biography. Even Harriet seemed to have felt the age-old proscription against sharing too many details from the personal life of a great society lady. She said only, "Allyce and Raymond Dunkirk had no children, other than a son who was stillborn in 1926. She is also rumored to have suffered a late miscarriage in 1925."

The silver rattle. Faye looked at the photo of Allyce with her gardening spade in hand and wondered whether there could be any doubt that she had buried her dead son's rattle and diaper pins in the rear garden of Dunkirk Manor in 1926. A profound sadness settled on Faye, and she wondered whether she herself was too pregnant to read about such things and still keep a level head.

She flipped through the photos of Allyce, paused, then flipped through them again. At times, Allyce had displayed the early twentieth century ideal of female beauty—apple cheeks, rosy complexion, full breasts—that Faye associated with Gibson girls and period Coca-Cola advertisements. At other times, she had the lean sharp glamour of a flapper. She thought of Harriet's analysis of Lilibeth's photos for signs of pregnancy, and she wondered…

Grabbing a pen and paper, Faye began sketching a timeline for Allyce like the one that Harriet had drawn for Lilibeth. She found photos of Allyce taken throughout the first twenty years of her marriage, but there was an obvious gap in 1926, when she would have been pregnant. Looking back at 1925, Faye saw a similar gap. No lady of the day would have allowed herself to be photographed in that condition. The only photo of Allyce taken in 1925 showed a heartstoppingly lovely woman with a glowing complexion and soft eyes. The blast of hormones that signaled the beginning of pregnancy could not have been more obvious on her face.

An early 1926 photo showed the same luminous glow, though Faye could have sworn she detected melancholy in those dark eyes. Becoming pregnant so soon after the loss of a child was hard on a woman, body and soul.

With her new insight, Faye worked her way backwards through Allyce Dunkirk's thirties and twenties, and the pattern was unmistakable. Again and again, the thin, sad woman bloomed into her full beauty, then she disappeared from the photographic record for months, only to reappear, thin and sad. The scenario even recurred in 1928, the year of Lilibeth Campbell's murder.

Faye believed to the very core of her soul that she understood the tragedy of Allyce Dunkirk's life.

In that day and age, medical science offered little help for infertility and miscarriage, beyond encouraging a couple to keep trying. If pregnancy resulted, then rest was prescribed—sometimes even bedrest—in hopes that the woman might go to term. Sometimes it worked.

In Allyce Dunkirk's case, it nearly *had* worked, twice. But in the end, her body refused to give her the thing she wanted, the thing that nature drove her to want so desperately...a child. Instead, she'd had no one to receive that bottled-up love, no one but a philandering husband and the ragged little boy who lived down the street. Perhaps she had poured that love into her art, but she'd been trapped in a time when society didn't want her to express herself in that way. She had lived among people who wouldn't even look at the passion she projected on the canvas. If society had bound and gagged Allyce Dunkirk, it could not have silenced her more completely.

Faye couldn't look at Allyce any more. She closed the book and picked up Father Domingo's diary instead. Perhaps the priest had been in as much pain as Allyce Dunkirk, but he seemed further away. And his tragedy wasn't so closely linked to Faye's own fears, as her delivery date loomed.

She would rather touch Father Domingo's pain, buffered through the cotton gloves she wore to protect his timeworn book, than spend another moment imagining herself in the shoes of the grieving Allyce Dunkirk.

From the journal of Father Domingo Sanz de la Fuente

Translated from the Spanish by
Faye Longchamp Mantooth, Ph.D.,
and Magda Stockard-McKenzie, Ph.D.

After the victory at Fort Caroline, our celebration
was shadowed by the knowledge of the hundreds of
French soldiers who fled into the wilderness. Our new
colony, called St. Augustine because land was first
sighted on the feast day of the Holy St. Augustine,
was vulnerable. It could fall before the onslaught of
the remaining French troops at any time.

The Captain-General dispatched men to secure
the area. After they had been gone for some days,
he felt God stirring his heart in pity for his soldiers. Resolved that he should not remain in the
comfort of our camp, but should join the men himself, our Captain-General and Admiral, Don Pedro
Menéndez de Avilés, set out with an entourage that
included Father Francisco, Father Esteban, and
this humble priest.

Marching through water that rose sometimes to
our knees, we traveled three leagues along the coast
in search of our comrades. The biting insects flew

so thick that it was a marvel any of us retained any blood in our veins.

When we found the war party, we learned that our enemies were encamped on the far side of a slow-flowing river. The Captain-General sent men to fetch our boats, and we arrived in time to see a great many of the enemy go down to the water to gather shellfish for food. Believing himself enlightened by the Holy Spirit, our Captain-General resolved to dress himself as a fisherman and go talk to the enemy. It could be, he reasoned, that they were without supplies, and would be glad to surrender without fighting.

As was his way, he put his plan into execution before he had scarce finished speaking. Quickly learning that our adversaries had not had bread for more than seven days, and that the greater number of them were Calvinists, the general revealed himself and ordered them to surrender on pain of death. They proposed to surrender, provided their lives would be spared, but Don Pedro would not agree to these terms.

After further parley, then gave their arms and flags up to the Captain-General himself and surrendered. Don Pedro then ordered the execution of every man among them, hundreds of them. Having mercy in his soul, Father Francisco begged permission to speak to the condemned men, in order to find out whether there were Christians among them who might be spared.

My French is halting, but I can make myself understood well enough. I knew that our

Captain-General was a man of quick and decisive action. There was no time to lose before blood began to flow.

I ran from one man to the next, asking each one if he loved God and believed in the one true church. Father Esteban was always in earshot, and even in my short acquaintance with him, I had learned that I dared not speak more clearly than that. If I could have been free of his judging eyes, I would have taken each man by the shoulders and shaken him, crying, "Say it! Just say it. Say whatever will make the Captain-General spare your life."

But I could not. Or I did not.

As I searched for men I could save, Father Esteban took his inquisition quickly from man to man. "Are you now or have you ever been a Calvinist? A Huguenot? A Protestant?" And one by one, the list of the condemned grew longer.

Father Francisco identified eight Roman Catholics in their number, while I succeeded in saving but four men. Father Esteban spared no one.

Those twelve were brought back to our camp. All the others were executed on St. Michael's Day, September 29, 1565. The river—pure, innocent, and clear as the day God made it—ran red with blood.

It has been fifty years since then, but that river still bears the name Matanzas, in remembrance of the terrible massacre committed that day on its shores. Perhaps it always shall. When the morning dawned on September 30, 1565, I packed up the possessions I could carry and woke Ocilla quietly, while my brother priests slept. I asked through gestures whether she would like to stay or go.

She did not acknowledge my question as worthy of an answer, only pointing to Chulufi as her way of asking for permission to take Father Esteban's serving woman with us. It is an everlasting shame to me that I needed a heathen woman to suggest this act of mercy.

Yaraha would not leave Father Francisco. She remained curled on her mat, raising only a hand to bid us farewell.

Ocilla, Chulufi, and I walked away from our encampment and disappeared into the thick jungle which Our Lord has spread over every inch of La Florida. It was a blessing for us on that day, for it covered our escape. If Father Esteban had seen us go, I believe he would have slain us on the spot in the name of the Most Holy God.

In the intervening years, I have forgotten many things. I have nearly forgotten the sound of the native tongue in which I now write. But I have not forgotten what happened on the shores of the Matanzas River in 1565. I do not know why Our Lord brought me to this foreign land, but it was not to watch His human creations be slaughtered. I know in my soul that I was most assuredly not brought here to spread His blessing over that slaughter.

I fear that He brought me here for no reason other than to be a witness to unprecedented destruction. I would have preferred to be His agent to stop that destruction. I would have preferred to be His face in this new world, comforting those who suffer, and perhaps I have fulfilled that role at times. But I fear that my true purpose is simply to tell the story.

In your hands, Reader, you hold the proof that I did try to do that. There have been many failures in my life, and one grievous and damning sin, but I have tried to serve Our Lord, as I promised to do at my ordination long ago.

My only defense when I face Our Lord's judgment will be this: I tried.

I, Father Domingo Sanz de la Fuente, attest that the foregoing is a statement of actual events.

Chapter Nineteen

If Faye had thought that it was impossible for Suzanne to be more over-protective of her as a pregnant woman than she already was, she now stood corrected. The woman had actually asked her if she needed help getting from the dining room to the bathroom.

Suzanne's husband Daniel was even worse. After Faye had managed to visit the ladies' room unaccompanied, Daniel had met her at the dining room door, fully loaded breakfast plate in hand, and herded her back to her room. He'd been pretty forceful about it, saying things like, "You shouldn't be on your feet, not after what you went through yesterday," and he'd waved the plate loaded with quiche and fruit compote like a matador guiding a bull with a red flag.

She'd regretfully turned her back on the noisy dining room, filled with happy eaters and a boisterous little girl crawling beneath the table. She'd been looking forward to a little time watching Rachel play and listening to her talk to her imaginary friend but, confronted with the opportunity to eat in her room in silence, Faye realized that her nerves might not be ready for a three-year-old's demands on her attention.

Maybe Daniel was right. Maybe she *did* need more time to recover from her adventure in the creek with Betsy.

Faye was reminded that Daniel, like Detective Overstreet, had spent months of his life as the husband of a pregnant woman. He was completely aware that she woke up so hungry that she could be led by the nose with nothing but the aroma wafting from the plate in his hands.

And apparently, Joe was aware of the same thing. As they passed the kitchen door, he emerged with an identical plate in his hand. The expression on his face made her laugh out loud, which was not the best response.

Faye was impatient and frustrated, and it seemed that Joe was suffering the same symptoms, even though he'd been spared the aches and the hormonal roller-coaster. She could tell that Joe wanted to yell at Daniel for rendering his food offering to Faye useless. And she could tell that Joe knew just how stupid it would be to yell at Daniel for doing something nice.

Since Faye was the only person involved who wasn't carrying a dish, her hands were free. She used one of them to squeeze Joe's forearm and say, "Thanks for fixing me a plate. Now we have two. You can eat the extra one."

Daniel, a model of tact, smiled as she thanked him for his help, then disappeared into the kitchen. Joe's scowl grew a little dimmer, but not much.

Faye was ridiculously happy to be standing in the early morning sunshine, watching her team work. Rachel was making mud pies under the shade of a hydrangea laden with blue mop-headed blooms, oblivious to the fact that her mother was watching her every move.

Faye couldn't blame Magda's babysitter for quitting. There wasn't much impetus for a young woman to stick with a low-paying job, not when someone her exact age had disappeared from her workplace.

Rachel was exceptionally well-behaved, and Magda was a formidable multitasker. Thus, there was some possibility that this very important project could proceed on schedule, despite having a three-year-old underfoot. It didn't hurt to have sympathetic clients. Suzanne had "given" Rachel an entire flower bed, so Magda and Faye had been presented with daisies and petunias at five-minute intervals, all morning long.

There would be no adventures in law enforcement today, because Detective Overstreet had made it clear that Faye had served her usefulness, until and unless something archaeological reared its head.

Half the morning had passed, and nothing particularly archaeological had even surfaced here, where a bunch of people were digging for such things. Faye had walked surreptitiously over to the garden shed and tried the door, because she was bored and because she felt compelled to check every day. It was locked and had been locked since the evening when Overstreet had gotten a search warrant, hoping to find Glynis in there.

Faye had spent many uneventful days like this, so she'd been lulled into expecting to uncover nothing on this day, nothing but uninteresting fill dirt. It was at times like this that lightning often struck.

"What in the hell…?" Kirk said, pulling something the size of his fist from the soil.

Everyone gathered around to look at the elephant figurine.

"Do you think it's African?" Kirk asked uncertainly, like a young man offering his best guess, but who is afraid that his best guess is just stupid.

"I do," Faye said. "The carving is intricate and the proportions are very good. This was no cheap souvenir."

Magda, looking over her shoulder, nodded in agreement.

"What's it doing here?" Levon asked. "Was it in the fill dirt where the pool used to be?"

"Nope," Kirk said. "It was under one of the paving tiles. Just like the spear point and the Spanish coin."

"And the baby things," Magda said.

"Yeah," Kirk said, still looking at the little elephant. "Do you think this stuff came to be here naturally—though I can't really imagine how—or do you think maybe somebody buried it all on purpose. Maybe a kid?"

Faye thought of young Victor, helping Allyce Dunkirk with her gardening. He would certainly have had access to shovels. Maybe he'd been a little bitty kleptomaniac, stealing cool stuff out of Dunkirk Manor and burying it, just for the hell of it. It would explain a lot...

"Faye?"

Detective Overstreet's voice had a sheepish note to it. She looked up from the elephant in Kirk's hands and saw Overstreet and Victor standing nearby.

"I know I said I wouldn't be needing your help any more—"

"You were pretty vocal about it."

"Yeah. Well, I've got another stash of artifacts for you to look at."

She raised an eyebrow at him.

"They're at Victor's house."

So Victor wasn't homeless after all.

Faye was relieved, up to a point. The fact remained that his house was so substandard that the old man almost might have been sleeping under the stars. She stood between Victor and Overstreet, looking over the house from threshold to rooftop and wondering how long it had been since there were panes in the windows.

Overstreet had expressed concern over whether Faye should walk to Victor's place, which was ridiculous. If Faye had lingered in the street in front of Dunkirk Manor, she could have seen the shabby house. She could have thrown a rock and hit it.

Faye was astonished that she'd never noticed the little shack. Though standing on a vacant lot overrun with vines and underbrush, it was nevertheless in plain sight at the end of the short street, if you knew where to look.

"Best I can tell," Overstreet said, "is that this was the gatehouse when Dunkirk Manor was first built. It was probably out of use by the time Raymond and Allyce Dunkirk owned the big house. Old Mr. Dunkirk sold a lot of this property around the turn of the century, so there wouldn't have been a gate on the street by then. The other houses on this street all stand on plots that used to belong to the Dunkirks. They probably held onto the gatehouse property a little bit longer, but Victor says he owns it now. He says he grew up in it. His parents rented it, but the Dunkirks gave it to him sometime after they died."

He leaned toward Faye, whispering in her ear. "He may not own it now. I can't imagine that he's been paying property taxes. I've been thinking that maybe Victor's mental issues aren't just due to old age. Maybe the Dunkirks gave him this place because they knew he'd never be able to take care of himself."

"It's possible," Faye said. "I got a title search on the Dunkirk property when I was doing my preliminary work. I was primarily interested in the plot where the mansion stands, but I remember seeing that big chunks of it were sold off over the years. It won't be hard to find out if they really gave this…house…to Victor.

"House" seemed like a strong word for the place where Victor stayed. Only a few traces of white paint remained unpeeled from its wood frame. Green vines shrouded the entire structure, and they provided enough camouflage to hide Victor's Piggly-Wiggly basket from passers-by. There was no bathroom, no kitchen, no running water. Maybe there was, or had been, an outhouse in the overgrown area out back. There certainly had been no such thing as indoor plumbing when the gatehouse was built, not in modest little dwellings like this.

And there was no kitchen, maybe because the gatekeeper's family had always eaten with the servants at Dunkirk Manor. Victor had said he ate in the dining room with the Dunkirks while they lived, at least sometimes. Maybe he ate with the servants the rest of the time. She wondered if his parents had been on staff at Dunkirk Manor while they lived, meaning that Victor had eaten every meal of his life in the mansion until the Dunkirks died and left him alone.

Faye couldn't imagine Allyce Dunkirk allowing "her" little boy to go hungry, or to fend for himself if she knew he wasn't able. But the day had come when Raymond and Allyce Dunkirk weren't able to shield Victor from the world and, for whatever reason, they hadn't made sure that someone else was going to do it.

Victor was beside himself with joy that he had visitors. He had danced down the street in front of them, crowing, "Come! Come in! Come see me."

The warped floorboards inside Victor's front door made it impossible for the door to swing completely open or completely shut. Victor seemed to think this was great, since he told them several times that he loved to be able to come and go at will without taking the trouble to operate the door. There was one window in each wall. Upon closer inspection, Faye found that a couple of them still had some panes.

The gatehouse stood at the end of the dead-end street, so anyone standing at the front window had a clear view of its entire length. This had made sense when the Dunkirks had employed a gatekeeper to monitor comings and goings. Now, it simply meant that Victor knew everybody's business.

"I saw those people yesterday closing Miss Allyce's gate, and I runned down there to put a stop to it. I did."

Perhaps to prevent Victor from suffering another emotional meltdown, Overstreet changed the subject. "Show Faye the things you showed me. She likes old stuff." Overstreet chuckled. "She likes you, Victor."

"'Cause I'm old stuff?"

"You bet."

Victor cackled softly as he pulled several ratty cardboard boxes from beneath a dining table that was missing a leg. As best Faye could tell, he stored the boxes there because the table kept them fairly dry. Faye could see blue sky through some of the holes in Victor's roof.

As Victor held his treasures up for her to see, one by one, Faye could see why Overstreet had wanted her opinion. Victor had probably found most of this stuff during his daily schedule of dumpster-diving, but not all of it. Beneath a moldy stack of romance novels, Faye saw a leatherbound edition of George Eliot's *Middlemarch*. In another box, there was a piece of Victorian bric-a-brac, carved in ebony, that might have been part of a music stand. There was a set of carving knives, sheathed in a red felt sleeve, with horn handles. Atop them was a pair of embroidery scissors embossed with the body of a tiny bird, the blades shaped like its dainty beak. A tarnished candlestick had the look and heft of real silver. The slick gleam of an ornate china snuffbox stood out among the dusty junk.

"What do you think of this stuff? Overstreet asked, pointing at the leather book, the scissors, the ebony carving, the silver candlestick, the knives, the china snuffbox.

"I think it's all from the 1800s. I'm pretty sure the candlestick and snuffbox match family pieces I've seen in Dunkirk Manor. I figure either Allyce and Raymond gave this stuff to Victor when they got newer, modern stuff. Or he pulled it out of the trash."

"Or he's got sticky fingers."

"Oh, I hope not," said Faye. "Do we have to ask that question? Nobody alive would know whether he stole these things. Can't we just let him be?"

"Sure. It's not like I see anything in this room that looks like it was stolen lately." He dragged out another box, obviously very heavy, that was hidden under a moldy tablecloth. The contents of the box settled with a metallic clank. "Take a look at this."

Faye peeked inside and started to laugh. Overstreet joined her. After peering at them for second, Victor chimed in with a weak giggle that told them he had no idea why they were laughing.

It wasn't that the contents of the box were all that funny. It was simply that Faye and Detective Overstreet had confirmation of something they'd both suspected. The box was full, almost to the brim, of dimes, most of them silver.

"Mister Raymond, he give me those," Victor said, between giggles. "Every day, he give me some. Nearly 'bout. They piled up, after a while. He said I was a good boy, and I deserved to get paid because I was so nice to his Allyce. I earned my pay. I did. When I got grown, he said I might as well have this house, since I was gatekeeping already. It was a nice house then. I don't know what happened to it."

His bleary eyes searched the room, as if to find cozy curtains at the windows, instead of limp, dirty rags. "I made sure I earned this place, you bet I did. Didn't nobody ever come down this street that I didn't tell Mister Raymond about it. Even still, nobody comes down here and I don't know it. These days, though, I ain't got no one to tell."

Overstreet was looking at Faye, daring her to understand the important point in this conversation. After a second, the answer struck her hard.

"Nobody, Victor? Nobody ever comes down this street without you knowing about it?"

"Nope. Not them locksmiths…" The look on Victor's face said that he wished Raymond Dunkirk had taught him a curse word to use on the people who locked the garden gate. "Not you and Mister Joe, when you came home all muddy yesterday. And not Mister Lex Tifton, on that day when Miss Glynis went missing."

Faye now knew the question that Overstreet had already asked Victor, the one he wanted to hear her ask. "Did anybody else come down the street that morning, anybody that didn't belong here?"

"Nope, only the usual folks. The gardener and the cook and the housemaids, they drove to work. Miss Glynis, she come to work in her car. A little early, she was, but sometimes she done that. Mister Lex Tifton, he walked in the gate, right behind her car. And that's all. Nobody else came until the police sirens came blasting up the street."

Faye thought through the movements of all the key players that morning. Something was missing. "Did anybody leave? Did you see Glynis leave? Or Lex? Or anybody you didn't know?"

Victor shook his head.

Faye turned to Overstreet. "So if Lex didn't walk out and wasn't carried out, then someone threw him over the back wall of the garden. That's the only way I can think of for him to wind up dead in the river. And Glynis…"

"She's either still in the house or an outbuilding, all of which I personally searched from top to bottom, or she went over the back wall, too."

A sick possibility presented itself. "Or she's buried somewhere on the grounds."

Overstreet nodded and, suddenly, Victor shook himself and let out a shriek.

"Dead? Mister Lex is dead? He was my neighbor. Lived right there." A clawlike hand waved in the general direction of the Fountain of Youth. "I didn't know it! Nobody tells an old man anything. And poor Miss Glynis…" He dissolved into hysterical tears.

Faye and Overstreet eyed each other. Victor was apparently telling the truth. Why would he not be? He hadn't understood the implications of the fact that he'd seen neither Glynis nor Lex leave. He offered no interpretations of what he'd seen. He wasn't capable of doing that. He'd just told them what he saw.

As Faye spoke soft, comforting words to Victor, she felt sure that his observations would be a help in solving this case. But how?

Overstreet knew he needed to face facts. Dr. Longchamp-Mantooth was a help to him, and not only on those occasions when he wanted to ask her about old things carved out of rock. He'd been born into the Leave It To Beaver era, and it stuck in his craw to think about endangering any woman. But she'd gotten herself into trouble while she was doing nothing more dangerous than checking out those old things carved out of rock that he'd hired her to study. And if he judged her character right, she was well able to get herself into trouble any old time. Doing contract work for the police department just gave her more convenient access to danger.

So after they'd left Victor in his hovel, he'd invited her to take a ride so they could talk about the case. All of it, not just the archaeology. They were sitting in the Starbucks drive-up doing that right now, while they waited for their coffees. But that didn't mean that he intended to let her drink anything but decaf.

"Catch me up on the case," she said, sucking on the travel cup like she thought she might be able to get some real, actual coffee out of it.

"We haven't found the first physical clue since we searched her car. That waist-length platinum hair Glynis has is a double-edged sword. If she left one behind, we'd surely see it. But so would the person who took her. If there was any time at all to clean up someplace she'd been, the hair would be as obvious as a neon sign. Any idiot would find it and get rid of it. So no hair evidence."

"What about fibers?"

"We're lucky to have the convenience store video, so we know what she was wearing—even down to the brand name, because one of our officers went to the mall and tracked down the outfit. Rich women like Glynis don't wear their clothes long. A new trend crops up and they send their old dresses off to Goodwill before they're even sold out at the mall. So we got lucky there. Her blouse was a black-and-white print silk. The pants were black with a small houndstooth check. Again, those threads would be easy to see, but we haven't seen any, except in her car and her house. Maybe we haven't been going the right places, or maybe the culprit did a good job of cleaning up. There's no way to know."

"No footprints?"

"Nothing beyond what I already told you. Footprints could eventually prove helpful, because both Glynis and Lex wore really pricey shoes. Not a lot of people around here spend that kinda money on their feet. So if we find the print of a five-hundred-dollar loafer, we won't necessarily be able to prove it belonged to Glynis or Lex, but it sure would be a solid hint that one of them had left it."

"And that's it for physical evidence?"

"Well, there was the questionable trace of blood in the garden shed. Remember? Coulda been blood. Coulda been boxwood or poison ivy. Those chemical tests are useful, but they have some damn huge drawbacks."

"What do you think about Victor's certainty that nobody steps onto Dunkirk Manor's property without him knowing about it?"

Faye's latté had left her with a little milk mustache. Overstreet knew that a real gentleman would tell her, but he apparently wasn't one of those, because he just answered her question without telling her to wipe her face. "I don't know. Victor lives in his own little world. But let's go with it. Say he's right. What does that really do for us?"

"Well, it lets Dick Wheeler and Alan Smithson off the hook. If they weren't on the grounds, then they didn't do the killing or the kidnapping."

"Do you really want to eliminate them as suspects?"

"Hell, no," she said, wiping her face with the back of her hand. Feeling the dampness on her upper lip, she shot him a dirty look. "We can't eliminate anyone, even if Victor is a hundred percent right that nothing went through that gate but Lex, Glynis' car, and the household staff's cars. A killer could have been lying in the back seat, with a gun pointed at Glynis' head. Victor wouldn't know."

"Or somebody could have been hiding in the trunk of any of the cars."

"Exactly. This isn't like some Agatha Christie locked-room mystery, where there's no way to get to the scene of the crime other than on foot or by driving one of the few cars known to have entered the property. It's more like a physics problem…a conservation problem."

"Come again?"

"Well, you know that matter is neither created nor destroyed. It is conserved. If you look in a big black box and you see a…um… dog, and you look in the black box later and it's empty, then you don't have to be a physicist to know the dog is somewhere else."

"Might be dead."

"Well, yeah. But the dog…or its parts…are *somewhere*. Fluffy the Poodle didn't go *poof* and disappear. That's not the way things work in our world."

"Dogs are neither created nor destroyed. Check. Except for puppies. They just…happen."

She looked like she wanted to choke him. "Would you focus?"

He nodded, so she could continue teaching him physics. "So we can treat this case like a black box. We have to presume that the people who came onto the Dunkirk Manor grounds are still there, unless we know they left."

"Like Glynis."

"Yes. And we have to think very carefully about ways people could have gotten onto or off the grounds without anybody, even Victor, knowing. Which means that Wheeler or Smithson or someone else could have come and gone over the garden wall. And they could have taken Glynis with them."

"It would have been hard for Wheeler to do that," she observed, "then get the river mud off himself in time to be at the Rotary Club in less than an hour."

"True."

"Like you said, someone could have been in the trunk of any of the cars that came in that morning."

"Or the day before, if he found a place to hide and wait."

Overstreet's new consultant Faye liked this line of reasoning. He could tell by the way she was draining her tall decaf latté before she spoke. "Yes. But then they'd have had to hide and wait for a chance to leave."

"We searched the place hard. Even in that big old house, I just can't believe we missed a place big enough to hide a person."

"Or two. Glynis has to be somewhere."

"You've checked Wheeler's alibi out at the Rotary Club?" Faye was obviously still trying to imagine the man coming and going over the garden wall in a business suit.

"Yep. He checks out."

"Damn. I don't like him. But Smithson hasn't got any alibi. Do we really think he would do anything to harm Glynis—his own daughter?"

Without waiting for him to answer her question, she plunged on. "But we don't really know Glynis is hurt. If Lex was standing in the parking lot yelling at Glynis, maybe hitting her once or twice—"

"—which would account for the little bit of her blood that we found—"

"Yeah." Faye nodded vigorously. "Yeah. Maybe Smithson stumbled onto an ugly scene between his daughter and her boyfriend. He killed Lex, then dumped his body in the river."

"But where's Glynis?"

"Maybe her father hid her, so that she couldn't testify against him in a murder trial."

"But how long could he possibly keep her hidden?"

Overstreet had a sudden image of Rapunzel alone in a tower with only her flowing golden locks for company. Wherever Glynis was, how very lonely she must be.

Faye looked longingly at the rickety stairs rising to the attic where Father Domingo's journal had lain hidden for who-knows-how-long. How much would she give for a day alone in that place, plundering for hidden treasure?

Instead, she'd ridden the elevator up to Daniel's office, for no good reason other than he wanted her to. He'd asked her how the excavation was going and whether the project was on budget. He'd asked her to tell him again about the artifacts they'd found. Then, like everyone else she encountered these days, he'd decided that she looked tired.

Over her protests, he'd taken her solicitously by the arm and escorted her back to the elevator, even going to the ridiculous extreme of riding downstairs with her. They'd paused in the entry hall, with his hand still gripping her elbow, to discuss whether she was capable of walking to her bedroom or to the excavation under her own locomotion.

Faye really thought she might scream. But who would hear her and rescue her from this nuttiness? Joe and Overstreet were just as bad. So was Magda. Levon and Kirk might have been, except they came from a generation that rarely guided a woman from place to place with a hand cupped around her elbow.

She pulled her arm closer to her side, hoping to disengage Daniel's hand, but it clung like a vise. Faye knew she shouldn't be so resentful of people who were trying to help her, but she was only human.

Then a shadow fell across the perfectly buffed oak floor of the entry hall. Daniel's hand relaxed. So did Faye. Maybe she *was* hormonal, but there were times when she just wanted to stand still and look at her beautiful husband.

Joe's skin glowed with the same bronzed brown of the oak floors. He was as solid and strong as Dunkirk Manor, but he was alive from his dark flowing hair and clear green eyes to his powerful legs and moccasin-shod feet.

"I'm glad you're back, Faye. Let's go get you off your feet."

He thanked Daniel for looking after her and ushered her through the atrium. Ever empty and ever cold, the light in the atrium always seemed wrong. Not quite the filtered light of late afternoon and not quite the warm, shifting glow of candle fire, this light made shadows where there shouldn't be any.

Before the thought was fully formed in her mind, Faye's eyes darted to the staircase, looking for Allyce. She saw nothing but shadows, and she felt nothing but the chill breeze of Dunkirk Manor's modern air conditioning system.

Then, once again, Suzanne stepped out of the shadows on the balcony above them. She reached for the shining clock, all glass and wood and brass, that sat on a shelf at the head of the stairs. After winding it and lightly touching a finger to a clock face that already displayed the correct time, Suzanne lingered on the landing a moment, extending a tentative foot toward the first step down to the atrium's ground floor, then drawing it back. She locked eyes with Faye in a way that made Faye pat her bulging middle, as if to make sure the baby was still there.

The manor's atrium was as austere and lifeless as ever...until Rachel scampered through. Multicolored light streamed through the stained glass overhead, and it broke into pieces on her shining auburn curls. Her softness soaked up the room's echoes and emptiness. Her tiny laugh made it simply alive.

The look on Suzanne's face tore Faye's heart out. Faye wondered if Annie's hair had been auburn. She wondered what Annie's laugh had sounded like.

Magda stomped through a dining room door and into the atrium, struggling to keep up with Rachel and calling mother words after her.

"Stop right where you are, young lady. Right this minute!"

Musical giggles trailed the little girl as she fled.

"I'll call your father. He'll drive all the way over here from Micco County and you'll be in big trouble!"

Rachel never hesitated. She kept running, unable to believe that her doting father would even scold her, much less punish her.

"Rachel Lillian McKenzie, you're going to give me a heart attack!"

Concern spread across the flawless little brow. Rachel stumbled to a stop and turned toward her mother, arms up.

"No, Mommy. No!"

Magda scooped her off her tiny feet and said, "Don't run from Mommy. How many times do I have to tell you that?"

"I be good." The tiny hand splayed across Magda's ample breast. "Heart okay?"

Faye wondered if the tiny child realized already what it meant to have parents who were old enough to be her grandparents. It meant that she would have less time to spend with them.

The fine lines at the corners of Magda's eyes softened as she said, "Yes, sweetheart. Mommy's heart is just fine."

Suzanne backed away from the balcony rail, fading into the shadows.

A hand closed like a vise on Faye's elbow, guiding her toward her room and her bed. This time it was Joe's hand, and not Daniel's, so Faye didn't mind so much.

Chapter Twenty

Faye and her work crew could hear Overstreet and his technicians rustling through the vegetation on the riverbank behind Dunkirk Manor's garden wall. She could hear their cursing as, one by one, they lost a boot in the muck or slipped in the slimy mud.

These sounds told her something about Lex's murder, something that Overstreet already knew. He had already led a search of the riverbank on the day Glynis disappeared, without finding a trace of human activity. Since a person slipping around in slimy, boot-sucking mud tended to leave a trail, Overstreet had drawn the conclusion on the day of the murder that no one had been sneaking around back there…probably.

His uncertainty was rooted in the simple limitations of time. Glynis had been reported missing by mid-morning. While others from the department began a search of all of St. Augustine, starting with the street in front of Dunkirk Manor and fanning out, Overstreet and his technicians had begun an immediate search of the manor's grounds, first by trying to track the movements of people in the vicinity of her car. When the footprints and blood trail failed, they had carefully searched the gardens, front and rear, looking for Glynis or her footprints or her blood behind every bush and tree.

Then they had searched the house from top to bottom, which was not something that could be quickly done in Dunkirk Manor. The public areas—the entry hall, atrium, dining rooms, parlors—were vast, but they offered no place to hide. The hidden warrens of servants' quarters and closets and butler's pantries on the first floor, however, were another story. And the upper floors offered bedrooms and more closets and tiny bathrooms added into odd corners when people began to demand more than one bathroom per floor.

Under the attic lay the storage room where Father Domingo's book had been hidden for decades. Faye had no doubt that searching this room had not been a quick job for the police. And then there was the room waiting at the far end of that storage room, behind the door that Faye hadn't gotten the opportunity to open.

When asked whether he and his crew had searched that mysterious room, Overstreet had sighed and said, "I see that you truly do think that I'm an idiot."

According to Overstreet, that room had also been used for storage, but only of large pieces of furniture, so it had been easily searched. Once all the trunks and armoires were found to be empty, the search was over.

After tallying up the time needed to search the parking lot, grounds, and house, Faye was not surprised to learn that it had been late in the day before Overstreet expanded his search to include the riverbank behind the manor's garden wall. In that time, the tide had risen and begun to ebb. The Matanzas River was tidally influenced here, so close to the ocean, and its level ebbed and flowed like the sea. Ordinary footsteps would have been washed away at high tide. Deep pits wallowed out by a killer navigating the muck while carrying a body might not have vanished so completely, but Overstreet had found none.

His best guess was that the body had been dumped over the back wall. Then the killer had gotten lucky. The tide had carried the body away, buying the murderer an extra day to…do what?

If Glynis was the killer, she'd had an extra day to run. If someone else had killed Lex and either killed or kidnapped Glynis, then Glynis could be in the river while her killer had enjoyed an extra day to escape. If her father had murdered Lex, then he'd had another day to make sure Glynis was hidden in a secure place and to hope that he'd obscured his trail well enough to avoid being nailed for Lex's murder.

Or, and Faye had trouble imagining this, if Glynis' father had killed her in a fit of rage over her environmental activism, she too might have gone over the wall. The Matanzas River might even now be deciding to give her back, the way it had given Lex back. This was also true if Dick Wheeler was the culprit, or someone else whose motives were yet unclear.

If somebody within the brick walls of Dunkirk Manor had done the deed, then that person had suffered through an entire day of knowing that Lex's body was lying on the riverbank, starting to decay. The killer had spent an entire day thinking about the monstrous thing he or she had done. Daniel, Suzanne, the household staff, the police, Faye, Joe, Magda, Rachel, Kirk—all of them had spent a day in the close vicinity of a corpse, but only one of them had known it. And Victor had presided over the entrance to their haven, watching to see whether a killer had come or gone.

A ruckus on the other side of the garden wall brought Faye running as fast as her tired legs would carry her.

"Look at this!" an unfamiliar male voice cried.

"Great work," Overstreet was saying as he splashed audibly toward the other man.

Frustrated by the brick wall, which was about as tall as she was, Faye called out to Overstreet. "Harry...it's Faye. What's going on back there?"

"A shoe. We found Lex's shoe. Proves what we already kinda knew—he went over the wall."

A scenario was playing out in her mind. Some of the scenes were fact. It was well-established that Glynis had arrived at Dunkirk Manor's employee parking lot alone on the day she went missing. Victor said that Lex had arrived on foot shortly afterward. She saw no reason for him to lie, and this put Lex in the right place to be murdered as part of Glynis' kidnapping.

At this point, her scenario left the realm of fact...well, except for the positive pregnancy test in Lex's pocket. Its existence was a fact. It raised the question of whether Lex had intercepted Glynis on the way to work so that they could argue about…what? Had she hidden her pregnancy from him? Had she told Lex, only to see that he wasn't taking the news well? Had he questioned whether the baby was his? Had he demanded that she get an abortion? Or had she announced her intention of seeking an abortion that he didn't want her to have?

There was no way to know, but an argument like this could certainly have resulted in Glynis being hit or slapped hard enough to generate the trickle of blood that she left smeared on the car seat. Then what?

Had she defended herself? She'd had a box of weapons on the seat next to her, and Joe had said that Lex's throat wounds could have been inflicted by the broken stone blade, but it had showed no trace of blood. Had she used the missing half of that blade? If so, where was that weapon hidden? And why hadn't the killer disposed of the bloodied celt, as well? Maybe, in the heat of the moment, he or she had forgotten about the weapon that had wounded Lex Tifton, but had hidden the blade that finished him off.

The grievous damage to Lex's body had left no trace beyond the puddle of blood in the parking lot. The damn sprinkler system had flipped on and washed away the killer's trail from the parking lot to the garden wall, leaving nothing but that puddle of blood, a faint smear of the same blood on the very old stone of the broken celt, and nothing more.

Faye enjoyed eating her lunch outdoors. The meal would have been an utterly peaceful moment with Joe, but the reality of their work meant that they were never alone during the daytime.

Levon and Kirk had eaten nearby, without uttering a word to Faye or Joe. Each day that Glynis was gone affected them more, but in different ways. Levon paced, head down, and Faye had twice seen him wiping his eyes.

Kirk just grew increasingly irritable. During their lunch, he had tried again and again to get the sullen Levon to speak, but had been rewarded with monosyllables and a total lack of eye contact. Faye wasn't sure what she'd do if a fistfight broke out. The how-to-manage-people book that she'd bought as soon as she opened her business had not included a chapter on how to behave if your workplace became the scene of a murder/kidnapping.

Magda had sat on the manor's back porch, watching Rachel run rampant. Magda was on the lookout for a replacement babysitter and, in the meantime, she was doing a good job of juggling work and motherhood. This didn't mean that she wasn't starting to look a little frayed.

Daniel and Suzanne also came and went during the meal, asking politely about their progress on the project. This was understandable, considering that they were paying by the hour. Sometimes it was a struggle for Faye to accurately account for her time, since Daniel and Suzanne could only be expected to pay her for hours spent working toward their objectives. Managing her crew was definitely billable to Daniel and Suzanne. Working with Harry Overstreet was definitely billable to the police department. Reading Father Domingo's journal wasn't billable to anybody, but it sure was fun.

Reading Harriet's book was billable when Faye was scrutinizing every last detail of Dunkirk Manor's construction and learning about the Dunkirks themselves and their illustrious guests. When she was fretting over the particulars of Lilibeth Campbell's murder...no, that was not billable time. Not by any stretch of the imagination.

When Betsy's smile and gray curls appeared at her side, Faye was really happy to see her, but her consultant's mindset went immediately to the question of "Who am I working for at this moment?"

When Betsy said, "I know something exciting about the artifacts at Alan Smithson's construction site," Faye's mental accountant said, "Police department. This conversation should be billed to the police department."

Then Faye herself said, "What do you know? How exciting is it?"

"Well, you remember our thrilling adventure in the wet ditch?"

"I do."

"And perhaps neither of us was at her best that day?"

"I sure wasn't."

"Well, I confess to filling my pockets full of something I shouldn't."

Since Faye had brought home a musket ball for analysis, she couldn't exactly take potshots at Betsy for this.

Betsy held out a plastic box, and Faye could hear things bumping around inside that were probably fascinating. Betsy opened the box and Faye laughed out loud.

There, nestled among broken pieces of European transfer-ware from the mid-16th century, there was a single bead. It was silver and filigreed, and Faye was prepared to swear that it was identical to the rosary beads that Glynis had wanted her to see. Joe leaned over her shoulder to get a look.

"Magda! Get over here!" Faye barked.

Magda scooped up Rachel, settled the child on her broad hip, and loped over to join Faye. Unbidden, Levon and Kirk joined them. Unlike the others, they didn't understand the significance of the tiny bead in terms of solving Glynis' disappearance, but they knew what they were looking at, from a historical standpoint.

"Damn," Kirk said.

Faye thought that this observation pretty well summed up what they were all thinking, as archaeologists.

As a consultant for the police department, Faye was thinking something completely different. She was thinking that Smithson's construction site was now inextricably tied to the artifacts Glynis was carrying on the day of her disappearance.

By three o'clock, Faye's energy was flagging. She knew it was true. She couldn't hide it. She hated these facts.

She'd been sitting in a lawn chair for an hour. She'd scolded Levon twice for sloppy technique, which had resulted in a quick improvement of Kirk's work. And she'd spent a pleasant few minutes looking over yet another odd artifact Magda had found beneath the tiles of the old pool deck—a lovely blown glass vase small enough to cradle in one hand and big enough to hold a single perfect rosebud. Though still crusted with dirt, its luminous blue glass looked old and expensive.

She'd also had a quick phone conversation with Overstreet, and that quarter-hour could clearly be billed to the police department.

He'd said, "The county's historic preservation guy has been alerted to the need for him to visit Smithson's project. It's a big place—acres and acres—but thanks to you and Betsy, he's going to know exactly what he's looking for and where it is. They're gonna shut that construction project down for a good long time. I feel kinda bad doing this to Smithson, what with the fact that his daughter's being missing and all—"

Faye wasn't about to let him get away with this bald-faced lie. "No, you don't."

"Well, you're right. I don't. I'll do everything I can to find that girl, but I don't like her father."

Faye couldn't argue with him. And she couldn't sit in this uncomfortable chair another minute, either. As much as she hated it, her company's president and CEO needed to go off the clock, so she could go inside and take a nap.

Faye was not a good napper. She lay on the bed, aware of every pressure point—shoulder blades, pelvis, skull, elbows, and heels—as it dug into the worn-out mattress. Other pressure points, mental ones, bothered her, too.

Now that she had an awe-inspiring view of a dingy ceiling, instead of the bright blue sky, she was wide-awake. Maybe Harriet's book would entertain her while she rested her aching bones.

Turning to the back of the book, Faye saw a floor plan of Dunkirk Manor. She'd certainly seen one of those already, though she'd concentrated more on the grounds where she'd be excavating than on the house. True to form, Harriet's book was value-added. She'd taken the bare-bones plan of the house that Faye had been able to find at the library, and added commentary she'd gleaned from research and from conversations with elderly folk who remembered the Dunkirks' glittering parties.

Harriet had hand-drawn the original footprint of the house onto the plan, showing where the bedroom wing had been added after ghosts disrupted the first owners' wedding night. She'd marked the location of each piece of furniture, as shown in old photos. Faye was struck by the fact that, in the house's public rooms, the original furniture still sat in its original locations.

She smiled. *We wouldn't want to disrupt the ghosts by moving things around, would we?*

A note near the manor's front door said, "Conversations in the 1970s with retired household staff yielded multiple statements that the original purpose of the turrets was to serve as cisterns. They are said to have provided running water to the first and second floors. Bathrooms were rare in those days, particularly on upper floors."

This was a cool fact that would add a bit of human interest to her report on the property. When people stopped to think about life without bathrooms, they unanimously agreed that life was better with them.

A room on the second floor was labeled, "The Nursery." It was closet-like, with no window, opening only into another large bedroom. By Faye's best guess, these rooms had been converted into the living room of the owners' suite where Daniel and Suzanne lived.

She remembered sitting in that area, surrounded by people worried about Glynis on the very day that she disappeared. Picturing the room, Faye remembered the wide bank of windows overlooking the front yard. She remembered the suite's front door, which opened onto the hallway and faced the windows. She remembered a door into the suite's kitchen and dining area. But she didn't remember a door on the wall facing the kitchen door.

Squinting at the floor plan, she decided that the wall between the living area and the old nursery had been removed to enlarge the space. Perhaps the Dunkirks had done it themselves, when they finally recognized the truth: there would be no babies sleeping there.

Faye remembered how lovely little Rachel had looked, running through the atrium, and she realized that no child had lived in this house since lonely Raymond had watched his mother walk away. Only Victor had graced the house with bubbling youth, and his presence must have hurt Allyce and Raymond in an undefinable way. He wasn't theirs. And, if Faye could believe her suspicions that his mental state wasn't just a function of age, he wasn't…*right.*

Allyce could love a child like Victor with all her heart, but she couldn't give him her hopes. She couldn't dream that he would grow up to be the handsome, intelligent, and masterful man that her husband Raymond seemed to be. He was a forever child, someone to love and grieve over. And he had other parents, whose rights superseded the rights of a woman with all the love and money in the world.

It was hard to imagine that he'd fallen through the cracks, with both his parents and the Dunkirks to care for him. His parents had died without providing for him, and perhaps they weren't capable of it. And the Dunkirks, who might have made sure that he never wanted for anything, simply didn't.

Her eyes stung a little, thinking of Victor and wondering if she could do anything to help his situation now. Maybe the best place to start would be to check with shelters that could provide a much better roof for his head. And food—now that she'd seen Victor's home, she had to wonder what on earth he ate. He'd lived in St. Augustine so long that he surely knew the location of every soup kitchen and charitable restaurateur, but this was no way to live the last years of a long life.

She picked up her laptop, planning to look around for social service agencies, then indulge herself by rambling around the web in search of Robert Ripley and his Believe-It-or-Not empire. She'd gotten as far as typing "s-o-c-i-a-l s-e-r-v-" when the door opened.

Joe stood there, loaded down with bed linens, towels, and a loaded plate. "I bumped into Daniel down the hall. He said that Suzanne sent you these."

"We will never again have clients who care so much about our well-being. You know that don't you? Usually, their attitude is, 'Would you finish this project already? And I don't know why you can't work for fifty cents an hour on Christmas!'"

"They're very nice people. And I think they're so, so sad about their daughter Annie. Always will be. Seeing you healthy and strong and ready to have a baby makes them happy, maybe. And that makes them want to help."

"They really are kind. But you know what, Joe? I'm not hungry and I think maybe Victor might be. He's just a few steps down the street. Would you take that plate to him?"

Feeling like maybe she'd staved off Victor's needs for a few hours, she went back to her computer and dropped a few emails to some people who might be able to help him for longer.

Then she crawled the web, reading about Robert Ripley's travels to places she wanted to go—China, Madagascar, Brazil, Morocco. She dozed off, dreaming of touring exotic lands with a baby strapped to her back, and she stayed asleep until Joe came back with another plate of food that she *was* hungry enough to eat.

So sleepy by the time she finished eating that the last forkful just looked too heavy to lift, she dozed off again. When she opened her eyes, Joe was asleep at her side. It was midnight and she was wide awake. Quietly, she pulled on her robe and a pair of cotton gloves. She crept out into the nearest dining room and laid Father Domingo's book on the ornate tablecloth.

The dining room was a bit spooky, perhaps, but Faye didn't believe in ghosts…much. At midnight, her logical mind was a bit less resistant to such things, but no matter. Faye felt sure that the ghosts of Dunkirk Manor confined themselves the atrium, walking endlessly in circles around the balconies and climbing for all time on staircases that had no end.

From the journal of Father Domingo Sanz de la Fuente

Translated from the Spanish by
Faye Longchamp Mantooth, Ph.D.,
and Magda Stockard-McKenzie, Ph.D.

I cannot say that my life among the Timucua has been unpleasant. It seems that Ocilla was of noble birth, as such is determined by her people. By walking with me away from the River Seloy, she left her homeland forever. Still, there are many Timucua villages within a few days' walk of the new Spanish settlement of St. Augustine. Many of their chieftains are Ocilla's kin, and we wandered for a time, staying first in one village, then another, but always as most honored guests.

Many of these chieftains told us of a fierce young man of God who had come to them looking for a runaway priest traveling with two women. There was never a mention of an older priest. I knew that Father Francisco would not hunt me down. For the rest of his life, he would pray for me, but he would let me be.

I also knew that Father Esteban would not forgive my desertion nor the heresy that surely prompted it. And he would never forgive me for the blow that I dealt to his dignity by stealing his woman.

The deerhide shoes covering Timucuan feet are far better for carrying news across the countryside than hard Spanish boots. Before many months had passed, Father Esteban could hardly have failed to know that I had stolen more than his woman. Chulufi delivered his daughter before the maize ripened. With the addition of an infant to our number, we could not continue our ceaseless travel. We picked a village and settled there.

It is also not possible that Father Esteban did not know where we were. Those deerhide shoes could not have failed to bring him that news. For a time, I wondered why he left us alone. Then a pair of those shoes brought us the news that he had been recalled to Dominica, and I began to dream of a peaceful life in my adopted home. For a long while, that dream was mine.

The village welcomed me with the respect due a shaman, since Ocilla told them that I was well-acquainted with magic and spiritual matters. In all my years with the Timucua, I was never certain that I communicated to them the difference between their blood-magic and Our Lord's Holy Communion.

I was educated in the medicinal arts in Spain, and my knowledge of herbs and tinctures made me useful in my new community, to the extent that I could find the herbs I needed. The Timucuan shaman, Humka, was mortally offended by my presence and refused to acknowledge me for the better part of a year, until one of my poultices broke the fever of the chief's young son.

Once so reticent to share his status of holy man, Humka now seized on every particle of knowledge I could offer. In return, he taught me to use plants no healer in Spain had ever seen.

Together, we brought God's blessed healing to some of the sufferers among us. Not all, for God's judgment is not to be questioned. We all must die, and He will determine the time and place, but I believe that the shaman and I served as God's comforting Hand for the sick and dying among us. And Merciful Mother, there were so many sick and dying.

As I learned to speak their language, I learned the truth about the sickness among us. When a young mother came to us with pockmarks covering her face, Humka told me that he had been a man before he ever saw such a sickness. He cannot tell me his age, but my eyes tell me that his shoulders are not hunched and that he still has many of his teeth. It has not been a great span of years since he became a man.

These people die of illnesses that make Spanish children whine and cry for a few days before returning to their toys. I am not as highly educated as Father Francisco, nor even Father Esteban, but I can count and do sums. I know when Spain claimed this land for herself, and I believe we brought these diseases with us. I fear such sicknesses will be the end of Ocilla's people, just as they have already been the end of her.

If every village across this wide land has seen as much death as I have witnessed here, then the destruction is greater than any war ever fought. It is greater than all our wars added together. How many people have we killed merely by stepping off our tall ships?

I spend much time in prayer these days.

I, Father Domingo Sanz de la Fuente, attest that the foregoing is a statement of actual events.

Chapter Twenty-one

Spending the night's small hours in Dunkirk Manor's public areas had taught Faye something. The house was full of clocks, and they were all accurate. Or, at least, they were all set to the same time. There were clocks on the mantelpieces of both dining rooms. There was a grandfather clock in the entry hall, standing against the wall opposite the new elevator, and there was a delicate and ornate clock on each balcony, sitting on shelves that were dead-center on the back wall.

Faye wondered whether there had been two grandfather clocks in the entry hall, before the elevator was added. The rest of the house was so utterly symmetrical. Had Daniel and Suzanne trashed one to make room for the elevator? Or had they added a clock to balance the visual weight of the elevator doors? She was a little surprised they hadn't just gone for broke and installed matching elevators, to avoid destroying the manor's perfect balance.

A late night spent listening to clocks tinkling and chiming at fifteen-minute intervals reminded her of something else—the sound-absorbing power of the poured concrete walls in this house. She'd never had an inkling that there was so much ethereal noise going on outside her bedroom every night.

When her eyes tired of the effort of reading Father Domingo's handwriting, and her mind tired of the labor of translating his words into English, and her hand tired of laboriously recording that translation, Faye found that she still wasn't sleepy.

She'd brought Harriet's book, knowing that she might need a moment of light reading before she was ready to go back to bed. Turning again to the Dunkirks' biographies, she noticed that Allyce had survived Raymond by six years. His 1950 obituary mentioned his bereaved wife. The fact that she had outlived him explained the fact that Raymond's family home, Dunkirk Manor, had passed to Suzanne, whose father was Allyce's great-nephew.

All that wealth, and no one but a not-too-near relative to pass it to…well, a not-too-near relative and a feeble-minded boy who lived down the street. Faye's heart clenched inside her a little, at the very thought of it. The echoes of all those clocks as they marked the passing minutes sent her mind down passageways of time, reminding her of all the little things it steals, one by one.

Dawn was pink in the sky outside her little bedroom window when she crawled under the covers beside Joe and, finally, she slept.

◇◇◇

Joe was on time for work. The crew had agreed to work a half-day to make up for the time lost to Glynis' disappearance, but just because it was Saturday didn't mean it was okay to drag around and waste half the morning.

Joe was always on time for work. This meant that his crew was also always on time, because they knew their tardiness would be noticed. Joe might or might not comment on that tardiness, but he wouldn't have much to say to them for the rest of the day. Their work assignment might not be the one they wanted. And it was just possible that, before he handed them their break-time water bottles, he might leave them out in the sun for just long enough to blunt their cool edge.

It wasn't so much that Joe consciously thought this quiet management strategy through. It was just that Joe instinctively understood animal behavior, even when the animals were human. He had never raised his voice to Levon or Kirk, but they treated him with respect. A portion of this respect might be due to the fact that Joe towered over them both, but another portion was due to his quiet confidence.

Another reason he never had raise his voice was because Magda showed up, she did her job, and then she did the job of anyone around her who was slacking. After that, she gave the perpetrator a good lashing with the sharp side of her tongue. It had occurred to Joe that maybe this job wasn't running smoothly due to his management prowess, nor Faye's. It was running smoothly because everyone concerned was tiptoeing around Magda. Joe loved her like a big sister—albeit an opinionated and crotchety one—but even now, Magda sometimes scared him a little.

Joe set out to circle the worksite, checking the crew's preparations for the day from every angle, then he stopped short in his tracks. Something was wrong.

The equipment was in its place. The excavated areas were exactly as they'd left them the previous afternoon. Levon and Kirk were bent, heads together, over the day's work plan. But Magda was nowhere to be seen.

Now, Magda had been happily late for work on the day that she and Faye spent glorying over the old Spanish diary. But other than that, the woman was a machine. She could get herself and her kid dressed and fed and out the door in less time than it took most sleepy people to figure out how to turn the coffee pot on.

Magda had not been at the breakfast table. She had not been in his room that morning, pestering Faye to quit consulting and be a professor, as God intended. He knew in his heart of hearts that she was not lounging in bed, hitting the snooze button again and again. When a reliable person slips, people notice. Joe noticed. He headed indoors, but not before wordlessly telling Kirk and Levon where they should be working, by the simple expedient of eye contact and a nod.

There was no place left to look but Magda's bedroom, and Joe was too much of a gentleman to barge into a lady's boudoir alone, not when the lady's best friend was right down the hall typing up the outline for her first big consultant's report.

Joe left his workers to their jobs and went to get Faye.

◇◇◇

After being forced to parade across Dunkirk Manor's back garden in her flannel pajamas, Faye had taken to sleeping in sweatpants and a t-shirt. Her maternity work pants were so snug that she was afraid she'd soon be wearing sweatpants around the clock. Remembering how trim her waist had always been made her want to swear.

When Joe stuck his head in the door, flustered and upset, Faye was glad she'd switched her sleepwear. She couldn't say exactly how she knew Joe was flustered. His body was still relaxed yet ready for action. His hands didn't show the slightest signs of a tremble. He wasn't sweating or pale. She truly believed he had conscious control over all his reflexes and bodily functions, which really came in handy when he wanted to stop breathing long enough to draw his bow and shoot something tasty. Right now, the look in those clear green eyes was enough to jolt her out of her chair and onto her aching feet.

"Magda didn't show up for work or for breakfast. Come with me. Let's check her room."

Faye paused only long enough to slide on her house slippers. The last time she'd met a crisis in her sleepwear, she'd been very sorry to be barefoot.

Magda's room was maybe five steps down the hall, but two words echoed in her head with each step.

"Where's Glynis?"
"Where's Glynis?"
"Where's Glynis?"
"Where's Glynis?"
"Where's Glynis?"

She was not capable of adding *Where's Magda?* to that list, not until she opened the door and saw that her friend was gone. And so was Rachel.

Rachel's toys were strewn exactly as you'd expect a three-year-old's toys to be strewn. Magda's morning cup of coffee was sitting half-drunk on the nightstand. That morning's paper was casually refolded, beside the cup. Everything was as it should be, except that two of the people nearest to Faye's heart were simply not there.

Entering the room with Joe, Faye saw that Magda's blue cotton shirt was still draped over the ironing board, and the iron had been left on. So had Magda's curling iron.

Magda used a curling iron? Who knew?

Something was wrong. Faye felt it.

Then her foot brushed something small, but heavy for its size. She couldn't see what it was, because her belly was in the way. Joe bent down easily and handed it to her: Magda's cell phone.

The last number dialed was 911, but the call had been dropped. Of course it had. Cell reception was nonexistent here in this pile of concrete. Magda had tried, but her phone hadn't been able to push that call for help out into the world.

Faye clutched the phone as if she thought its navigation system would take her straight to her friend. Her first thought was to question how someone could kidnap Magda. How could anyone simply take her, with no sign of a struggle and no sound? Glynis, young and dainty and innocent, might have been easy to abduct. But Magda? She would fight to her last breath.

That last thought took Faye's own breath. She shoved it out of her head.

The absence of sound was easy to explain, here in the fortress that was Dunkirk Manor.

But why did the room show no sign of a struggle?

The answer to that question was easy and heartstopping. How hard would it be to take a mother, if you already had her child?

Faye's knees wanted to buckle, but she held firm for Magda. Her body was wrecked by this pregnancy, but there was nothing wrong with her mind. To find her friend and her godchild, Faye needed to get to the truth. And the fastest way to the truth was to ask the right questions.

Who could possibly be so inhuman as to hurt a woman and her child?

No. She didn't know that they were hurt. She only knew that they were gone. Faye reached again, looking for the simplest possible question, the one that most clearly addressed the facts.

Who could possibly be so inhuman as to *take* a woman and her child?

As soon as that silent question sounded in Faye's mind, she knew. Short, dumpy Magda and tall, wispy Glynis were separated by more than twenty years in age, and they were separated by light-years in terms of money and glamour and privileged upbringing.

They had only two things in common. They were both women. And they both had a child. Glynis' unborn baby looked nothing like Magda's rowdy toddler, but Faye knew they looked much the same to a woman desperate for a child of her own.

Less than a year ago, Faye had been nearly that desperate for a baby herself, though not so much so that kidnapping one would have ever crossed her mind. Perhaps Allyce's sad story had given her some insight into a psychic pain so deep that it was almost physical.

Perhaps it is physical, she thought, *this business of a woman's body craving the chance to do what it was made to do.*

And there was yet another woman in this house, one whose loss of a child might well have driven her to do the unthinkable.

Faye looked at Joe and said, "I know who has them. And I know where they are."

Five steps back down the hallway took them to their room, where Faye showed Joe the floor plan of Dunkirk Manor. She tapped on the tiny room labeled "nursery," and said, "Remember? We were in that room, but this door wasn't there. I noticed the discrepancy last night, but I just figured Daniel and Suzanne had taken out a wall to make their living room bigger. But that's impossible. This house is built of poured concrete. That wall ain't going anywhere."

"You think they closed up the door to the nursery?"

"I think somebody, maybe Daniel and Suzanne or maybe somebody long ago, closed that room behind a hidden door. Lots of houses like this have secret rooms. What better place than an old nursery to hide a woman who's going to give you a child?"

"But Glynis is barely pregnant. Hide a woman for nine months? Faye. That's insane."

Faye thought of the dimming of the light in Allyce Dunkirk's eyes. She thought of the way she retreated from life in her latter years, secluding herself in this barren home that was not a haven and not a comfort. She thought of the disturbing images in the paintings Allyce chose for the house and of the paintings that she made herself. And she wondered about Allyce and her great-great-niece Suzanne, the trial attorney who had retreated into a world so limited that a wilted flower or a misplaced piece of parsley or a wound-down clock became critically important.

"Yes," she said. "It is insane. And I'm beginning to think that insanity runs in this family."

The plan was simple and it would unfold immediately, because the time since the abduction was being measured in minutes, not hours. Maybe even seconds. The "on" light on Magda's curling iron showed that it hadn't even been abandoned long enough to switch itself off. It was possible that Suzanne hadn't had time to hide Magda and Rachel yet.

And Daniel? Was he involved, too? There was no way to know, so she had to presume that he was.

Joe was going to go upstairs to the owners' suite, and he was going to do it now, in hopes that he could snatch Magda and her child out of danger before they'd ever really gotten there. Faye didn't even argue with his flat, unyielding position that she was not going with him. She'd be no help to him, physically, it was true. But more than that, Faye needed to protect herself for their baby's sake.

She couldn't allow herself to be harmed, not now. Magda would understand that. If Faye showed up to rescue her now, Magda's first response would be to bark, "Faye. Are you nuts?"

If Glynis had been kidnapped because she offered the promise of a baby in nine months, and if Magda had been kidnapped because she offered the reality of a young child now, then how much would Faye be worth to their kidnapper? She could deliver an untouched newborn, almost immediately, one who wasn't already bonded to its mother. In Faye's womb, she carried the most human of dreams.

Was this why Daniel had taken her, alone, to the storage room? Had he been planning to kidnap her? Joe's arrival might have prevented that, and Suzanne and Daniel might then have turned to their backup plan—stealing Glynis, a woman who could provide a baby, eventually, to a couple willing to wait nine months.

Faye remembered Daniel bringing a meal to her and then being interrupted by Joe. She remembered that Joe had intercepted Daniel just the day before, while he was carrying food and sheets and towels to Faye, who certainly had not requested them. She especially remembered the vise grip of his hand on her arm on the elevator and in the entry hall on the day he had urged her to come with him because she needed some rest. Again, Joe had intercepted Daniel's attempt to get Faye alone.

Had the man been trying to take Faye, who had her attentive husband to thank for the fact that she wasn't trapped wherever Glynis was right now? More to the point, had Daniel been trying to take her baby, so that Suzanne could be happy again?

Joe's eyes showed his naked need to get Faye out of Dunkirk Manor. For once, she was going to let him protect her.

It only took a few words to map the best way to get Faye out of the house and to get Joe straight to Magda's side. Quietly, they would move past the guests eating breakfast in the nearest dining room, through the atrium, and into the entry hall. From there, Joe could step on the elevator and ride sight unseen to the second floor, just a few steps from the owners' suite. Faye would be out of the front door immediately and down the street, dialing 911 as soon as she got out of Dunkirk Manor's signal-hampering bulk and into the open air. Once the call was made, she could wait for help with Victor in his hovel.

It was the simplest of plans, and it just might work.

Dunkirk Manor's clocks were sounding as Faye and Joe crossed the dining room. She heard the clatter of plates and the chatter of guests around her, but the sound was dim. It was as if she were wrapped in a transparent bubble of clear air. She could see through it. She could hear echoes of the world outside. But she was almost as insulated from the world by her fear as she'd been by the thick walls that had kept her from hearing Magda being led away.

The baby squirmed inside her as they entered the atrium, and Faye was grateful for the human contact. Joe, intuitive to the bone, slipped an arm around her and rested his hand on the place that used to be her waist. Even his warm body wasn't enough to buffer her from the chill of the beautiful room. Her heart was breaking for Magda. In the atrium, she was shocked to find that she could still reach deep into the dark well of her emotions and hurt for Allyce, too.

They were only in the atrium for a silent and timeless moment. Then Joe opened the door into the smaller, intimate entry hall, and the reality of their mission struck them. Joe was going to do what was necessary to save a woman and child they both loved. And Faye was going to do what was necessary to save their own child. And they would have to separate in order to do that.

Luck was with them, in that the elevator was waiting on the first floor. Joe was aboard before the doors were fully open but, with his customary easy grace, he had leaned down to kiss Faye as he left her, without delaying him from his mission by even a millisecond.

If Faye had reacted as effortlessly as Joe, if she hadn't paused for a fraction of a second to watch the elevator doors close in front of him, if she'd moved swiftly instead of with the leaden stride of late pregnancy, then maybe things would have been different.

Instead, she left herself unguarded, for the briefest period of time, in the home of people who so desperately wanted what she had. As she grabbed the handle of Dunkirk Manor's heavy front door with both hands, she heard a shushing grind as it slid across the inlaid wood at the threshold…and she heard the same sound behind her, along with a slight metallic click.

She had no chance to turn her head to look, because an arm encircled her beneath her big belly like a steel band. A hand clamped itself over her mouth.

The hormones that were already swamping her mind surged, and her body failed her. The arms that had always been so strong, moving tons of earth in her years as an archaeologist, dangled at her side like ribbons. Her legs, the ones that had spent those years crouched in the dirt and had spent the past months hauling her ever-growing baby around, buckled under her, making it easy for her assailant to drag her…somewhere. Violently nauseated out of sheer terror, her empty stomach spasmed. She gagged and retched, but her attacker was undeterred.

Even her mind was leaving her, and it had never failed her before.

Chapter Twenty-two

Joe hesitated outside the door to Dunkirk Manor's owners' suite. His back was to the wall beside the door and he was flattened against it, because the suite's front door opened onto the second-floor balcony encircling the atrium. The balcony was deep and the sturdy railing partially obscured the view from the atrium floor. He wasn't achingly obvious to anyone walking across the atrium, but if someone stood in the right spot and looked up then, yes, he could be seen from below.

He placed the back of his hand against the door, knowing that the bones of his knuckles would conduct any sound from inside the suite that was loud enough to vibrate the door, even slightly. If someone were just inside, sitting quietly on a couch, there would be no vibration and he'd never know anybody was there until he opened the door, but this was the best way he had of getting some notion of what was going on in there.

He got nothing, which was disappointing. If Magda were in there fighting a kidnapper who wanted to put her and her baby in a windowless room and lock the door, then he should be feeling some mighty big vibrations at the moment.

Well, he was going to have to go in blind. He twisted the doorknob slowly—and it turned. He didn't know whether to consider the unlocked door a stroke of luck or not. It likely meant that Daniel or Suzanne or both were still in there, but he'd known all along that he'd probably have to confront somebody to get Magda back. He just hoped they didn't have a gun.

Joe was always armed. The leather bag he wore at his waist always carried weapons he'd made from stone, and right now he was holding one of them in his hand. It was a flint knife, chipped to an edge sharper than surgical steel. It would slice flesh and open up a windpipe, and if Magda were bound and gagged, it would set her free.

It would not stop a bullet.

For this reason, Joe was going to make his stand right here in this doorway. If a gun went off when the door was closed, it was possible that no one would hear, or that they would hear without being able to figure out where the shot came from. But if it went off when Joe was standing right where he was, in front of this door that he was even now opening, then help would come. It might even come soon enough to save Joe, depending on where the bullet caught him.

More importantly, help would come for Magda and Rachel and, if she was still alive, Glynis. Someone would hear the shot and call the police, and surely they would realize that the shooting had some connection to the kidnappings. Even if Joe weren't able to tell them about the hiding place, even if he were dead, surely his shooting would lead the police to search the suite long and hard enough to turn up the secret room.

He turned the knob slowly and silently, and the door opened.

Faye's feet dragged helplessly over the slick wooden floor. She was bent double over the arm wrapped around her middle, and she could see that she was still wearing her house slippers. They were fur-lined moccasins that Joe had made for her last birthday, and her adrenaline-charged mind took note of every pore in the soft leather.

Details. She was in survival mode and her brain was convinced that noticing details would save her life. She noted the direction she was being dragged, not toward the door into the atrium nor toward the elevator, but toward the wall where the grandfather clock stood. Why?

Then she watched her feet as they were dragged over a shallow threshold and onto a concrete floor that she'd never seen before.

She could hear the ragged breathing of the person restraining her. Who was it? Suzanne? She seemed too…birdlike…to haul Faye around like a sack of potatoes. But maybe…

Daniel?

She assessed the size of the person behind her by the feel of the body at her back and of the arm at her belly. Yes. It could be Daniel. It made sense that he and his wife could be working together to get the baby that Suzanne's madness craved. She had seen the depth of their love for each other with her own eyes. How could such love be so perverted that it would lead two people to kidnap a woman and her child? How could love drive them to murder?

Daniel—and now she saw that it *was* Daniel—set her down firmly but gently on the floor and backed out the doorway into the entry hall without a word. She fell to her hands and knees, doing her best not to collapse utterly. Then the shushing grind sounded again and a heavy door closed in front of her blurry eyes. The outside world was gone, every ray of light and every breath of sound, but there was a surprising degree of life in this room. Her ears said so.

Focus. She needed to focus her eyes so that she could assess her situation.

There were sounds behind her. A little girl's whimper and a mother's soothing murmurs. Magda and Rachel!

And there were long sighing breaths to her right, coming from someone who was sitting or lying on the floor. Still stunned, Faye lingered on all fours, trying to shake the dizziness and nausea. She cut her eyes in the direction of those quiet breaths and could only see a long slim foot and the hem of a pair of black checked pants. *Glynis*. She didn't sound good, but she did sound alive.

It took everything she had, but Faye raised her head and turned it, and she managed to do so without vomiting. She was sitting in a square room with smooth concrete walls and a smooth concrete floor. The room extended up and up, and light entered from windows far above her, maybe three stories in the air. She was in one of the turrets.

One turret had been converted into an elevator shaft. How could she have failed to wonder what was in the other one, now that it was no longer being used to store water? It was the perfect prison, a modern castle tower where a princess could be hidden.

Magda and Rachel grabbed hold of her. Rachel clung to her thigh, a little girl who was scared and confused but who knew a familiar and protective friend when she saw one. Magda, always practical, was checking Faye for broken bones and pressing her belly to see whether it was contracting.

She wasn't, not yet. Praise God. The thought of delivering her baby here chilled Faye's blood.

Clinging to the comforting touch of two much-loved people, Faye looked again at Glynis. She found her alone, eyes closed and curled on her side, with her body nestled into the corner of the turret wall. Her breathing was labored, and there was a black bruise on her cheek and a scabbed cut at the corner of her mouth. It looked like someone had wiped the blood from her face, so at least her captors hadn't left her in a bloody pool.

Glynis was still wearing the expensive and elegant black-and-white outfit that Overstreet had described. Her long pale hair was spread about her like a splash of light. It was stark against the gray concrete and Faye could see individual strands flung everywhere, loose on the floor. Glynis had shed so much hair that it was visibly thinner at her temples and along her hairline. In patches, Faye could see clear through to her scalp. Her skin was pallid and damp and, even in unconsciousness, her arms were wrapped tight around her vulnerable belly and her fists were clenched shut.

This was no fantasy-kissed sleeping beauty. Faye knew now that the story of Rapunzel was a myth. *This* was what a princess held captive in a tower really looked like.

◇◇◇

Joe found the suite's living room empty. He heard nothing. The room was so silent and still that he found it impossible to believe that first Glynis, and now Magda and Rachel, had been hauled kicking and screaming across its thickly carpeted floor. Surely that kind of terror would leave its mark on a place. But he felt nothing, no panicky tremble to the air.

No matter. Faye said they were here, and he had never had cause to doubt her judgment. He was going to find them.

"We've gotta get Glynis out of here," Faye said.

"No shit," Magda answered. "I've only been here long enough to look this place over a little. The big door's there." She nodded toward the door Faye had just entered. "There are little windows way, way up there letting the sun in, which are gonna be zero help to us." She pointed straight up. "There are two little wooden doors about three feet across up there—" she said, pointing to square holes in the walls above them. "They look like they might have been for maintenance access, one on the second floor and one on the third floor."

Faye nodded.

"But since this place has twelve- or fifteen-foot ceilings, I can't see any way to get up to them. If they're even unlocked."

Faye couldn't argue with her.

"And then there are these things, which are interesting but use-less." Magda pointed to a series of small holes in the wall near the floor. They were about the size of her palm. Then she opened a nearby trap door to reveal a hole in the floor leading exactly nowhere.

"If this tower was used as a cistern, then the water had to go out to the house somehow," Faye said. "I guess maybe the pipes went through those holes in the wall. And the hole in the floor… hmmm. The weight of the water in a cistern this tall would have given great water pressure, but I guess you'd still want a pump for times when the water was low or if you wanted to drain the thing. Maybe the pump went in that hole."

"The important thing is that the hole doesn't lead anywhere, and nobody but Rachel could possibly get in it. Especially not you and your big stomach."

"Thank you for your sensitivity."

"Don't mention it."

A rustle of silk caught their attention. Glynis reached a hand up to touch her battered face. The other arm remained wrapped around her, tight. She said, "Is somebody here?" and her voice was so faint that the walls nearly absorbed it all.

Faye fell to her knees by the wounded woman's side. "It's me, Faye. And Magda, and her little girl Rachel. How are you, Glynis?"

"Ankle…broken. Knee's pretty bad. Ribs…probably broken. Some of them. Head hurts something terrible."

"Are you hungry?" Faye saw several full bottles of water near Glynis, alongside an untouched plate loaded with an omelet identical to the ones the bed-and-breakfast guests were happily eating in the dining room.

"Don't want food. But he makes me, sometimes. Shoves a spoon at my mouth until I open it and swallow. Says he's got to feed his baby." She gave a weak sigh. "He comes at night. Late, late at night. I can tell the time, sort of, by the light coming in those windows up there. It's been dark a long time when he comes. I guess there's not much risk of someone catching him then. They're all asleep in their rooms…in their beds…soft clean beds…"

Faye noticed a sodden rag beside Glynis' head. She reached to pick it up and Glynis' eyes opened. "He brings those every time. He soaks them in ice water and wipes my face and hands. Says he's sorry it's warm in here and he's trying to figure out a way to run electricity in here for a fan. Because I'm going to be in here nine months and it'll be even hotter soon than it is now. Nice of him to worry, I guess…" The eyes drooped shut.

"Does Suzanne know you're here?"

"…don't know…" The voice drifted into a wordless breath.

Glynis was slipping back into unconsciousness and Faye didn't want her to go. She needed all the information the poor girl could give, if they were to have a prayer of getting out of this cell alive.

Faye touched Glynis on her silk-clad arm. "Can you tell us how you got here?"

The eyes flew open and the imprisoned princess rallied. "We fought. Lex and me. I told him about the baby the night before and we argued all night. He didn't want me to keep it. Worried... he was worried about getting his practice going first. I left as soon as it was light. Got some coffee, 'cause I didn't know how on earth I was going to get through the day. I've been so tired lately. I can't tell you how tired..."

"I remember, sugar." Magda reached down to smooth a hand over Glynis' hair. "For the first three months, I was too tired to breathe most of the time. It gets better."

Faye remembered, too.

"When I got to work, Lex was right behind me. Guess he wanted to yell at me some more. Tried to get out of the car but he yanked me out first...foot got stuck in the doorframe. When I fell, my leg got all twisted...heard some things break." A little sigh escaped her. "Then he hit me, hard, in the face. Never did that before. Think it scared him. He backed off for a second while I pulled myself up on the door. Got my top half back in the car, lying across the car seat. My face was bleeding all over it."

So that was the source of the small amount of Glynis' blood in the car.

Glynis shivered a little and kept talking. "Then he just leaned in my car door. Loomed over me...grabbed my shoulders...beat me...shook me till I could hardly see. "

Tears leaked onto the bruised cheek. "I had some stuff on the seat beside me. I couldn't see, not with him up in my face. Just felt around until I found something big and heavy, made out of rock...hit him in the head with it as hard as I could. It knocked him out and he fell. I shoved him out of the car. Had to climb over him. Fell on the ground. Couldn't do anything but crawl, but I crawled to the house, as hard as I could go, because I was so scared he'd wake up. And because I knew Suzanne and Daniel would help me. I trusted them...trusted..."

Weeping, Glynis closed her eyes and wrapped both arms around herself again, drawing her good leg into a fetal position.

Something was missing from Glynis' story.

"You hit him in the head. Not the throat."

"Forehead. Or nose, maybe. Made a big damn noise."

"Was he bleeding when you left him?"

The eyes flickered open again. "Maybe a little bit oozing out. Not much. Why?"

There was no way that Faye was going to tell this wounded creature that the father of her child had bled himself empty on the ground. If God was good, she wouldn't have to tell Glynis that Lex was dead until after she was out of this desolate place.

"I'm just trying to find out what happened that morning. So you left Lex and went to Daniel and Suzanne for help."

"Just Daniel. I crawled to the front porch and up the steps. Had to pull myself up and stand on my good leg to open the door. Tried to open it, anyway. Should've rung the doorbell so everyone in the house would hear, but I just wanted to get inside. To get away from Lex. But the door's too damn heavy for somebody with one good leg and a bunch of broken ribs. Opened it a crack and it slammed shut on me. Did it again. And again. Daniel was in the kitchen and I guess he saw the door opening and shutting on the security system. No other way for anybody to know, not when the door between the entry hall and the atrium is closed. Nobody saw me outside. Nobody could see into the entry hall from the inside—"

This was true, because none of the guests and staff had reported seeing Glynis that day, even for an instant.

"He pulled me into the entry hall. Talked me down, 'cause I was hysterical. I told him what Lex had done, and he whipped his cell phone out of his pocket, ready to call 911. If I'd just shut up then...but I didn't. I told him why Lex had beaten me. When I said I was pregnant, the weirdest look came into his eyes. He just said, 'A baby. You're going to have a baby.' And there was another weird second, like he was thinking this thing through. I should have run then. Only I couldn't have run if I tried."

"How could you possibly have known what he was thinking?" Magda said in her best don't-be-ridiculous voice. "This..." She gestured at their concrete prison. "This is insanity."

Glynis shook her head back and forth once, twice, too many times. The motion made the tears on her face take one crazy turn, then another. "There had to have been some way to keep this from happening. I don't know. But as soon as he learned I was pregnant, the phone went back in his pocket and he changed his tune. He said, 'Domestic abusers are unpredictable. I need to hide you. Let me put you someplace he'll never find you, until we can get the police here.'"

Faye looked around her at the impregnable walls hidden behind an invisible door. Daniel had been right about one thing. Lex would have never found her here.

"So he reached behind the grandfather clock and did something and that door opened up. I walked right in. Well, I limped right in, with Daniel's help, but I got in here just as fast as I could go. I was so scared and so glad to be safe. Can you believe that I put myself in this godforsaken hole?"

Magda plopped down beside Glynis and placed the girl's shining head gently in her lap. A loose strand of hair slipped from that head and floated to the floor. "Yes, I believe you. When the man you love threatens you and hurts you, you'll run anyplace to be safe. But it never works. You still love him, wherever you are. And you're trapped there until you figure out that you've got to leave him."

Faye's jaw dropped and Magda said, "Don't look at me like that, Faye. You thought maybe I was some kind of middle-aged virgin when you introduced me to Mike? Yes, I had a life before you met me, and yes, it wasn't a walk in the park, surrounded by roses and petunias." Turning her attention back to Glynis, she said, "You did the right thing, going for help. It sucks that you ran to a psychopath, but this is not your fault."

Magda opened a bottle of water and lifted Glynis' head. "You need to drink something. For the baby. Can you do it?"

Glynis nodded and did as she was told. As she drank, Magda gestured at the little girl clinging to her leg. "I will never, ever let this child see me let anyone mistreat me, and I certainly will never let her watch me go back for more. I love Mike with all my heart, and I can no more imagine him lifting a hand to me than I can imagine the sun stopping in its tracks. But if he ever did it, even once, he would be treated to a good clear view of the front door slamming behind me. Behind me and Rachel."

Glynis let the water bottle drop and Magda pushed it back to her lips. "Drink up. Faye and I are going to get you out of here, so that you and your baby can have the good life you both deserve."

Faye looked again at the impregnable fortress around them and wondered how in the hell they were going to do that.

Rachel left her mother's side and sidled up to Faye, whimpering, "Want a story, Auntie Faye. Tell me a story."

How many stories had she told Rachel over the past three years? Why couldn't she think of just the right one for this occasion? Faye herself was terrified, but there wasn't a chance in hell that she would fail to offer Rachel any comfort she wanted. A story…what story could she tell her here?

Her mind went straight to Rapunzel and then to Sleeping Beauty. She couldn't stop it from going there, but she pushed those fairy tales as far back in her skull as they would go.

Snow White…running for her life from a murderous woodsman?

Cinderella…imprisoned and forced to slave for her hateful stepmother?

Hansel and Gretel…driven from their home to starve, then fattened for the dinner of a witch?

Why were children's stories so terrifying? Because children couldn't be allowed to wait until they were grown-up to learn that the real world harbored danger?

Faye couldn't think of a single traditional story that she was willing to tell Rachel right now. Her mind wandered toward the true stories that had occupied her mind lately.

The murder of Lilibeth Campbell.

The betrayal and slow deterioration of Allyce Dunkirk.

The destruction of America's native people when the Old World collided with the New.

Faye rejected the truth in favor of singing Rachel her ABCs and following that up with some innocuous nursery rhymes, the ones about candlesticks and cats and fiddles and plums. There might be adult themes buried in those old songs, but Faye didn't know them and neither did Rachel.

Unfortunately, singing nursery rhymes didn't occupy Faye's entire brain. Her voice might be delivering a spritely rendition of "Mary Had A Little Lamb," but her mind refused to stay out of those shadowy passageways where priests participated in massacres and where gold trumped God.

From the journal of Father Domingo Sanz de la Fuente

Translated from the Spanish by
Faye Longchamp Mantooth, Ph.D.,
and Magda Stockard-McKenzie, Ph.D.

My path to hell was not long nor crooked. I fell from God's benevolent grace in a single instant.

For some years, I pursued my shaman's work, but I comforted myself by saying that I did it for God. Each tincture of an unfamiliar herb, dropped into the mouth of a grievously ill infidel, held the hope of saving that infidel's life so that he might someday find the grace of God.

And some of them did. I did not preach conversion to my gentle hosts. It seemed somehow wrong to flee the vengeful faith of men like Father Esteban, only to try to create it anew here. Instead, I set aside my role as priest and sought only to worship Our Lord quietly.

Despite my silence on matters of faith, the Timucua grew curious about my time spent in prayer. They asked endless questions about the rosary that I touched with such veneration and the worn book of scriptures that rarely left my hand.

The time came when some of them asked to be like me, and I was a priest once more.

I began celebrating the Mass as best I could. The bread was made of maize and the wine was squeezed from wild grapes and berries, but I believed. I believed in what I was doing. A priest without belief is nothing.

My prayers came to center around the Timucua and their future. As best I could tell, they had no future. There were murmurings among the men, rash murmurings that preached war. They were so sure that they could drive the Spanish away through sheer valor. I know exactly how much valor armed with stone weapons is worth when it is aimed at men wrapped in chain mail. Nothing.

The voice of God echoed in my prayers and told me what I must do. I must seek peace, even though the peace would end badly. The Timucua would be ground into the earth by the Spanish, regardless of whether they fought back. If I could convince them of the futility of war, then perhaps more of them would live a little longer. This was the best hope I could find for them, and it is not much.

I devised a ceremony that was warmly accepted by these people who so loved ceremony. When a wild-eyed young man preached war and fear, I taught him to break his spear into two pieces and bury it. If he had managed to scavenge a bit of Spanish war gear—a knife, a musket, an ax—I implored him to bury it with his own hand-made spear. Sometimes, those wild-eyed young men agreed.

I traveled the countryside, free of the fear of retribution from Father Esteban, exiled as he was in Dominica. Many weapons were broken and hidden in the ground, never to be used again, but other warriors were making more ceaselessly.

In the end, there are always more weapons. But, perhaps because of me, there were people whose lives were longer and happier than they would have been with fewer weapons above the ground. I can hope for no more than that.

I became an old man and never noticed, because I was preaching peace and tending to other things. Then came the cold winter day when Ocilla ran to me, weeping and wrapped in a Spanish blanket I didn't know. She had seen Father Esteban, who had returned from Dominica to build missions for the Church. With him was Yaraha, who Ocilla said now lay in the house she had shared with Father Francisco, covered with the pox.

Ocilla wept bitterly, because she knew that Yaraha would die, but her face shone with gratitude to Father Esteban, who had given her this blanket. He had told Ocilla to bring me to see him, and he would give us more blankets than we could carry, enough for the entire village.

The Timucua were in a grievous state of poverty, and I with them. The waves of pestilence, year after year, had killed the young men and women who should have been growing food and making clothing for the rest of the tribe. Ocilla could not have imagined refusing the great gift of a blanket, no more than she could imagine the murderous intent in the man who gave it, but I knew in my soul that it carried the pox. Why, other than revenge, would Father Esteban have sought us out again after all those years?

I had known the man for a short time, decades in the past, but I had no doubt that he had taken a blanket from a corpse and wrapped it around my Ocilla. Days would pass before I had proof, but the gift of a blanket told me all. Father Esteban was not a generous man.

I spoke to Humka of my fears, and this was a sin. None of the Timucua would have considered that Ocilla's sickness had been, in its way, an act of murder. They would never have conceived of the necessity for revenge without my words. Humka and I decided that Ocilla and I would remain in our hut, alone, until all danger of infection was past. He would leave food and water outside our door every morning. This was a generous use of days that might be his last, if the pox had come to our village. He had been standing beside me when Ocilla ran to us with her news. If she was to die, he very likely would die, too.

Unspoken was our knowledge that these precautions were useless if the plague was upon us. There was no possibility that the sickness could be contained. Ocilla had shown Chulufi her beautiful new blanket before she showed it to me, and Chulufi had run to all the other women to share the news. Perhaps we could have ordered everyone in the village to remain in their own huts, but the damage was done. And in this time of famine, who could have found the food to feed them all while they sat alone with their families, waiting to learn their fates?

I spent those days of Ocilla's quarantine in conversation with her, my lifelong friend. I watched her face for the deadly pockmarks, and thought ceaselessly of all her years of faithful kindness to me.

No Spaniard would have called Ocilla beautiful. Her face was curiously flattened, with broad cheeks and protruding teeth, and she was taller than me by a handspan. But no Spaniard ever knew such sweetness. When it was too late, I came to believe that it would have been no sin to love her. Even if it had been sin, my other wrongs would have far dwarfed that small one.

For I spent those last days with Ocilla contemplating a most monstrous sin.

I, Father Domingo Sanz de la Fuente, attest that the foregoing is a statement of actual events.

Chapter Twenty-three

Joe had rubbed his hands all over the wall that Faye said was hiding two terrified women and a child. He had removed and replaced picture frames. He had pulled a sofa away from the wall, checking behind it and every other stick of furniture. He had stood back and studied the wall and the crown molding above it and the baseboard where it met the floor. As best Joe could tell, it was all solid.

If someone had closed up a door in that wall, then it had been done right, by filling in the open frame, then plastering over it. This meant that the former nursery was completely inaccessible, unless someone had carved an opening in the concrete wall on its far side, opening into the room one door down from the owners' suite. Joe doubted it, but he was going to try to get in that room and check, just as soon as he was finished in here.

On the other hand, if someone had filled a frame in this wall with a hidden door that could be opened, then that had been an amazing job of masonry and carpentry.

After studying every square inch of that wall a second time, and again failing to find an opening, Joe had studied all the others, even the one with the window in it, trying to figure out where three human beings could possibly be hidden. Thwarted, he was now trying to choose his next step: search all the other rooms? Or roll up the carpet and study the floor in this one? Maybe there was a trap door leading to a secret passage that led into the old nursery...

Then he heard the click of a latch being released. Still focused on getting into the nursery, Joe whipped his head in the direction of the solid plaster wall, but there was no slowly opening secret door to be seen.

Then the door to the hallway, the non-mysterious door that Joe had just entered, began to swing open. Light on his feet and silent-moving in his soft-soled moccasins, Joe leapt to the wall, flattening himself behind the opening door.

Suzanne stepped through.

"Daniel said I could always have another baby, after I gave this one to Suzanne. He said it lots of times, like that should make me feel better," Glynis said. "And he said I was young and that nine months wasn't such a big piece of my life to give up, so that Suzanne could have my baby and be happy again."

"He's crazy, sweetheart," Magda said. "Don't listen to him."

Faye was only half-listening. She was assessing their options. They weren't getting out through those little holes where pipes had once run. They weren't getting out of the hole in the floor that went nowhere. Faye's eyeball calculations said that even if she stood on Magda's shoulders, and then Magda stood on Glynis' shoulders, they'd never reach the lowest of the maintenance doors above them.

Besides, Glynis could hardly be expected to hold anyone up, not with cracked ribs and a messed-up leg. The thought of big-bellied Faye supporting anyone else *or* balancing on top of a human pyramid was comical in a painful way.

One thing was clear—if they were going to get out of this place, they would be leaving through the door that brought them in. Faye had run her hands over the door and the wall around it, time and again, looking for a way to spring their trap. She'd found no openings except a tiny, metal-rimmed hole in the door about five feet from the floor.

It was a peephole, and it was probably the answer to Faye's question of how Daniel could be absolutely sure there was no one around before opening the door. Even the peephole was camouflaged with a small metal disk. Faye would bet money that the disk, smaller than her smallest fingernail, had a fool-the-eye woodgrain finish on the other side. She'd painted many a faux woodgrain in her day, reproducing the decorative paint finishes her home had boasted in its payday. A good artist could make that peephole practically invisible.

Faye looked around the room and didn't see anybody who could pour herself through a hole smaller than a dime, not even Rachel. It was a fair measure of her desperation that she even looked, but there was a solid reason for that desperation. Another horrifying facet of their situation had occurred to her.

When Magda went missing, Faye had been so sure that she knew where Daniel and Suzanne were holding her that she'd sent Joe running headlong into danger. He'd probably already burst into the very home of her kidnappers. They could be holding him at gunpoint right now. If he'd miraculously missed walking into that trap, then he was probably searching that apartment high and low for an entrance to a secret room housed in the old nursery…which certainly might exist, but Magda and Rachel weren't in there. Neither were Glynis and neither was Faye.

Not that Joe had any inkling that Faye was in trouble. And not that he had any inkling that she hadn't called the police, so the cavalry was not going to be topping the hill, with its bugles blowing and its flags flying. Unless Faye could find some secret latch to pry this door open, Joe was on his own. And he didn't know it.

She kept looking, but all she saw was a stout wooden door embedded seamlessly in a concrete wall, with no weakness but a tiny little peephole.

Stomping on his revulsion at the notion of manhandling a woman, Joe stepped from behind the door and had a hand over Suzanne's mouth and her arms pinned at her sides before she'd taken a breath. He used his foot to close the door quietly behind her.

"You're going to tell me where they are, and you're going to do it now. Quietly." He eased a hand from her mouth, ready to clamp down if she took a breath to scream.

She answered him, obediently quiet, but with a surprising fierceness. He should have known that a woman who had made a career as a trial attorney had not morphed completely into a meek thing with no thought beyond the beauty of her gardens and flower arrangements. She looked him in the eyes and hissed "Where who are? What are you talking about? Let me go!"

Suzanne seemed to have taken a self-defense class, because she launched into a sequence of moves that she'd obviously rehearsed. He could tell she was trying to stomp on his instep, drop into a crouch, shift his center of gravity over her leg, and shove him down, because he'd taught Faye to do the same thing.

Unfortunately, he'd known at the time that Faye was the size of a hummingbird. No amount of leveraging one's weight was going to do much good when one weighed a hundred pounds on a good day. And Suzanne was tall, but she wasn't any more muscular than Faye.

Joe was twice Suzanne's size. He had her pinned so thoroughly that she wasn't going anywhere, not an inch in any direction. He leaned down, preparing to state firmly and clearly that, until she agreed to free Magda, Glynis, and Rachel, his intentions were assuredly not good.

He pulled his hand from her face and said, "Keep talking. And whisper while you're doing it."

Her whisper was as intense as any shriek. "I knew it was you! You showed up here, and poor Glynis disappeared. And Lex… even Lex didn't deserve to have you slice his throat with…one of those." She shrank from the stone knife in Joe's hand and dissolved into sobs. "Please don't hurt me, too."

Joe had been poised on the balls of his feet, ready for action. At Suzanne's words, he rocked back onto his heels, needing a minute to process what he'd just heard. His grip slackened slightly, so she tried her self-defense sequence again, but the effort was as futile as it had been the first time.

Joe's intuitive nature told him that Suzanne was telling the truth, but he wasn't so foolish as to let her go.

"You're telling me that you didn't kidnap Glynis or kill Lex? What about your husband?"

She was shaking her head, refusing to speak, and he could see hysteria setting in. He closed his hands on her arms one degree tighter and gave her a single small shake. Joe had always known that he would stink as an interrogator, but he just didn't want to hurt this woman whose emotions had always seemed even frailer than her body. He would have to rely on the intimidation inherent in his sheer size. He leaned down, way down, and put his mouth next to her ear.

In a low, quiet voice, he murmured, "Where…are…Magda… and…Rachel?"

He was unprepared for the whipped-up frenzy that this question provoked in Suzanne. "Where are they?" she hissed. "What do you *mean* asking 'Where are they?' That little girl and her mother are in the back yard right now. The mother's working and the child is just…being a child. Aren't they?"

Joe's belief that Suzanne was telling the truth grew stronger. No actress was this good.

He watched her a moment, unsure that she could stand to hear the truth. Because if Faye was right, it was very likely that Suzanne's husband was the person who had interrupted Rachel in the act of just being a child.

"Aren't they?"

Suzanne's legs had collapsed under her, and Joe was now hefting her entire weight, which wasn't much.

She'd given up on whispering, no matter what Joe said. Her voice rose into a low, groaning monotone, and it seemed that she was talking to herself more than Joe. "Did someone take that mother and child? Did they take Glynis? Did somebody do to them what was done to Lex? Oh God, you can't let someone hurt that baby girl. *Oh…Annie.*"

Joe lowered Suzanne to the couch, where she curled into a tiny ball and wept, repeating the word, *"Annie… "* with every breath.

Joe wondered what he would do if Faye were ever in this much pain. He wouldn't kill someone, or harm them physically. He knew that. He wouldn't steal someone's child, or imprison anyone against their will. But he might be capable of almost anything else, if it would make Faye happy and whole again. Watching Suzanne's agony and remembering Daniel's devotion to her, Joe knew in his soul that Faye had been right.

Glynis and Magda had indeed been taken by someone who wanted a child enough to kill for one. Suzanne was the one with the crazy aunt, so Faye had leapt to the conclusion that she was insane enough to act on those urges. But having insanity in the family didn't necessarily make a person insane. And even a person with a Norman Rockwell family could be crazy as hell. Was that person Daniel?

Joe was good at asking himself these questions, but Faye was the one who was good at answering them.

Joe's intuition said that Daniel had taken Glynis and Magda, out of a twisted belief that stealing their children would salve his wife's pain. Now what? Joe needed to get Suzanne to tell him everything she knew, and he needed to get out of this apartment pronto, because Daniel did *not* need to know that anybody was onto him.

He helped Suzanne to her feet and said, "Ma'am, I hate to say this about your husband, but I'm not a hundred percent sure you're safe here. And I know I'm not. Let's go someplace where we can think…someplace where we can talk to somebody lots smarter than me. Let's go find Faye."

Suzanne went with him without arguing. Not, it seemed, because she agreed with him that her husband was a kidnapper and a killer, but because she'd dropped into an agony of grief that didn't let her argue.

In seconds, they were at the elevator, which moved so slowly that Joe thought it was lowering them a millimeter at a time, stopping frequently to decide whether they actually deserved to reach the first floor. If they could have taken the stairs without being seen by anyone in the atrium, he'd have thrown Suzanne over his shoulder and taken them three at the time. Traveling at Joe's top speed, they could have been down the street and in Victor's shack quicker than this damn elevator could lower them fifteen short feet.

But, finally, it finished its task and Joe guided Suzanne out of Dunkirk Manor, whispering words of comfort in her ear all the while.

He gave himself some words of comfort, as well.

Everything will be okay in just a minute. Faye will know what we need to do.

"What do you think he'll do?"

Glynis' voice was thready and weak. Perspiration was beading on her forehead and running through her once-glorious hair. The morning was passing and the angle of the sun shining through the windows above them was slowly changing. It was certainly warming up their prison cell, but not enough to account for the sweat flowing out of Glynis' elegant body. Faye laid her hand on her forehead again, checking for fever, but she just couldn't tell.

What would it do to a human body to be battered and menaced, then to be thrown on a cold prison floor? And how much worse would it be for a woman in the early stages of pregnancy?

Daniel had brought blankets into the cell to cushion Glynis where she lay, but Faye was sitting beside her on those blankets right now, and her own hipbones were digging into the hard concrete. This was not a fit bed for a woman who needed to heal. If a princess could feel a pea through a mountain of mattresses, then Glynis must be suffering terribly. And every breath disturbed her broken ribs. Days spent lying on this damp floor, taking one shallow breath after another to avoid that pain, might well have brought her to the brink of pneumonia.

"What do you think he'll do?" Glynis asked again. "After the baby comes, I mean."

The still air in the turret soaked up the terror in her words. Glynis had spent days in here, absorbing the idea that she would be here for nine months and then…what? How could Daniel possibly let her go? He would have to kill her, just like he killed Lex.

Glynis would find out her fate sooner than that. Faye would cease to be useful in just a month, when her own baby came. And Magda was useless now, except for the fact that her presence kept Rachel calm. When Glynis saw what happened to them, then she would know what was coming for her.

Faye was settling her mind into the horror of her situation. *A month in here. Childbirth without the help of a doctor. And then…*

She jerked herself off the edge of that precipice.

"Glynis, he comes every midnight? Right?"

The silvery head nodded.

"Does he come in? Or does he just shove your food through the door and leave?"

"He comes in. He takes out my…that thing…and brings me a fresh one." She nodded at a bedpan near her bed. It was early in the day and Glynis wasn't eating or drinking much, so it was still empty. Faye couldn't imagine what it took out of Glynis, in terms of pain and effort and humiliation, to make use of it.

Faye had been studiously avoiding the thought of bathroom necessities.

"On the second day, I tried to crawl around him and get through the door while it was still open. He grabbed me by the arm and just that little tug twisted my ribs. I screamed. I couldn't help myself. And I saw that the door was still open a bit and I thought the noise might get out. So I screamed and screamed, long after the door closed off the chance that somebody might hear. But the door closed and then he cried, because he saw that he'd hurt me."

"What a prince," Magda mumbled.

"He started thinking out loud about how maybe he should gag me, but that I'd have to wear the gag twenty-four hours a day, just to keep me quiet for those seconds that the door was opening and closing. He looked deep in my eyes and explained things to me."

As Glynis spoke, she stared high into the turret, where the ceiling should be. "Since it would hurt him to think of me bound and gagged around the clock, he was just going to start carrying a knife. 'Just so we understand each other,' he said, 'my first priority has got to be the baby. If you scream when I come through that door, I can't afford to kill you, but I *will* hurt you. Think about this rationally. There's nobody outside that door. Everyone is asleep on the far side of this big house. It's not possible for someone to hear you scream, but if you try, I will cut you. If you scream again, I'll do it again. Do you really want that?' Since then, he's always got a butcher knife in his hand when he comes here."

Faye thought of the hole in Lex's throat. However mildly Daniel had behaved in his role as Glynis' jailer, none of them needed to forget that the man's madness could cross the line into murderous violence. It had happened before. If they tried to escape and failed, then it could happen again.

Her eyes landed on Magda, sitting with her arms curled around her child. Faye, Glynis, Rachel—they all enjoyed some immunity from Daniel's madness, because they all gave Daniel the ability to give his wife the child she craved.

Magda, on the other hand…Faye figured that Daniel had only taken her so that Rachel would go quietly.

Magda was expendable.

Chapter Twenty-four

Joe looked Suzanne up and down and decided that the best way to escort her down the street was to simply walk very closely at her side. Throwing her over his shoulder would have attracted attention. Even guiding her with a hand on her waist ran the risk of looking inappropriate. If Suzanne decided to run, Joe knew that his long arms and lightning reflexes wouldn't fail him. But she didn't.

They walked to the end of the street, so slowly that it twanged Joe's nerves to a high-pitched hum, but they got there. Victor, sitting in his customary watchdog position at the window, rushed out to meet them, burbling words of welcome.

Joe cut him off. "I need to talk to Faye."

"Ah, Faye, she's so lovely. What a beautiful mother she will make—"

"Where is she?" Joe stood in the doorway of Victor's home, looking at its single empty room.

Victor's face was utterly vacant. There was no information there about Faye, no information about where she was, no information on whether she was okay, no information on whether she was even…

Joe reached out and grabbed Victor's shoulders. The urge to shake the truth out of the old man was so strong, but he remained in control. There was no one home behind Victor's sad eyes. Or, if there was anyone remaining in that feeble brain, there was only a little boy who could not be blamed for any looming disaster.

"Where is she?" Victor asked, but Joe couldn't tell whether he was asking the question or just echoing the last thing he'd heard.

Joe whipped his cell phone out of his pocket and dialed Overstreet. He said "Do you know where Faye is?" instead of saying hello.

The rising tones of Overstreet's questions mirrored Joe's skyrocketing worry.

The officer's first response was "No, I don't. *Should* I know where she is?"

His second response was, "What do you mean she dialed 911? From Dunkirk Manor? If there's trouble there and nobody's called me, there'll be hell to pay."

And his concerned tone reached its peak with "*Why* did she call 911? Faye wouldn't do that without a serious reason. And when did she call? Is anybody there yet?"

Time expanded and contracted for Joe. The first slow elevator ride. The search of the room where he'd thought he'd find Magda. The encounter with Suzanne. The second slow elevator ride down. The slow walk down the street. The interminable moment spent looking in Victor's eyes, knowing that the addled old man could do nothing to help him find the woman that he loved. The mother of his child…

He couldn't get his brain around how long any of these things had taken. He just didn't know.

"I don't know how long it's been since she called to report Magda missing. Fifteen minutes, easy. Maybe half an hour. Maybe more."

"Then nobody called 911, or they'd be there already. I'll double-check on my way over and I'll get the emergency vehicles over there. Now."

"No. Wait."

Joe wished for Faye to be here, with her sober and flawless logic. But she was not. All Joe had on his side was his own hunter's intuition.

Joe knew predators. He knew how their minds worked. It was time to put that knowledge to work.

Mary Anna Evans

"Maybe we don't want a bunch of sirens surrounding the house just yet. Not until we know where Faye is. And the other women. Faye has to be in Dunkirk Manor, or on the grounds somewhere. Unless she got out the front door and someone kidnapped her on the street." He refused to voice the possibility that she had gone over the garden wall and into the river. He clung to the hope that, in mid-morning, someone would have seen it happening and stopped it.

Joe looked at Victor, who shook his head. "No cars on the street this morning except the cook and maids coming to work. They drove into the parking lot. Nobody's came out of the house at all. Nobody's drove away." His ancient vocal cords gave the words a shrieking, grinding sound, like failing brakes on a collision-bound car.

"Then Faye's still in the house. Magda and Rachel are still in there, too," Joe said.

"Considering how much time Victor spends looking down this street," Overstreet offered, "Glynis is more than likely still in there, too."

Joe turned to Victor. "You never saw her leave, did you?"

Victor shook his head hard.

"We can't go in that house looking for them until we've got Daniel under control." Joe found that he was thinking of Daniel as he would think of a mother bear, who might turn and make a stand before letting anyone take her cubs.

"We don't want to scare him into hurting them, or holing up with them in whatever secret places he's got them hidden."

"Exactly."

"Joe," Overstreet said. "Are you absolutely sure Daniel did this? We don't have many other plausible in-house suspects, but there are the two men who work for you. And the household staff. And the guests. We need to get them all out of the house, not just Daniel. Ask Suzanne where they keep their evacuation plan."

Joe asked her.

"There's a copy in my desk. Another posted by the kitchen door and by the emergency exits in the guest wing."

Joe felt the plan unfold in his head. As it did, he told Overstreet how things were going to go. If this irritated the policeman's professional sensibilities, then that was just too bad.

"Okay, here's how we do this. You get your people in place, but don't let Daniel know. He could take hostages. He's already *got* hostages. We have to get him out of the house before he takes more, and we need people with rifles hidden all around the house in case we don't manage it. But he can't know they're there."

"Agreed."

"You and I can go into the house, because we have an excuse to be there. But nobody else. We don't want to tip him off."

"Also agreed."

Victor had shyly taken Suzanne by the hand and taken her into a corner of the room to look at his collection of silver dimes. Joe was okay with this, because he was standing between them and the door, but he kept an eye on them both.

At the same time, he was still spinning his plan for Overstreet to hear. "Next, we get Daniel away from everybody else and out of there, before he has a chance to disappear to wherever he has the women hidden. Can you ask him to go with you to the station or something like that?"

"I'll tell him that we've...um...constructed a timeline of Glynis' activities during the week before she was taken. I'll say that, as her employer, we need him to come downtown to check it over and see whether he thinks it's accurate."

"That'll work. Once he's gone, I guess I'll pull the fire alarm and get everyone else out of the house. If he gives us any trouble, well...we have the snipers. And the women will be out of his reach, once he's outside. Then we can search the place from top to bottom. If you people at the police department can get hold of some equipment that can detect secret rooms, it would help. I don't know...x-ray, maybe..."

"No." Suzanne looked up from Victor's coin collection. "Nobody's pulling the fire alarm and throwing my guests into a panic. I'll tell the staff that we're doing a fire drill. They'll get everyone out of the house and gather them up so that we'll know exactly where they all are, but they'll be very clear that it's just a drill. I'm not willing to risk the safety of my guests, not when there's a way to get them out of the house that's just as efficient as your way. A lot of them are old. They'll get hurt or have heart attacks or…no. I'm not willing to risk anyone else's safety because of what my husband has done."

Joe looked at the slim woman. The events of the morning had left her swaying on her feet. This actually wasn't a bad plan, but could she be trusted? Was she stable enough to do this, and had she really been so easily convinced of Daniel's guilt? Was she willing to lay a trap for her own husband?

She saw the concern on his face, and she answered him. "I've known something was wrong with Daniel all week. I've blamed it on worry over Glynis, but something just wasn't right—something deep and ugly that he couldn't tell me about. There's always been a part of Daniel that I couldn't reach. Since Annie…that part has nearly taken him over."

She looked at Joe and read his doubts. "We've been married twenty-seven years," she said as if that explained everything.

Joe had been married a year, and that was long enough for him to know the depth of the marriage bond. The part of him that knew when Faye had a headache, before she said so, believed that Suzanne had sensed Daniel's deception.

"His response to Glynis' disappearance has been just… wrong," she said. "He's ordinarily a very protective man, very concerned about women, but he's been very brisk and business-like about this, until I cry. Then he freaks out, saying 'She's fine, baby, she's fine. I just know it. You can't tear yourself up this way.'"

She looked at Joe and Victor as if she'd just offered inarguable proof. Joe was trying to think of a nice way to ask her to be more convincing.

Again, she saw his doubts, so she tried. "It's like someone took my husband and put someone else in his bed…in his body. He paces. He hovers over me and asks if I'm okay about twelve times a day. He's taken a midnight walk every night since Glynis has been gone. He never does that."

Joe thought the midnight walk was marginally more convincing evidence. Daniel had to visit Glynis sometime, to take her food and water and make sure she was okay.

Suzanne seemed to sense that she was making better headway with Joe by giving him documentable facts instead of feelings, so she plunged ahead. "The maids told me yesterday that several blankets have gone missing."

Joe nodded. Blankets could be counted and Glynis needed something to sleep under. This was a reasonable clue for Suzanne to hang her suspicions on.

Then she returned to the realm of intuition, but she went to a particularly bone-chilling part of that realm. "The day after Glynis disappeared, Daniel started telling me that he thinks maybe we can adopt after all, even though we gave up on that years ago. 'I just feel in my heart that we can get a newborn. And maybe a brother or sister, too…an older child, instead of an infant,' he said."

So he'd had his eye on Rachel for days.

"Other times, it's something like, 'It would probably be easier to get a baby who wasn't white…biracial, maybe.'"

The man had been calmly discussing the kidnapping of his child. Faye's child. Joe felt his heart turn to iron.

"It all adds up." Suzanne squared her thin shoulders. "I know Daniel. Sometimes I know him better than I know myself. I believe I know what he has done. I care deeply for Glynis and we have to do whatever it takes to find her. And Faye. And that poor little girl and her mother. Let's stop wasting time and just do it."

It had taken the better part of an hour for Glynis, drifting in and out of consciousness, to tell Faye and Magda about Daniel's creative methods to keep her captive and alive. Or at least Faye thought it had been an hour.

Time didn't mean very much in the dim light of Dunkirk Manor's tiny prison. It was possible that the angle of light coming through the tiny windows high at the top of the turret had changed, but Faye couldn't tell. She couldn't even bring herself to care much, and this worried her. Curiosity and attention to detail had saved her life in the past, and she couldn't let them fail her now.

"He brings food and water in a brown paper grocery bag. There's always one plate of hot food—leftovers that he warmed up in the kitchen—and a bunch of protein bars. Lots and lots of vitamins in protein bars…" Her voice took on a mocking edge. "He's very concerned about my health. Since I'm making his baby and all. See the medicine bottles over there? Prenatal vitamins, plus an extra bottle of Vitamin D. Because he knows I'm sure as hell not getting any sunshine in here."

Faye was actually glad to hear the anger in Glynis' voice. They were all going to need some fight in them today. Because Faye did not intend to sit here for a month, eating protein bars and waiting to have her baby, so she could die.

Glynis wrapped her arms even tighter around herself and clenched her fists harder. Faye wouldn't have thought that possible. "How many nights have I been here?"

"You were taken on Tuesday morning," Faye said. "It's Saturday morning now."

"So that's four nights." Glynis looked like she was trying to remember a series of nights that had all been the same, trying to count them and make them her own. "He brings a fresh bucket of water every night, so I can wash my face and hands, and he leaves it, so I can have a wet cloth to help keep me cool in the daytime. It takes him two trips—in with the bag of food and maybe some blankets or whatever. Then out with the bedpan. And then back in with the clean bedpan and the bucket of water."

Faye was thinking, and she was very glad that her brain had returned. Tonight, there would be two able-bodied women waiting for Daniel…well, one able-bodied woman and Faye.

"A little at a time, he keeps bringing me stuff to make this place liveable. A couple of nights, it was blankets and towels and a pillow to fluff up my bed. One night he brought me some books." Glynis pointed to a stack of paperback novels that probably came out of the bed-and-breakfast's library. "Today, he brought an iPod, loaded it with this week's Top 40." A wry smile peeked through. "I like metal. Suzanne would have known that. That's why I think she has no idea what he's done."

"That's useful information. Not sure what we can do with it, but it's good to know that he's working alone." Magda patted the sleeping Rachel's head. "I suspected it already, though. A woman would have done a better job of making this cell homelike for the mother of her child. Suzanne's so domesticated that she would've been knitting you some doilies for this charming little apartment."

"I'm so glad…no, relieved…that Suzanne didn't do this to me." Glynis reached up a hand to twiddle with her hair. "She's been almost like a mother since I came to work for her. I was so little when Mom died. I'm worried about Suzanne. She's sleeping beside a crazy man who's capable of…well, look around you."

Faye didn't want to look around her. She wanted to come up with a plan to get all four of them out of this hellhole.

"Okay, ladies," she said. "We've got a jailer who's not very good at his job. If Glynis could get up and walk, she'd have already figured out a way to get out that door when he leaves to get his second load of stuff."

Magda nodded. Faye could tell that she'd already come to the same conclusion.

"We outnumber him. If he had any good sense, he'd have tied us up. If he *has* any good sense, he's already worried about that critical moment when he opens that door for the first time tonight. What will we have in store for him? But we know he's unbalanced, and he might have convinced himself that we're all happy to stay in this cell and make babies for him. I say that Magda and I position ourselves on either side of the door, ready to rush him when he comes back. It could work. What's the worst that could happen?"

Nobody answered, but all three women remembered the butcher knife.

◇◇◇

Joe had fled, leaving Suzanne in the relative safety of Victor's little house. Overstreet had wanted him to wait there until he arrived, but Joe couldn't make himself waste even those few minutes. Suzanne was critical to their plan, so Joe told Overstreet to pick her up at Victor's and meet him in Dunkirk Manor's back garden. The garden shed had been bothering him ever since Glynis disappeared. Ever since Daniel had inexplicably locked it. He needed to search the shed one more time for clues, and he desperately needed to see whether Faye was in there.

Joe went straight to his and Faye's corporate toolbox in the back garden of Dunkirk Manor and grabbed some boltcutters. Overstreet might need a search warrant to search the shed, but Joe just needed the right tools.

One snip, and the padlock was gone. Joe let his eyes adjust to the dim light in the shed. He saw that Faye was not there, and his heart broke.

He assessed the size of the space. It looked right. So there was no secret room in the shed where his wife could be hidden.

The sprinkler system controls on the wall mocked him. Those sprinklers had obliterated Lex's killer's trail. Daniel's trail. Realizing that Daniel knew full well where the controls were, Joe wondered whether anyone had thought to ask the gardener about the irrigation schedule. Maybe it hadn't been a coincidence that the killer's trail was washed away. Maybe Daniel had simply stepped in here after disposing of Lex's body and turned on the water.

Daniel had certainly locked this shed on the evening Glynis was kidnapped, after the police searched it, and it had been locked ever since. Why? The police had found nothing.

Was Daniel moving Glynis from place to place? That seemed dangerous and unnecessary. Maybe there was some other reason for the lock. Maybe there was something in here worth finding…

His eye rested on a towel-sized piece of blue tarpauline, wrapped around a pipe leading away from the sprinkler system. Lex's body had been wrapped in a blue tarp.

Joe's eyes scanned the shelves and saw a stack of multicolored towels, and another stack of drab brown coveralls. The colorful towels stood out in the drab, dirt-floored space. If a tarp—a full-sized, bright-blue tarp—had been folded and stored on one of those shelves, it would have shone like a beacon. The absence of that bright blue object would only be obvious to someone who expected it to be there.

Suzanne clearly had spent a lot of time in this shed over the years, arranging flowers and potting plants. Did Daniel decide she needed to stop those visits, because something had changed and he knew she would notice?

And maybe there had been other subtle changes. Maybe the pile of greenery in the middle of the shed had been moved or spread out to cover something suspicious, like the slightly bloodied spot where a murdered man was wrapped in a tarp before being dumped in a river.

Joe had killed a lot of animals. It's not that easy to drive the life from a large, strong being. Lex's injuries had included a terrible throat wound and a head wound that was significant but not lethal. He was confident, based on the smear of blood on its surface, that the broken celt had delivered the wound to Lex's head.

The killer had left that celt at the scene. Daniel. Daniel had left it at the scene. Was there something else he needed to hide? Why was Daniel limiting access to this shed?

Joe pictured Lex, unconscious on the ground, as Daniel cast the celt aside. Or Glynis. Maybe she'd struck back at a bullying Lex with the broken celt and then dropped it as Daniel happened on the scene. That might explain why Daniel hadn't hidden that weapon—he'd never used it.

No matter who dealt the blow to Lex's head, seconds would have passed. Maybe a minute. And still Lex was not dead. Unconscious, but not dead. Panicked, maybe Daniel had picked up something sharp and precise to deliver the killing blow. This was the bloodletting that had left a great amount of B-positive blood soaked into the parking lot's soil.

No physical evidence that Overstreet's investigators had found at the scene explained the throat wound. Where was that weapon?

Perhaps it had left the scene with Daniel and his victim. Daniel was aging, but he was tall and still strong, and he retained a bit of the light grace of a tennis player. He could have hauled Lex's body to its feet, bent forward, and carried him on his back, arms over his shoulders and feet dragging on the ground. It would have looked like a scene from an Old West movie, where a cowpoke was dragging his dead friend from the range, but who would have seen it? The route from the parking lot to the garden shed wasn't visible from the street or the guest wing or the service wing or the kitchen or the dining room.

What would Daniel have done about the blood? Surely he would have gotten blood on his clothes.

The brown jumpsuits on the shed's shelves gave him that answer. So did the garden hose and the drain in the floor where Suzanne repotted and watered her plants.

If Daniel had been lucky enough not to be seen by an arriving employee, he could have gotten Lex to the shed and wrapped him in a tarp to contain the blood. Most of the back garden wasn't visible to people inside the house. Presuming Daniel moved quickly, he could have loaded the body on a garden cart and dumped it over the rear garden wall within a few minutes. It was only an okay hiding place, but the tide was with him. The shifting waters of the Matanzas River had taken Lex Tifton off his hands.

He would have needed to hose himself down and get rid of the wet clothes. Probably he did that before dumping the body, throwing them over the wall where the river had taken them. Did he do the same thing with the murder weapon? Probably.

But what if he forgot? Overstreet's people hadn't found a murder weapon on the river bank or wrapped up in the tarp with Lex's corpse. Joe needed to remember that Daniel was not a hardened criminal. He had almost certainly made some mistakes.

Overstreet had said that his techs had found traces of something that might or might not be blood on the shed floor, but only traces. That tracked with the notion that the body had been wrapped in a tarp that captured most of the trace evidence. What other evidence might remain?

Joe's eyes alit on the pile of landscaping rock. The first weapon, the broken celt, was made of rock. Maybe the second weapon, the sharp object that had destroyed Lex's throat, had been made of rock, too.

He studied the rocks for color and shape and surface texture. They were mostly limestone, chalky and mottled gray. He turned the rocks over one by one. None of them looked dangerous. None of them seemed to have a history of murder. And then, hiding beneath a large chunk of limestone, he found a smaller piece of brown rock that was smooth and honed to a fine edge.

Joe lifted the big chunk of limestone from the rock pile, so he could get a better look at the sharp rock beneath it. He refrained from touching it, because he recognized it for what it was: a murder weapon. It was a chunk of flint with a vicious point, and he would bet money that its fracture plane would mate with the broken end of the stone blade that Glynis had wanted to show Faye.

If Suzanne had harbored any doubts of her husband's guilt, this cold piece of rock should ease her mind. This was good, because they needed her cooperation if their plan to get Daniel out of the house before he could harm his hostages was to succeed.

Joe backed out of the shed, just in time to see Suzanne and Overstreet approach. He gestured for them to come in the shed and see what he'd found.

As soon as Overstreet had all his officers in place, they were going in. Joe intended to have Faye and Magda and Rachel and Glynis out of that place before Daniel knew what hit him. It was time.

◇◇◇

Faye stirred from her somnolence. How long had it been since someone spoke?

She'd been thinking through their plan. She was positioned by the door's hinges and Magda was waiting on the side that opened. Magda would be calling the shots on the timing of their attack, based on whether she thought she could get control of the knife.

Options for weapons of their own were slim. She and Magda had busted open a water bottle and crafted the sharpest shards of plastic that they could manage. They had pulled the pillowcase from Glynis' pillow, and Magda waited with the pillowcase in hand. If she could manage it while avoiding the knife, she would drop the pillowcase over Daniel's head and kick him hard in the groin, hoping to immobilize him long enough so that she and Faye could get Glynis and Rachel out. Faye, hiding behind the door, would help her restrain him in any way she could.

This was the weak part of the plan, because moving Glynis was not going to happen quickly. The best way seemed to be for Faye and Magda to each grab a corner of the pile of blankets where she lay and simply tug. If the door could be kept open and if Daniel could be eliminated as a threat, then they could haul the princess out of her tower on a litter of blankets and towels.

The effort of this might throw Faye into labor, but if having her baby a month early in the safety of a hospital was the worst outcome of this predicament, she could live with that.

There was an alternative plan, and Faye wasn't sure that she didn't like it better. If Magda judged that she couldn't control that knife, then Daniel would be allowed to make his first visit as usual. Faye hoped that he would be lulled into security by their apparent docility. But as the door closed behind him, Magda would surreptitiously position a water bottle cap in the frame of the closing door. If Daniel were sufficiently preoccupied by transporting the bedpan, then maybe he wouldn't notice the door fail to close completely. After waiting a minute to let him go someplace to empty the bedpan, then Magda might be able to get a grip on the slightly open door and pull it toward her. If she could tug it open, they'd make a rush for freedom.

This plan required Daniel to overlook the fact that the door was slightly ajar but, otherwise, Faye liked it a lot.

Faye's eye fell on Rachel. Here was the fatal flaw in any plan they might make. If Daniel grabbed Rachel, then they would surrender immediately, no questions asked. And he knew this.

With Rachel's safety in mind, the little trapdoor in the floor that led exactly nowhere…this little trapdoor began to look very different. Faye knelt beside it and lifted the door.

She squinted at the hole and she squinted at Rachel. Yes. The child would fit, with a little room to spare for comfort.

"Rachel! I've found you a playhouse!"

The child toddled over and Magda stirred, fixing a "What in the hell are you up to?" stare on Faye.

"Let's see if it's big enough for you. You're getting to be such a very big girl."

Rachel had grown so much, and Faye had grown so much in a different way, that she could hardly lift the child. Little feet dragged the concrete floor as Faye moved Rachel to the little pit and lowered her in.

Perfect. When seated, Rachel's head was several inches below the trapdoor. There were inches of clearance around her in all directions, so she didn't look cramped. The concrete floor, however, looked hard and Faye needed Rachel to be comfortable in this hole for an indefinite period of time.

"Glynis, do you need both those pillows? Could I borrow one for Rachel?"

"Of course you can." Glynis lifted her head, so that Faye could take her pick.

Faye left the bed pillow for Glynis—she'd already taken the pillowcase from it—and reached for the square sofa pillow that was just the size to wedge into this hole. Its cover had a Moorish design carefully chosen to blend with Allyce Dunkirk's exotic Jazz Age décor. Faye lifted Rachel out of the hole and jammed the pillow down into its bottom.

"Look! It's like Aladdin's magic carpet, Rachel."

The little girl clapped her hands and crowed, "Want to get back in my playhouse, Auntie Faye!"

Faye locked eyes with Magda and they both smiled. This plan—convincing a three-year-old that she *wanted* to hide in a dark pit for an extended period of time—was ridiculous. But if it worked, Rachel could be invisible and safe while they launched their jailbreak. There was nothing more important than taking care of the child in this room. Children. Faye and Glynis needed to take care of their children, too.

That task wasn't going to be nearly as easy as making Rachel think that her dank pit was a fabulous playhouse.

Chapter Twenty-five

More time had crawled past. Faye didn't know how much.

She'd shown Rachel the trapdoor and told her it was her playhouse's "roof."

"Put my roof on, Auntie Faye!"

Faye had said, "Let me ask Mommy's permission."

Armed with Magda's maternal experience, they had slowly dropped the trapdoor, then raised it quickly, despite Rachel's pleas for them to leave it closed.

"Mommy likes to look at you, honey. We'll just close it now and then."

And they had, for increasing periods of time. Rachel had been in ecstasy over this new game.

During periods when the door was open, the women had scoured the room for objects that could pass for toys. An empty water bottle and its cap. Protein bar wrappers made of a glittery foil that Rachel loved to shred and toss like confetti. The cough drops out of Faye's sweatpants pocket, which Rachel had happily sucked on while shredding their wrappers. The paperback thriller that occupied her for a solid fifteen minutes while she removed its pages one by one, then admired its lurid cover.

Oh, how Faye wished she'd grabbed her cell phone and stuffed it in her pocket when she'd rushed to Magda's room that morning. Granted, there was no reason to expect that it would work here, when it hadn't worked in any other part of the house. But it would have amused her to burn up the battery trying. After that, it would have amused Rachel to open it and close it and poke its worthless buttons. Instead, Rachel had to be satisfied with shredding stuff and demanding that Faye lower her "roof."

It was critical that Rachel be in her hole and out of sight when Daniel arrived, but no one knew when that would be. Glynis was of the generation who used their cell phones for timepieces, so she wore no watch. Her cell phone had been abandoned on the floorboard of her car, leaving her floating free in time for her entire period of captivity. She couldn't tell them when to expect Daniel, other than to say that it was late at night.

The group could, however, infer when he might come. All three women knew the schedule at Dunkirk Manor. Guests came and went freely through the house, starting at breakfast time and continuing until the front door was locked at eleven p.m. There was certainly no curfew, which would have been ridiculous for any business hoping to attract tourists, but guests were told to use the door on their wing after eleven.

The front door stayed locked until six a.m., when the cook and maids arrived at work. So it was altogether likely Daniel made his nightly visits to Glynis beween the hours of eleven p.m. and six a.m.—more likely between midnight and five, to allow a safety margin in case there might be stragglers or early birds about.

Pinpointing that window of time wasn't necessarily a simple matter. Faye's watch was on her nightstand with her cell phone, because she had been interrupted in the act of working in her bedroom on a Saturday morning.

Magda, too, had been interrupted while going about her morning chores, so she had no watch, either.

Rachel, however, was sporting a vintage-design Minnie Mouse watch, a going-away gift from her doting father. The thought of Sheriff Mike's suffering when he learned that his wife and child were missing made Faye want to curl up in a ball. She'd made a pact with herself not to even imagine Joe's reaction to the same news.

So Faye's plan was to entertain Rachel, both in and out of her playhouse, until Minnie's hour hand pointed to eleven. Then she planned to plunk the child into her hiding place, with the roof firmly closed. She'd likely go to sleep there, which would be a very good thing.

In the meantime, Faye and Rachel could practice a very important game. When Faye said "Now!", Rachel crawled into her hole and Faye shut the lid. Then Rachel waited, quietly and patiently, for Faye to say, "Rachel…go!"

At this signal, the child stood, pushing the trap door open with her own little head. She crawled out of the hole. This was easier after Faye folded up a couple of towels to serve as a step-stool. Once out, she ran at top speed for the door.

"If I ever say, 'Rachel…go!' and you see that the door's open," Faye had instructed, "then you run through it and you keep running. Don't stop for anybody but me or Mommy or Daddy or Uncle Joe. Or Detective Overstreet. You can go to him or any of his police friends. Then you tell them to call 911 and send someone to get Mommy and Auntie Faye and their friend Glynis."

Faye was optimistic that she and Magda could occupy Daniel long enough for Rachel to make a run for it, even if they couldn't get themselves out. Unfortunately, she knew that there was no way in hell that Rachel could open the massive front door of Dunkirk Manor. So she instructed the child to run as hard as she could for the guest wing. She wasn't to let anybody there come near her. She was simply to keep running down the wing, hollering, "Mommy said to call 911!" and right out the back door.

It was hard to believe that Rachel might get this far without being recaptured or rescued, but Faye covered all the bases. If the little girl actually escaped the house, she was to find the sidewalk in front of the house and run toward town, urging everyone she saw to call 911.

Rachel looked happy, leaning against the wall of her pit and hugging her knees.

"Want a story, Auntie Faye! Or a song!"

Good. Rachel was giving her the option of singing something mindless, instead of forcing Faye to rack her brain for an acceptable story. Looking down at Rachel in her pit, Faye found her mind circling biblical stories.

Young Daniel in the lion's den.

Young Joseph, thrown into a hole by his brothers and left for dead.

A song. It would be much better to sing a song. But which one?

A song from long-ago Sunday School classes bubbled to the top. Slavery was hardly more cheerful than stories of trapped children waiting for death, but at least the story of Moses and the children of Israel ended well. Unless you were a firstborn Egyptian…

Go down, Moses,
Way down in Egypt land.
Tell old Pharoah
To let my people go!

Every time Faye reached down and bellowed out the low notes, "Let my *peo*-ple *go*!", Rachel laughed hysterically. Maniacally, actually. So Faye, who knew an awful lot about three-year-olds for someone who had reached forty without reproducing, sang it again and again. And again.

"Hey," Magda murmured in a discouraged monotone that worried Faye. "If you even sing one note of 'Swing Low, Sweet Chariot,' I promise you I'm gonna slit my wrists with this broken piece of water bottle."

Faye just nodded as she reached down into the baritone range and once again belted "Let my *people…GO!!!!*"

But the song didn't take up every cell in her brain. It left space for another sad story about people with no place to go and nowhere to hide.

From the journal of Father Domingo Sanz de la Fuente

Translated from the Spanish by
Faye Longchamp Mantooth, Ph.D.,
and Magda Stockard-McKenzie, Ph.D.

When the first of the pox erupted on my Ocilla's face, I called the village's men to me.

A span of ten days had passed while I waited to know her fate, time enough for me to ask myself why Father Esteban would have done this. The Timucua were valued for their labor. The colony at St. Augustine would not have survived without the food the natives produced at the missions springing up across the countryside. If the pox gained a foothold here, it would spread to other villages and to the missions. Why would a man of God deprive St. Augustine and its cathedral of desperately needed supplies?

There could only be one reason. Father Esteban had revealed himself when he told Ocilla to bring me to him. Spain and the Church may not have come to collect payment for my crimes, but Father Esteban had chosen to collect it for them. This murder of countless innocents was calculated to be a heretic priest's punishment. In a single stroke, it would also eradicate those natives tainted by association with that heretic priest.

The pocked scars on my face had told Father Esteban that this disease would not touch me. Perhaps that knowledge figured into his decision on which pestilence to send. It would have been a mercy to send a plague that would carry me away with Ocilla and her people. My enemy is not a merciful man.

In the days I waited for the pox that I knew would come, I told our warriors what man had sent it and where he could be found, but I waited until I knew beyond doubt what Father Esteban had done before I told them when to strike. When the fever seized Ocilla and she lay shivering on her mat, I told them.

I told them that their enemy was a priest of Our Lord God, just as I am. He came from Europe in a tall ship, just as I did. He was born and educated there, just as I was. And he lives his life according to the same discipline.

They looked at me, still questioning. They still needed for me to tell them when to strike.

Asking God's forgiveness for a sin I knew to be unpardonable, I asked them if they had not seen me deep in prayer in the mornings and in the evenings and before taking my meals.

They had. Still, they did not take my meaning.

Looking them each in the eye, one by one, I told them that our enemy would also be praying at those same times. Understanding dawned on their faces. They should slay the man who sent them the pox while he was intent on communing with the Most Holy Lord.

I sent them to murder a man of God while he was deep in prayer. I did this, not because I was unwilling to kill him myself, but only because I was old and because I did not know how. When a man lives an entire life as a man of peace, he never gains the ability to make holy war when such a war is justified. So I sent my flock to avenge a lifetime of outrage. Then I went into my house and bade farewell to the only person in this new world who has loved me.

May God have mercy on her soul. And on mine.

I, Father Domingo Sanz de la Fuente, attest that the foregoing is a statement of actual events.

Chapter Twenty-six

Joe Wolf Mantooth had walked from Oklahoma to the Appalachians alone before he was twenty, tracing the Trail of Tears and pondering the big questions in life. He had decided that there were three.

What are you going to do?

Who are you going to love?

And what are you going to do to make God happy that you spent time here on Earth?

He'd spent some time in North Carolina after that epic walk. He had apprenticed himself to a master flintknapper and he'd learned that he was very, very good at making stone tools in the ancient way, but this didn't seem like a good answer to the question of making God happy. It didn't even seem to be a very good way of making a living, so he'd still been stuck on that first question of what he was going to do. And the issue of who he was going to love had been an open question.

Then he'd wandered for awhile and found himself in Florida, with no possessions to his name but a john boat and a tent. Praise God that Faye lived on an island. He'd dragged his boat ashore there, pitched a tent someplace where he thought no one would notice him, and was forever blessed to have been wrong about that.

Faye had found him. She'd let him stay. She'd befriended him and nagged him into working on his education. This had answered the first big question of what he was going to do with his life. In the archaeological world, he was finding that there were actually a lot of people who thought his archaic skills were valuable.

Then after years of his loving her without the first notion that she even noticed, she'd found herself loving him back. It had taken a bullet through each of their bodies to get them to this point, but Joe would happily let himself be shot again if that's what it took to keep Faye in his life.

And now they were going to have a child, and Joe was sure that taking care of Faye and their baby was the one certain thing that would make God glad he was alive.

Faye had answered all his questions for him, without asking anything in return, nothing but his love. She only needed one thing from him right now. She needed him to find her.

Overstreet had men with rifles on boats in the river, ready to scale the garden wall at his signal. He had men on the street, too. They were as unobtrusive as they could be on a street where traffic was rare and where unfamiliar cars parked on the street were rarer. A hostage negotiator was standing by.

The thought of a hostage negotiator bargaining for Faye's life made Joe retch.

Overstreet had accomplished all of this in an astonishingly short period of time. The sun was high overhead as Joe and the police officer wiped their feet on the welcome mat and prepared to enter Dunkirk Manor. If Joe had been alone, he would have strolled right in, since Dunkirk Manor was his temporary home. It *was* Suzanne's home, but it would have looked funny for her to walk in with Joe and Overstreet, so she'd gone around back to enter through the kitchen door. Since Overstreet's excuse for coming was to ask Daniel some official questions, then he couldn't stroll right in. Instead, he reached out and rang the doorbell.

Dunkirk Manor's doorbell was somber and expensive-sounding, which was hardly surprising. It echoed for a long time. Joe stood there and listened to it, and he thought that no sound in the world could have done a better job of reminding him of the soul-chilling reality of his mission.

Get Faye. Get Rachel. Get Magda. Get Glynis.
Bring them out safe. Bring them out alive.

Faye had developed a fascination with the peephole in their prison door. It was hard to imagine much sound seeping through its glass barrier, but the peephole still represented the weakest point in their prison. If she pulled the metal cover back, there would be nothing but glass between her and anyone in the entry hall. More accurately, the peephole was two lenses of glass separated by air, which would be a pretty darn good sound barrier, but it was better than trying to shout through the solid concrete wall.

If she put her mouth next to the glass and screamed when there was someone in the entry hall, was it remotely possible that she could be heard?

The peephole had a wide-angle lens, giving her a decent view of most of the entry hall. No one was there.

Of course they weren't. The entry hall was almost never used. But sometimes…

New guests sometimes came in the front door. Other guests sometimes wandered through this room like tourists. Sometimes, Harriet brought her ghost tours into this very room. Faye decided to stand here by the peephole and watch for passers-by. Then she could test the theory that her screams might be audible through this little chink in their prison's armor.

Out of sheer nervousness, she started twiddling with the metal lens cover. It made a slight metal-grinding sound as it slid across the lens, ending with a metal-on-metal clink.

That clink made Faye stand up straight. She slid the cover open again, then closed it. *Clink.*

She had heard that sound before.

Methodically, she slid the disk back, then slid it closed, over and over. Was it possible that this little noise could be heard in the entry hall?

It was more than possible. Faye had heard it, just as she heard the secret door slide open…just before Daniel stepped out of this very room and grabbed her.

She put her face close to the peephole, hoping that she'd see even a shadow that would tell her someone was out there. Then she started opening and closing the peephole, over and over again.

Grind. Click. Grind.
Grind. Click. Grind.

As Faye repeated the sound, again and again, monotonously and continuously, Magda opened her eyes and turned them in the direction of the noise. Her expression spoke of either murder or suicide.

Faye waved away Magda's irritation. "This sound can be heard out there. I *know* it can. So I'm going to keep making it until somebody hears me. If you can't stand it, then try singing Rachel a song. Your caterwauling might drown out this noise."

"You don't like my singing?"

"Nobody likes your singing. Your own child doesn't like your singing."

A voice wafted out of the hole in the floor. "I don't, Mommy. Really."

Magda launched into "The Eensy Weensy Spider," anyway. Faye felt sorry for Glynis as she lay in the floor, knowing that she would spend her fifth day in captivity listening to out-of-tune nursery rhymes and a crazy-making string of mechanical noises.

A ripple, a vibration, an echo. Faye felt it coming through the peephole. She felt it as much on the skin of her hands and face as she did with her ears.

A bell. A chime.

Was the grandfather clock ringing a new quarter-hour? Were all the other clocks in the house chiming in?

Or had somebody just rung the doorbell?

Faye ramped up her assault on the peephole cover. She slid it back and forth, clicking it hard when it reached the limit of its range of motion, then twisting it back and trying again.

She was going to *make* somebody hear this thing.

It occurred to her that Daniel might be the someone who heard, and it might bring him into their prison before his regular midnight visit. They needed to be prepared for this possibility. "Magda. I hear something. Close Rachel's roof. Drag Glynis over here close to the door. And get in your position."

Glynis cried out when Magda lifted both corners of her makeshift bed and tugged. Without Faye's help, she wasn't strong enough to move the wounded woman gently. She could only lean back with all her weight and pull hard. Faye wished that she believed it possible that anyone outside could hear Glynis scream.

Grind. Click.

Faye called out for help in the only way she knew, by making a little tiny noise, over and over.

Daniel didn't so much hear the clicking. It was more that he felt it.

Someone was at the door. It made him nervous to usher them past the place where the three women waited with his children, but it shouldn't be a problem. There was no way anyone could hear them scream.

But the metallic clicking penetrated their prison walls just enough to rattle him.

He needed to answer the doorbell. His guests might just barge in, if he left them out there too long.

Would they hear the clicking? Would they write it off to the ticking grandfather clock? Would they comment on it to him? Would they mention it to anyone else?

He knew the anxiety showed on his face, but he had no choice. He pulled open the front door and said, loudly and brightly, "Welcome to Dunkirk Manor!" Then he kept talking—prattling, actually—saying anything that crossed his mind, just to cover the barely discernible noise. He reached in his pocket and began fiddling with his loose change, in hopes that the metallic clinks would mask the tiny noise his captives were making.

And he began weighing his options.

He had too many prisoners. Magda would have to go. And, regrettable though it was, the other two women would need to be bound and gagged until he had their babies in hand. Then he and Suzanne could take her family fortune and flee to some foreign country where no one asked questions and where the American dollar still went a long, long way.

The echo of Dunkirk Manor's doorbell rang in Joe's ears. He suspected that his ears were ringing, anyway, out of panic and dread.

Joe was accustomed to being able to hear wild animals breathe. Now, all he could hear was the rush of blood in his ears.

The mansion's door swung open, quiet as a breath, and Joe followed Overstreet into the entry hall. Daniel was talking, asking Overstreet if he'd made progress on Glynis' case. His high-pitched voice, his flushed face, and the incessant jangling made by his hand shuffling through the coins in his pocket... all these things made Joe crazy.

Something else was jangling. Joe moved his head from side to side, trying to pinpoint its location, but it was too faint.

Overstreet didn't hear it. Joe could tell. His eyes were completely focused on the kidnapping suspect at his side.

Something about the rhythm of the faint noise made him think of Faye.

The three of them passed through the entry hall and into the atrium, and Joe lost the sound. There were two clocks in the atrium, one on each balcony. Both of them ticked loudly, for precision-engineered timepieces. But he didn't hear anything that sounded like Faye.

Faye saw three people move past the viewfinder. They were blurry but, if forced to guess, she'd say that two of them were

Detective Overstreet and Daniel. One of them, beyond a shadow of a doubt, was her husband. No one moved like Joe.

All three of them had passed into the atrium now, joining Allyce Dunkirk's ghost.

Anybody but Faye would have stopped her noisemaking foolishness after that, since it had so clearly not worked. But Faye knew that Joe was out there.

Grind.

Click.

Daniel's beloved wife Suzanne appeared in the atrium, standing in the dining room entry. She greeted the three of them warmly, and Daniel saw an opportunity.

He gestured at Joe and Detective Overstreet, saying, "Darling, would you take our guests into the dining room and pour them some coffee? I've got some things upstairs in my office that I want to show them."

Daniel was confident that his wife would show her habitual hospitality skills, buying him ten minutes alone. He backed through the open door behind him into the entry hall, knowing that they'd presume he was taking the elevator. In a single motion, he retrieved the butcher knife hanging on a hook behind the grandfather clock, slid it into a barely visible seam in the paneled wall, and triggered a latch hidden within that wall.

The hook had been designed to hide a long thin sliver of metal that served as a key, but Glynis, by throwing a screaming fit, had forced him to arm himself. Fortunately, his weapon opened the door just as well as the key had.

The hidden door swung open and he was inside the turret within five seconds of leaving Joe and the policeman with Suzanne…less…so quickly that the little pregnant woman standing on the other side of the door sprawled in the floor. Why couldn't she be more careful when she was carrying his child?

Daniel brandished the knife. "How hard is it to sit in here and *be quiet? All of you.* I heard you making that noise. *I heard you.* You have to stop it." He focused his eyes on Faye. "You *must* stop it, because you're going to make me hurt you. You've *already* fixed it so that I have to tie you all up, even…"

His eyes raked the room.

"Where's the child? Where's the *little girl?*"

Suzanne needed a child. Suzanne was everything in his world, everything. Nothing had been right since Annie died, and Daniel was doing everything he knew how to do to make it right. There were two babies in this room, waiting to be born, and they were guarantees of a family. He and Suzanne had always wanted a big family, but no child had ever come to them except Annie, and even she only stayed ten years.

The babies were…*necessary.* He wanted the babies desperately. But they might turn out to be boys. The only way to make things right, really right, was to replace Annie. Little Rachel was unquestionably a girl, so she was essential.

And she wasn't here.

◇◇◇

Faye shook her head, trying to gather her wits after suddenly being knocked hard to the ground. Her body hurt from navel to knees after striking the concrete floor with her pelvis. She thanked God that she was sitting on Rachel's trapdoor, because she could think of nothing worse than for the little girl to appear right this minute.

Then something happened that was almost as horrible as watching Rachel reveal herself to a killer. Her whole middle spasmed, as if her body were trying to cave in on itself. So this was what a labor pain felt like.

"*Where…IS…she?*" he bellowed, reaching for Magda as she crouched by the door.

Faye watched in horror, breathless and panting. She needed to do something, anything, but she couldn't. Not until this contraction passed and she could rise to her feet.

Daniel reached down and yanked a blanket from beneath Glynis, who shrieked in pain. Using the knife to slash the blanket into strips, he said, "You will all *sit still* while I tie you up, and somebody is going to tell me where the little girl is *right now* or…"

He waved the knife at Magda, and Faye prayed that he didn't finish his sentence, because if Rachel heard him say, "…or I will kill her mother," then nothing would keep the little girl in her pit. Not even Faye's substantial weight on the trap door would do it.

"I *heard* you make that noise," he raved at Faye, still slicing fabric. "Do you want to bring this whole thing down around my ears?"

Well, yes. Faye did, and Daniel should know it. But this man was not rational now, if he ever had been. The fact that he'd taken the risk of entering this room in the daytime, knowing that he'd have to risk being seen when he left…these things told her that the situation had reached an ignition point.

Daniel went down on his knees and reached for Magda with his right hand. In his left hand, he held a knife.

Chapter Twenty-seven

With a wordless glance, Joe and Overstreet agreed to cover Daniel by splitting up. Overstreet put the lie to his tubby frame by taking the atrium stairs two at a time. If Daniel had gotten on the elevator to go to his apartment, Overstreet would be waiting for him when it opened. If he'd, for some reason, gone to the third floor, then Joe and Overstreet couldn't cover him. But he'd have to come down through the second and first floors to get out, and they'd be waiting for him.

Joe crossed the atrium, reaching for the door to the entry hall. If Daniel was still in there, Joe intended to subdue him. If he'd gotten out the front door, there were officers with rifles waiting out there for him.

Daniel was trapped. There was no place for him to go. Still, Joe cursed the inattention that had brought them to this point. Not inattention, actually—they had made their mistake by role-playing too well. When Suzanne had appeared, both he and Overstreet had hurried across the atrium to shake her hand, instinctively covering the fact that they weren't at all surprised to see her.

Daniel, looking for a chance to flee, had lingered at the door behind them and taken that opportunity. He'd had no way of knowing that Joe and Overstreet were onto him, so he'd expected them to wait patiently for him, sipping coffee with Suzanne in the dining room. So while he might have hoped to gain ten or fifteen minutes—to do what? Joe couldn't think about it—he had in fact only gained a few seconds.

Because it only took a few seconds for Joe to cross the atrium, open the door...

...and find the entry hall empty.

The elevator was sitting open, so Daniel had not boarded it. Joe flung open the front door. The officers waiting so unobtrusively in their parked cars were still sitting there, waiting for something to happen. No fugitive had fled out the front door.

Daniel had walked into this room and simply evaporated.

Joe wasted a few seconds by sticking his head into the atrium and calling to Suzanne, "He didn't go upstairs. Get Overstreet and tell him that Daniel's somewhere down here."

The entry hall was a hollow cube of polished wood. It shouldn't be empty, but it was. Joe stood in the center of the cube and tried to make sense of what he'd just seen.

Where was Daniel? And where was Faye?

Faye had been trying to reach him with that funny little noise. He knew it.

He called out to her. "Faye. I know you're here."

Nothing.

"Help me find you!"

Nothing. No voice. No faint clicking. Nothing.

He looked up at the balcony, lined with old and beautiful books. The noise he'd heard had been closer at hand. And Daniel had not had time to climb those stairs and vanish. Faye was down here on the ground floor somewhere.

Joe began checking the elevator carefully for latches that might open into a hidden shaft beyond the elevator shaft. Maybe the elevator didn't take up the entire turret.

Overstreet appeared, and Joe said, "They're here. Somewhere near this room. And he's with them. Get some tools. We need to take this elevator apart."

Overstreet rushed out the front door. Joe crawled all over the floor, running his hands over the ornate inlaid wood, praying for some sign of a trap door. The carpentry was flawless, without a

single seam wide enough to shove even a piece of typing paper
into. Pounding on every square inch of that flawless floor yielded
no hollow sound to hint at a space beneath.

Joe stood and yanked priceless artworks from the walls, throwing them in a corner. He worked his way around the room, tapping
and rubbing his hands on the sleek oak. The wood was adorned
with ornate moldings and raised panels. To Joe's sensitive hands,
each piece of carved wood felt seamlessly joined to the next one.

It was hard to believe that this woodwork had withstood a
century in such good shape. Maybe it had been restored. Maybe
during the restoration someone had taken the opportunity to
add a secret room. Or maybe the secret room had been there
the whole time.

All of the panels around the room were identical and perfect.
All of them were the same…except for one.

Just to the right of the grandfather clock, Joe found a single
seam almost concealed by the grain of the wood. Two feet to the
right of this seam was another seam, and this one was slightly
out of line. If he ran his thumbnail horizontally in front of him,
it caught on the slightly raised panel to the right of the second
seam. The two-foot panel was slightly depressed on that side,
which made it feel to Joe like a door that was slightly ajar. Very,
very slightly ajar. Like maybe a millimeter ajar.

It wasn't much. It was infinitesimal, actually. But maybe it
could be more.

Joe backed up and prepared to use his shoulder as a battering ram.

Daniel had taken his sweet time in binding Magda's hands and
feet. Faye had felt the contraction in her belly ebb, but she
didn't dare interfere with Daniel's work. The knife was rarely
far from a vulnerable part of Magda's anatomy—throat, heart,
belly. Glynis lay on the floor, eyes closed and sobbing, but Faye
couldn't make herself look away from Magda.

Magda's eyes caught Faye's. Then they twitched slightly in the direction of the door.

Making sure Daniel wasn't looking at her, Faye sneaked a glance. Then she blessed her friend's presence of mind and sheer cussedness. Despite the fact that Daniel's appearance had been a total surprise, Magda had managed to execute one part of their plan. She had shoved the water bottle cap into the doorframe.

Faye knew she shouldn't have been surprised. She'd never known anyone else with Magda's clear-headedness and strength of will. No one else other than Faye herself, that is.

There was just a teeny problem. The slamming of the heavy door had obliterated the bottle cap. Bits of plastic protruded from the gap between door and frame, but Faye had no confidence that enough plastic had jammed into that gap to keep the door from closing and latching.

Worse, the door opened inward, so even if it hadn't latched, they were going to have to figure how to pry it open. This was going to be a problem, once they were all trussed up like turkeys. If it had opened the other way, Faye and Magda could have taken turns running into the door like little battering rams, but they hadn't been that lucky.

Inside the entry hall's concrete wall was a delicate but strong latch, designed to guard a secret room and its secret contents. When firmly engaged, the door was so sturdy that it might as well have been a part of the wall. But a tiny sliver of plastic jammed into the door opening had interfered just enough to stop it short of closing. Not far short, perhaps. The distance was vanishingly small between the door as it was now and the door as it was when it was closed. But that distance was enough.

A body the size of Joe's carries a good bit of momentum with it when it careens full speed into another large object, like a heavy door. Bracing himself, he crashed hard into the concealed entry. Nothing happened.

He did it again. Nothing happened.

He backed up to try again, wishing like hell that Faye would give him some kind of sign. If she would only answer him. He had been calling for her since Daniel vanished, but there was no answer, not even that faint metallic clicking.

He hit the door again, and the impact rattled the keys in his pocket. Hearing Faye call his name, telling him she was alive, would be the best possible thing to happen at this moment. But it didn't happen.

Joe was very clear about the second best possible thing that could happen. He needed this door to open, or at least to budge a tiny bit. And it did. When his bruised shoulder struck the door, again, he felt motion. The door only swung a millimeter in the right direction, but it did swing.

Joe backed up so he could throw himself at a nearly solid wall, one more time.

The door shuddered. Daniel, crouching beside Magda as he finished tying her bonds, whipped his head in that direction. He had the presence of mind to maintain his grip on the knife, but he took his eyes off his hostages.

In the case of hostages like Magda and Faye, this was a big mistake.

In a heartbeat, Faye was on her knees, going for the knife and knocking Daniel onto his butt in the process.

Magda did her part by headbutting him in the mouth. Then she rolled onto her side, so that she could use her powerful but bound legs, mermaid-style, to pound him in the stomach. This approach would have worked, if Daniel hadn't had the reflexes of a lifelong tennis player. He, too, rolled onto his side, taking the blow on his hip, instead of his vulnerable abdomen.

Taking this defensive posture, instead of grabbing or striking at Magda, left Daniel with one free arm. He wrapped it around Faye's throat, and squeezed hard.

Faye's mouth gaped open as she struggled for air. Magda backed off.

The door shuddered again. Faye thought she could hear someone shouting outside, but she couldn't answer with Daniel's arm squeezing her windpipe shut. How much longer could she stay conscious?

Even more importantly—how was this affecting the baby? Maybe her best plan was to go ahead and "pass out." If she feigned unconsciousness, Daniel would probably quit choking her and her baby could keep getting oxygen.

As she closed her eyes and went limp, she heard two things. She heard Daniel announce, "I am getting out of here, and this woman is going to help me do it."

And she heard the door shake and vibrate yet again.

"Wake up, Faye." He poked her earlobe with the knife. "You and I are walking out of here. You and me and the little girl." He poked the lobe again, and she felt a trickle of blood drip onto her neck. "You need to tell me where the little girl is. Right now."

She thought of Rachel, cowering beneath the trapdoor under Faye's feet.

Stay put, baby. Please stay put.

Still feigning unconsciousness, Faye let her eyes open a crack. Magda was still bound and gagged, but she wasn't hurt. Rachel was still hiding. And Glynis still lay on her pallet, ignored by their assailant. He'd written her off as so very helpless that he'd turned his back on her.

This was another big mistake.

Glynis' eyes were no longer closed. They had the bright cunning of a cornered panther.

With an effort that brought an agonized scream from her pale mouth, Glynis rose to a half-sitting position, reached her right hand over Daniel's shoulder, and yanked at the knife with all her strength. It clattered to the floor and Magda used her mermaid legs to kick it across the room.

But Glynis wasn't finished with her captor. Daniel's head jerked back and Faye felt his arm grip her harder for a timeless time, then relax. She scuttled on hands and knees to the knife, but she couldn't grab it. Another contraction, bigger than the last, had seized her. Nauseated and terrified, she looked down at the knife and an old wives' tale popped into her brain.

"If you put a knife under your laborin' bed, you'll cut your pain in half."

A guttural sound from Daniel forced her to look up. Eyes bulging, he clawed at the silvery garrote encircling his neck, but this only made Glynis pull harder.

The door shuddered again.

Daniel was fighting for air, but his brain clearly hadn't shut down yet. He had the presence of mind to fight the instinct to yank the garrote from his throat, because anyone could see that it wasn't going anywhere. Instead, he grabbed for Faye. Nearly immobilized by the contraction, there wasn't much Faye could do about it other than throwing herself to the floor, hoping she could slither out of Daniel's reach.

Glynis responded to Daniel's attack on Faye by crossing the ends of the garrote and pulling it even tighter. When she did, Faye finally got a look at the fine cord in her hands. It was two feet long, braided of tightly wound cables that Glynis had twisted from the finest of fibers—her own hair. The free ends spilled like silk over her hands.

During the hours and days when she had lain in this room, alone and in pain, she'd plucked her hair out, strand by strand. She'd gathered it into hanks and given them a tight twist, then braided those twisted hanks into a slender rope as thick as her thumb. And then she'd waited for an opportunity that her brutalized body would let her take.

Daniel went limp, but Glynis didn't loosen her grip.

The door shook again, then it burst open.

Simultaneously, Magda and Faye roared, "RACHEL... *GO!!!*"

The child clambered out of her tiny prison and ran toward the door, straight into Joe's loving arms.

Chapter Twenty-eight

It was too soon.

Too soon for the contractions clenching Faye's middle. Too soon for her water to break. Too soon for the grinding pressure that weakened her knees and turned her stomach and brought tears down her face in streams. Too soon for terrifying amounts of blood to flow.

It was five weeks too soon, but Faye's baby was coming now.

Through the haze of pain and fear, Faye heard the paramedics use words like "placental abruption" and "significant hemorrhage" and "life-threatening" and "emergency cesarean." She heard them say, "Get back. All of you. She's going on the ambulance. Now. Now!" And she heard someone, maybe Suzanne, ask Joe, "Are you Catholic? Should we call a priest?"

Part of her knew exactly what those words meant. A placental abruption meant that she could bleed to death. It meant that the baby could die or be forever damaged by lack of the oxygen stored in the blood that was being wasted on the floor beneath her.

Another part of her was thinking about leaving. That part was pulling away from her icy-cold body and floating up, away from the pain, away from the blood, away from Joe's tears.

Away from Joe.

As much as she wanted to leave the pain and the blood, she couldn't leave Joe. And she couldn't give up on their baby.

She reached for the faith of her childhood, praying for her baby to live, even if she didn't. The effort gave her some comfort, some feeling of God cradling her and keeping her warm.

But there were others with her. One of them was Allyce Dunkirk, who simply held her hand and wept. Allyce had labored over children and lost them, right here in this house. Her presence frightened Faye, but she gripped the spectral woman's hand anyway.

She derived more comfort from the visitation of Father Domingo Sanz de la Fuente. She tried to tell him that she wasn't a Roman Catholic, but he waved away her concern. Father Domingo had spent his life tending nonbelievers with the tenderest of mercy. He dabbed something cool and sweet-smelling on her forehead and simply lingered, supporting her with his presence.

Someone tangible and solid grasped her arm gently and dabbed on something sharp-smelling and acrid. He said, "This will hurt a second. We're going to get your baby born. After that, we're going to take good care of you both." His faint Cuban accent made Faye think maybe Father Domingo had come for her in the flesh.

Her mind, always overactive, wanted to rest but couldn't. She found herself remembering Father Domingo's story, day by day and page by page. Its tragedy was overshadowed by the Spanish priest's unwavering love for his people and for his dedication to God. That dedication had only wavered once.

Faye hoped God had forgiven him. She had.

Cold water closed over her head. She was alone with Allyce Dunkirk and Father Domingo. And God.

From the journal of Father Domingo Sanz de la Fuente

Translated from the Spanish by
Faye Longchamp Mantooth, Ph.D.,
and Magda Stockard-McKenzie, Ph.D.

It was too late for Ocilla and all her kin, and I well knew it. When the village's men returned from exacting their vengeance on Father Esteban, I began ministering to my flock for the last time.

I prepared willow water for their fevers and poultices for their angry flesh. I made weak broths for those few who could eat. I administered the Last Rites, time and again. And, one by one, I buried them.

The children fared better than most. Not the babies. They perished as quickly as the village elders. But the strongest youngsters and a few of their mothers and fathers did heal. I did not expect this.

My intention had been to bury the last of my Timucuan friends, and then find a way to die. My plans were murky, for I had never once considered committing this most final sin. But now? If I leave these few survivors, they will have no hope.

I am certain there is a message from God in the fact that among the survivors are two of Father Esteban's grandchildren. Perhaps they will live long enough to do great things and expunge the world of a small piece of his sins.

In my heart, I believe they have no hope, with me or without me. If I do not choose to die now, then I may live to see a day when there are no more Timucua. Perhaps this is my penance, to watch over a doomed people. If I do it well and faithfully, perhaps Our Lord will absolve my grievous sins and open the gates of Heaven to His most flawed servant. Despite the fact that she remained heathen to her dying breath, perhaps I shall see Ocilla there.

But in my heart I doubt that I shall see Heaven. I doubt it because I know that Our Lord sees into the depths of our souls. I know that He knows what will happen if I arrive at the Throne of God and see that Father Esteban, too, has also been offered that mercy: I will kill him again, this time with my own hands.

Because He knows this, I believe that Our Lord will consign us both to the deepest circle of Hell. And if I know that Father Esteban suffers agony for all eternity, I will be content to suffer it myself.

I think I will write no more in this book. I have people to tend.

I, Father Domingo Sanz de la Fuente, attest that the foregoing is a statement of actual events.

Chapter Twenty-nine

Post-cesarean recovery was not fun. The pain radiated, so Faye hurt pretty much everywhere. Everything hurt, even breathing. But there was one part of her recovery plan that she thoroughly enjoyed—the doctor's instruction that she was to lift nothing heavier than her baby.

He was so tiny, not even six pounds, but the doctor said he was as healthy as a horse. This had made Joe smile, but Faye knew what he was thinking. This child of theirs would be no domesticated animal. He would be as healthy as a bear, a fox, a wolf. And she would love him until the sun burned out.

He had remained nameless for days, until Joe was ready to leave Faye's side. The abruption, the emergency surgery, and an infection had teamed up to keep Faye in the hospital nearly a week. Only when the doctors started talking about releasing her did Joe agree to go start making preparations for the baby's early homecoming.

Part of those preparations had been a few hours in the woods with a campfire, some herbs, a bowl of water, and a hand-rolled ceremonial cigarette. After some time spent cleansing himself, body and soul, Joe had meditated until the baby's name presented itself. A circling bird of prey had delivered it:

Michael Hawk Longchamp-Mantooth

Faye agreed that it was perfect. It honored little Michael's godfather, Sheriff Mike. It honored both their parents. And the high-flying, fierce hawk would be as good a totem for their baby as the wolf had been for Joe.

He was a fine, strong child, with a sleek cap of black hair and a full set of black eyelashes. His eyes were the newborn's usual murky noncolor, but when they were open, they viewed the world with a calm and intense interest. He slept comfortably, wrapped in a summer-weight blanket and cradled under one of her breasts.

She'd wondered how she would feel, walking back into Dunkirk Manor with its terror-filled memories, but it couldn't be helped. At least Joe was at her side.

Magda, Levon, and Kirk had used their time well during her hospital stay and the site work was complete. There were several days of billable time on the project left for her to write the report, then she could put Dunkirk Manor behind her forever, but she needed to go back one more time. She needed to say good-bye to Suzanne, who had been willing to believe the worst of her own husband and to do what was necessary to save Faye and her friends. And Faye's baby.

Suzanne couldn't put Dunkirk Manor behind her. She could leave it for the nonprofit corporation to run, and she planned to, but the old house would haunt her for the rest of her life.

Faye wanted to reach out to her. She wanted Suzanne to know that there were people out there who cared about her, who wanted to see her find a way to be happy again.

Suzanne greeted Faye and Joe with a coffeepot in one hand and a tray of pastries in the other. "Welcome! Come in the dining room and eat something. I want to get a look at that gorgeous baby!"

The B&B guests had cleared out of the dining room for the day, but there were others sitting there, waiting for Faye's arrival. Magda, Levon, Kirk, Detective Overstreet, Betsy, and Harriet were deep in conversation. Victor hovered over them all, with a china teapot held carefully in both hands.

One of Suzanne's glorious flower arrangements adorned the table. Faye knew enough of the language of flowers to know that the woman had put thought into the choice of every stem. Daisies and baby's breath spoke of innocence. Holly branches carried a wish for domestic happiness. Trailing tendrils of ivy signified wedded love, and so did fragrant orange blossoms. Suzanne had reached outside her own garden and purchased pussy willows, the emblem of motherhood and the perfect adornment for a baby shower. There were wrapped gifts in front of each of the guests' plates.

In a plush armchair nearby, surrounded by pillows, lounged Glynis. A cast was visible below the hem of her flowing red silk pants. Faye was thrilled to hear her ask Victor for herbal tea, because she wasn't drinking caffeine until her baby came. After all she'd been through, Glynis was still pregnant. This was, in its way, a miracle.

"It's a baby shower!" Victor crowed, pulling out two chairs and flapping his hands in their direction. "Sit down and open your presents!"

Levon and Kirk had gone in together to buy a picture book about an American housecat who time-travels to ancient Egypt and helps discover King Tut's tomb. Overstreet had brought a waffle ball and a plastic bat, saying, "It's never too soon."

Suzanne had slipped a gift certificate for a downtown baby boutique into an envelope, along with a photo of a pregnant Faye standing on the lip of an open excavation. "For Michael's baby book," she said.

Harriet had found an ethereal dreamcatcher in a gift shop in the historic section, woven of twine and adorned with beads and feathers. She'd written in the card that "This child will have more dreams than he can catch in his hands."

Betsy had brought a mouth-blown stoppered bottle, small enough to stand on the palm of her hand. It was full. "Water from the Fountain of Youth. Because you never know."

Faye tilted the bottle and watched the water flow. "No, you don't. You never know."

Glynis had brought an adorable piggy bank and a Morgan silver dollar. After Faye opened it, Glynis grinned at Victor, signaling him to give his part of their gift. He carefully laid a silver dime next to the bank. "1918!" he said. "The oldest one I had."

Faye cradled the dime in her palm and admired the image of Liberty with her lovely winged cap. She held it down for Michael to see, but his perfect eyes were closed.

Magda gently laid her gift, a crocheted blanket, over Michael as he slept, and handed a wooden box to Joe. "From my husband, for his namesake." Inside was a collection of worn and well-loved alphabet blocks carved of wood. "They were his, when he was a kid. Mike's kids have all played with them, and Rachel's ready to pass them along."

Joe fumbled through the blocks until he found the seven he wanted, then he spread them across the table in front of Faye. "M-I-C-H-A-E-L," he said, pointing each block in its turn. "Open your eyes, kid. It's never too soon to learn this stuff."

Michael, recalcitrant, remained asleep.

"Can I show you my room, Faye?" Victor asked.

Faye gave Suzanne a questioning glance.

Suzanne said, "Victor, why don't you and I take Faye back there together?" Then she reflexively refilled everybody's tea cups, whether they'd asked for more or not. Victor ran ahead of them to the service wing where Faye and her crew had been staying.

In the kitchen, out of earshot of the others, Suzanne said, "Ever since...since that terrible day...I can't keep my mind off Victor's situation. Maybe I'm just distracting myself. Could I have stopped Daniel from doing what he did to Glynis? And to you? It keeps me awake nights. And that gives me time to worry about the old man living in a hovel at the end of my street."

Suzanne waved away Faye's attempts to reassure her that she didn't hold Daniel's widow responsible for his actions.

Michael burbled in his sleep. Suzanne leaned down and studied his flawless little face for a second.

"First, I had Victor move into one of the rooms on your hall, but just getting him out of that squalor didn't quiet my mind. I needed to know how this thing happened. Raymond and Allyce Dunkirk had practically adopted Victor as a child. They gave him that little house, and it was probably pretty nice when they did. How could people so educated and wealthy have failed to foresee that he wouldn't be able to take care of himself financially? I don't think Victor has ever really been much more than a child, mentally, and surely they knew that. So I reverted to being a lawyer, at least for a little while. I looked in the public records for their will, but it wasn't there."

"Was it lost? Or destroyed?" Faye asked. "Public records are supposed to stick around. They're…well…public."

"Not when rich people have something to hide," Suzanne said. "Since then, I've learned that my Great-great-aunt Allyce was committed to a mental institution shortly before her husband died."

"That explains a lot about the second half of her life," Faye said. "I'd noticed that she disappeared from the society pages years before that. She just faded away."

"That makes sense. I'd guess that her mental illness began earlier, but he waited to institutionalize her until he came to the end of his life. That way, he knew she'd be taken care of."

"Is that when he gave Victor the gatehouse—after he knew he was dying and needed to get his affairs in order?"

"Yes. I found the property transfer before I found the will, because there had been no reason to hide that."

The treasure hunter in Faye perked up her ears. "You found the will? Where?"

"In that room upstairs, the one that's full of junk."

"Yes," Faye said, remembering her odd encounter with Daniel that day. She'd never really known why he took her there in the first place, but now she suspected that he'd wanted her baby from the moment she took the consulting job. Perhaps he'd even hired her firm so that he could have a chance to steal her baby. She leaned down to kiss Michael's forehead.

How many times had Daniel taken her aside to ask a question or hand her some food, only to be interrupted by her hovering husband? If Daniel had been successful in his earliest attempts to kidnap her, perhaps Glynis' ordeal would never have happened. And if he hadn't taken her to the attic storeroom, trying to kidnap her, Father Domingo's journal would still be disintegrating in the heat and humidity.

"There's no telling what you might find in that room, if you set out to look, but I can't imagine that you'd ever find something you were actually looking for. Like a will."

"Well, I'm not sleeping nights. And there were only a few places where family records had been stored, so at least I knew where to start looking."

Suzanne clasped her hands together in front of her abdomen. It was a controlled pose, and it brought the lawyer in her back to life. Suddenly, Faye was certain that Suzanne would survive the tragedy of her husband's madness. She had survived the loss of a child, so she was stronger than she looked. Suzanne might do any number of things with the rest of her life. She might decide to continue operating the B&B. She might go back to practicing law. Or she might do something completely different, like open a florist's shop. But she would be okay.

"I found that Raymond *had* set aside money for Victor," said the attorney who was emerging from retirement very nicely. "Quite a lot of it. Income from that money went to an account at a bank not a quarter-mile from here. The bank tellers there were instructed to give Victor his money in cash every Friday when he came for it. And at least a dollar of it was always supposed to be in dimes."

"That's amazing service."

"Remember, it was the 1950s, and this is a small town."

"Did Victor just get lost in the shuffle over the years, as the old bank tellers retired and died?"

Suzanne nodded vehemently, and Faye knew that she'd reached the crux of her story. "Yes. But it was more than that. Raymond left instructions for his law firm to pay Victor's property taxes and other bills out of his account, then distribute the rest in cash for his food and incidentals. Faye, that's riverfront property. Do you have any idea what the taxes are like?"

Having struggled to pay her own property taxes, Faye did.

Suzanne continued her story. "Raymond was a brilliant man who handled his money well. He came through the Great Depression smelling like a rose. But he had no way to know how long Victor would live. And he had no way to know how low those property taxes would drain Victor's inheritance. These days, it's easy to pay Victor his income in dimes."

"Dimes! I have a whole lot of dimes!" Victor said, poking his head in the door. "When are you coming to see my room? That's where I keep my dimes."

"Raymond Dunkirk's will was carefully and lovingly laid out. Allyce was sent to the most comfortable asylum in Florida, and fresh flowers were sent to her room every day for as long as she lived. Victor was given a place to live and a financial legacy."

Suzanne smiled at the impetuous old man, who was jumping up and down in his eagerness to show Faye where he kept his dimes. "He loved them both, I think. I've come to forgive him for betraying my Great-great-aunt Allyce."

The archaeologist in Faye began to think in terms of time. The events in a person's life stacked up, bit by bit, just as surely as layers of soil covered the past. The last layer of Allyce Dunkirk's life was represented by the asylum, and that starkness was softened by her dead husband's flowers.

Digging deeper in time, the layer below the asylum was represented by Allyce's twenty years as a recluse. Her years spent as the hostess of glittering parties had ended when Lilibeth Campbell died, as suddenly and surely as the closing of a garden gate.

Excavating the layer below those reclusive years brought Faye to the early years of Allyce's marriage, a time when she was young and beautiful and rich, but she couldn't save the children she lost, one after another. The parties, the friends, the jewels, the beautiful clothes…in the end, they hadn't meant that much. But the watershed moment that coincided with abandoning that socialite's life hadn't been the death of her last child. It had been the death of her husband's mistress.

Something horrifying began to nibble at Faye's mind. Suzanne kept talking, and her words served only to solidify Faye's suspicions.

"I think Allyce's mind was already gone by the time her husband met Lilibeth Campbell. Great-great-uncle Raymond was a human being and he needed companionship and romance, but my heart—and the detailed provisions for her in his will—tell me that he never got over loving Allyce. He died thinking he'd taken care of her, and of Victor, too. The image of flowers being delivered to an insane asylum, year in and year out, from a dead man to his widow…that image softens my heart toward Great-great-uncle Raymond."

"Flowers. Oh, she loved flowers." Victor beckoned, and they followed him to the servants' wing. "And she loved to paint. So much." He opened the door with a flourish. On the room's far wall was an oil painting of a small boy with Victor's eyes. "After she stopped going places, she didn't do much but paint and plant things." Lowering his voice, he leaned in their direction. "Sometimes…sometimes, she planted things that wasn't flowers."

The sad little shrine made of baby things leapt to Faye's mind and she held Michael closer.

Leaning in still closer, Victor said, "After awhile, she got to where she'd take things, just to have something to bury." Quickly, he added an excuse for his almost-mother. "O'course, she wasn't in her right mind by then. She was a lady, not a thief. But nobody coulda resisted the wonderful things Mr. Ripley used to bring over here to show Mr. Raymond. Stuff from India and Zanzibar and Siam, all of it carved out of wood and ivory and jewels and covered in gold. You couldn't blame Miss Allyce for taking some of it."

Faye would have given her eyeteeth to have dug up some of Robert Ripley's exotic plunder in the back garden of Dunkirk Manor. Or maybe she had. A knife carved of carmine stone and an exquisitely proportioned little elephant came to mind…

"Mr. Ripley loved her, too. No man could help loving Miss Allyce. He always spoke to her so kind, so respectful, even after she stopped talking back. He stopped bringing the really good stuff here, but he kept bringing interesting little things for her. They was gifts, but he didn't tell her. He'd just leave them laying around and let her take 'em. Such a kind man."

Faye thought of Allyce Dunkirk, deep in madness, prying up tiles around her backyard pool and burying her treasures there. She did her best to admire Victor's box of dimes and listen to him enthuse over his comfy new bed, but Allyce's story was playing in her mind, year by year. Distracted, she followed him and Suzanne as they trooped back toward the dining room where Faye's baby shower was going on without her.

"It tore Miss Allyce up when Mr. Raymond filled in that swimming pool. She did love to swim."

Raymond Dunkirk had sent flowers to a wife too deep in madness to even speak. The evidence said that she was already dropping into madness when he destroyed that pool, shortly after Lilibeth Campbell died. Why would such a tenderhearted man have taken away one of the few pleasures his fragile wife could still enjoy?

A cold finger touched her spine. Faye finally understood, deep down, why Raymond Dunkirk had destroyed his wife's cherished pool. And she was pretty sure she knew why the description of Lilibeth Campbell's body had said that her wounds had been wiped clean. Perhaps those wounds hadn't been wiped at all. Maybe the blood had been rinsed away, even as they were being made. Maybe Lilibeth had been knifed to death while submerged in Allyce Dunkirk's beloved swimming pool. And nobody had more reason to want Lilibeth dead than the lady of the house.

Victor prattled on and confirmed every awful image in Faye's mind. "After Miss Lilibeth died in that pool, Mister Raymond couldn't stand to look at it. It was a long time before he could even look at Miss Allyce, after she killed that young lady. She was wrong to kill her, o'course, but so many people had told Miss Lilibeth to be careful. She would do most anything to get pretty things, little Miss Betsy would, and I think she wanted Miss Allyce's pretty things. Wanted her husband, too. Maybe that's why Miss Allyce buried stuff. So's she could keep it to herself. And maybe that's why she killed Miss Lilibeth. So's she could keep her husband to herself."

Suzanne stood gape-jawed in the dining room door, staring at an old man who was oblivious to the effect of what he'd just said, but Faye just clung to Michael. Allyce Dunkirk's guilt was no surprise to Faye. Part of her had known the truth since the day she made the timeline of Allyce's life by studying the photographs documenting her slow deterioration. The answer had been waiting in her subconscious until Suzanne delivered the last telling bits of information: Allyce's madness, her final days in an asylum, and the river of flowers that flowed to her from her loving husband.

Every head had turned in their direction. There was no sound, other than the sumptuous clink of someone's silver fork hitting a china dessert plate.

Harriet was on her feet. "Allyce Dunkirk killed Lilibeth Campbell?"

"Well, o'course she did. I thought everybody knew that. Mister Raymond did, and me, because we was both there. And those Hollywood people knew. Well, maybe everybody didn't know, because I remember hearing the Hollywood men saying stuff to Mister Raymond like, 'This can't get out!' But I know the police chief knew. 'Cause he told Mr. Raymond that he would be holding him to the promise of a gentleman. I heard him say that. People don't think I'm listening. Don't even see me standing behind them. Lots of times, I am."

"What promise was that?" Faye asked.

"That Miss Allyce would never set foot off this property. This would be her jail and Mister Raymond would be her jailer. It was the right thing. You couldn't imagine a lady like her in jail or locked in the asylum." A shadow crossed his face. "My folks used to talk about putting me in an asylum. They did. Miss Allyce and Mister Raymond wouldn't let 'em. They gave me my house, so I'd always have a good place to live. It woulda been wrong to lock Miss Allyce up, not when she couldn't help what she did. That's what the police chief said."

Faye remembered the Dunkirk's glittering wealth and thought that, yes, money could buy justice in those days. It still could.

"On the day he finally did send her away, because he was dying, Mr. Raymond opened that garden gate and walked outside to the car with her. He was so sick and frail. He didn't even get dressed. Just walked beside her in his pajamas, leaving the gate open for the first time since he dived down under the water and tried to save Miss Lilibeth from Miss Allyce and her knife."

Harriet drew an audible breath.

"He give me everything sharp in the house to keep for him after that, everything but the knives locked up in the kitchen. He did." The old man gave an emphatic nod. "Nobody coulda stopped her, you know. They thought she was asleep, him and Miss Lilibeth, when they snuck out there to swim under the moon. Mr. Raymond was high in the air, doing a jack-knife dive, when Miss Allyce ran out of the shadows and started stabbing that poor young lady. Both ladies fell in the pool, and still she kept a-stabbing. They all thought I was in bed, too, but I wasn't. I saw."

Faye found herself feeling pity for Raymond Dunkirk. Maybe Suzanne was right. Maybe his wife, the Allyce who he'd loved, was already dead when he betrayed her with Lilibeth. Maybe the real Allyce had been lost to madness long before.

"Mr. Raymond was a man of his word. He made sure Miss Allyce was locked up for always, but he was good to her. She had nice people with her all the time, and their job was to make her smile. It was my job, too."

Harriet sat down with a plop.

"After the car drove Miss Allyce away, he said to me, 'Victor, you live in the gatehouse, and your job is to guard this gate. Don't you *ever* let anybody close it again. Ever.'" He gave an emphatic nod. "I didn't, not until this week. And I did try to stop them."

Suzanne put a hand on his shoulder. "Yes, Victor. You did."

Faye turned her eyes to the open passageway from the dining room into the atrium. She had denied it to Harriet, and she would continue to deny it to anyone but Joe, but she *had* sensed Allyce Dunkirk's presence in that room. On the day that she'd stood in the doorway with Harriet while a cold wind swept past her, she'd felt a presence whose grief and pain was almost three-dimensional. She didn't know what that presence was, but it had been *real.*

At times, while she'd sat imprisoned in Dunkirk Manor's turret, she'd felt that presence again, grieving over her, grieving over the plight of Magda and Glynis and all three of their children. But she didn't feel it any more.

And what of Father Domingo? Was he resting?

Faye didn't know. But she thought of the broken celt and blade that Glynis had brought to her. She remembered Betsy's statement that she, too had unearthed a broken weapon in this same county. And she thought fondly of the two halves of a shapely spear point that Levon had dug up while Faye rested in the hospital. The broken weapon had been buried in a portion of the garden thought to have been undisturbed in recent centuries, even by Allyce Dunkirk and her little gardening shovel.

She liked to think that Father Domingo had presided over the burial of these weapons, during the years when he traveled among the Timucua and urged them to lay down their arms and live in peace. She liked to think that she had walked on the same ground as the renegade priest, alongside the self-same river.

Maybe the old heretic was at rest, but Faye would rather believe that he lingered here, watching over the sick and the weak. The world could use a few more heretics like Father Domingo.

Faye looked around her at the fine interiors of the old mansion. Dunkirk Manor was newer than Faye's ancestral home, Joyeuse, and it was even more stoutly built. There seemed to be no good reason for the fact that Joyeuse felt warm and alive, yet Dunkirk Manor seemed to steal the life from the very marrow of Faye's bones. She was glad that Michael would never pass a single night here.

It was time to go. Faye intended for Michael's first night alone with his parents to be spent at Joyeuse.

Guide for the Incurably Curious: A Personal Note to Teachers, Students and People Who Just Plain Like to Read

This readers' guide is my chance to talk directly with the people who enjoy reading Faye's adventures as much as I enjoy writing them. Composing the "Guide for the Incurably Curious" has become a rite of passage for me. It means that I've finished a book that has consumed a year of my life. And it's my chance to put some thought into what that book means.

I always want to know what questions my books leave behind in the minds of the people who read them. Because no book can answer every question for every person. Certainly no novel can. Part of a novelist's art is deciding what to reveal and what to withhold. It is part of my job to leave you with space for wonder.

I write fiction. I make a lot of this stuff up. But I write stories about a woman who loves history and archaeology, and it's important to me that my made-up stories about Faye coexist plausibly with the real world. As a novelist, I also put a high value on the facts that underpin my story. If my readers recognize that the laws of physics and the flow of history are not violated too terribly in my stories, then they can believe the more implausible twists that are inherent in fiction. In other words, if Faye behaves like a real-life archaeologist, my readers are much more likely to swallow the notion that she stumbles across a murder victim every now and then.

When I do speaking engagements, certain questions get asked over and over. "Are the Choctaw folk tales in *Effigies* real?" (Yes.)

Or "Where, exactly, is Joyeuse?" (Reader, Joyeuse exists only in my imagination and yours.) In this guide, I'll try to anticipate questions I'd expect to hear from readers of *Strangers* and I'll ask some questions of my own. I visit many classrooms and book groups over the course of a year, and these are the kinds of ideas people like to toss around. If you or your class or your book group would like to chat further, contact me at maryannaevans@ yahoo.com. I answer all my e-mail, when humanly possible, and I'd love to hear your responses to some of these questions.

1. What did you think of Faye's transition into a Ph.D.-holding business owner?

Faye's struggle to find a way to finish her education was a central theme in *Artifacts*. *Relics* was probably the book that illustrated most clearly her struggles to be taken seriously as a student of archaeology. In the next three books, *Effigies*, *Findings*, and *Floodgates*, Faye was doing archaeological work that she hoped would help her finish her dissertation and her doctorate. Still, I didn't want to leave her in school forever.

I've resisted settling comfortably into a predictable format for the books in this series. I loved the Florida island setting of *Artifacts*, but I purposely took Faye on the road to Alabama and Mississippi before setting another book on Joyeuse Island. I sent her back to school, so that I wouldn't fall into the rut of writing book after book about a black-market archaeologist working on the edge of the law. (And sometimes falling off.) I took a big risk in resolving the romantic tension that sizzled between Faye and Joe for four books, but I didn't want to take the mirror-image risk of letting their relationship grow stale.

So Faye's professional life has now progressed through a six-book story arc, from an amateur archaeologist to a student to a Ph.D.-holding consultant. I really couldn't see Faye as a professor, so I gave her a corporation to run. My editor liked this plan, because she said she thought it would be interesting to watch Faye juggle the demands of a business-owner. As the book progressed, I realized that Faye and Joe would make good partners, but that they probably would take different approaches to running a business.

The thing about Faye's new enterprise that pleases me most as a storyteller is the fact that a consultant does what she's hired to do, and those jobs can vary widely. If I want to send her to Rome for a job, I can do that, as long as there is a plausible reason for someone to hire her. Even better, she is now in a position to be hired by police departments for cases that require the expertise of an archaeologist. Imagine how happy I am to realize that her new career has eliminated the problem of explaining to you why my intrepid heroine has stumbled over a dead body...*again.*

2. Could you tell that Faye was sick and tired of being pregnant?

I'm not sure I've ever read a book written from the point of view of a woman who is entering her ninth month of pregnancy. As a mother of three, it was an interesting exercise to imagine how advanced pregnancy would affect the things that Faye must do for her work and, in the end, to save her own life.

For a time, I intended for Faye to be in the earliest stages of pregnancy in *Strangers*. She might even be unaware of it until the final scene, when she realizes why she's been feeling so weird and redoubles her efforts to save herself from the bad guy, because now she has to protect herself *and* her baby.

But it just didn't work. I tried to write it that way, but realized that the reader would be in on the secret as soon as I mentioned that Faye was feeling queasy or tired. Then Faye would be looking like an idiot for about three hundred pages, while my readers were yelling, "Take a home pregnancy test, dummy!" I was rather proud of myself for making one of those tests an important clue.

As I launched into a story about a woman on the verge of becoming a mother, I learned something very quickly. Being extremely pregnant is like having an elephant in the living room. You can't ignore it, and neither can anybody else. It affects your ability to do your job. It affects your ability to even move through a crowded room or up a flight of stairs. And even when I wrote scenes from other characters' points of view...well, *they* couldn't ignore it, either, and it affected their behavior toward Faye.

I decided to just go with it. The key to writing realistic characters is having them behave like real people, and real people do notice when someone in her thirty-fifth week of pregnancy waddles by. When I was in that condition, a stranger once said within my earshot, "She looks like she's about to pop." Gee, thanks.

As a part of Faye's character arc, this pregnancy is very important. She admits as early as *Artifacts*, six years before the events in *Strangers*, that she wants a baby very much. In the meantime, we've watched her suffer some significant romantic travails, and her age is much on her mind. After writing six books about Faye, I found that I wanted her to have this baby almost as much as I would if she were a flesh-and-blood, real human woman who was suffering from the demands of her biological clock.

Last but not least—I think Joe is going to make a really cool father.

3. How did the long history of St. Augustine work as a backdrop for this story? And did you enjoy Father Domingo's journal?

I like to work with nooks and crannies of history that are interesting, but not very well known. It's hard for Americans to get our modern brains around how far away in time the 1565 founding of St. Augustine is from us. For example, I originally wanted Glynis to bring a bayonet to Faye. "Spanish bayonet" is such a common phrase in Florida that we have appropriated it to name a very sharp-pointed plant. But I learned that bayonets, which seem a bit primitive to us, are relatively modern weapons. The Spanish did not have them when they came to Florida in 1565.

Another way to get perspective on the age of St. Augustine is to realize that it was founded more than two hundred years before the American Revolution. So its Spanish founders were as remote to our powdery-wigged, knee-pants-wearing Founding Fathers as those Founding Fathers are to us.

This antiquity presented me with a unique problem. There was just no way to shoehorn all of it into one book about a modern-day archaeologist. So I had to pick and choose. I loved the glamour of old Hollywood, so when I learned that silent movies had been filmed in St. Augustine, I knew I would use that fact, without a doubt. The story of Lilibeth Campbell, Raymond Dunkirk, Allyce Dunkirk, Victor, and the Hollywood moguls is completely fictional, but I hope it reflects the glamour brought to St. Augustine in the Gilded Age by railroad baron Henry Flagler.

When I stumbled across an English translation of the real-life journal of Father Francisco López de Mendoza Grajales, telling of his adventures on the way to the founding of America's oldest permanent European settlement, I knew that I wanted to use his story. But how?

It has been my personal policy not to muck about with the lives of real people in my books. It's disrespectful and, in the case of historical figures, it clouds the facts. My solution to this problem was to create my own Spanish priest and put him at the real Father Francisco's side, gathering experiences that he would record in his own fictional journal. I also created Father Esteban to serve as a foil for my sympathetic renegade priest, Father Domingo.

Father Domingo's story of his tumultuous trip from Spain to Florida is modeled closely on the real journal of Father Francisco. (If you're interested in reading his reminiscences, a quick web search for "Father Francisco López de Mendoza Grajales" will take you there.) When I depict Father Francisco's actions during that trip, they are very near to the actions he described in his real-life journal. And Father Francisco really did save some men destined for massacre at Matanzas in the way I described. Still, the real Father Francisco was a man of his era in his views of people of different faiths from himself, and I wanted to tell the story from the point-of-view of a man ahead of his time. I wanted someone to bear witness to the tragedy of the Americas—the death and destruction of her native people.

In the end, I found that I couldn't tell the story of St. Augustine without touching something old and painful, the unimaginable suffering of Native Americans due both to warfare and to disease. In a way, I think those diseases were the biggest tragedy. Even if armed conflict over territory and gold could have somehow been avoided...even if the people from Europe had come in utter peace…the diseases that they brought with them would have still killed the native people in droves.

The last full-blooded Timucuan died in Cuba in 1767.

To receive a free catalog of Poisoned Pen Press titles, please contact us in one of the following ways:

Phone: 1-800-421-3976
Facsimile: 1-480-949-1707
Email: info@poisonedpenpress.com
Website: www.poisonedpenpress.com

Poisoned Pen Press
6962 E. First Ave. Ste. 103
Scottsdale, AZ 85251